The New Europeans

James Ward

COOL MILLENNIUM BOOKS

3

Copyright © James Ward 2016

James Ward has asserted his right to be identified as the author of this Work in accordance with the Copyright, Designs and Patents Act 1988.

This is a work of fiction. All names, characters, and events are the product of the author's imagination, or used fictitiously. All resemblance to actual events, places, events or persons, living or dead, is entirely coincidental.

First published 2016.
This edition published 2021.

A CIP catalogue record for this book is available from the British Library.

ISBN: 978-1-913851-30-9

Front cover picture shows the Victoria Memorial. Rear shows Mansion House EC4.

This novel was produced in the UK and uses British-English language conventions ('authorise' instead of 'authorize', 'The government are' instead of 'the government is', etc.)

To my wife

Chapter 1: Springtime for Planchart

Outside, the sun shone on a perfect spring morning. Shoots turned to leaves, birds sang, flowers opened. A fresh warmth penetrated the soil and freed everything dormant from the last constraints of winter.

All this new beginning was fully sensed indoors, even though the walls here had been built to withstand a siege. On the third floor of the north tower of the Château de Javier Maroc in the French Alpes-de-Haute-Provence, thirty men sat round an antique table with their hands in front of them either folded or taking notes. Their business had just come to an end. Jean-Paul Crevier, a Lyonnaise billionaire and the group's chairman, summed up the agreements reached. A shaft of natural light fell across his memoranda and ended beneath a gilt-framed picture of Louis Antoine, Duke of Angoulême, on the wall opposite the window.

Anyone magically entering through the room's single locked door at that moment would have assumed this was a once-in-a-blue-moon meeting of some kind: very wealthy businessmen or influential politicians, or a mix, all with widely varying diary commitments that made their congregation a rarity. The sumptuous Bourbon Restoration décor, the way the incumbents sat up in their chairs, the cut of their clothes, their shiny leather shoes placed flat on the carpet, the way each had a notepad and pen and a glass of water in front of him, and especially their age and appearance – all were male, over fifty with expensive haircuts and well-fed faces – would have confirmed that impression.

What our invisible entrant could never have guessed were the deeper truths. That here, in this space, this very particular group had gathered with the intention of taking sole charge of European history for the foreseeable future; that since (notwithstanding their impressive wealth and connections) they were all relatively powerless at the moment, this entailed wresting the reins of power from others; that they knew how to do it, or thought they did; and – as a corollary of all the above - that this gathering was merely about dotting the *i*'s and crossing the *t*'s.

Of the ten British representatives here, none had informed their employers of their involvement. To do so would not only have been professional suicide, but would have set alarm bells ringing in the highest echelons of state security. To all intents and purposes they belonged to a group that did not exist.

As Jean-Paul Crevier continued to speak, the man on his right went round with wine glasses, one of which he placed before each representative. Then *Domaine Leflaive Montrachet Grand Cru* was poured. Finally, Crevier picked up his glass and bowed slightly from the shoulders to a sallow, black-haired man in the chair opposite.

"May I propose a toast," he said. "To Charles Planchart, the next Prime Minister of the United Kingdom."

Three hours later, Planchart was on his way home to London by high speed train. Opposite him sat a grey-haired thin man with a crooked mouth and small, penetrating, grey eyes. Martin Cheswick, Planchart's sole collaborator in MI7. Outside, the French countryside shot past in a perpetual interchange of green and yellow fields, vineyards, dilapidated farmhouses and screens of Lombardy poplar.

"From what you're telling me," Planchart said, "Our biggest problem is likely to be Red department. Blue and White should come over to us fairly automatically. Black's an unknown quantity."

Cheswick smiled sheepishly and shrugged. "Believe it or not, Black may not even exist. Either way, we're best dealing with it post-transition."

"Talk me through the so-called 'problem of Red', then."

"I've managed to obtain an overview of what we in Grey already know about them," Cheswick said, as if it had been procured at great risk to himself. He reached into his briefcase and pulled out a document. "Information's in there. I'll talk you through it, then I'll need it back."

"Of course."

"Normally, it's not necessary to inquire into Red's affairs, so a lot of what's in there is information we've accrued incidentally in the course of more direct exchanges of information. Their department head is a black woman called Ruby Parker. Her core team comprises four agents, whose details you can see on page three: Phyllis Robinson, ex-army, hard-working, bright, ambitious, but not particularly imaginative; Annabel al-Banna *née* Gould, recruited fifteen years ago by the late Celia Demure: a former repeat young offender, now a martial arts and firearms expert; Alec Cunningham, another ex-army individual and the department's most experienced officer, rather set in his ways, and finally, John Mordred, of whom more in a moment. All four officers transferred from Grey to Red under the auspices of the head of Grey in 2014, Ranulph Farquarson, now retired."

"I've met Phyllis Robinson," Planchart said. "I called her in over poor Frances. We spoke for over an hour. All very amicable, I'm happy to report. Enjoyable, even."

"There's no reason whatsoever for anyone to suspect anything. We've taken every available precaution. Talbot might kick up a bit of a fuss, but we've covered that. He'd be on a hiding to nothing."

"I'd quite forgotten about Ian Talbot."

"He's easy to overlook. Second-rate academic, over-inflated view of his own importance. He won't talk. He's made big mistakes, we know all about them, and he has too much to lose. Lovely wife, two adoring daughters. Job, possibly."

"This 'John Mordred'," Planchart said. "You said, 'more in a moment'?"

"He requires separate consideration. In many ways, he's their most dangerous asset."

"Their international assassin, I assume?"

Cheswick smiled. "Far from it. They don't really go in for that sort of thing in Red, never have. No, he's not trained in karate like Annabel al-Banna, and he doesn't have the survival skills of Phyllis Robinson, or the roundedness of Alec Cunningham. He's an expert in languages and he's a brilliant detective. That's all."

"Any chance of you re-employing him?" Planchart quipped. After the triumph of the Château de Javier Maroc, he was uncharacteristically upbeat.

Cheswick met his remark with a grim chuckle. "I'm not sure we'd want him. He's highly eccentric and known to be wayward. Ruby Parker knows how to keep a tight rein on him, but I'm not sure any of us would. We tend not to indulge idiosyncrasy down in Grey. It's amongst the things that's kept us robust. Farquarson mollycoddled him, which was one of the reasons he was shunted into an honourable resignation."

"Karma. What goes around comes around."

"Post-transition, if I'm to assume control of Grey, as agreed, and we're to dissolve Red, we need to begin with John Mordred. Once he's out of the way, the others should be biddable. Ruby Parker may pose a problem, but she's sixty-one this year, and there's no reason to think she won't accept the same deal Farquarson did once she knows she's finished. We can even go one better if our new connections turn out, and dangle her a peerage. Phyllis Robinson's a long-standing member of the Conservative party, and may be won round with a vigorous appeal to her patriotism; Alec Cunningham's about ripe for a desk-job-with-pay-rise; he can be put out to pasture if necessary. Annabel al-Banna we can threaten. Her father did time in prison, and she probably should have done, and we can argue she may pose a security risk. Yes, she's fiercely loyal to Ruby Parker, but once Ruby Parker's gone, that may not be an issue. She's recently been diagnosed as OCD - Obsessive Compulsive Disorder - and the job means

8

everything to her. I mean, *everything*. She'd be ideal for Grey. I could rehabilitate her."

"Yes, I'm sure you'd enjoy that."

"The only problem might be her husband," Cheswick said, ignoring the wink-wink-nudge-nudge. "A 'Tariq al-Banna', Red's principal IT coordinator. He has limited access to the MI7 mainframe, but of course not to any significant content, not on our floor, nor even on Blue's. His precise allegiances within the obvious parameters aren't known. Or how much influence he has over his wife."

"We'll mark him for investigation, then. Which just leaves John Mordred."

"Unfortunately, there's no *kind* way to deal with Mr Mordred," Cheswick said. "His 2013 psychological evaluation demonstrates an inflexible allegiance to classical moral virtues, even above Queen and country. I'll spare you the detail, but I think it's highly unlikely he can be persuaded to join us. Fortunately, of course, this same inflexibility gives him an Achilles' heel. I've managed to accumulate some pretty damning evidence against him. Little things which, put together, could constitute evidence of radical unreliability."

"If it's material you've accumulated, presumably his boss – 'Ruby Parker'? - already knows about it. Never underestimate the knowledge of spies, nor their ability to sidestep traps."

"Indeed," Cheswick half-agreed. "In any case, one of my main stratagems for discrediting him is already in the pipeline. He should find out about it today, or tomorrow at the latest."

"What are we - you - aiming to do with John Mordred?" Planchart asked. "I mean, ultimately? Thus far, all I've heard is vague intimations. So we can't accommodate him; yes, point taken. In that case, what?"

"I'd like to say, 'let him go'. He knows a lot, but he'd be bound by the Official Secrets Act, and I'm pretty sure he'd respect that. No, it's not his potential leakiness that worries me. It's his powers of detection."

"I'm not sure I follow."

"He'd know I'd disbanded Red, and he'd come after me, and he'd find some way of exposing me - *us*. He wouldn't need to appeal to classified information to do it. We could lose everything."

"Really? He's that good?"

"Moreover," Cheswick went on, "once he's dismissed, we wouldn't necessarily be able to find him to monitor his movements. His exceptional linguistic skills mean he could settle virtually anywhere in the world undetected. He'd pass as a native. We might never find him until it's too late."

"You're talking about killing him. Let's not mince words."

"It may be irregular," Cheswick replied, "but we may well regret it otherwise."

"Presumably then, you should do it now and get it over with."

Cheswick smiled. "That's not possible. If an agent of any department in MI7 is killed, all others are obliged to cooperate in tracking down the murderer. And something analogous to the freedom of information act comes into play. I can't permit that." As if anxious it wasn't yet clear, he added: "No, completely out of the question."

"It doesn't have to be traceable to you," Planchart replied. "I could apply to any one of those men round the table we've just been sitting at. You can give yourself a watertight alibi. If the worst comes to the worst, and any investigation does point in your direction, it won't happen for some time. Post-transition, we'll bury it, you have my word."

Cheswick nodded. "Let's try my way first. First, I'll discredit him, reduce his currency in the eyes of his colleagues. In the end, of course, I'll force his resignation: those uncompromising moral principles again. We can kill him when he's stepped down."

"The key would be to make it look like an accident. Sorry, I know that's stating the obvious, but we've got to lay everything on the table here."

"Naturally."

"What about other significant members of the department? You said earlier these are the core members. Are there others we should be concerned about?"

"Possibly their two newest recruits, Edna Watson - the former the MBE Olympic gold medallist - and Ian Leonard."

"Gold medallist?" Planchart said scornfully. "What sort of a spy is *she* likely to make? Must be pretty hard for *her* to go undercover!"

"John Mordred's not exactly obscure," Cheswick said. "His sister manages a highly successful … 'pop band', if that's the right term nowadays."

Planchart gave a contemptuous grimace.

"'The public agent often does better than the man who has to spend a lot of time and energy keeping undercover'," Cheswick quoted. "James Bond in *From Russia With Love*. And Kim Philby and Anthony Blunt were two of the greatest spies Russia ever had. Hidden in ultra-plain sight. I don't think Red's necessarily out of its mind. In any case, Edna Watson and Ian Leonard are undergoing training in Molenbeek right now under the supervision of Alec Cunningham."

"And Mordred? What's he doing?"

"I don't know. As I say, a lot of what I've supplied is information we in Grey have accrued incidentally in the course of more direct exchanges of information."

"I'd like to at least set some men on Mr Mordred," Planchart said. "Soften him up a bit. There's nothing that provokes a fall from grace better than disorientation, and there's nothing to produce that like a good hiding – especially when it comes out of nowhere."

"That can be arranged through Horvath," Cheswick said. "The private security firm. So long as I don't have to arrange it."

"Leave it to me. Is Durand still in London?"

"I believe so. Waiting, in case you had any last minute orders arising from the conference."

"I haven't. Tell him to get out. He's far too reckless. And he's known to the police, although they haven't anything that would justify their holding him. Tell him to leave the country at once and lie low till further orders."

"He's not under my control. You'd need to contact our French partners."

Planchart sighed irritably. "I'll do it the minute we get back." He shook his head and his annoyance seemed to grow for a moment. "What are we doing about the journalist?" he asked.

"Again, she's a matter for our continental partners. From what I know, she seems to be rarely at home. And she's good at evading a tail. However, my guess is it's only a matter of time before she comes back to you looking for a scoop. Either way, she's in our sights and her days are numbered."

Planchart nodded. It was a miracle she was still going. "We'll keep each other informed," he said flatly, and began to read the file he'd been given.

They settled into silence. A good long while yet till they reached Paris. Cheswick lowered his seat slightly and took a nap. Planchart looked out of the window. Lovely weather, lovely countryside. One day he'd retire here, maybe. The rustic life.

Ten minutes later, as he closed the file, he reached a decision. Never mind what Cheswick thought. Cheswick was nice enough, but he was prone to over-caution.

Of course he was entitled to be, poor man. You didn't have to have read the collected works of John Le Carré to know a mole's life is never a happy one.

The truth was, with Durand dawdling and the journalist still at large, there were already too many ominous variables. Another was out of the question.

This 'John Mordred' had to die, and quickly.

Chapter 2: Before the Lord Mayor

Burgundy walls hung with gilt-framed pictures and mirrors, a glass-domed ceiling, varnished wooden railings, ornamental coping, and an island bar. Everything in The Counting house – once a banking-hall, now a pub deep within the old City of London - came together to give the impression of a nineteenth century hotel crossed with a Soho bordello. Mordred was here with his MI7 colleague, Phyllis Robinson, to kill the thirty minutes or so before their afternoon appointment with the new Lord Mayor of London, just a short walk away in Mansion House. Both agents had been given a half-day off work for the occasion.

Mordred ordered a gin for himself, and a white wine for Phyllis, then they removed their coats and sat at a small leaflet-covered table by a frosted window. Lunchtime, and the floor was beginning to fill with excitable City employees in suits and watches. These were men and women much like themselves – young, attractive and smiling - only in more expensive get-ups: Gucci, Armani or Chanel, as against their M&S and Next. Plenty of tall, well-built, blond haired men like Mordred; plenty of dark haired, tall, athletic women like Phyllis.

"Do you think it's wise to be drinking before we meet Willie?" Phyllis asked. She sipped her wine. "Note to self," she went on: "mustn't call him 'Willie' to his face. It's *William Chester*, Lord Willoughby de Vries."

"We didn't ask for this meeting," Mordred said. "He did. Besides, we're not drinking because we're alcoholics."

She smiled. "Comforting to know."

"Alcohol's supposed to lighten you up. I don't want to get into an argument with him. This is supposed to be a 'bury the hatchet' meeting. If he's got any sense, he'll have had a drink too."

"Alcohol doesn't 'lighten you up'," she said. "It makes you more aggressive."

"It always makes me want to go to sleep."

"That should help bury the hatchet, yes. You nodding off in the middle of a fresh cream meringue."

"I'm not saying I'll actually *go* to sleep, obviously."

"I hope you do. It'll be another for the scrapbook."

"What do you mean, 'another'?"

"I meant one. *One* for the scrapbook. For God's sake, chill out, John. Get another gin if you think it helps. I'm not your mum. I'm just saying."

They sat without speaking or drinking for a few moments. Twice they made eye-contact with each other and smiled. Phyllis looked a lot more relaxed than him, especially given what she'd been through last year in so-called 'World War O'. *Not a kidnap in the true sense,* she said afterwards. *I was well treated.* Still, the Lord Mayor's office had a lot to answer for. Probably, though no indisputable connection had yet been proven. She picked up one of the leaflets – 'Leave' in big yellow letters against a blue background – and read it indifferently.

"Would *you* like another drink?" he asked. "After this?"

"Any thoughts, John?" she replied, ignoring him. "Shall we stay in or shall we come out?"

Her leaflet. The EU. He shrugged. "Stay in. But I'm open to persuasion."

"You don't think Brussels is too big for its boots?"

"Better the devil you know. What about you?"

"Come out. I'd like Britain to be great again."

He laughed.

"What's so funny about that?" she said.

"We *are* great. Think about *The News Quiz* and Grayson Perry."

"Bless." She leaned forward. "Blunt question: how about a date?"

"A - date? That's a bit sudden, isn't it?"

"Or are you seeing someone?"

"Er, no. I'm not."

"I'd love to go out with you, just see what it was like."

He couldn't see how they'd got here. A second ago, it had been all about the EU. "Yes, I'm a real curiosity. I don't usually get that offer after only one glass of wine."

"I've been thinking about it for a while, as a matter of fact. It was just a question of the right time to bring it up."

"I thought you had a boyfriend. Toby."

"Not any more."

They sat looking hard at each other for a few moments. He had no idea if she was being serious. String 'em along and dump 'em might be her style for all he knew. She'd been in the army, so she probably wasn't a confirmed sentimentalist.

"Toby was a thug," she said eventually. "It took me a while to see that, but when I finally did, I performed a post-mortem to see what had set me considering. It was you. I can do better. You're the future of men, John. A good conversationalist with a strong conscience who likes the company of women and doesn't see it as a weakness to defer, even to capitulate, given good enough reasons."

"You've heard of the curse of Mordred, right?"

"Remind me."

"The first woman I loved turned out to be a member of Black. So once our joint mission was over, I never saw her again. Then there was Gina. The less said about that the better. I even thought about marrying Annabel for a while."

"Annabel? Oh, yes, I remember now."

"She said she loved me. Then she married Tariq. Don't mention this conversation to her, by the way."

"Let sleeping dogs lie."

"She married someone else. I'd hardly call that a *sleeping dog*. More dead in the water."

"What a poignant image."

"And the tragedy is, there's nothing the RSPCA can do."

Phyllis drained her glass. "In sum, no one can live long in the brilliant light that is John Mordred. Luckily, I love to flirt with danger. And I'm a born survivor."

"I'm flattered you're even considering the possibility."

"You find me attractive, yes? I won't cry if you say no."

"You *are* attractive, but I think we should be concentrating on the Lord Mayor."

"It's decided then. At least something good will have come out of today now, whatever happens at Mansion House, and I'm not optimistic about that. Now, concerning the time and place."

"And ... something tells me you've already made your mind up about that?"

"Promise you won't freak out? Come on, talk a bit more quickly, John. We've got to be at Mansion House in a few minutes."

"I promise I won't freak out."

"Two weeks in July. The island of Capri. In the Gulf of Naples."

He laughed. "Er ... *what?* Are you being serious?"

"Yes or no?"

"It's not a very conventional first date."

"Yes or no?"

"Just us two?"

"And the Italians, yes. I'm not bringing Toby, or my parents, or any of my friends. Just you and me. Look, I've been in your flat. I know that in addition to all your other endearing qualities, you're house proud. There's no catch. Say no if you like, but I warn you, you'll never see me again."

"That should be quite difficult, us being coll - "

"Yes or no? Yes or no? *Yes or no?* Sorry to be persistent, but most men would have decided by now."

"Yes, definitely. Is it already booked?"

"Already *arranged*. Look, the villa belongs to Annabel. Part of her recent inheritance from her father, old Pa Gould. She agreed to let me stay there a fortnight *gratis* on one condition: I could get you to come with me, and I wouldn't take anyone else. I guess she'll come and check on us sometime during the holiday, just to make sure I'm fulfilling her matchmaking terms and conditions."

The bitter truth sank in. He nodded. "So it's not me you want, it's Annabel's villa."

"I knew if I told you the details, you'd come over all holier-than-thou."

"So what are *your* 'terms and conditions'? I assume sex is out of the question."

"I didn't expect you to ask that. I'm disappointed."

He glowered. "But since I *have* ..."

"It *is* a first date."

"So let's see. It's April now. You're asking me out on a date. But in three months' time. Just so we don't have to breach the no-sex supposed 'rule' pertaining to first dates."

"Two. Two months' time. The beginning of July, not the end." She rolled her eyes irritably. "Okay, look, you can have sex if you like!"

"I don't *want* sex. I just need to know exactly how you're looking at this whole thing."

"Look, John, I'm not *that* desperate for a fortnight in Capri. Coming up: a bit of a reality check, if you don't mind. It's the twenty-first century. I'm an independent woman and I'm not famed for my parsimony. I can easily buy my own holidays when I want to, and still have change for anything else that takes my fancy. Can you imagine how that might be, an entire fortnight sharing a villa with someone you don't particularly like – or even someone you're broadly indifferent to? I'd actually pay good money to get out of that, thank you, and so would you - and so would just about anyone I know. When Annabel made her offer, it sounded like a dream come true. So yes. *Yes*, we can have sex. We can have sex on the floor now, if you like! Get it out of the way!"

They suddenly realised the whole pub had stopped to listen to them. Mordred looked at the barman, then back at Phyllis.

"I'm not sure it's allowed," he told her.

She stood up and bowed deeply to the assemblage. "*No Sex, Please, We're British*. Theatre Royal, Drury Lane, until the end of April. We do matinee performances every Thursday and Friday at 2pm. Pick up a leaflet on your way out, and thanks for listening. Sorry if we alarmed you, but hey, that's showbiz. Got to get bums on seats somehow. Have a great afternoon."

She sat down to an almost universal 'Aaah!' of appreciative enlightenment. A few people applauded. The conversational roar resumed.

"Well done," Mordred said.

"I'll have another glass of wine. A large one. Then we're going." She caught sight of something behind him and her jaw dropped. "Good God. Don't turn around."

He looked at his watch. They still had five minutes. After that, it would have to be a taxi. "What is it?" he asked.

"*Farquarson.*"

"Sir Ranulph?"

"How many Farquarsons do you know?"

He smiled. "One. But I'm guessing you know at least five."

"Funny. Very funny. I'm not a toff, John, just a Tory. I actually went to school at a comprehensive, if it helps."

He laughed. "It's really, really useful. Thank you."

"People assume that because I wear nice clothes and took elocution lessons when I was sixteen and once had a boyfriend called Toby, I must be some sort of Sloane Ranger. Well, I'm not. We need to get past all that if we're going to have a meaningful relationship, as opposed to a mere teenage one."

"What's so terrible about Farquarson being here?"

"It's just awkward, that's all. He's the ex-head of Grey, and we used to work in Grey, and he left under some sort of cloud."

"No, he didn't."

"Yes, he did."

"He was pensioned off," Mordred said. "There was no implication that he was involved in any wrongdoing."

"What's he doing here?"

"Is he with anyone?"

"An old woman," Phyllis replied. "About his age. His wife, I assume. Maybe he's just enjoying a day out."

"That would be the best explanation, yes."

"Well, the rules state that in this sort of situation, he's not allowed to acknowledge us, nor we him. I guess that's what makes it awkward. I quite liked him."

"I'd imagine we all did. Listen, all we have to do is stand up and leave. Keeping our heads down. It's time for us to go, anyway."

"Sit still. He's coming over. Don't make eye-contact. Here." She passed him the 'We're Better Off Inside' leaflet. She resumed reading 'Leave'. They kept their eyes glued to their pages until after he'd passed. He left a strong smell of *eau de cologne* in his wake.

"That was close," she said. "I half expected him to make some oh-so-droll aside about the Theatre Royal. I know he's not allowed to, but in his position, I'd have found it irresistible."

"What happens if we *do* acknowledge him? Will there be an explosion?"

"I don't want to find out. But yes, I expect so. Give him a minute."

"We're going to be late."

She drew a sharp breath. "He's coming back. Bloody, bloody hell."

They picked up their leaflets and pretend-read again. Farquarson's elderly head appeared between them. They jumped violently.

"Oh, er, hello, sir," Mordred said. They sat up like disobedient children.

"I know this is a serious breach of protocol," Farquarson hissed sourly, "but there's something you need to see. Phyllis, you stay there. John, follow me."

They didn't argue. Phyllis took their empty glasses back to the bar. Mordred saw a man of about his age offer her a drink. She accepted. When it arrived, it was a spirit of some kind with ice. She downed it in one.

Mordred didn't know how, assuming – what now seemed more than possible - Farquarson wasn't in his right mind, he was going to break it to him that they had an urgent appointment just round the corner. His misgivings increased when Farquarson drew him deeper into the pub. He'd been expecting to be led outside onto the street.

"Turn around," the old man said, when they were almost against the wall. "Look out of the window."

He clocked Farquarson's sight-line and tried to follow it. A small-ish café on the other side of the road with two tables outside. Each table with a couple. The nearest, two men, the foremost of whom had his back to them. Something disturbingly familiar about the other one, though, and -

"Good *God*," Mordred said.

"Tell me I'm not seeing things."

"But it can't be. What would he be doing back in London?"

"Should I call the police, do you think?"

Pierre Durand. Mordred hadn't seen him for over a year. The last time their paths had crossed, the Frenchman was working for one of MI7's longest-standing adversaries. He'd suddenly disappeared – apparently from the face of the earth

– at the conclusion of a major investigation which had very nearly ended in disaster for the whole secret service. He was still high on British Intelligence's Wanted list. Bringing him in trumped everything, even the Lord Mayor.

Phyllis appeared alongside them. "We're actually one minute late now," she said, short-temperedly. "I'd rather not lose my job, if it's all the same with you two. What are you looking at?"

She did what Mordred had done, and followed the direction of their gaze. Her mouth popped open.

"Never!" she said. She whistled softly, and took a moment to digest the evidence of her eyes. "Well, at least now, we've got an excuse. How are we going to play this?"

"No point in calling the police," Mordred said. "He's not known to them. No point in calling Thames House either. By the time anyone gets over here, he'll be long gone. It's down to us."

"Count me out," Farquarson said. "I've just had a new hip fitted, and the one hundred metre dash isn't an option."

"Have you a smartphone?" Mordred asked him.

Farquarson held one up. "I thought you might say that. Nokia Lumia. The best."

"We need pictures," Mordred said. "Especially of who he's talking to. Phyllis and I will keep a watch. You move out. Keep it discreet, obviously. You're just a snap-happy tourist, that's all."

"Thank you," Farquarson replied drily. "I *was* going to go over there and point it right in his face. I completely forgot I used to be a head of section and before that, in charge of recruitment and training. So thanks awfully for your wise advice."

"Apologies."

Farquarson sighed, muttered something about ageism under his breath, and moved away without a farewell. His wife met him at the door. They linked arms.

"Are we absolutely sure it's Durand?" Phyllis whispered, as if the Frenchman might overhear.

"About fifty, tall, lean with a hangdog expression, sparse, jet-black hair, slicked back, and black rings under his eyes. Doesn't mean much on its own, but it's that thrill of recognition that counts. You felt it too, yes?"

She smiled. "It's him all right. To repeat my earlier question: do you have a plan?"

"There are two of us, but depending on who his companion is, that may not give us an advantage. Durand's twenty years older than us, but I don't think he's a weakling. We may have our work cut out."

"So the answer to my question is, 'no'."

"Thanks to the bloody Lord Mayor, we're in a real jam."

"Forget poor Willie. If we bring this guy in, we'll get a medal. Medals are what make life worth living and what mayors understand above all. We won't be in trouble, John."

"Granted. I didn't mean that."

"So what the hell *are* you talking about?"

"Normally, I'd say, let's shadow him and find out where he goes, then come back later with a reliable army. That's risky anyway. He used to work for the French secret service, so it's not like he won't be on high alert. We stand a high chance of losing him. If that were to happen, what would we tell the Lord Mayor? It'd look like an excuse."

"Farquarson would back us up."

"Right now, there's no love lost between MI7 and the City of London Corporation. Farquarson's one of us. Willie might not necessarily believe him, and we've been given the afternoon off to kiss and make up."

"We're already late. I think that particular ship may have sailed."

"Right now, the only way we can salvage it is if we're *seen* to be apprehending Durand. We can't do that clandestinely. We've got to make it as public as possible, so when we have to make our excuses to Willie, we've got public evidence that prevents it looking like a shaggy dog story. Which is going to be equally difficult, because I haven't got handcuffs or a gun."

"So what are you saying? Stop calling him 'Willie', by the way."

"That we're going to have to make a display of apprehending him, hope he makes a dramatic run for it, hope we catch him, hope he puts up a fight, hope we beat him, hope the police take us all into custody. Even William, with all his suspicions, will have to believe that."

She sighed. "So it's all about William."

"Looks like he's forcing our hand again."

"You go over and make a citizen's arrest," she said soberly. "Or try to. I'll go wide, ready to cover either direction."

"Can you sprint in those shoes?"

"I'll take them off, stupid. Take your phone out and ring me. We'll keep in touch that way."

He did as instructed.

They put their coats on, went outside and split up, holding their phones to their ears. A bright day, a fresh wind from the west, a traffic jam. Phyllis walked straight along the pavement at a trot, keeping her head down until she was level with the two tables. Mordred walked across the road between the traffic. It was obvious from the outset that Durand was jumpy enough to bolt at a moment's notice. He didn't look like he felt remotely safe in London. He looked like he thought the city was crammed with people who wanted to hunt him to oblivion.

He looked at Mordred no less hard than he looked at everyone who passed. Long before the two men were within touching distance, Durand was out of his chair and staring wildly at his would-be apprehender as if he both could and couldn't believe his eyes. *Could* because it was what he'd been expecting all along. *Couldn't* because he hadn't specifically prepared to meet his own maker on this particular street at this precise hour. He threw his chair to one side and ran east at top speed.

Mordred went after him. Durand turned hard right at Gracechurch Street, and suddenly they were both going full pelt.

For a moment, it looked like Durand might be heading towards London Bridge, but he turned sharp left and kept going. The crowds made running at speed difficult, and Durand was barging through bodies as roughly as he could, obviously trying to fell people and hinder the pursuit. Phyllis probably couldn't keep up, not in bare feet. Mordred put his phone to his ear.

"Phyllis, if you can hear me, we're in Fenchurch street, heading for Tower Bridge. I've still got him in sight. Get in a taxi and meet me over there. Call Ruby Parker, see what she can do."

Down by the Thames, Durand kept going east. He looked like he thought he had an idea and he'd promised his body it wouldn't be long now. He was putting everything into his legs, and once they reached the quay walkway, he actually began to pull away slightly. Did he have rescuers to hand? What about the man he'd been with, outside the Counting House? Could he be about to reappear from somewhere, pull off the rescue of the century?

Then Mordred saw. The Tower of London. Of course, providing he managed to barge past security, there were lots of places to hide in there. For a man who trusted in his cunning more than his brawn, a maze of buildings, hillocks and verdure probably looked as safe a bet as he could conceivably expect. The two men hurtled down the main entrance between the two towers.

Mordred's phone rang. He must have put it down. "Yes?"

"Where are you, John?" Phyllis.

"The Tower of London."

"I'm in a car. *Tower of London, driver*. Ruby Parker knows. I'll be there in two minutes. Don't do anything stupid. He might be … "

She obviously couldn't say 'armed' in front of the driver, and Mordred hadn't time for a discussion anyway. Durand bundled past a group of primary school children, tossing them out of the way like little furry animals. A Beefeater, obviously stymied with disbelief, lunged half-heartedly at him, but he replied with a Karate move that left the guard winded and nose-bleeding against a wall. Girls screamed. Durand yanked a gun from his coat pocket without a seeming object in view, but without breaking stride, and headed straight for the main tower.

"Police," Mordred said, flashing his phone at whoever-on-the-gate as if it was a card. No one tried to stop him. He jumped over a pair of crouching, whimpering bodies then accelerated. They were heading for the White Tower, right in the centre of the fort.

Another scramble past tourists and they were inside. Just a matter of time, surely, before Durand started brandishing that gun. The only way to stop him was to close the gap between them to make the three-stage process of stopping, turning and pointing his weapon impossible to complete before Mordred was on top of him.

Several floors and suddenly, they were on top of a tower. Not a high one with a cover. He couldn't envisage where it was from the outside – mostly, up here, you saw the sky - but they were alone, thank God.

Durand ran away across the floor space and raised his gun. Mordred froze, raised his hands. Whatever happened now, it was over for the Frenchman. The question was whether he'd want to take his pursuer with him. Murder versus …

Well, versus what? What were they going to charge Durand with? Possession of a firearm? Assault? 'Known to the security services' didn't necessarily mean outside the law. Holding on to him was going to be a problem. For all his jitters, he'd know that. He almost certainly wouldn't shoot.

Then Mordred saw. It wasn't even a real gun. They didn't even have that on him. Did that matter? Couldn't they detain him without charge for a long while? He couldn't think.

Durand dropped his replica weapon and put his hands up. He didn't look happy, but neither did he look defeated.

Mordred was already on the phone to Phyllis. "Durand's just surrendered. The police should be here in a moment. I'm at the White Tower. Get someone to message my credentials over. If I can get out of here fast, we might be able to catch the tail-end of tea with William. Better that than nothing, and at least we've got a whole city full of witnesses to our excuse."

He heard Phyllis sigh. "Farquarson was mugged," she said. "By the guy who was with Durand. Who's now got his mobile."

Behind Mordred, two elderly Beefeaters and a clutch of what looked like security personnel arrived in haste to take charge of the situation. They grabbed Mordred and Durand from all sides – six men apiece – and wrestled them unnecessarily to the ground. As he went down, Mordred dropped his phone. He watched it skid away.

"You're in big trouble, son," one of his apprehenders told him.

Chapter 3: Tea With Chester

Mordred never discovered exactly how it happened, but by the time he'd reached the ground floor of the White Tower, he was free to go. No one shook his hand or apologised. They just released him and told him to be on his way. He stepped onto the lawn, walked in between the visitors for a while, then turned, dusted himself down and examined his general appearance. They'd torn his jacket at the shoulder. Even if the Lord Mayor gig was still on, he couldn't go dressed like this. Neither could he go home and get changed: it was too far. It'd have to be Thames House if it was anything. They kept spare sets of clothes there, amazingly, something for every occasion.

But what was he thinking? Lord Mayors were busy people. It obviously wasn't going to happen now. Not today, anyway. Maybe not ever.

He stood to watch a police car crawl along the path to receive Durand. Once the Frenchman had been handcuffed and accompanied onto the rear seat, Mordred double-backed and went up the tower stairs to retrieve his phone. It was still lying where he'd dropped it. Ringing. *Ruby Parker*, his boss.

"Where are you now?" she asked when he picked up. She sounded neither pleased nor displeased.

"Still at the Tower. On my way back to base now. I assume Chester - Lord Willoughby - knows why I couldn't come."

"He's been informed. He says the invitation's still open."

"Great. When?"

"He'll see you at three."

"Three?"

"It's only one thirty-five now. Is that a problem?"

"Only that the arm's hanging off my best jacket. I assume Phyllis is still going too."

"It's the same arrangement as before, only two hours later."

28

"I can't go there looking like this."

"He knows what you've been doing. It'll give you added kudos."

"Sorry, I feel uncomfortable going to a formal meeting in a torn suit. Call me fussy."

Pause. He expected a smack on the wrists, but her voice, when it came, was conciliatory. "I call it professional, as a matter of fact. I'll get Amber to pick you out a replacement suit at Thames House. And I'll send Kevin to fetch you in the car. Go and wait outside the Tower entrance. Oh, and John?"

"Yes?"

"Good job. Phyllis has explained why it had to be such a high drama. I agree. You were right to play it like you did." She chuckled. "Risky, though. Good job you caught him."

"He was a challenge. I'll give him that."

"See you over here in about twenty minutes' time."

Amber Goodings was Head of Wardrobe, a stout fifty year-old with big spectacles. The suit she'd chosen for him was in just about every sense what he'd have selected for himself. Grey, nicely fitting and modern without being too trendy. And a matching tie, shirt and shoes. He asked her if this particular piece of kit had been ordered specifically with him in mind. "You're an important member of the organisation now, John," she'd replied. "We've got lots of clothes in your exact size. More than you can imagine."

"Can I see them?" he asked.

"No."

It was getting on for half two. There wasn't time to press the matter. But he would one day. Meanwhile, it was disturbing that there was someone who knew more about what he should wear than he did himself. He looked at his reflection in Amber's full-length mirror. God help him, he looked a damn sight better than he had in The Counting House. Or probably any time in the last six months.

He wondered if Amber was available outside work as a professional shopper. And if so, how much she charged.

More than he could afford, without a doubt.

When he was dressed, he went downstairs, checked out with Colin at reception and went to the grey C Class Mercedes-Benz Coupé outside. Phyllis sat on the back seat looking exactly as she had at the pub, only more disgruntled. She was examining her face in a hand-mirror and refreshing her lipstick. She made a show of moving up when Mordred opened the door, even though she'd already left ample room for him. Kevin was driving.

"Hi, Kev," Mordred said. "It's me again."

Kevin ignored him.

"Nice weather we're having. I mean, for the time of year."

Kevin ignored him.

"You're quite the hero, I hear," Phyllis said tartly.

"Yep."

"Why does nothing exciting ever happen to *me*?"

"You were kidnapped last year, possibly by men connected to the Lord Mayor. I wouldn't call that 'nothing'."

"Pretty passive, though. Incidentally, you look good in that suit. I assume it's one of Amber's."

"What makes you think it's not one of my own?"

"Don't get touchy, John. I'm not suggesting you've no style, but Amber's in a class of her own. Who do you think chooses my clothes? I don't do it myself. I used to. People used to say I had taste. Then I wore something Amber picked out for me. An official function at Guildhall, strictly work-related. She took me to a whole new level. I've never looked back."

"She claims she's got more clothes for me than I can possibly imagine."

"Me too. If only we could gain access."

They stopped speaking and looked out of their windows at the river. London Bridge was unusually quiet. The buildings either side of them were mainly office-functional: cuboid concrete with rows of parallel, vacant-looking windows. A passenger plane flew high overhead.

Five minutes later, the car drew to a halt in front of Mansion House, a large old grey building with six Corinthian columns in a portico. This was the heart of the financial centre, and populated by the kinds of skyscrapers beloved of bankers everywhere: ninety-nine per cent smoked glass with reinforced steel frames. Kevin got out and opened the door for Phyllis. Mordred waited for a gap in the traffic, let himself out into the road and came round to join her.

"Why doesn't Kevin like you?" Phyllis asked as the car drew away.

Mordred did up the middle button of his jacket. "If you ever find out, let me know."

They went up the steps at the front of the building and into reception where they gave their names and sat down. 2.57. Three minutes.

"Switch off your mobile," Phyllis said.

A middle-aged man with a pile of straight grey hair and a bulbous nose came to get them. Because he wore a suit, Mordred's first impression was that he must be the Lord Mayor, but he adjusted when the man called him "sir". He realised for the first time that he had no idea what William Chester looked like. In all his considerations up till now, he'd employed a completely invented image: a thin, nondescript man of about sixty with swept-across grey hair and square wire-rimmed glasses. How would the real Chester match up? The guide led them up two flights of stairs. He knocked at the fourth door along after they'd turned left into a corridor.

"Come in, Philip," a plum voice from inside called. The man opened the door to admit them, then closed it from the outside.

They found themselves in a room with two large bookcases, and three armchairs arranged around a table laid with a teapot, three cups, milk and sugar and a variety of cakes on a three-tier plate stand. The walls were dotted with pictures and a huge mullioned window in the opposite wall was flanked by two sky-blue curtains. The room's sole occupant was a thin, nondescript man of about sixty with swept-across grey hair and square wire-rimmed glasses. William Chester. Luckily, there was enough of a disjunct between the mental image and the reality to stop Mordred feeling overwhelmed by *déjà vu*.

Chester came across the room to meet them, saying his name and extending his hand. "Sit down, sit down," he said, when introductions had been exchanged.

Mordred liked the fact that there was tea available, but no coffee; that it had been brewed and brought in before their arrival; that the cake-stand was cheap-looking and the cakes unremarkable. He imagined himself telling Phyllis this when they got out, then thought better of it. It gave him the sense of Chester as fundamentally unpretentious, the kind of man who didn't understand what networking was or how to use arcane arrays of cutlery and/or designer crockery to overawe his enemies. What used to be called 'a decent sort'.

Once tea had been poured – and the Lord Mayor poured it: he didn't call Philip back in to do it for him – and cakes distributed, Chester delivered the speech he'd obviously prepared earlier.

"I want you to know," he said, "that I consider the events of last year to be something of a black mark on the City of London Corporation. We should have cooperated with you from the beginning and next time, we will. I brought you here today to offer my apologies in person, because I know that you were both put to a lot more trouble than you should have been."

Mordred had been briefed as to the proper response to this, so it wasn't a free conversation as such. He wasn't allowed to say, *Is there going to be an official inquiry?* He had to say, *Thank you, sir. We look forward to working with you.* The words stuck in his throat.

"Thank you, sir," Phyllis said. "We look forward to working with you."

"Outstanding icing on this," Mordred said, mainly to prevent the ensuing silence gaining the upper hand. "Hint of coconut."

"My wife made all the cakes here," Chester replied.

"They're marvellous," Phyllis said.

Before he arrived, Mordred wondered what they'd all talk about once the apology had been offered and the olive branch tendered, but Chester was prepared for the transition, and asked them in general terms about their 'exciting day'. Mordred recounted his pursuit of Durand without going into detail about the who or the why, then the conversation turned, as it often did in this sort of situation, first, to the intelligence service generally, what it was like to work there, then the new James Bond film, then to a comparison of different Bonds, then to who should play Bond next. Almost before they knew it, an hour had passed, and it was time to leave. Handshakes were re-exchanged. Philip arrived and escorted the two agents back to reception, where they picked up their coats.

"Well, that was fun," Phyllis said, when they were outside.

"You'd never think he was king of the crooks," Mordred said.

"They're not crooks."

"Corporate tax-avoiders. Libor-fixers. Manipulators of democratically elected governments."

"You don't know what you're talking about, John. Would you like to share a taxi back to base?"

"I'm going home now," Mordred said. "We were given the half-day off, remember? I haven't anything at Thames House that can't wait. I told Amber I'd bring the suit back tomorrow."

"Lucky you. Unfortunately, I'm knee-deep in the Frances Holland case. I'm working serious overtime at the moment. Still, it's good for my career."

"I understand you're in charge of the investigation. Why haven't I been roped in? Don't you want me or something?"

"I was keeping you in reserve."

"Thanks," he said drily.

"It's a compliment. Ruby Parker agrees with me too. When John Mordred gets into an investigation, he starts seeing things the rest of us can't. It's not good to have one person who's too insightful. It prevents the rest of us developing. I'll call you if things get too intractable. Besides, you've work of your own to do."

"Examining junior agents' reports. It's supposed to give me an 'overview'."

"Professional development, it's called. Don't knock it. I assume you want to get on at work."

"Do you?"

She shot him a disgruntled look. "Of course. I'm sane."

"What if 'getting on' puts you in a position where you don't like what you're doing?"

"E.G.?"

"Would you like Ruby Parker's job, for example?"

"At her age, yes. Not now."

"How old do you think she is?"

"Could be anywhere between forty-five and sixty. I don't know. Black people age better, so they say. Listen, John. If someone offers me a job that involves nothing but looking at other agents' reports, I'll say no. So will you. But even that isn't how it works. Jobs come up, you apply if you want them, you don't if you don't. What's the matter with you? You've come over all moody."

"Funny day."

"And yet you could have been doing paperwork. Hard life."

He laughed. "Roll on July."

"That's more like it. Now, stop moaning and push off home, loser."

She saw a cab and hailed it. It almost screeched to a halt. She had that power over taxis, no one knew who'd taught her, when, or even whether it was a transferable skill. She gave him a little wave, an affectionate, "Be seeing you!" and was gone.

There was a bus to where he lived from here. But maybe he should wander round the town for a bit. Nothing more calculated to increase his despondency than sitting alone in front of *Young and Obese – Confronting the Crisis?* with only a bowl of mushroom soup and a stale bun for company. Even staying within the Square Mile wasn't as bad as that. Call Alec, perhaps? Go and see a film? Go to the top floor of a high building and drink a cocktail by the window with the best view? Something crazy like an ice-skating rink somewhere? This was London in the 21st century. Nothing was out of the question.

But home – such as it was - was calling him. For some reason, it seemed the only meaningful option. Common sense told him he didn't have to have soup: there were other choices. And he didn't have to watch TV. He could read a book. He could even download a new one on his e-reader. Treat himself. Something by that Man Booker prize woman with the golden armlet.

He suddenly knew what was troubling him. The Counting House. *I assume sex is out of the question.* A stupid remark, the memory of which made him squirm with embarrassment. The truth was, he'd done all the one night stand stuff when he'd been a teenager, and he hadn't enjoyed it. Nowadays, he didn't want sex with someone he didn't love. And he didn't love Phyllis.

Which meant their going to Capri together was going to be difficult, if not impossible.

She'd cornered him, though. *I warn you, you'll never see me again*. She'd been joking, but not entirely. 'No, I don't want to go to Capri with you' wouldn't have been well received, that was for sure.

Maybe he could *try* to fall in love with her. He had till July. Two and a bit months. She was attractive, witty and intelligent. What used to be called 'a catch'. You could love to order, surely? Definitely with someone like that? He'd just have to push himself.

The supreme irony was, she was completely out of his league. The once minor supermodel and the – well, he didn't even *know* what *he* was: there wasn't a word for it. Even if someone invented one, it wouldn't be a good word. It'd be somewhere between 'scarecrow' and 'clown'. He ought to feel colossally grateful.

He was about to pick up an *Evening Standard* – the headline, *Planchart launches scathing attack on Cameron's 'Euro-Grovelling'* looked like a forget-your-problems read for the tube – when he suddenly felt someone take his left elbow. At first, he thought he must be mistaken, but the grip tightened and he turned to find a man of about his own age – no one he knew - in a suit-minus-tie, leering into his eyes. Someone took his other arm. He turned. A clone of the first. City types, possibly drunk after some works bash.

"Hello, *John*," the man on his left said.

"Going anywhere special?" the other asked.

Mordred tried to stop, but they kept propelling him forward. They were obviously prepared to drag him if need be, and they had tight hold now. A hundred thoughts crowded into his head at once. About how, since they knew his name, this probably wasn't a casual meeting; and how, given that, they probably weren't what they looked; about how they wouldn't be doing this if they thought they could take him freely; and how, given their bulk and youth, and that there were two of them, they probably had violence in mind.

While one part of his mind processed all this with a view to formulating a plan, another part told him it would be a good idea to find out what they wanted before turning on them.

"What's going on?" he asked, trying to sound frightened.

"What did you go to see the Mayor about, *Johnny boy?*"

"Who are you?" Mordred persisted. "Why do you want to know?"

"Let's just say we're friends of the City. With Lord Willoughby's best interests at heart."

He doubted that. "Why don't you ask him yourself?"

"We're asking *you*," the one on his left said, in a syrupy voice. They sped up. There weren't any deserted alleyways in London, which was going to make beating him up a challenge, since they probably didn't want to do it in broad daylight. They must be taking him to either a car or a building. He couldn't tell which: no obvious candidate in view yet. Either way, they probably had reinforcements to hand.

So far he'd played compliant in the hope of augmenting their sense of security. Now he put all his strength into reversing and throwing himself backwards to the ground. He calculated their forward momentum against his backward would bring them to a halt, and the deliberate fall would throw them off-balance and ideally, into each other. In the past, he'd seen it done effectively enough to crack the two men's heads together. Unlikely to work as well this time.

It didn't even catch them particularly unawares. Obviously professionals. As usual in these sorts of situations though, his brain was ahead of his thought-out plan, and at a certain point, things just seemed to happen of their own accord. He was on his back now. He twisted round and squeezed the groin of the man on the left like it was a bunch of grapes and he was Bacchus. The two men finally cracked heads, and he sensed their panic.

With his other hand, he grabbed the ankle of the man on his right and rived it up into the air. Not quite the clincher he was hoping for, but from the side, he head-butted the one leg the man still had planted rigid on the ground, and felt the kneecap go.

He'd never known he was capable of anything like this. Contortionism. And so odd to be winning a fight against superior numbers from ground level.

He sprang to his feet. A clutch of passers-by had stopped to watch, horror written on all their faces. He released the first man's groin, waited the split second till he'd clambered to his feet, then punched him hard in the face. The man went down and lay still, His comrade was still gasping on the ground, clutching his leg like he'd been dismembered. He wouldn't be getting up any time soon.

As Mordred walked away, he wondered who they were. Perhaps he should go back and take photos of them. Obviously, the police would then arrive and he'd be bundled into a Paddy Waggon, but that didn't matter. He'd probably been caught on camera already – ten or twelve cameras, for that matter.

But so had they. He'd report back to base and deal with the police from behind the protective shield of MI7. He hadn't started it, they had. And since they knew who he was, it probably wasn't best interpreted as a private matter.

He took his phone out of his pocket and switched it on. *Missed call.*

Then it began to ring. *Ruby Parker.*

So she'd heard already? Bloody hell, talk about fast. He wondered how she'd found out, and what sort of a slant she'd got on it.

"John," she said. "We've got a problem. Durand's out."

"Er - *what?*"

"I don't know the details, but I believe a veritable army of lawyers was waiting for him at the police station. Somehow, incredibly, our prevention of terrorism communique was disregarded. We're still hazy about the details, but I'm going over there now to create merry hell and get some answers. I thought I'd better let you know before you found out from someone else."

"Who the hell would hire a team of lawyers to get Durand out?"

"That's partly what I aim to find out."

"Which lawyers?"

"A strictly upmarket outfit by the name of Simpson, Musgrave and De Groot. Who also work for the Lord Mayor, although that may be coincidental."

Mordred chuckled darkly. "It may also be chance that I've just been attacked in broad daylight by two heavies claiming to represent him."

"Attacked?"

"They came off much the worse, although I may need you to plead my case to the police when they arrive."

"Where are you now?"

"On my way home. There didn't seem much point in hanging around. I'm a member of the security services. According to the manual, in these sorts of cases, I'm supposed to make myself scarce before the press arrive and start blowing things up out of all proportion."

"Absolutely right. Go home and file an encrypted report via the website. I'll take care of the rest."

"Thanks."

He put the phone down and made for the tube. Perhaps there was something to be said for paperwork, after all.

Chapter 4: The Radical

Mordred awoke at four o'clock the next morning, unable to sleep. *Durand*. What was he doing in London? How untouchable was he? How far in advance had he known the police wouldn't be able to keep him? What was his – or their - next step, if anything? Wild questions, produced by conventional early morning, dark-outside morbidity.

He had to talk to Ruby Parker, but obviously that wasn't possible at this time. Someone, somewhere was laughing at him. Certainly, Durand would be. Maybe Simpson, Musgrave and De Groot too. At how he'd raced across London and torn a perfectly good suit all for nothing. Had he known at the White Tower what he knew now, he'd have put up more of a fight when they wrestled him to the ground. He just looked like a dud.

To Phyllis, amongst others. Another passenger on board his insomnia wagon.

He got out of bed, made himself a coffee and walked through into his living room. Phyllis was right. He *was* quite house proud – or he'd become so lately. For a long time, the floor here had been occupied by boxes – mainly of language resources – but nowadays, he had everything he needed at Thames House. He'd shipped some of his own things over there, and binned the rest. What he'd been left with was minimalism - sofa, TV/ DVD player, table and chairs, and hardly anything in the way of ornamentation. Which could – yes, probably would – give the outward impression he was the tidy sort.

He wasn't generally one for graveyard hour angst. Probably more frequent when you reached middle-age: all those opportunities you'd never grasped, places you hadn't visited, relationships that might have been. Or so you thought. He was only thirty-one, and he quite liked his job. Durand – or Phyllis - or both - must really have spooked him.

He sat on the sofa. Netflix, that should distract him. He flicked through the options for five minutes, then switched the TV off. He went into the kitchen, poured his coffee away, and got back into bed.

He suddenly realised he didn't care about Durand, not really. There were seven billion people on earth. What did it matter if one of them was laughing at him? The Frenchman might think himself pretty clever now, but in the end, they were both going to die, and no one would ever remember what had happened in the White Tower one sunny April day in 2016.

But still he couldn't get to sleep. He turned onto one side then the other, and couldn't keep his eyes closed. Willpower, that was what counted. Force yourself to stay still and ignore all the little suggestions of bodily discomfort, whether you'd be snugger on this or that side, with your arms here or there. Prayer as a last resort.

Suddenly, he knew what was troubling him. It wasn't Durand at all. Much less Phyllis.

It was the Lord Mayor.

He'd been … not quite right somehow. What was it? Mordred mentally reviewed the micro-expressions connected with basic emotions. Deception, probably. That would fit with those two bouncer 'friends' of his.

But no, it wasn't that. What was it?

It was *fear*. He'd been afraid. And not just slightly. Very.

Suddenly, things made sense. Some things. It was the reason tea had been such a lethargic affair. Because, at bottom, Chester couldn't be bothered with it. It was the reason they'd had that kooky conversation about the next 007. He was too scared to care what he looked like, and he didn't want to talk about himself.

Mordred was wide awake now. Sleep wasn't even vaguely possible any more. One: the Lord Mayor was scared; two: his lawyers were the same as Durand's; three: two men claiming to represent the City had accosted Mordred on his way home. What was the connection?

Impossible to discern. It was like the first round of *Catchphrase*, trying to guess the bonus board when you only had three outside squares.

Which assumed there *was* a connection, that they were just three little parts of a much bigger puzzle.

Which might not be the case at all.

Only, he felt sure it was.

He arrived in Thames House at 8.50, not knowing where the day would take him. After checking in with Colin at reception and handing the suit back for storage, he went to his desk where his itinerary for the day would be waiting. As expected, a meeting with Ruby Parker at nine sharp. Nothing after that. Good: that probably meant his schedule was up in the air. The significant possibility of no more junior reports for the time being. He'd had enough of an overview, anyway. It was beginning to get him down.

8.58 already. He went straight to Ruby Parker's office and knocked on the door. A voice from within commanded him to enter.

Her office was small. Just big enough for a desk, a few house plants, a small black woman in a skirt-suit and one other item of the occupant's choosing. For reasons he'd never enquired about, her chosen item was a tank full of tropical fish. It always looked well-cared for. Who cleaned it out was a mystery. Ruby Parker somehow seemed too important, but that couldn't be right either. The government paid for everything in here and it wasn't prone to subsidise idiosyncrasies. Maybe it was *self*-cleaning. This was the second millennium after all, and he knew next to nothing about the maintenance of aquaria. It could well be. Maybe the fish cleaned it themselves.

"Are you interested in tropical fish, John?" Ruby Parker asked drily, calling him back to more important things.

"Not in general," he said. "But when they're to hand, yes."

She sat down and gestured for him to do likewise. "Durand's lawyers had rounded up a group of witnesses from outside The Counting House, including the proprietor of the café he'd been sitting outside. The police claim they didn't receive our communication asking that he be detained until *after* the lawyers had removed him."

"Didn't they even want to keep him for questioning?"

"They interrogated him informally on his way to the station. He claimed you tried to mug him, and he ran for his life. The witnesses didn't quite back that story, but they weren't in a position to contradict it either. From their point of view, you just came at him, and that's what they told the police. He doesn't have a criminal record. The police actually asked him if he wanted to press charges, and when he said no, they released him without further ado."

"God help us. What about Sir Ranulph?"

"No injuries. A straightforward snatch of his phone. I gather he was rather sarcastic when you tried to give him instructions."

"Did Phyllis tell you that?"

"No, he did. Said you'd be in 'seventh heaven' when you found out he'd been made."

"I'd have preferred the photos. So what now?"

She sighed. "I don't know. Can I ask why you wanted to apprehend Durand? I don't mean to imply you were wrong. I just want to make sure we're on the same wavelength."

"Unanswered questions from last year. His suspected association with Sopa for a kick-off."

She nodded. "In a way, the police were right to release him. We couldn't have held him, and we couldn't have made him answer our questions. I'm not even sure we suspect him of anything concrete. We just think he knows things we'd like to. And we vaguely imagine he'd give us information. But we're almost certainly wrong about that."

Mordred shrugged. She was right. "Yes, probably."

"We're better off than we were before you spotted him. We now know he's involved in something it's important enough to send in a crack legal team for."

"Something shady. Well I never."

"Something current, and something big. That's worth knowing. Now we need to find him again and this time, instead of apprehending him, we need to put a tail on him."

"He's probably hot-legged it back to the continent by now."

"Well, cross-border cooperation's something we've got to thank the EU for."

"With the best will in the world, he's still a needle in a haystack."

"It must have occurred to you that we have two things here that might, just might, be connected. Those two men who attacked you yesterday afternoon, and Monsieur Durand."

"The link being the Lord Mayor."

"It's highly tenuous and I've no idea what to do with it. The two men you crossed swords with aren't speaking. They say you attacked them, and the phone camera evidence, as well as the eye-witness testimony, seems to back that up. Obviously, we're not entertaining the possibility for a minute, but it may be that, in the end, we've no option but to let them go too."

"Bloody hell. Why not just let *everyone* go? Have we ID-ed them yet?"

"Now this is where it gets interesting. Yes, we have. And we know something the police don't. Those two men are ex-Grey department. Timothy Manners and Shafiq Effanga. Right now, they're working for Horvath."

He smiled humourlessly. "The 'corporate intelligence consultancy'. What happens to MI7 agents when they die."

"It took us a while to make the connection, because, of course, Horvath is an alias. A trading name of the bland-sounding Hollingford Group Ltd. Based in the City."

"I'm pretty sure the Lord Mayor isn't behind it. But I'm equally willing to bet he knows something."

She paused to look him gravely in the eye. "In order to justify that conclusion, you must possess some piece of evidence I don't."

"It struck me in the early hours of this morning. Throughout our interview, he was petrified."

She looked sceptical. "Are you sure?"

"I wouldn't have said so otherwise."

"Of what? I mean, what could he *conceivably* be scared of?"

"I don't know. It's another bit of the jigsaw. I reckon we've only got another four hundred and ninety-seven pieces to go. Then we've got to start putting it together."

She put her elbows on the table, interlaced her fingers, rested her chin on her knuckles and sat thinking for a while. When she finally looked up, her expression was resolute. "I'm assigning you to the Frances Holland investigation," she said. "Phyllis is in charge. I'll let her know you'll be coming and I'll get Brian to brief you. Follow her instructions."

"I'm not sure she'll be one hundred per cent pleased."

"It's the biggest inquiry we've got right now. If there is a 'bigger picture' to be discovered behind Durand-Horvath-Chester, there's a possibility it'll overlap with whatever emerges from Holland. It offers a possible way of proceeding on the former, in other words. Given what you've been through, you're entitled to claim it as partly your business, and I don't have any other ideas."

He stood up. "I'll get right on it."

"Not quite so fast, John," she said gently. "There's another matter I want to discuss with you."

"Oh?"

"This will only take a minute, and it's only for information. I want you to hear it from me before others. Not that I think anyone else in this department knows yet, but there is such a thing as a leak, and it may be in another department's interests to instigate that. I'm going to deal with it."

What was she talking about? He sat down.

"You've been flagged up as vulnerable to radicalisation."

A surprise – it was the last thing he expected her to say – but the sudden upsurge of a million memories showed him it wasn't entirely absurd. And yet it was. On top of the memories, he experienced a rush of contradictory emotions, most of them mixed with indignation.

"Not Islamic, obviously," she went on. "More, left-leaning. More than once, you've been overheard saying you won't necessarily obey Queen and country. And you do seem to have a thing about bankers and Westminster politicians."

"Me and about three quarters of the British population."

"Three quarters of the British population aren't working for MI7."

"Can I ask who flagged me up?"

"Someone in Grey department. I don't know his or her name, and I don't expect to find out. The accusation is that you've got I.I.C. Ideology, intent and capability. At least potentially."

He scoffed. "Intent? To do what?"

"Whatever it is radicalised left-wingers do."

"I'm not a 'left-winger'. Yes, I have a strong distaste for our world-class politicians' propensity to take well-paid jobs with our rapacious finance industry, as also for the wormy revolving door at the heart of government, but that hardly makes me a Marxist. And for the record, I quite like the Queen."

She smiled. "It's not me you'll have to convince. You're probably going to be interviewed about it, just as a formality. By that time, I'll have kicked up such a stink that you'll survive unscathed even if you attend in a Kim Jong-un suit singing the North Korean national anthem. This is a thinly disguised attack on my department, that's all. It happens from time to time. It's got nothing to do with you, not really."

"Can I ask a further question?"

"Go ahead."

"You say it came from Grey. Could its ultimate source by the City of London Corporation? Specifically, the Lord Mayor's office?"

"I won't say that thought hadn't occurred to me, John. It might even be why the Lord Mayor was looking so frightened yesterday. Maybe he thought you might be on to him. If so, and if our previous conjectures are right, putting you on the Frances Holland case may be fanning the flames."

He smiled. "Which is why we're doing it, right?"

"Attack is the best form of defence."

They'd reached the discussion's natural end. He stood up, let himself out and went upstairs to find Brian.

Chapter 5: Brian's Realm

Briefing room five was big enough for about ten people and felt like a last-resort seminar room at an underfunded university. The windows were dirty, the paint faded, and the tables functional and slightly rickety. Its sole concession to modernity was a brutal interactive whiteboard at the front: ugliness plonked on top of shabbiness. This was Brian Penford's realm. He wasn't here yet. Mordred went in, sat down and read *The Guardian* on his phone.

Five minutes later, the door opened and Brian entered, carrying a document wallet and a mug with *The London Dungeon* printed on. A bearded, bespectacled fifty-two year old in a worn tweed jacket and trousers. Mordred put his phone away and stood up.

"Morning, John," Brian said. "Would you like a coffee? The kettle's just boiled. Or we've also got tea, if you want tea."

"I'm fine, thanks."

"So how are you these days?"

"Good. You?"

"Good."

Verbal pleasantries out of the way, they shook hands and each took a seat. Brian picked up the remote and pointed it at the whiteboard. A posed portrait picture of Frances Holland came up. A slim woman with shoulder length brown hair and a white Alice band. Heavy eyebrows, blue eyes and a thin mouth. She wasn't smiling. She wore a suit jacket and a scarf.

"The Brexit Queen," Brian said.

"The what?"

"Brexit. British exit from the European Union, John. Surely you must have heard of bloody *Brexit*. God help us, there's a referendum just around the corner!"

"I meant, I'd never heard her called that."

"By her colleagues, not by the general public."

"And she's supposed to have disappeared, right?"

"Gone for seven days now."

"Who reported her missing?"

Brian put his notes aside. "Her parliamentary colleague, Charles Planchart, Conservative MP for Bromley and Chislehurst. She lives in London during the working week, so her family weren't aware. By 'family', I mean her parents and her brother. Her husband's out of the picture. They divorced a decade ago, and he re-married, she didn't. And she doesn't have any children."

"This is a police matter, presumably."

"And a national security one. Her disappearance hasn't been publicised. It's been kept under wraps. She's a rising star in the party, but, well, it's come to light recently that she's had mental health issues in the past. That's not going to be a problem for her if those issues are not seen to be affecting her capacity to do her job. But if the press get the idea she's likely to go awol at the drop of a hat, she's probably finished. The party consensus is that she's worth taking care of. At least, provisionally. Review that when they find her, I suppose."

"Has she gone missing before?"

"On that particular question, her parents haven't been very forthcoming. Neither has her brother. Neither has the Conservative party."

"So yes, in other words."

"That's the word on the street."

"Are we ruling out foul play?"

"So far. Go with the simplest explanation consistent with the facts. Obviously, that may – probably will - change if new evidence is uncovered."

"What leads are we following?"

"You'll have to speak to Phyllis about that, John. It's not my department. I'm just here to bring you up to the starting line."

"What's she done to earn her title?"

"The Brexit Queen? She's one of seven founding members of a Tory campaigning organisation called 'The Get Out Clause'. She's been anti-European for quite some time. She was one of the first to insist that the Conservative party could only side-line UKIP by becoming UKIP – or at least requisitioning its title-policy. At the time, just before the last election, she was sticking her neck out big time. Now far more people are behind her."

"I bet David Cameron loves her."

"She won him an important seat in 2010. But no, not so much any more."

"Where was she last seen?"

"King's Cross Station, by a Network Southeast guard coming off duty. He didn't see her board a carriage, though. Apparently, she was standing in the middle of the shopping area looking 'unhappy'. We've got CCTV footage that confirms that."

"You probably don't go to King's Cross unless you've formed the intention of catching a train."

"That's the assumption we're working on. But of course, that would mean she could be anywhere."

"And presumably we can't appeal for sightings, because that would alert the press. Isn't it quite likely that she'll just turn up?"

"She'll have to at some point. The question is, in what sort of condition?"

"Could she have a lover?"

"This is the UK's most sensible woman. Sensible shoes, hairstyle, facial expression, highly practical bag - "

Mordred held up his hand. "Sorry to be pedantic, but sensible's a psychological attitude. It's not about clothes and accessories. If she's prone to mental illness, she can hardly have a relatively emotion-free, balanced state of mind. At least not all the time."

Brian shrugged. "Fair point."

"It might be in her interests to disguise herself as a sensible woman by adopting the outward trappings."

"What do you mean?"

"Don't you see? She's aware of the beast lurking within and knows she has to adopt fairly rigorous measures to keep it down. Attempt to fool herself every time she looks in the mirror. If that's the case, then, on her own assessment, there's a constant danger of her 'other' side breaking out."

"Possibly," Brian said. "I think you're over-thinking the matter. And I'm not sure where it gets us."

"If she sees it, someone else might have."

"Okay … And …?"

"Let's say I'm a predator of some kind. Not necessarily sexual. Someone already known to her, not necessarily well. I tag her as vulnerable and I start subtly pestering her to give me what I want. Not in an unpleasant way, although, for the sake of argument, let's assume I have all of my own interests at heart, and none of hers."

"Go on."

"She knows she's being harassed; she's half-tempted to report it, but being 'sensible' implies being independent, being in charge, so she doesn't. And the less well-balanced side of her feels drawn to whatever it is that's on offer. One day, she just cracks."

"Maybe after a few drinks."

"Possibly."

"Or blackmail."

"Or both. Or neither."

"You know what this reminds me of?" Brian said. "The disappearance of Agatha Christie. Eleven days in December 1926. When they finally found her, she was in a hotel in Harrogate. She'd lost her memory. Hang on, I've got something here from the BBC website. Let me read it to you. 'According to biographer Andrew Norman, the novelist may well have been in what's known as a "fugue" state or, more technically, a psy-

51

chogenic trance. It's a rare condition brought on by trauma or depression'. She never spoke about it afterwards. But she was perfectly normal."

There was a knock at the door. Phyllis entered wearing a red suit and no expression. Probably here to complain about him muscling in on her investigation. He sat up.

"I understand you're joining us, John," she said noncommittally. "Good morning, Brian."

"Would you like a coffee, Phyllis?" Brian asked. "The kettle's only just boiled. We've also got tea, if you want tea."

"Nothing for me, thank you," she said. "Well, John?"

"I'll, er, take this opportunity to go and refill my mug," Brian said in a tone that suggested he foresaw a row. "If you want me, I'll be in the kitchen. Otherwise, I'll be back in a minute." He shot a 'here's hoping you survive' look at Mordred and left.

Phyllis didn't sit down. She put her fists on the table and leaned over him.

"Well," Mordred began, "I was attacked last night right after we parted. Two bruisers who claimed to be pally with the Lord Mayor. Later, I realised Chester had looked frightened all the way through our tête-à-tête. Then Pierre Durand got a Get Out of Jail card courtesy of the Lord Mayor's own law firm, name of Simpson, Musgrave and De Groot. Stop me when you've had enough of the Chandler-esque euphemisms."

She said nothing. Not, obviously, because she couldn't think of anything, but because she was processing a heap of fresh information and mentally filing it for later use.

"And all that relates to you joining us – how, exactly?" she said eventually.

"If you don't want me to join, just say. It's your investigation."

She softened and laughed. "You'd better not start bloody solving things, that's all. Has Brian given you the lowdown yet, or is he still going? I notice you're only on slide one of his Powerpoint."

"What are the other slides?"

"You say you were *attacked*?"

"An awful lot's happened since last night."

She sat down. "I heard about Durand getting out. And, for what it's worth, I didn't think Willie looked at all frightened, although I concede you're more of an expert than me. But the attack, I didn't know about. So tell me. And let me ask you again, more sympathetically this time: what's it got to do with my investigation?"

"I'll answer that last one first. I don't know. But something big's going on. And the only other big thing in town is Frances Holland. Statistically, it seems unlikely that two such big things are going down at exactly the same time, ergo it's possible they're part of a single whole."

He told her about the two men and explained matters roughly as he'd relayed them earlier to Ruby Parker. Then he told her about his discussion with Brian. "It's only speculation," he said, "but I think some third party may have compromised her."

"Like who?"

"I don't know yet. I'd like to start by speaking to someone who knew her."

"Who do you have in mind?"

"I'd like to see the rest of Brian's Powerpoint before I decide that."

She gave a wry smile and made to get up. "See if any of her acquaintances looks particularly shifty? They all do."

"Phyllis, stop," he said.

She turned a puzzled frown on him. "Stop what?"

"Just stay there. Only for a minute. Please. I want to ask you something."

She sat down again, looking concerned. "Anything you like."

He hadn't prepared this and 'Phyllis, stop' wasn't exactly an auspicious beginning. It sounded like a command. Luckily, they'd been colleagues long enough for her to know it wasn't. She put her head patiently on one side.

"You remember yesterday," he said, "when we parted at Mansion House, and I called the Lord Mayor 'the king of crooks'? You didn't mention it to anyone, did you?"

"What do you mean? You can't think *I* had anything to do with those two - "

"Not them."

"Then what?"

"I've been flagged up to Ruby Parker as 'vulnerable to radicalisation'. Obviously, I know it wasn't you. That's not what I'm asking. I just wondered whether you'd, say, mentioned it in passing to anyone?"

She hooted. *"'Vulnerable to radicalisation'? You?"*

"Me."

"Oh my *God*, someone's put their jobsworth's hat on! Bloody hell, we all know you're a muesli-eating, sandal-wearing hippy, John, but no one in his right *mind* thinks you're a threat to the organisation!"

"Okay, well - "

"I can't *believe* it," she went on. "What the *hell's* society come to? Don't get me wrong, I'm a fully paid-up member of the Conservative Party and, for what it's worth, I happen to think most of your ideas are completely barmy, but at least you bloody *think* about the world we live in!"

"In that case - "

"I don't suppose *anybody* would flag you up if all you did with your life was what all the other *bloody zombies* nowadays do. Post picture after picture after picture of yourself on bloody Facebook and Instagram. It's incredible!"

He counted four bloodies and two hells and, to her credit, she seemed a lot more upset about it than he did. He began to regret mentioning it.

"What's going to happen now?" she asked. "I mean, what are the faceless ones intending to do about it?"

"I've got to be interviewed."

"When?"

"To be announced."

"Who reported you?"

"Someone in Grey, apparently."

"We've got to find out who. Annabel can probably help with that. She's - "

He held his hands up. "Ruby Parker says she'll take care of it. It's not in my interests for any of us to go probing. My friends especially. That may be exactly what they want. The pretext for a war."

"You make it sound like gangland. Mind you, that's what it is, sometimes. It's what all workplaces are. Anyway, don't worry. If anyone talks to me, I'll give you a glowing reference. And don't worry about Annabel, Edna, Alec, Tariq, even Young Ian. I'll give them a heads-up."

"Thanks."

"It'll be fine. Meanwhile, welcome to my investigation. *Our* investigation."

"Thanks."

A knock at the door. Brian. He and his London Dungeon mug put their heads round. "Is it okay to come in?" he asked.

"I'll stay and watch the rest," Phyllis said. "Everyone needs a refresher from time to time. Then you can tell me who you want to interview, John, and I can arrange the necessary paperwork. Save you having to find me."

So she was being nice to him now. She probably felt sorry for him. He definitely shouldn't have told her. What a mess.

The rest of the Powerpoint consisted of four more photos of Frances Holland from different angles, the CCTV footage of her at King's Cross, plus two embedded videos of her doing interviews on BBC South West, one outdoors, one in the studio. She seemed severe but well-informed, and no one's fool.

Probably headed for great things before she collided with Cameron, and before this. However, nothing was decided yet. There had been more astonishing comebacks.

The other slides consisted of the remaining six members of The Get Out Clause, including its nominal leader, Charles Planchart, MP, a ghoulish looking man with a long, pale face, dark rings under his eyes and black hair swept back from a widow's peak. Then the three members of her family: mum, dad and younger brother.

"I'll begin with Planchart," Mordred said, when Brian switched the whiteboard off. "Might as well start with *numero uno*."

"I'll let him know you're coming," Phyllis said.

Chapter 6: Interview With Planchart

Portcullis House was a seven-storey modern building, consisting mainly of offices, and just across the road from the Palace of Westminster. Mordred's first impression was of a coal-burning power station, though Charles Planchart later said it was meant to evoke a ship. On the ground floor, he counted four shops around a courtyard with two parallel rows of trees in concrete planters in the middle. The roof was glass.

He checked in early and sat where Planchart had told him to, on one of the rectangular benches between the trees. It was midday and most people here were MPs. To general indifference, an overhead annunciator broadcast the latest business in the House of Commons.

Mordred wore a grey sports jacket, pale trousers and brogues. He had a picture of Planchart in his inside pocket and he'd seen him once or twice on TV, so he didn't think he'd miss him. At the moment, though, the MP was nowhere in view.

Two men in business attire sat down a metre away and began to discuss safety measures at agricultural shows. They turned to face each other and gesticulated as their conversation grew animated. A smell of freshly ground coffee wafted over from the café. Mordred looked at his feet, then around him again, then at his watch. It was time now; more than. Maybe he'd been stood up. Or maybe Planchart had been shanghaied at the last minute for a crucial vote of some kind.

He'd have phoned, wouldn't he? He had Mordred's number.

Not necessarily.

Give him another ten minutes – at least. In Mordred's experience, the more important you thought you were, the more you believed unpunctuality was a forgivable offence. Your own, not that of others. There had to be plenty of MPs - especially the safe-seaters - who were late all the time. He yawned and started to build an airport on his phone using an app he'd downloaded last night in an attack of boredom. Good grief, so much swampland to deal with. Years before he could even think about constructing a runway.

Someone sat down next to him. A woman - so not Planchart. She alighted sufficiently inside his personal space to make turning to look at her a natural response. A messenger? Planchart's PA? An acquaintance of Mordred's even?

Someone he'd never seen before. Smart casual trousers and blouse, about his age, with brown eyes, big lips and a small nose. She smiled and offered a handshake, but didn't give her name.

"First of all," she said, "you need to dig a few trenches – ten metres apart maybe – to allow the water to drain to accessible ground."

"Er, excuse me?"

"Only then can you consider building that runway."

He grinned and put his phone away. "Oh, right. Yes."

"Are you with the police?" she asked. Something like hope was in both her eyes and her tone of voice.

"Do we know each other?" he replied, trying not to sound discouraging. She might have information. She was a journalist. Something about her body-language made it almost certain.

"Sarah Riceland," she said. "With the recently deceased *Independent*. Or at least the print-version's dead. We're in online heaven now."

She was nervous, he didn't know why. He shook her hand. "Jonas Eagleton," he said, giving his cover name.

"Are you with the police?" she repeated.

"I'm a detective inspector," he replied, giving her the rest of his cover. "How did you know?"

"I happened to see you chasing a man through central London yesterday. It *was* you, wasn't it? Did you catch him?"

He shrugged in an attempt to conceal his interest. "The Mounties always get their man."

"Who was he?" This was the question she'd been building up to. For some reason, it was the cause of her nervousness. She tried to make it sound casual, but it didn't.

He needed to forestall her – at least for now - if he was to find out what was going on. "I can't say."

"What had he done wrong?"

"I'm afraid I can't tell you that either."

"How did he escape from custody?"

Now it was he who was on the back foot. "How did you know that?"

"I can't say," she replied archly.

Suddenly, Planchart appeared in front of them, a tall, forbidding figure all in black, more like a butler or an undertaker than a people's representative. "DI Eagleton?" he enquired coldly.

Riceland looked up and seemed to shrink with horror.

"That's me," Mordred said, standing up and accepting the handshake.

The journalist gathered her things hurriedly, got to her feet without making further eye-contact and left at speed.

"Do you two know each other?" Mordred asked, noting the MP's clear animosity.

"I believe she's a journalist," Planchart said.

Mordred nodded. Later. He'd ask again later.

Once civilities had been exchanged, the two men went upstairs to Planchart's office, a plain affair with a wooden desk, what looked like plasterboard walls and two fitted oak cupboards. A copy of the *Telegraph* lay half-folded on the desk with the headline, *Chancellor accuses Planchart of using referendum to launch leadership bid*. Beside it, a telephone and a stationery organiser. A door in the far wall led outside to a balcony.

"Not as fancy as some of my colleagues' offices across the road," Planchart told him, closing the door behind them.

"A good example to the electorate," Mordred replied.

They sat down. "So what can I do for you, Mr Mordred?" Planchart asked. "I'm assuming it's acceptable to dispense with the 'Detective Inspector' now we're alone? I've already talked to the police and to one of your colleagues, but I'm quite happy to talk to you as well, because getting Frances back trumps everything, doesn't it? I appreciate your discretion so far. We all do."

"There are seven of you in The Get Out Clause, is that right?"

"Six, now. I don't suppose it's connected to that, though. As you're probably aware, Frances was bipolar. I didn't know myself until recently. Mostly, she seemed to go on okay. But of course, from time to time, these people have mood swings. Extreme depression or euphoria. I suppose it must have been the former. I hope she's okay."

"She was on medication, from what I understand."

"So I've heard. Your colleague, Ms Robinson, seemed to know everything about her. That *is* her job, I suppose. Very good at it too. Is it 'Miss', by the way, or 'Mrs'?"

"Er ... You mean Frances Holland, or Phyllis?"

"Phyllis Robinson. Your colleague. Just out of interest."

"Miss." He felt awkward saying it, but Phyllis would probably bawl him out otherwise. It was another potential entrypoint to an important source. "Let's talk about Frances Holland."

"Indeed. Right now, I'm feeling optimistic about Frances. Suicides are usually found fairly quickly, because they plan it that way. I assume it's the same reason they usually write notes. The attention. If you're seeking your fifteen minutes of fame, you generally want it now."

"I'm not sure what you're saying."

"Roughly six thousand people a year commit suicide in the UK," Planchart said. "That's an average of sixteen a day. In other words, it's not an unusual phenomenon, and this is a very overcrowded island. There aren't that many places in Britain you can be alone for long. Arguably, there aren't *any*. Not any more, not with all the immigration. She's been gone seven days. If her corpse hasn't been found yet, that probably means she's still alive. Even if she set off with the intention of topping herself, if she hasn't done it by now, there's a strong likelihood she's not going to do it at all."

"With respect, you're ignoring the possibility she may have gone abroad, among other things."

"Perhaps, but as I say, suicides usually want to be found. If they don't care about that, then presumably they don't care one way or the other; in which case, why not do it anywhere? I can't think of any reason why she positively *wouldn't* want to be found, can you?"

Mordred nodded. "It's a good argument."

"She must be hiding out somewhere."

"Then why are you so concerned to find her? Surely she has a right - "

"I'm not as concerned now as I was when your colleague interviewed me three days ago, and even less than I was two. You're absolutely right. She's an adult. She can do what she likes. As for her being mentally ill, half the population of the country's on prescription drugs for some kind of mental disorder, and in my experience, the well-to-do, respectable classes are worst of the lot. She's in very good company, even here in the Houses of Parliament. I'd be surprised if three-quarters of the cabinet weren't on anti-depressants, quite frankly. We're living in a science-fiction kind of world, Mr Mordred, and it's only doctors' confidentiality that prevents us seeing it."

"So presumably, you think we should just wait till she comes back."

"That's my latest assessment, yes. If we can find her, we should. But she's a highly intelligent woman, so if she's decided she doesn't want to be found – which she obviously has – I'd say there's very little we can do about it."

"Do you think it's possible she's been blackmailed?"

Planchart put on an irritated expression. "Is there anything in what I've just said to suggest so? Who would be blackmailing her?"

It was suddenly Mordred's turn to attack. "She's on medication. Assuming it's effective, if she keeps taking the tablets, she should be immune to the sort of mood swings that would persuade her to up sticks, hop on a train and lie prone in a darkened bedsit for a week. Now I admit, people do forget to take their medication from time to time. But this is the Brexit Queen. She's knee-deep in a career make-or-break campaign in which she also happens to passionately believe. Negligence therefore seems unlikely. But negligence is precisely what we're – you're - assuming."

Planchart rested his nose on his index finger and looked at the floor for a few moments. "You're right," he said. "Maybe … I don't know … so many factors …"

"That's what the police and intelligence services are here for."

"But she was alone at King's Cross. Looking unhappy."

"'Unhappy' doesn't necessarily imply clinical depression. And the physical absence of a blackmailer in any given location doesn't mean anything whatsoever."

"I get the impression you're quite good at your job, Mr Mordred. You're certainly good at making deductions. Well, now, let's see, this opens a whole new can of worms. From what I understand, so far the investigation's focussed on her mental condition and the various ways in which that renders her vulnerable. Extortion's a new angle. We'd need to ask who has most to gain from her disappearance? Well, the most obvious candidate would be a political opponent in one of the various pro-EU campaigns. But how would that work? If you've got something sufficiently damning to blackmail her with, you'd use it to get her to withdraw from the contest respectably. That way, you'd minimise the chances of drawing attention to yourself. You wouldn't use it to put her onto a train to Nowheresville."

"Granted. Maybe she'd been presented with the heart-breaking end of the story, but wanted to delay it. And this was the only tactic she could think of."

"Hide her head in the sand, you mean? That doesn't sound like Frances."

"People aren't usually themselves when blackmail's involved."

He put his nose back on his index finger and looked at the floor again. He sighed. "This puts – yes, it does – a whole new spin on things," he said dourly. "A completely fresh light."

He suddenly stood up and opened the doors onto the balcony. He strode outside, put both hands on the rail, and looked down onto the internal courtyard without speaking. Mordred began to think their interview was over, that Planchart's last words had been his highly oblique way of ending things, when suddenly the MP turned around. He came back into the room as abruptly as he'd left, sat down again and looked Mordred directly in the eye.

"I'm going to tell you something now that I was once told in confidence," he said. "Obviously, if I'd thought blackmail might be involved before, I'd probably have recalled what I'm about to divulge earlier. I'm going out on a limb, as it were."

"The whole point about involving MI7 is our capacity for discretion. We haven't let you down so far."

"How well do you know Bill Ashbaugh?"

"I don't recall ever having heard the name."

"Most people have. I get the impression you don't watch a lot of news, Mr Mordred. He's the Labour party coordinator of VSI: Vote Stay In."

"And?"

"He and Frances had a 'history', apparently. They were at Sussex together in the nineties, doing the same course. Lovers."

"Okay ..."

"I don't know what happened to their little 'fling', but I can guess."

"Go on."

"The physical attraction, the love of *penne in salsa di cipolle* and the touching mutual interest in the life and works of Christina Rossetti eventually wore thin. Thereafter, they argued constantly about the advisability of taxing the rich, the loathsomeness or otherwise of Rupert Murdoch, the real cost of cutting benefits, etcetera, etcetera, *ad infinitum*, and eventually broke up. Acrimoniously. That's usually how it works in Con-Lab relationships. In the end, your shallow middle class tastes are never enough to keep you going as a couple. You need something deeper."

"I should probably speak to Mr Ashbaugh."

"Don't tell him I sent you. And I warn you, he's not the discreet sort. If he gets wind of the idea that Frances has suffered some sort of breakdown and shipped out on a fast train to the provinces, he'll be straight on the phone to the papers. Be careful."

"Excuse me if this sounds presumptuous, but I get the impression you and Ashbaugh are at loggerheads personally as well as professionally."

"Perhaps."

"Were *you* having a relationship with Frances Holland?"

Planchart took a sharp breath. He flashed a new look on Mordred as if considering whether to punch him. The look intensified, then out of nowhere, it dissipated. He smiled bitterly. "Yes," he said. "Not that it's relevant. But yes. If this is your roundabout way of asking whether my view of Ashbaugh is coloured by my feelings for Frances, then yes. Again, yes. Maybe. *Partly.*"

"I'm only asking because it's my job."

"Of course. Of course it is, yes." He was behaving like a man on the ropes now, which wasn't what Mordred had intended. He seemed to sense how discomfited he must look, and tried to deflect attention away from it by changing the subject. "Can I ask which way you're intending to vote in the referendum, Mr Mordred? Just as a matter of interest? You're not obliged to answer of course."

"I haven't made up my mind yet."

"As I said earlier, in another context: so many factors to consider. The only thing is, if you're pro-EU, you might end up giving Ashbaugh an easier ride than he deserves. People are often deceived about what's at stake here. Supposedly, people like me are 'Europe-haters' and therefore xenophobes. People like Ashbaugh are tender-hearted universalists."

"People used to think like that a few years ago. Nowadays, I think most people believe it's considerably more complex."

"I love Europe and the Europeans. My first wife was French; my second, Italian. I speak four continental languages. But I don't like the EU. And I know lots of people in this country and abroad feel exactly the same. We don't like corruption. We don't like the endless tide of economic migrants. We don't like having to tread on eggshells where Erdogan and his thugs are concerned. We do want to rebuild bridges with Russia. We do want a rational middle-eastern policy - which may or may not involve supporting Assad, but certainly centralises the Kurds, the only non-basket-case militia in that part of the world. Don't be fooled. It's not about how 'nice' you are. And Ashbaugh's not nice. I'd say the same thing even if he and I were on the same side."

"Er, right. I'll bear all that in mind."

Planchart ran his hand over his hair. "Sorry to address you as if you're a public meeting. It's just there's a lot at stake. I tend to get carried away sometimes."

Time to throw the last question in. "That journalist downstairs. She looked a little embarrassed at meeting you - "

"She's a *pest!*" Planchart snapped back.

Mordred held his hands up. It looked like Holland wasn't the only one with mood swings.

"Sorry," the MP said. "It's been a long day. I expect she was asking you about me. Ignore her. I don't know what she wants. I don't suppose anyone does. She's probably on drugs too. She's one of the many reasons a formerly great newspaper went down the pan, I'd imagine. Talk to her if you like, but I warn you: you'll waste a hell a lot of time, and probably end up with a stalker. Friendly advice. Whatever you do, don't give her your real name. *At your own risk.*"

"Understood," Mordred said. There had been lots of interesting things in this interview, but this topped them all. He stood up. "Thank you for our time. I'll be back in touch if I need to clarify anything. And of course you can contact me through Ruby Parker."

Planchart seemed infinitely relieved that it was at an end. He rubbed his neck and offered a final handshake. "Always a pleasure," he said.

When Mordred left, Planchart sat in his chair for a long time, looking at his desk and trying to think. He'd quite enjoyed their little meeting. A change to meet someone so obviously intelligent. In another life, they'd have been in the army together, or perhaps they'd have mountaineered, or joined up for an expedition to the north pole. Something ambitious and daring. In this one, they'd landed on different sides of destiny. Mordred had been fortunate in the City the other day: they'd underestimated him. He wouldn't be so lucky a second time.

This time, the luck was all Planchart's. Sarah Riceland suddenly turning up, and that she now thought Mordred was a policeman. She'd go after him because she'd imagine he'd be willing to help her. Obviously, that was a forlorn hope, given that he was a spy and therefore secretive by profession. But where he went, she would probably follow. Two birds, one stone.

He picked up the telephone and dialled the number he'd been given. After he'd exchanged the scripted civilities with the man who answered, 1940s-spy style, he relayed a single sentence message. "I think we should hold back on our City friend for the time being. I'll explain when we meet face to face."

Chapter 7: The Green Woman

Mordred walked back across the courtyard of Portcullis House and outside wondering who to contact first, Ashbaugh or Riceland. He emerged into early afternoon sunshine. The traffic was steady now, the long lull before the rush hour. He inhaled the familiar smell of exhaust fumes and registered the roaring of engines, grinding of gears and hiss of hydraulic brakes as if it was medicine; a cure for the dreary whiff of Planchart's office. Directly opposite, the Palace of Westminster sat brown and craggy like an old bear.

The first person to contact, surely, was Phyllis. Her investigation, he couldn't just go off on his own. He took out his phone and was about to call when he spotted someone across the road, just standing looking at him. A woman in a lime green jacket, matching trousers and a cream fedora. All around her, people came and went.

Sarah Riceland? But that didn't seem …

She certainly hadn't been wearing those clothes last time they'd met. Who the hell wore all lime green anyway? She looked like she'd dropped out of the avant-garde section of London Fashion Week.

Was it her? She was a good seven hundred yards distant, just far enough to make her features not quite determinable. If so, why was she looking at him so fixedly? Why wasn't she moving – making any attempt to come and meet him, for example? What the hell was she up to?

He put his phone away. One of those times where instinct was your best guide, and his told him to cross the road to meet her.

As soon as she saw him coming, she turned and headed off across Westminster Bridge. He broke into a jog to catch up with her – the crowds were too dense for anything more strenuous - but she followed suit by accelerating. Once she was on the other side of the river, she turned left into Belvedere Road, and by the time he'd caught up sufficiently to round the corner, she'd gone.

He didn't give up that easily. He increased speed, looking to his right and left.

Then he saw her, about five hundred yards in front. She was getting into a taxi, but didn't look as if she was in any particular hurry. He flagged a minicab down and got into the passenger seat beside the driver, a man with a triangular head, a pointy beard to emphasise it, and a pink shirt with a black stain on the breast pocket.

"Follow that taxi," he said.

"Who is it?" the driver asked. "I can't just go following people. You - "

Mordred showed him his DI Eagleton card. "There isn't time to call a police car. If you won't drive me, I'm entitled to commandeer your vehicle and drive myself."

He had no idea whether this was true – probably not – but it had the desired effect. The driver shrugged and stopped asking questions. They pursued the taxi.

"You will pay me, won't you?" the driver said suddenly. "I don't want to be filling in expenses forms. I want to be paid in cash or credit card like a normal fare."

"Like I said, I'm authorised to take over your car."

"On what grounds? Obstructing the police?"

"Something like that."

"But I wouldn't be. I just wouldn't be assisting. Not assisting isn't the same as obstructing."

Mordred laughed. "Are you a lawyer or something?"

"Just because I'm a taxi driver, doesn't mean I'm stupid."

Bloody hell, The Great British Class War, now. "I've got cash."

"How much?"

Mordred drew a breath and turned to look at him.

For some reason, this had the effect of completely unnerving him. "Okay, okay, you've got cash," the driver said. "I was only asking."

"If you speak again, I'm going to get my colleagues to test your car for roadworthiness and general safety. And if it doesn't pass with top honours, we'll impound it."

"Sorry. Sorry again. Point taken."

It didn't feel good, making threats. Bloody hell, why couldn't people just trust you? He had his magic card, for God's sake. Why did it always have to descend into unpleasantness? As if Sarah Riceland wasn't enough.

Then it occurred to him. What was he even doing out here, playing her ridiculous catch-me game? If he wanted to talk to her, he could just ring *The Independent*, or what was left of it. He'd been hoodwinked into thinking he had something to gain by the pursuit. Yes, he wanted to talk to her, but she didn't know that yet. And last time they'd met, she'd made the approach. Let her come to him.

And for all he knew, it might not even *be* Sarah Riceland in that taxi.

"Stop the car," he said.

"Hang on, we haven't lost her yet."

"Stop the car."

"I said, *hang on.*"

"Look, if you don't stop the car, I'm going to get my colleagues to impound it."

The driver slammed the brakes on. He swore under his breath – something about the police, almightiness and arse – and grabbed the steering wheel so hard his knuckles turned white.

Mordred looked at the meter. Which didn't seem to be working. "What's the damage?" he asked.

This was apparently the last question the driver was expecting. "Bloody hell," he said. "Ten pounds forty", as if it was an afterthought.

Mordred gave him fifteen pounds and told him to keep the change. He got out and began to walk back to Thames House. He'd make for the river and walk along the embankment. He took his phone from his pocket and rang Phyllis. He told her all about Sarah Riceland.

Phyllis made the obvious point. "But you're not even sure the green woman was her?"

"I didn't have my binoculars."

"Funny joke. Who else could she have been?"

"I don't know. I've no idea how she got changed so quickly, or why into something so garish. She wasn't Frances Holland, if that's what you're thinking."

"But you abandoned the chase?"

"I can't keep pursuing someone just because they're staring at me from across the road."

"I'll check Sarah Riceland out on the database, see if we've got anything on her. Otherwise, I'll ring the *Indy* and make you an appointment. You see if you can get in touch with Ashbaugh."

"I have a feeling I'm going to see her again."

"You'll have to be the one to interview her," Phyllis said. "She's obviously taken a shine to you. Forget about the lime lady. People do look like other people. It happens all the time."

"It wasn't just that. Look, I'm more than seventy-five per cent sure it was her."

"It's academic now. Isn't it?"

"I don't think so. You don't get done up like that unless you want to be seen."

"And you don't run away unless you'd rather not meet."

"Maybe she's trying to lead me somewhere."

Phyllis laughed. "Odd way to go about it. Look, what exactly are you trying to say, John?"

"If I'm right, she'll be back any minute now. I'll see her. She'll have monitored my pursuit in the minicab, and registered that I've apparently thrown in the towel. But she's not going to give up. I'm not following her. She's following me."

"If you're right."

"If I'm right."

"And she wants *you* to follow *her*. Right, well if she re-appears - "

He looked towards the bridge. Then the shock of recognition. Colour before person. "She's back," he said.

"Where are you?"

"Waterloo Bridge, south side of the river. She's standing on the eastern rail, facing Temple tube station. Or rather, she isn't. She's not looking at Temple, anyway."

"She's looking at you, right? Follow her, and keep in touch. Remember those men in the Square Mile. It could be a trap. I'm coming over, and I'll bring Annabel. Ring me in *ten minutes*. Don't forget."

He put his phone down and met her gaze directly. The same instant, she turned and walked briskly away from him.

He did the opposite of what his body wanted. He went to a bench and sat down. Phyllis might be right. Either way, he needed to think. Whoever those two men had been, they'd wanted to take him somewhere. Probably someplace highly specific, since they wanted information, and you couldn't just torture a person any-old-where in London. You'd probably require a detached house in the suburbs. Drug the victim first, yes.

In order to achieve all that, you'd have to set a trap. It would have to be far subtler than your first trap – getting two men to frogmarch you to a car in broad daylight – because that hadn't worked. It might well involve a 'journalist', name of 'Sarah Riceland' wearing lime.

That was the first thing to check then. He got back on the phone to Phyllis.

"Where are you?" she asked. "We're in the car. Kevin estimates about a minute."

"I'm sitting on a bench under a tree in front of the National Theatre."

"You decided not to give chase then?" She hmm-ed. "Probably wise."

"We can easily corner her if you get to the north end of the bridge. I can't see her any more, but she can't have gone far."

"Easily spottable in all green."

"I need you to get in touch with Tariq. I need to know whether there really is such a person as Sarah Riceland from *The Independent*. Ideally, I'd like him to send a photo of her to my phone."

"Will do. Let me know if you move."

If someone was intent on abducting him, they could easily do it here.

But then, they could have done it outside the Houses of Parliament. Even better, Belvedere Road, or one of its side-streets. Or even – the park. That's right, Jubilee Gardens abutted the western side nearly all the way along. If she'd been part of a kidnap team, that would have been the perfect place. Instead, she'd got into a taxi.

That was it, then: wherever she was leading him, it wasn't into a trap. He got up and walked briskly across Waterloo Bridge, sweeping his eyes but trying to keep his head still. No sign of her anywhere now, but he wasn't worried. He didn't have to find her. She'd find him. He saw a car pull to a stop on Victoria Embankment. Phyllis got out, looking casual, followed by Annabel.

What was the plan? His phone rang.

"Laugh gently like I'm a personal friend and you're pleased to hear from me," Phyllis said. "We don't want her to think you've called reinforcements."

He pretend-beamed. "It may be a bit late for that."

"She can't have you in view all the time. Besides, you sat down. And before that, you got out of the taxi. She probably believes you've lost interest. True, you're on the bridge, but maybe she thinks you're just heading home."

"What are we going to do? Like I say, we've nothing concrete to reproach her for, and we can't just go pulling people in off the streets for no reason. We're not the FSB."

"When she comes back, you follow her, and so will we. The only difference is, we won't try to catch up. As far as we know, she's not trained in spycraft. The chances of her making us are negligible." She hung up.

Mordred's phone pinged. *Tariq.* 'Sarah Constance Riceland, born North Yorkshire 4 May 1986. Multiplatform News Journalism Diploma, Harlow College, 2007. Middlesbrough *Evening Gazette*, 2007-2009. *London Comet*, 2009-2013. *The Independent*, 2013-2016.' He opened the attachment. A head-and-shoulders shot of the woman who'd approached him in Portcullis House.

That was it then. The only question was whether she and Lime Woman were the same. His phone pinged again. *Phyllis.* Another text: 'Gotcha'. He opened the attachment. A ten-seconds-old picture of Sarah Riceland sitting on a bench, dressed in lime. Case closed. His phone rang.

"Riceland, yes or no?" Phyllis asked.

"That's her."

"Better come and get her then. Listen, Annabel or I could accidentally bump into her if you like, give you time to catch up."

"I want to find out where she's going. Ideally, I'd like her to think she's in charge. She wants something from me. I've the feeling she's hiding something."

"About Durand?"

"I know you think it's off-topic, but I think Durand may somehow be connected to this case. The Holland case."

"Convince me."

"I can't. It's just a hunch I've got."

He heard her sigh. "Okay," she said. "We'll help you tail her on foot. Let's get it out of your system. Soon as you've found whatever it is you're after or she wants you to find, you're to go and see Ashbaugh, okay? Or would you rather I did it?"

A test, to see whether he had ambitions to take over her investigation. "Why not?" he replied innocently. "You're in charge."

"The only reason I let you go and see Planchart," she snapped, "was because you asked, and I wanted to give you a little welcome-to-my-investigation-no-hard-feelings present. Strictly speaking, I should be the one who deals with Tories: I understand them, they instinctively see that, so they're more open. That's the theory. For the same reason, you'll be better with Ashbaugh. He'll twig I'm not a Marxist Leninist Trotsky-ite fruitcake as soon as I walk though the door. It'll take him a lot longer to suss you out."

"You're forgetting that all politicians are the same nowadays."

"Let's not take that risk. Look, let's get back to Sarah Riceland. Annabel and I will help, but let's treat it as an amusing diversion till something more concrete raises its head. Then you go and see Ashbaugh."

"Done."

She hung up again. For the third time in twenty minutes, his phone pinged. *Tariq.* 'Sarah Constance Riceland, medical record 2010-16. Conditions: sleeplessness, depression, alcohol-induced mild psychotic behaviour. Medication: Citalopram, Prochlorperazine, Dosulepin. From November 2015, one-weekly Cognitive Behavioural Therapy at St Luke's Centre for Health and Wellbeing, NW1.'

He could see her now, sitting on the bench Phyllis or Annabel had photographed her on, more like a venomous green chilli than a friendly lime. She fixed him with her stare then rose and was off again.

His phone rang. *Phyllis*.

"I assume you got the latest Tariq bulletin," she said wearily.

"Quite a catalogue."

"I've had enough, John. We're on a wild goose chase here. She saw you running after Durand, and now she's latched on to you for reasons that have nothing to do with anything. I'm heading back to Tracy Island, and if you've any sense you'll do the same."

"I'd like to see this one out, if that's okay."

"Exactly what I thought you'd say, you moron. Annabel says she'll keep you company then. But I'm warning you both, she'll zig-zag you all over town, then ditch you when you're completely knackered. Why not just wait till tomorrow, then ring the *Independent* and set up a proper meeting with her? If she won't play ball, we can lean on her employer."

"Because this is more fun. Come on - "

She rang off. Riceland was on her way to the other side of the bridge by the look of things. He paused to allow her time to reappear as she passed beneath him, then watched her turn the corner on to Savoy Street. She disappeared from view again, but he was in no hurry now. Sooner or later, he'd catch up with her. Because whatever she might think to the contrary, she wanted him to.

He spent the next four hours in exactly the same way. She led him north as far as Tufnell Park, then headed west until they reached Olympia, then south. He lost her countless times, but she always reappeared again, and always in the same way – staring hard at him. It was like hunting a goblin. After about an hour, he thought he might be the one who was mentally ill. As for her, she didn't exist. She was all in his mind. It was only the fairly infrequent sightings of Annabel – and he got the impression Annabel was far less at sea than he was – that kept this impression from intensifying to fever pitch.

It was a rare old tour of the town, from the upmarket promenades to the sordid dives, the tourist haunts to the loneliest wastelands, from the old and ghostly to the new and frivolous, and it all somehow added to her enigma.

Not that there was anything particularly deep about that enigma. What was it with all the mental illness in society? It wasn't just her and Frances Holland. What had Planchart said again? *I'd be surprised if three-quarters of the Cabinet weren't on anti-depressants.* Probably right. A century ago they'd have been called mad. But you couldn't institutionalise seventy-five per cent of the population, nor would you want to. Yet it must say something about what the world had become.

Unhappy, mostly. That was the least you could say. Why? It wasn't as if most people lacked for things. At least, not in this country.

Some did. He passed lots of homeless people along the way, and stopped thinking about it. The world was just too complicated, and no one really saw that, they just carried on in their own little bubbles. Just like he'd be in his if it weren't for all the destitute people popping it.

The sky darkened and a fleet of grey clouds arrived from the east like spaceships, stopped over central London and unloaded their rain. People ran for shelter or put up umbrellas, or just carried on as always, pretending not to notice or to care. The homeless people drew their knees up and gave an extra bit of blanket to their dogs, and it was all sad, sad, and sad again. His phone rang. *Annabel.*

"I'm going home, John," she said gloomily. "I've had enough fun for one day."

"Thanks for helping."

"You coming? We could get a slice of pizza on the way back. Well, *you* could. I could do with a cup of tea."

He could see Riceland about seven hundred yards ahead. They were at opposite ends of a well-to-do residential street.

She stood on a set of stone steps staring at him like a leprechaun.

He looked at his watch. 7pm.

He'd had enough. He was soaked. Sarah bloody Riceland could take a running jump. He should have listened to Phyllis earlier.

"Count me in," he said.

Chapter 8: Annabel With A Plan

No sooner had he abandoned the chase for Sarah Riceland than he regretted it. Rain, melancholy and hunger. How pathetic that those three things, working together, were all it took to stop him in his tracks. He met Annabel on Sloane Street. She wore a grim expression. "We lack stamina," she said, as if it was a question.

"Do you want to get a taxi?" he asked.

The rain had eased off, but for some reason, she didn't look wet at all. She probably carried a micro-umbrella in the lining of her jacket, devised by M, and which doubled as a rapier in emergencies. The traffic roared by and people hurried to and from buses or the tube with their shoulders hunched and their eyes down as if it was winter. A street light had come on. The shops and cafés looked warm and inviting. The deceptive allure of commercialism.

"A taxi to where?" she replied. "I thought we were going to get pizza and tea."

"Wherever you can get that combination then."

"Like … here?"

"There's no pizza takeaway on Sloane Street. It's too up-market."

"You're from the north, John. You don't necessarily know everything about London."

He bit his tongue. He'd never had her down as An Expert on the Metropolis bore before. *Let me show you around, London is my natural home, I'll lead, you follow.* He might not have lived here all his life, but he knew there wasn't a pizza takeaway on Sloane Street.

No point in fighting, though. Let her find out. He put his hands in his pockets and they set off in the direction of Knightsbridge. She linked arms with him as a peace-offering.

After a minute, they came to a narrow tea-shop with plaid curtains and two empty tables inside.

"In here," she said. "I'll order. You sit down at the table by the window."

He did as he was told, glad he hadn't challenged her to a bet. Two minutes later, his slice of Margherita arrived with her tea.

"They do anything you like in here for a price," Annabel said. "Mrs Hennigan sends out for it and charges fifty per cent commission. Would you like some tea?"

"I wouldn't mind a glass of American cream soda."

She smiled. "So you want to *challenge* Mrs Hennigan?"

"Tell her if she can bring it before ten minutes have elapsed, I'll pay her four times whatever she'd normally ask."

She frowned. "That's the sort of game City traders play, John. I'm surprised at you."

"You're right," he said feeling his face warm up. "Sorry, it's been a long day."

An old woman appeared from the door leading to the back of the shop. She carried a jug and a glass. Without looking at either of them, she set the latter on the table and filled it.

"Your United States cream soda, sir," she said impassively.

For a moment, no one did anything. The old woman stood motionless. Her two customers stared disbelievingly at the fizzing drink.

"That'll be ten pounds, please," she said, after what seemed like an age.

"Give her a tip, John," Annabel whispered, even though she was standing right in front of them; and, given that she'd heard their conversation from behind the shop, her hearing was unlikely to be defective.

He pulled out a note from his wallet and unfolded it. A twenty. Too late to put it back and look for anything else. "Keep the change," he said.

She took it without thanking him, and shuffled back into the darkness.

"Let's go," Annabel said, a minute later.

They went outside. Somehow, it felt a lot later than it should be, given that they'd only spent twenty minutes in Mrs Hennigan's. Headlights and street lights and shop lights all came together to make the sky look dark. Commuter time was over and going out time hadn't yet begun. There was a smell of cooking oil from somewhere. It was cold.

"Right, so what are we going to do about Sarah Riceland?" Annabel asked.

He suddenly realised she hadn't gone. She was right in front of them, about four hundred yards away. He groaned. No, not again. No.

"Nothing," he said.

"I should be getting back to base," she said. "Tariq's doing overtime tonight, but he finishes at eight. I said I'd be there to meet him."

"Thanks for the pizza slice. And for keeping me company today."

"It's not over yet. In fact, it's only just beginning."

"Oh, really?"

"We've been working on the premise that she wants you to follow her; that she's leading us somewhere. She isn't. If she wants anything at all, it's for you to catch her."

He laughed. "So that's why she keeps running away?"

"She doesn't know me. Which is how I managed to get up close to her earlier. There's a tracking device on her lapel." She took out her phone and switched it on. "Look."

Her screen showed a little light at the end of a labelled satellite map.

"What's going to happen now," she went on, "is you're going to 'disappear' and come up two feet in front of her. Then she's going to run away, and I'm going to trip her over."

"I'm sure she'll be delighted."

"Oh, it doesn't end there. She'll tell you to go away, and you'll hail a taxi and get in it. I'll make sure there's one available. Once she knows she's on the verge of losing you for good, my guess is she'll change her tune. Then she's all yours. Tell me tomorrow how you got on."

He took his phone out, went to the MI7 website and keyed in the tracking number she gave him. "I see her," he said.

"Be sure to retrieve the device afterwards."

They split up. There was a sense, even in the little dot of illumination that was all Sarah Riceland was right now, that she was confused. She wandered up and down a little and eventually turned right on to Knightsbridge. He shadowed her movements via the various adjacent side streets and came out in front of her at the end of William Street. According to his phone, she was walking fast towards him now. He stepped up his pace and put his head down.

Suddenly, she appeared five feet in front of him. She froze, her face filled with confusion and terror, and turned to run. But someone collided with her, clipping her feet from beneath her and leaving her prostrate before moving on in a hurry.

He rushed over, and grabbed her arm. "I saw what happened," he said, solicitously. "Are you okay? I can call an ambu – wait, haven't we met before? You're - "

"*Get off me!*" she shrieked, wrenching her arm free and clambering to her feet. "*I don't need any help!* Leave me *alone!*"

He backed off with both hands in the air. "Sorry, I was only trying to help. My mistake. *Taxi!*"

As if by magic, a taxi pulled to a halt alongside him. Annabel, its only passenger, let herself out through the roadside door as he opened the pavement one.

"Well, goodbye," he said. "Apologies again."

"*Wait!*" she shrieked. "Where are you *going?*"

She got in beside him. The driver pulled out into the westbound traffic.

"Well, this is nice," he said.

She took him back to her flat, a half-converted garage in Stratford without heating or proper toilet facilities. He'd heard about such things on *Panorama* and *Dispatches*, but he'd never seen one before. It was freezing, and probably not very secure.

"Where do you go to wash?" he asked.

"There's a tap round the back," she said. "A public convenience in the park across the road, and a laundrette in town. I want to live in London – it's a conscious choice - and beggars can't be choosers. Mega-rich people own everything decent for a ten-mile radius, most of which they leave vacant. But I can't complain. I don't *have* to live in London. I could live in Essex and commute, but then there'd be the train fares. I'm better off this way; financially. I don't come back here very often. I'm an eccentric, you see. A real British eccentric. We're a dying breed. I have green days where I go out and follow random people, and red days where I just move from café to café, and blue days – summer days - where I sit in parks. Green days, mostly winter days, are kind of fun and they keep me warm. And every so often, you come across a story. Really, I'm not joking. A *bone fide* story."

He sat on her single bed, the only piece of furniture in the room, beneath a bare light bulb, and wondered what kind of car used to go in here. A small one.

"Do *Shelter* know you're here?" he asked.

"Don't tell them!"

"What if someone breaks in at night? It doesn't look very secure."

"I've got a little notice I hang on my front door," she said. *"Nothing valuable kept in here overnight."*

He didn't laugh. God, no wonder she was mentally ill. He went back to his phone. *London Comet, 2019-2013. Medical record 2010-16.* An almost exact congruence. She'd succumbed a year after she'd got here. Probably the sense that she was going nowhere combined with the realisation that she was one precarious notch above sleeping rough. Enough to unsettle anyone's nerves.

"Do you have any family nearby?" he asked.

She grinned. "My mum died when I was eighteen. My step-mum disowned me. My dad's too weak to count. So no. Turn your back, I'm going to change my trousers."

Given that she'd led him all over London, and how she'd shrieked when he tried to help her up off the pavement, they were getting on surprisingly well. He accidentally caught her reflection in his phone. She'd put her trousers on. Now she was eating tablets. She swallowed.

"You can turn round now if you like," she said.

"Do you have a boyfriend?" he asked.

"Nosey, aren't you?"

"I'm a policeman."

"Why aren't you asking me about criminal stuff then?"

"I'm trying to make small talk."

She hooted. "Prying, some people might call it. Have *you* got a boyfriend?"

"I've a girlfriend," he replied.

"Are you now, or have you ever been, married?"

"No."

"Any family nearby?"

"Mostly in Newcastle. I've got a sister in Norway and another in Syria with *Médecins Sans Frontières*."

"Cool. I wish I had siblings." She laughed. "Or anyone." She shivered, rubbed her hands together, put them over her mouth and exhaled warmth onto them. "I've got friends, obviously. Everyone's got friends. I haven't seen any of them lately for reasons I'll go into later."

"What's the plan for this evening? I mean, why have you brought me back here?"

She shook her head. "You're not very bright, are you? Rewind a bit to when I first met you. I've got information you could use. In return, I want anything you've got that I can work into a story. But first, I want something to eat. I want you to take me to a tall building where I can look out over the whole of London. And I want fine wine, good food and a jazz singer, preferably female."

"Sounds expensive."

"You're unmarried, you're a detective inspector and I've got something you want. Don't tell me you can't afford it."

"I could just take you down to the station."

"Feel free. It's probably warmer than staying here."

He smiled. She'd won. "One-nil to you, then."

She picked up her bag. "The Mounties always get their man."

He rang Thames House and got them to arrange a table at Searcy's at the Gherkin, the only tall building place he could think of. He wasn't keen on re-visiting the Square Mile after his last experience, but needs must, and he had no reason to think he was any more vulnerable there than elsewhere in London. If someone wanted to grab him, they could do it virtually at any time and place of their own choosing.

They arrived at 9.30 and gave their names at reception. A lift took them 180 metres to the top floor. He took her coat from her and with it, the transmitting device Annabel had attached. They sat at a window table and looked out over the city. She sighed with pleasure. They ordered pasta and a bottle of chianti.

"Thank you for bringing me here," she said emotionally. "I'm sorry I forced you to. I just had to know who you were, that's all. You're not a policeman. You're a spy."

He laughed. "What makes you say - "

"I expect you to deny it. Don't worry, your secret's safe with me. If anything, I feel safer. A detective inspector wouldn't have the resources to set this up at the drop of a hat. This has MI5 written all over it."

He gave her a noncommittal smile. "So what have you got?"

"Let's do this one piece of information at a time, shall we? Let's begin with me asking you a question. Who was the man you were chasing?"

He could tell from the way she looked at him that she already knew. Sometime between their meeting in Portcullis House and now, she'd accessed a source of some kind and acquired the correct information. She was asking him as a test.

"His name's Pierre Durand," he said.

"Spot-on. What had he done wrong?"

This, she almost certainly didn't know, but he might as well go with the truth. Nothing hung on it now. "It was over a year ago. We suspect he was involved in the Horvath-centred attempt to frame the fringe politician, Chapman Hill. Horvath the private intelligence firm, based in the City."

She nodded. "I know you're telling the truth. I did a course in micro-expressions. Level voice, and you looked to the left. And your eyebrows didn't move."

He picked up his glass. "Well done me. Cheers."

"It's my turn now, isn't it?"

"I don't want to sound pushy, but yes."

"Promise you won't just leave me when you've found out?"

He folded his hands on the table. "I'll be honest. I'm not sure what else we have to gain from each other beyond the exchange of information. But I'm not going to run off without paying the bill, if that's what you mean."

"I need protection," she said.

"What do you mean?"

"Somebody wants what I'm about to give you. And they won't mind hurting me to get it. That's why I spend a lot of time outdoors. Easier to avoid them or see them coming. That's why I led you around today. Partly because I wanted to know if you were one of them."

"One of who?"

"I don't know. They've searched my flat, but I've hidden the goods elsewhere. All they need to do to find out where is torture me."

He suddenly remembered her mental illness. *Mild psychotic behaviour.* Not necessarily conclusive, but hardly irrelevant.

The best way of judging was to find out what she had.

"I know what you're thinking," she said. "You're thinking, 'she's mentally unstable'. Don't deny it. You're from MI5, so you'll already have accessed my medical records. I should never have given you my real name, but you'd have found it out sooner or later. Thanks to Theresa bloody May, you guys can do anything you like nowadays, and that wasn't meant in an admiring way. Before you go leaping to conclusions, why don't you have a look at what I've actually got?"

He grinned. "Whatever it is, it's a long time coming."

They stopped talking as their pasta arrived in two steaming bowls and the waiters did the conventional fussing, putting parmesan sprinklers and pepper and little bowl of pesto to hand in a way that suggested they had to be just *here* on the table and nowhere else. When they'd finished, they interlaced their fingers, bowed almost imperceptibly from the neck – a genuine 21st century bow – said 'enjoy your meal', and re-tired.

"Prepare to be blown out of your seat," Riceland said. She reached into her bag, pulled out three or four large black and white photos and passed them across. "I don't usually take my own pictures, but I'm investigative, so sometimes I need evidence. This is just the tip of the iceberg, by the way. I've got others. You'll have to look after me if you want to see the complete set."

He browsed through them. My God.

Frances Holland together with Pierre Durand, four separate locations, outdoors, looking furtive and intensely engaged in each other. He tried not to let his mounting excitement show, but she'd studied facial expressions, so she'd probably gathered something of his reaction already.

Next, as always with remarkable photos, the almost instinctive one-word question: *Photoshopped?*

But no. He'd been following her all day – when could she have done that? And even if by some miracle she *had* mocked them up, wouldn't that be just as interesting?

One thing was clear: her claim that someone was after her didn't look so far-fetched any more.

"What do you want?" he asked.

"A partnership. Frances Holland has disappeared. I know that. Right now, I'm the only journalist who knows where to dig, or that there's anything worth excavating. That'll change to my detriment as soon as I go to my editor. I want the whole story with my byline, and I want you to give it to me."

"I don't know the whole story. I'd hardly be sitting here if I did."

"I accept that. So we work together."

"Let's assume you're right for a moment. Let's say I'm a spy. It's normal in this situation for a spy to report back to his superiors. The situation's then out of his hands. What happens next is that MI5 despatches its best agents to recover the information by whatever means necessary. Thanks to Theresa bloody May, it can do anything it likes nowadays. Don't fool yourself that it won't find you."

"Thank you, I had thought of that."

"And?"

"Firstly, there's a limit to what it can do if the subject won't talk. Much more importantly, it would have to be incredibly stupid to go down that road. Once it cleans me out as a source, it effectively eliminates any chance of finding out who *else* is after me. Which could be the most valuable lead of all."

She was right, but something told him he'd lost her trust. She finished her pasta and snatched up the photos from the table.

"I don't even know your real name," she snapped. "No, don't bother telling me. You've made it abundantly clear we can't work together, that I can't trust you. I've been an idiot."

She still had five pieces of fusilli to go, and she wasn't going to leave them. She obviously had no expectation of eating again for a while. While she was stabbing them, he wrote his phone number on a napkin and gave it to her.

"I was only *what if*-ing," he said. "I didn't mean to sound threatening. I'd like us to work together."

She scraped her chair back, wiped her mouth and stood up. "Up yours."

"My name's John."

She laughed at his insouciance, then turned round and left.

He did an audit of the table. Good, she'd taken his phone number, which probably meant she'd be back in touch. He hoped whoever was after her wouldn't find her, but there wasn't much he could do right now. Not following her, not making a grab for the photos, just staying where he was – they were the best means of regaining her trust. She needed him, and since she didn't want his company right now, forcing it on her would probably backfire. Besides, he'd had enough chasing her for one day, and he still had pasta left.

Meanwhile, whatever else she had in reserve, he already knew the most important part.

Chapter 9: More 'DI Eagleton, Special Branch' Flannel

"And you didn't have to sleep with her to get that information?" Phyllis asked. They were in the lift to the canteen, heading towards a working breakfast. Annabel was already up there with Tariq.

"I'm not allowed to have sex with anyone we're investigating," Mordred replied. "I don't know how many times I've explained that to I don't know how many people in this building. Everyone pretends not to get it."

"You think people are making fun of you?"

"If they're that hard up for amusement, good luck to them."

"To be fair, it's why most men probably joined MI7. The opportunity to sleep with binders full of women, as the phrase goes."

"I grew up in a family of females. I know a thing or two about them."

"Such as?"

"They're human."

She laughed. "No wonder people find you incomprehensible."

The lift doors opened and they walked along the corridor to the canteen. A large serving area in zinc with what looked like an industrial size kitchen behind it. In front, rows of padded benches enclosing Formica tables, everything fixed to the floor in the style of an American diner. A mingled smell of fried bacon and eggs and fresh coffee. Annabel and Tariq had already annexed a seat where they could talk in privacy, plus a muffin each and some orange juice. They registered their friends' entry, but didn't wave.

"What are you getting?" Phyllis asked when she and Mordred had picked up a tray. "Don't drag it out. I want to make this quick."

"How could I drag it out? It's not like I can place a bespoke order. It's the works canteen."

She laughed. "You could order black pudding."

"You're in a funny mood this morning. Bowl of Rice Krispies, please," he told the serving lady. "And a cup of tea, stirred not shaken."

The serving lady laughed like she'd heard that one at least fifty times since seven-thirty.

"An orange juice and a piece of toast, please," Phyllis said.

They paid, walked over to their two colleagues, and sat down facing each other, Mordred next to Tariq, Phyllis next to Annabel.

"I heard you made an important discovery last night," Annabel said. "I hope you didn't breach your 'no sex' commandment."

Mordred rolled his eyes. He stood up, clapped his hands and asked if everyone could just stop eating for a moment, he had an announcement to make. In the time it took to put a knife, a fork and a spoon down, everyone in the canteen stopped what they were doing and looked blankly at him, leaving only the humming of the ovens and the faint sound of frying.

"I discovered some very important information from a member of the public last night," he said, "and at no point did I sleep with her."

The silence continued. A few people exchanged quizzical looks.

"Thank you, that'll be all." He sat down.

A light smattering of applause, a few more perplexed expressions, six or seven looks of irritation, and a sardonic groan or two. When he resumed his Rice Krispies, he noticed Phyllis was blushing. Annabel looked completely oblivious, as if it was what she'd been expecting all along.

"So Frances Holland and Pierre Durand have been meeting," she said.

"Looks that way," Mordred said. "Which is a very good outcome."

"I don't see how," Phyllis said gloomily. "You realise you've got a reputation in this place?" she said, raising her voice to change the subject. "See how people reacted? *That's bloody John Mordred, that is; he's a facetious git.*"

He sipped his tea. "Jealousy. In my defence, I'm never unpleasant to anyone. People don't like me because I undermine the James Bond thing, that's all."

Tariq laughed. "Personally, I admire the way you've got the canteen staff behind you, especially Cilla."

"Inverted snobbery," Phyllis said. She seemed genuinely annoyed.

"Much as it would fit your view of me that I should want us to sit here all morning talking about me," Mordred said, "I really think we ought to concentrate on Ashbaugh. You're in charge of this investigation. Don't you want to brief me?"

"Sorry," Phyllis said, softening. "I'm frustrated, that's all. Frustrated with myself and I'm taking it out on you. You're right. You're never unpleasant to anyone. What's it matter if all the little hobgoblins in here resent you?"

"Thanks," Mordred said. He could guess what was upsetting her. He hoped someone would change the subject back to Ashbaugh in such a way that it would stay there.

"Why are you frustrated with yourself?" Tariq asked.

"If it's any consolation," Annabel told her. "I actually agreed with you at the time, Phyllis. I only stayed on because the alternative was more desk-work."

"Yes, but I'm supposed to be in charge," Phyllis said. "I should have known something useful might come of it."

"You had a look at her medical record," Mordred said, "and you had no reason to think that yesterday would be the last we'd ever see of her. It wasn't a bad decision. At worst, it was an insignificant gamble with money you could afford to lose."

She put a thank you hand on his. She seemed on the verge of saying something but changed her mind about what it was. "Back to Ashbaugh," she said. "What's your plan? How are you going to avoid giving away the fact that Holland's disappeared?"

"Simple," Mordred said. "I'm not going to ask him about Holland. I'm going to ask him about Durand. I wish I'd got hold of those photos last night, but she seemed determined to take them, and I didn't want to worsen the situation."

"You think she'll call you?" Annabel asked.

"She took my number. She must be leaving it open as an option."

"Let's hope she doesn't turn up while you're with Bill Ashbaugh," Phyllis said. "What are you going to do if he simply says he's never clapped eyes on Durand before? Which he might do."

"I may not have the original photos," Mordred said, "but I have persuaded Reprographics to mock me up a few counterfeits. Just Durand and Holland together in various places. I'm picking the results up at lunchtime. I don't suppose they'll be perfect, but they ought to survive a cursory glance. Ashbaugh may or may not know Durand, but he certainly knows Holland, and that should be sufficient pretext for a useful conversation."

"You didn't find out why Planchart was so het up about Riceland?" Phyllis asked.

"Not really," Mordred said.

"I thought Planchart himself had explained that," Annabel remarked. "She's a journalist and she keeps pursuing him. It's what journalists do. There needn't be a mystery about everything."

"The question is," Phyllis said, "what is she pursuing him *for*? He's a backbench nonentity – or was, until The Get Out Clause came along. Now he's big in Brexit."

"So there's your answer," Tariq said.

Phyllis frowned. "No. That would mean you'd want to interview him *once* at the most, maybe for a feature. But from what you said, John, I got the impression he thinks she's after him relentlessly, like she works for *Heat* and he's Zayn Malik. And rather than take out a restraining order, he's decided to grit his teeth and put up with it. Why?"

Mordred nodded. "And then there was *her* reaction when she saw him. She didn't look like she wanted an interview. She looked like she couldn't get away fast enough."

"The plot thickens," Tariq said. He stood up. "I'd better get going. IT calls."

Mordred turned to Phyllis. "With your permission, I'd like to show my mocked-up photos to Planchart once I'm done with Ashbaugh."

"Sounds like a plan," Phyllis replied. "Meanwhile, I'm going to put a tail on him. See what it reveals."

"Bags I that job," Annabel said. "He doesn't know me, and I like fresh air."

Phyllis stood up. "Agreed. I've got a meeting with Ruby Parker in five minutes. Everyone keep me updated."

2.15pm. Mordred stood in the central lobby of the House of Commons. The floor was tiled with what looked like a blue mandala extending outwards into squares. Above it, a vaulted ceiling supported a three-ton chandelier and was ornamented with tracery. Entrants found themselves immediately surrounded by marble statues of patron saints. It was here he hoped to meet Bill Ashbaugh. He'd declined Phyllis's offer to ring ahead and make an appointment. He wanted the advantage of surprise.

For the second time in two days, he had a photograph of the interviewee on him: in his briefcase this time. Ashbaugh was in his late thirties and looked like a 19th century mill owner. Greying hair down to his shoulders, bushy sideburns and a six-inch chin-only beard. He habitually dressed in three piece suits with a watch-chain but no tie. His views were Blair-ite and broadly conventional, but his appearance meant the press considered him an eccentric.

There were lots of people around: MPs and peers on their way to one or the other Houses of Parliament, tourists, alone or in packs, and one or two concerned looking people with documents – either journalists or constituents. According to what intelligence he had, the location of Ashbaugh's office meant the MP had to pass through here every lunchtime to reach the bar. An hour ago, Mordred had registered his journey there; now he awaited his return. He'd be in a better mood then, and perhaps less guarded. That was the theory.

And here he came, thank God alone. Even better: he didn't look in any hurry to get where he was going. Mordred made eye contact and stepped out to intercept him. "Mr Ashbaugh? I wonder if I could have a word."

Ashbaugh stopped. His right hand rose an inch from his waist and twitched. He clearly didn't know whether this was handshake-worthy or not. "Are you – a constituent?"

Mordred produced his card. "DI Eagleton, Special Branch," he said quietly.

The blood drained from Ashbaugh's face and collected in his neck. "What do you want?" he asked.

Fear. Mordred knew enough to realise it probably wasn't connected to Holland. More likely his expense account or something as-yet wholly private.

"You're not under suspicion of anything. I just need to ask you a few questions."

"This is very irregular," he said angrily. "Just come in here and flash a card. Why didn't you ring ahead if you simply wanted to talk to me? Are you a journalist of some kind? A card doesn't mean anything. Anyone with a colour photo-copier can make one of those." He took out his phone and took a photo of Mordred's face. "What did you say your name was, again?"

"DI Eagleton."

"First name?"

"Jonas."

"Wait there. If I find you're anyone other than precisely who you say you are, you'll be the one who's on the receiving end of the full weight of the law."

He strode off, full of the anticipation of righteous indignation. Mordred had half-expected this, and he'd made the necessary arrangements. He calculated Ashbaugh would be back within ten minutes at the outside.

In fact, it was eight. Whether deliberately or not, he crept up on Mordred from behind and laid a gentle hand on his shoulder. Mordred turned round to a face not exactly filled with righteous indignation, but not entirely devoid of it either.

"You check out," Ashbaugh said. "I'm not going to apologise, though. You're at fault, not me. You can't just ambush a person like this. I'm at work. It's a bloody busy life here, contrary to what people think. What do you want? No, no, don't answer that," he said, apparently conscious that people were beginning to stare. He began to walk. "Follow me. We might as well go to my office. Don't expect a cup of tea or coffee, though."

"I thought it would be easier if I kept it informal. I assumed that way, I wouldn't alarm you."

"Well, you were wrong. It had the opposite effect. Remember that, in future."

"I wouldn't have been able to tell you what it was over the phone, and that would have placed you in limbo."

"You're assuming I've a guilty conscience." They were climbing a set of stone steps now. "Look, let's just put this conversation on hold till we reach my office, shall we? People are going to overhear. Then talk."

They walked along a corridor and into a small office with a desk, Edwardian in décor except that it was hung with gilt-framed pictures of Pink Floyd. It was much smaller than Planchart's, but somehow more overawing. Ashbaugh gestured for Mordred to sit down before the desk. He sat down behind it.

Mordred reached down and opened his briefcase. "I'm just here to ask you some questions," he said. "You're not under suspicion of anything."

"So ... I could see you anytime I like. I don't necessarily have to see you now. If I'm, say, busy ..."

"That's correct. But you can't put it off indefinitely. Even if you could, it probably wouldn't be good for your reputation."

Ashbaugh laughed incredulously. "Is that meant to be a threat? May I remind you, you're talking to a Member of Parliament here."

"I meant, it wouldn't be good for your reputation as a Member of Parliament."

"I probably know your boss," Ashbaugh countered. He grinned. "You see, two can play the threat game."

Mordred stopped what he was doing and looked at the MP. Ashbaugh met his gaze. Just like being children again. Planchart had warned him - in vague terms, but even so.

"Might as well get it over with, I suppose," Ashbaugh said suddenly, rolling his eyes. "Go on, give it your best shot."

"As I said, this isn't meant to be a confrontation." He passed the mocked-up photos over.

Ashbaugh flipped through them cursorily, grinned sardonically and put them down on the desk. "So what was I meant to see?"

"I want to know if you recognise anyone."

"You mean Frances Holland?"

"Anyone else? Take another look."

He picked them up again and again went through them at speed. "No."

Mordred stood up. He'd come prepared for this. Ashbaugh was almost certainly expecting him to argue, insist on a third look, express frustration. Instead, he picked up his briefcase and stood up quickly, looking as if this was the best outcome he could have expected. "That's very useful," he said. "Thank you, that was all I needed to know. Sorry to have interrupted your busy schedule, Mr Ashbaugh. I *will* ring ahead next time."

He left without a backwards glance and walked briskly along the corridor as if he had to get somewhere fast. He heard the door open and close behind him and hurried footsteps, then Ashbaugh's voice, only half-commanding:

"Detective Inspector!"

Mordred stopped and turned with an expression of mild indignation. "Er, yes?"

"I – sorry, what's going to happen next? Could you give me a bit of background?"

He turned to face the MP. "Mr Ashbaugh, you weren't very cooperative, if you don't mind me saying so. I'm quite happy to discuss my case with you, but it's a two-way process. As I'm sure you're right in saying, you probably know my boss. I'd rather not leave you to find out about it that way, but that's really up to you."

Ashbaugh looked like there was trouble at the mill. He wasn't prepared to apologise, but he certainly wasn't going to beg. And he couldn't think of any intermediate course. "I, er …"

"Shall we press re-set?" Mordred asked.

"That would be good, yes. I'll ask Maureen to put the kettle on. Tea or coffee?"

Chapter 10: A Nice Drop of Whisky With Ashbaugh

"Let me make something clear at the outset," Ashbaugh said, when he and Mordred were seated again, "and please don't take this the wrong way: I've called you back in here not because I'm scared. Not for myself, anyway. I've called you in because … well, it's Frances you're after, isn't it?"

"Yes," Mordred said.

"What has she done?"

"You'll forgive me if I leave that until after I've questioned you. Otherwise, something I say may prejudice one of your answers."

"Shit."

"What?"

"Let's talk to each other like human beings, shall we?" He leaned over his desk and pressed the button on an intercom. "Maureen, that tea, *s'il vous plait*, now. What do you want to know?"

"You're absolutely certain you know no one in those photos besides Frances Holland?"

"I notice she was talking to the same man in each photo. A man I've never seen before. I see Frances fairly regularly. Not to speak to, just across the chamber, or around the corridors. We don't even tend to say hello nowadays."

"Purely ideological differences?"

"Probably not. We were an item at uni, that's a matter of public record, but uni was a long time ago. There's been a hell of a lot of water under the bridge since then. She's the Brexit Queen and I'm her nemesis. Or I like to think of myself that way. There's no love lost between us any more. Quite the opposite."

"We don't know exactly who the man in the photos is, except that he once worked for the French secret service. He was thrown out. Since then, he's done a variety of shady jobs. He's wanted by the police for questioning, and he's got a team of very expensive lawyers behind him. And although he was arrested two days ago, there was a major cock-up, and he's now back on the streets again."

"What's his name?"

"Pierre Durand."

"Is he dangerous?"

"Not in the physical violence sense," Mordred said, "although I wouldn't recommend attempting a citizen's arrest. He's not a terrorist, if that's what you mean."

"What's he doing with Frances?"

"That's what we'd dearly like to know."

"I assume you've asked her."

Mordred paused. Given the direction of their conversation, there could be no hiding it now. "We don't know where she is."

"What? You - 'don't know where she is' right now, or - ?"

"We'd be grateful if you could sit on the fact for a while. She disappeared just over a week ago."

Ashbaugh said nothing. Maureen – a middle-aged woman with red hair in a bun – entered with a tray and placed a tea-set on the table, item by item. She smiled thinly and left. Ashbaugh showed no sign of noticing she'd ever been there. He stared miserably at the desk.

"Your secret's safe with me," he told Mordred eventually. "She and I may be on opposite ends of the political spectrum – insofar as that characterisation still has any meaning in modern politics – but we're colleagues. I'm not going to exploit what could be a tragedy. I mean, maybe I'm jumping to conclusions: 'disappeared' – it *could* be a tragedy, couldn't it? Or have I got the wrong end of the stick?"

"It could be," Mordred said.

"I know about her mental condition," Ashbaugh said. "At one point in our lives, we shared everything. I've never mentioned it to anyone else. I won't mention this either."

"Have you any idea where she might have gone?"

"I don't actually know her any more. Who reported her missing?"

"Her political colleagues."

Ashbaugh laughed humourlessly. "You mean Planchart and his cronies? I heard she and he were seeing each other. Maybe he did something to her."

"We're not ruling anything out, but we don't think it's likely."

"Don't let his supposed power deflect you. Why isn't this in any of the papers? If it's important enough to send a DI to Westminster Palace for, I'm pretty sure it's big enough for page five of the *Mirror*. Oh" - he rubbed his head – "oh, of course, yes. The mental illness. Ah, yes. Planchart asked you to be 'discreet', that's it, isn't it? Doesn't want to jeopardise her career. Or his own stake in it."

"Her family has the decisive say."

"Oh, really. Her ex-husband, Martin the Magnificent? Snivelling little creep he was."

"Her parents and her younger brother. We're dealing with the situation in accordance with their wishes. People in this country disappear every day. They don't usually get a full police investigation this quickly. They don't usually get a mention in the national press. People have to be looked after, but they also have the right to privacy. It's the family that usually knows best how to square those two."

"You need to concentrate on Planchart. He's been mixing with some very dodgy types lately, so I've heard."

"Tell me more."

"Members of the French National Front, and the German National Democratic party, for a start. It's no secret that Planchart sees The Get Out Clause as a stepping-stone to the Tory leadership. If Britain votes to leave the EU, David Cameron becomes a dead man walking. George bloody Osborne too. The party will call for fresh blood, right now. Planchart's got a lot of support. Moreover, he's building a certain kind of international credibility in anticipation: forging alliances with people who want Exit for their own countries. Or – as I say - that's what I've heard."

"Heard from who?"

"It's common knowledge around here. And of course, it's been in *Private Eye*." He put his hands on the table, looked at them as if they were someone else's, and made two fists. "Not that anyone takes any notice of a rag like that. Bloody public school know-alls, think they can tell you how to live!" He seemed transported to another world, full of accusations and furtive sniggers. Then he came back. "Sorry. Got on the wrong side of Ian-butter-wouldn't-melt-Hislop and his crew a few months ago. Don't ask me the details. All lies, every word they wrote."

"Right."

"So there we have it. Many hands make light work. Against all the odds, we seem to have solved your mystery. My guess is your Pierre Durand's an emissary of Marine Le Pen. Which makes me very sad, to be honest." He drained his tea-cup, opened a drawer in his desk, took out a bottle of whisky and poured himself one. "I'm disappointed in Frances. I didn't think she'd ever stoop this low. Want one?"

"I'm on duty, but okay, yes." Mordred had learned from long experience that joining an interviewee in a drink was nearly always an effective stratagem. He passed his cup across. Ashbaugh poured two or three measures and set the cap-less bottle in the middle of the desk.

"My advice to you, Jonas," Ashbaugh said, "in a nutshell: look for Frances in France. I assume you've shown Planchart these photos?"

"I've only just received them, but he's next on my list."

"Where do you stand on the EU, Detective Inspector? Personally? I mean, you can tell me, now we're having a drink together. Just out of interest."

"I'm undecided. I still haven't digested all the evidence."

Ashbaugh scoffed. "Good luck with that."

"There are still another two months or so."

"I might as well warn you now then. You're on a hiding to nothing. The problem isn't that there isn't enough evidence. It's the opposite."

"I'm not sure what you mean. You mean there's too much? How is that a problem?"

"It has to be sifted, that's what. Society's too complex and there are too many analysts."

"Maybe."

"The fact is, there's enough evidence for everyone to keep his or her prejudices intact, and always a huge pile of apparently redundant stuff left over. We're drowning in bloody evidence – the newspapers and the internet are overflowing with it - and it doesn't make anyone more able to reach a decision. We're asking about something unknowable and scary: what's going to happen in the future. A lot of people will cling hard to their own little piles of evidence and close their eyes to all the other little piles. It's happening all over the free world."

"That's quite a sceptical view. And yet you're committed to staying in Europe."

Ashbaugh smiled. "Well, yes. Because what we do know is that there are an awful lot of crooks in the British establishment. A general election every five years isn't capable of reining them in. Do you want to give them completely free rein? Or would it be better for them to be reined in by the more abstract crooks in Brussels? In the end that may be the only question."

Mordred laughed.

"What's so funny?" Ashbaugh asked.

"You've just broken the world record for alcohol producing melancholy."

"I had whisky for lunch as well. This is just a follow-up. Cheers."

Mordred stood up. It had been a useful conversation really. It put the ball firmly back in Planchart's court. "Thank you for your time."

Ashbaugh stood up. "Good luck making your mind up. Don't forget, by the way, you also need evidence about the evidence. You need to know who's providing it and how truly independent they are. And because of the secrecy in which the establishment's traditionally cloaked, that may be impossible to discover. But hey, good luck."

He offered a handshake. As Mordred closed the door behind him and left the building, he didn't know whether it had been a friendly or a sardonic gesture.

He switched his phone on. *2 messages*.

He was about to access them when it rang. *Ruby Parker*. He picked up.

"John," she said, "I want you to return to base now. Report to Colin at reception and follow his instructions."

She rang off before he had the chance to reply. Whatever it was, it sounded urgent – and not good. Both of his messages were from her, one ten, one fifteen minutes earlier, issuing the same order.

He crossed the road to the tube station.

Chapter 11: Spies Don't Like Being Spied On

When Mordred reached Thames House, he went straight to reception as per instructions. Colin Bale, a large bald man with an unambiguous sense of his own importance, signed him in and directed him to briefing room five, where Brian Penford usually dwelt. When he got there, Phyllis and Annabel were already seated, facing each other in silence, while Ruby Parker sat at the front and between them, like a teacher at a reconciliation meeting between two pupils at loggerheads. Was that what this was? Could Phyllis and Annabel have had a professional falling out of some kind? Why would that have to involve him?

"Thank you for coming so quickly," Ruby Parker said. "I hope I didn't interrupt your session with Ashbaugh, but this is urgent. Close the door and sit down."

He did as instructed. Phyllis and Annabel seemed to relax now that the meeting looked to be under way. Obviously, they knew as little as he did, only they'd had longer to dwell on it.

"I won't beat about the bush," Ruby Parker said. "Tariq's uncovered evidence that some of our internal signals are being intercepted *from within this building.*"

"Someone in MI7's spying on us?" Phyllis said. Incredulity turned to horror as one possible implication sank in. "You – surely don't think it's any of us three?"

"It's not any individual," she replied. "It's one of the other departments: Blue, Grey or Black. Black probably monitors us all the time anyway, that's the received wisdom. Which leaves Blue or Grey – or both."

"How did Tariq find out?" Mordred asked. "If it isn't too technical a question?"

"It is," Ruby Parker said. "Something to do with information tagging, an interceptor so light it ought to be undetectable, etcetera. It's irrelevant as far as we're concerned. Tariq knows what he's talking about, and if he's concerned, so should we be."

"What can we do about it?" Annabel said.

Ruby Parker put her fingertips together. "I've recalled Alec, Edna and Ian from Belgium. Until we get more information, it's a job for Tariq and his team. But we need to be prepared. Ordinarily, I might not be concerned – departments in this building do attempt to spy on each other from time to time, mainly when difficult investigations overlap and trust wears thin – but this is different. John, I'm afraid I'm going to have to ask you to continue from this point. I'm sure you know what I mean."

"Phyllis already knows," he replied. "I didn't tell Annabel because I forgot about it in the gruelling quest for Sarah Rice-land."

"Tell me what?" Annabel asked.

"John's been flagged up as vulnerable to radicalisation," Ruby Parker said.

Annabel didn't flinch. "By who?"

"Someone in Grey," Mordred replied.

"So now we know who's spying on us," Annabel said. "The question is, how are we going to retaliate?"

"The way MI7 works," Ruby Parker said, "they know more about us than we ever can about them. So we're at a definite disadvantage."

"Do they know that we know they're spying on us?" Mordred asked.

"If not, we need to start feeding them false information," Phyllis said.

"Specifically about John," Annabel chimed in. "They only need three or four of their accusations to fall flat for the whole investigation to come crashing down."

"The thought had occurred to me," Ruby Parker said. "But making it look plausible could be well nigh impossible. Why should we suddenly start opening up online about John's supposed ideological and political indiscretions? They'd see us coming a mile off, then they'd adjust accordingly. No, it's much more important to find out what they're looking for. Establish their probing patterns sufficiently to draw conclusions. That requires time. Meanwhile, I think it's important to review what we're all doing."

"Sarah Riceland," Phyllis said.

"You think she's some sort of Grey plant?" Annabel asked. "Designed to lure John?"

"Her credentials check out," Mordred objected. "I think she's bona fide."

"Credentials can be manufactured," Phyllis countered. "You ought to know that."

"The whole Durand episode could have been manufactured," Ruby Parker said. "We need to be very careful with regards to this 'Sarah Riceland'. If, and when, she contacts you again, John, I want you to make it a condition of your meeting her that you're not alone. If she declines, we need to find out where she is, then we do some proper shadowing. This time, she won't know we're there, and we'll tail her in shifts until we get some kind of result. I want to know who she really is and what, if anything, she's actually got. John, this morning, you got Reprographics to mock you up some photos of Holland and Durand. I've got copies. They're good, but they wouldn't survive a close-up examination. Since she retrieved the ones she showed you, we've no way of knowing whether they're similarly manufactured. She may have taken them away solely to stop you finding out."

"Durand himself could be a pawn of Grey," Annabel said.

"That would strongly implicate Simpson, Musgrave and De Groot, the law firm that came to release him," Mordred said. "In which case, we may need to start spying on them, see where it takes us."

"Sounds like a very good pretext for a burglary," Annabel said.

"That might be difficult," Ruby Parker said. "They're on the thirtieth floor of One Canada Square."

Annabel shrugged. "The higher they climb."

"Maybe we should go back even further," Phyllis said. "It was Ranulph Farquarson who pointed us in Durand's direction. Coincidentally, or otherwise, the ex-head of Grey. Could he be in on it?"

"I see your reasoning," Ruby Parker said, "but I don't think so. He wasn't inclined to dirty tricks when he was in office; it'd be odd if he'd suddenly developed a taste for them now he's retired. Besides, there were other ways your attention could have been drawn to Durand. No, I think Farquarson's appearance was mere chance."

"In that case, our coming across Durand himself was probably chance as well," Phyllis said.

"He certainly gave me a run for my money," Mordred said. "I didn't get the impression he wanted to be caught. And if he had, I'm pretty sure we'd have held on to him a lot longer. Instead of: not at all."

"So the first real manifestation of Grey in all this occurs via Simpson, Musgrave and De Groot," Annabel said. "They're the ones we need to attack now. The more so because they won't be expecting it. How soon till Alec gets back? We're going to need the extra bodies, especially Edna. I've a role for her."

"This is your burglary proposal again?" Ruby Parker asked. "I need to see a proper plan before I approve it. Not necessarily on paper."

"I've already got a basic idea," Annabel replied. "I'll get back to you in a few days. I'll need to do some research so, if it's okay, I'd like you to ask Ian to tail Planchart."

"Do you still think that's worthwhile?" Phyllis asked. "I'm pretty sure Planchart's hiding something, but will following him around uncover it?"

"I think it'd be premature to assume otherwise," Annabel said.

"Riceland and Planchart looked horrified by each other," Mordred said. "Maybe they're both acting for Grey somehow, and they didn't expect to meet. An unexpected encounter could be awkward in front of someone you're both trying to deceive. Especially if you haven't compared notes beforehand."

"You just said you thought she was bona fide," Phyllis said.

"I'm open to counter suggestions," Mordred replied. "Including my own."

"Everything's speculation right now," Ruby Parker said. "We don't know anything at all yet. Phyllis, you continue in charge of the Holland case, but I'm taking charge of the possible incursion by Grey. Obviously, it may ultimately turn out that your investigation comes entirely within my field, but we tend to see eye to eye as a rule, so I don't expect there'll be occasions where I have to use my power of veto in order to make executive decisions. Bear in mind, however, I'm not ruling it out."

"Understood," Phyllis replied.

Chapter 12: THE Interview!!!!!!!!!!!!

Three days went by without anything significant happening, then a lot of things happened all at once. Mordred received 24-hour advance notice that his 'vulnerability interview' had been scheduled. He was to report to a Dr John Murgatroyd at 2pm in Office Z14, to answer questions about his record with a view to determining whether he had an 'at risk' case to answer. The next day, on his way to the top floor of Thames House, where Z14 was situated, he called in at Ruby Parker's office. As arranged, she sent him straight to Tariq. Once Tariq had finished with him, and he was back *en route*, he got a phone call from Annabel.

"I need you to meet Edna and I at Canary Wharf," she said. "It's urgent."

"Now? I can't. I'm on my way to be interviewed."

"*The* interview?"

"The same. I'll call you as soon as I get out, but I've no idea how long it's going to take."

"In that case, mine's no longer so major. Call me as soon as you're out, though. Don't forget. Good luck."

Z14. Funny, the names they gave these rooms. It wasn't like there was a row of Z's on the top floor, or any numbers one to thirteen. He switched his phone off and knocked.

"Enter!" a voice called.

He went in to find a small, long-disused space with an empty bookcase on each side, and only two chairs in the way of furniture, one of which was occupied by a small, stout man in a black tie, scuffed shoes and a suit too small for him. Hair protruded from his ears, but failed to appear on the top of his head. This man stood up and offered a handshake, but his friendliness didn't extend to coming across the room to receive his interviewee. "Sit down, sit down," he said quietly, looking at the floor, as if he was very disappointed it had come to this. He didn't introduce himself. The letter had said a John Murgatroyd. Presumably, this was him.

Mordred sat down facing the window. You probably got quite a good view from here, but once he was seated, it was gone. Meanwhile, the sun was in his eyes.

Murgatroyd picked up a clipboard and a pen. "I'd like to start off by asking you a very general - "

"Do you mind if I move slightly to the side?" Mordred asked. "I'm a little blinded."

Murgatroyd sighed. "Fine, fine."

They shifted seats slightly, so they were both side-on to the window. The light here was still irritating, but less so than before, and this time the interviewer had to put up with it as well. Mordred got the keen impression the original placement of their chairs hadn't been a matter of chance.

"Fire away," he said.

"You're a vegetarian," Murgatroyd said. He waited for Mordred's nod, and continued: "I have it on good authority that your reasons are what might loosely be called 'moral'. Wouldn't 'squeamish' be a better word?"

Mordred shrugged. "Only if you think the two terms are interchangeable."

"Yet you have killed in the past. People, that is; not animals."

"True."

Murgatroyd gave a sardonic grin. "I also understand you've adopted a donkey in Sidmouth. Doesn't all this strike you as somewhat perverse in an intelligence officer?"

"I don't necessarily draw the line at killing animals," Mordred said. "It would depend on the circumstances. Just as I suppose you wouldn't necessarily draw the line at eating a human."

"I beg your pardon?" Murgatroyd didn't wait for an answer. "I can assure you, Mr Mordred, that is something I would never do!"

"Why not?"

"Because I wouldn't ..." He tailed off, obviously seeking a defence that wouldn't invoke 'moral' or 'squeamish'.

"The donkey's called Robert, by the way," Mordred said softly.

Murgatroyd drew himself up and seemed to press a re-set button deep within himself. "What does the word 'radical' mean to you?" he asked. "What I mean is, do you see being 'radical' as, in general, a good thing, or not?"

"It's a relative term," Mordred replied. "So it depends partly on what it's relative to. And also, of course, its specific content."

"So you wouldn't say it was *good* to be radical?"

"Not necessarily."

"'Not necessarily'. So it *could* be. In what *circumstances* would you say it was good to be radical?"

"Well, let's say I live in a community of white supremacists, and I come up with the radical idea that none of us are any different to black people. So I start working for the social inclusion of Kanye West and Frank Bruno."

"Yes, yes." The way the first affirmative was drawn out, it was obvious that this wasn't an acceptable answer. "That's not a very real example, though, is it? What I mean is, in what *real life* situations do you think it's good to be radical?"

"Well, let's say I'm a woman in Saudi Arabia, and I get the car out of the garage and go for a drive round the block."

"Yes, y - "

"It *is* a real life example."

"Yes, I know, I - "

"Or let's say I'm Rosa Parks."

"Right, okay, I think I see. Do you think MI7 is a radical organisation?"

"No."

"Would you like it to be?"

"In what way?"

"For example, would you like it to go round righting injustices?"

"I'd like everyone and everything to go round righting injustices. Wouldn't you? Or would you prefer injustices to stand?"

"It's not about me, Mr Mordred. It's about you."

"Call me John."

"'John'," Murgatroyd said, as if it was a piece of gristle.

"That's right, and in return, I hope I can call you by your Christian name. You're …?"

"Also John. But of course you knew that from the letter, didn't you? Am I to take it you're being flippant?"

"Shouldn't there be someone here to take minutes of our meeting? Because I'm beginning to suspect you're a little paranoid."

"This is MI7, Mr - "

"John. So, what? Everything's got to be secret even between ourselves?"

"So long as you're under investigation within this organisation, you're not entitled to the rights and privileges of an ordinary citizen."

"So you could write anything you like about me."

Murgatroyd didn't reply. He wrote something down. And kept writing. Three minutes later, he looked up again. "Let's get down to specifics, shall we?"

"How do I know you're John Murgatroyd?"

"Pardon?"

"You haven't introduced yourself. No one's vouched for you. You could be anyone. I don't actually know who John Murgatroyd is, anyway. Even if it were to be proved that you *were* John Murgatroyd, I'd be none the wiser."

"We can terminate this interview whenever you want to. All you have to do is walk out of that door. But you won't get a preview of the charges against you. They'll come at you later, out of the blue. You surely don't want that, do you? John?"

Murgatroyd's whole demeanour had changed. No longer the slightly pompous academic; suddenly, the seasoned interrogator. Mordred suddenly realised where he'd come from, and whence the mystery. Black. Only Black would have the authority to arbitrate a dispute of this nature between two departments. Only Black would appear suddenly like this, alone, devoid of credentials, with no apparent fear of being challenged. He'd better behave himself.

"Go on," he said.

"Let's go back to last year," Murgatroyd said. "You approached one of our newest recruits in the gents' toilet in this building, and told him you were a Communist. Is that right?"

"Ian Leonard, yes. It was a joke. I was trying to put him at his ease."

"At the time, he took your claim seriously enough to report it. He thought you were trying to recruit him."

"Well, ask him now. He's realised the error of his ways."

"Because he knows you're the 'office joker', right? There's a multitude of sins can be hidden under that soubriquet. Anyway, let's move on. Earlier than that you were part of a group within MI7, two of whom left to join Kurdish fighters in Syria."

"True, yes."

"Did you approve of their actions?"

"At the time, Ruby Parker instructed us not to comment one way or the other. She never countermanded that order, so: no comment."

"I'm countermanding it. Now."

"You've given me no reason to think you possess the authority."

Murgatroyd gave a 'let's move on' sigh. "You have been heard to say in the past that you won't necessarily serve Queen and Country if you think it involves injustice."

"Did I?"

"Are you claiming you didn't say that?"

"Has anyone made a formal complaint to that effect?"

"I'm asking you *now*, then. Would you put Queen and Country ahead of justice?"

"Always."

Murgatroyd sneered and grinned at the same time. "We do have such things as lie detectors in this building, you know."

"Well, we don't have one today. And if there's ever a choice between, on the one hand, preventing ISIS from committing genocide, and, on the other, mowing the lawns at Buckingham Palace – which would, of course, technically count as 'serving Queen and Country' - I'd always opt for the former. Good luck in devising a lie-detector test that contextualises your question precisely enough."

"Last year, you joined a group of radicals in Jersey who were protesting against tax avoidance."

"I was despatched there by my department, yes."

"Some people might say you went above and beyond the call of duty."

"I helped save lives. Of course, in London, Grey department was busy abducting one of my colleagues. Would you describe *that* as radical?"

"It's a matter that's already been dealt with."

"And yet the obvious lesson behind this interview is that matters previously considered under the bridge can be re-opened on a whim."

"Do you think the issue of tax avoidance urgently needs to be addressed?"

"Me and the Chancellor of the Exchequer, yes."

"*Urgently?*"

"I get the impression you're becoming a bit desperate now, John. If that's your real name. The overriding point is, I helped save British lives. And next time you're down in Black, or wherever it is you come from, maybe look up Red department's remit. 'Very roughly, Red exists to disrupt despotic and protect democratic regimes'. Then perhaps ask yourself a question. Does that sound in any way 'radical'?"

Murgatroyd didn't look fazed. He set to writing again. The sun had gone behind a cloud now, and the true dinginess of the room was beginning to make itself apparent. After three minutes, he made a loud full stop on his page, and looked up and smiled.

"Thank you for your time, Mr Mordred. That'll be all."

Mordred closed the door behind him and went straight downstairs to Tariq who helped him off with the wire he'd been wearing. If Murgatroyd later overstated his case, that little recording would spell the end of his involvement, and possibly the entire investigation. Because of it, he didn't have to report back to Ruby Parker: she was set to listen to it later. Instead, he was free to ring Annabel.

"How did it go?" she asked.

"Good and bad," he replied. "Good in that I met him blow for blow. Bad in that he didn't seem particularly keen on me."

"Edna and I are at Charing Cross now. Come and meet us at Trafalgar Square. We'll be under Nelson's Column with a packet of fig rolls. I'm just about to fulfil a plan. You're going to like it. Did you get Ian's message?"

"I've had my phone switched off for the last forty minutes."

"Oh, boy. So I get to tell you the news."

"What news?"

"You'll never guess who Planchart just met for a coffee and a croissant off Chancery Lane."

"Surprise me."

"Monsieur Pierre Durand. And I know nothing beyond that, nor does Ian. So don't ask. But ... well, well, well, eh?"

"Does Phyllis know?"

"She's the boss on this one, John. So obviously. She's with Ian now."

Chapter 13: The Red Lion

Things were beginning to happen. You often got that in an investigation. For a long time, everything seemed very slow, and sometimes even stationary. Then, all of a sudden, things sped up, and you could hardly keep up as event piled on event.

He got on the bus to Charing Cross and sat at the back where he could watch the other passengers. *Manual of Effective Spycraft, Rule #404.* Yet all he could think about now was the interview. He'd given as good as he got – hadn't he? The hope now was that Murgatroyd would turn out a distorted version. Then they'd be in clover.

But what was he thinking? *So long as you're under investigation within this organisation, you're not entitled to the rights and privileges of an ordinary citizen.* So far as he knew, there was no obligation on anyone to write anything up, much less to make corrections if there was a mismatch between any finished document and some clandestine recording.

Still, there'd been no mention of a second meeting. Just 'Thank you that will be all', or words to that effect. And no questions about his willingness, or otherwise, to resort to violence. He'd left the room genuinely uncertain of what impression he'd made. Given how he'd baited Murgatroyd, it should have been negative. But then at no point had the interviewer seemed riled, not really. Odd, odd, it was all very odd.

What would he do when he was thrown out of the service? Better start thinking about it now. Everything changes, nothing lasts for ever. Probably a good thing. Languages, his one talent. Maybe go and work for Linguaphone. Or perhaps the Foreign and Commonwealth Office. Bit more prestigious.

But no. That would be more of what he was doing now. Busy days with no particular good karma to show. Better to work for a charity. Maybe his sister could get him into MSF. He imagined her reaction – 'But you've got no medical skills, John!', said in the most cheeriest, most tactful way possible, of course. 'But you *must* need interpreters', he'd say. Then her: 'Let me see what I can do then. I'll get back to you'. The end.

All his sisters thought he was unemployable. Parents too. A few years ago, when he'd told them he'd landed a job as a sales rep selling machine parts, there was general relief. Like that was way better than they'd expected. Occasionally, his dad gave him a 'You should be looking for promotion' talk, even though his dad didn't know exactly what it was he already did – and couldn't, since his cover job didn't exist. But those talks were becoming less and less frequent.

Maybe make a clean break. Work with animals. Dog rescue centre, something like that. Get a dog of his own, even. A Labrador or a Greyhound, ex-racing. Go on holidays together to Wales and the Lake District. Drive up to Scotland with Tubby on the back seat. Yes, that's what she'd be called. Fat or thin, it didn't matter. With a dog, the name didn't have to match the weight or figure. No rules. Anarchy in the UK.

The bus grumbled along, crawling behind cars and bikes, then suddenly lurching forward or pulling out or both, occasionally giving a loud hiss like a sigh, as if to say it was fed up doing this. Outside it was a cloudy, dry, nondescript afternoon. Men and women plodded along in opposite directions at different speeds, none of them looking glad to be alive. Because they weren't smiling, and because the sun was in, they all looked shabby. That's what no smile plus no sunshine did to people. Made them look unkempt. Pretty good job he couldn't see himself in the mirror.

He got off at Charing Cross and walked down to Trafalgar Square. He saw Annabel and Edna before they saw him: a petite, severe-faced woman with long blonde hair in unusual bunches, and a tall, thin black woman with a shaven head. Sitting side by side on the edge of the fountain with a packet of biscuits. They didn't look shabby, but that was probably because he knew them and Edna was laughing. He checked his own clothes. Interview suit, not bad. Still, the sun was in and he wasn't smiling.

He advanced across the square to meet them. They saw him and got up. Before he could make up the distance, though, a little boy of about eight came up to Edna and said something to her. The boy's family came over, introduced themselves, took out their phones for selfies with the gold medallist. Yet more people arrived, attracted initially to the curiosity, then to Edna.

Annabel peeled off and came over to meet Mordred.

"Edna's coming in a minute," she said, looking behind her at the still gathering crowd. "Or maybe ten. She'll meet us in The Red Lion."

"I take it you've finished the fig rolls."

"We had to. I remembered after I called you: as soon as you're allowed near anything edible, you start feeding pigeons. Sorry, but it's your own fault."

They crossed the road and began to walk down Whitehall towards the Houses of Parliament. "So how did your interview go?" Annabel asked. "Sorry, you've already told me that. 'Good and bad'. But I was so eager to tell you about Planchart, I changed the subject."

"I didn't disgrace myself."

"What did they ask about?"

"Not 'they'; 'he'. One man, on his own. Not even someone there to introduce him. Could have been anyone."

"Sounds like Black. That would be just their style."

"Exactly what I thought."

"The good thing is, you've someone down there to vouch for you."

"Oh?"

"'Dao-ming Chou' aka Maggie Barclay. Your first real sweetheart, remember? Love in Siberia then never seen again. Whom we all remember with affection."

"I can do without being teased. It's been a difficult day."

"Seriously, though. She may have left you, but I doubt she wants to see you impugned."

"She may not even be working there any more."

"No one leaves Black. Ever."

Mordred frowned. "All the rubbish that's bandied around about that department. I've no idea how it's managed to survive all these years without a severe debunking. Someone needs to dial 999 and ask for James Randi."

"What I suppose I'm trying to say is, look on the bright side. Incidentally, I suppose they – sorry, *he*, your interviewer – brought up the time you went up to Ian, in the toilets, and told him you were a Communist?"

"I didn't 'go up to him'. Anyway, how did *you* find out about that?"

"Everyone knows about that, John. The only surprise is it didn't make the *Evening Standard*. I suppose he also asked about when Ian Woodward went to Syria with Thelma from White?"

"He did mention it, yes."

"And how you've been heard to admit you prefer feeding pigeons to serving the Queen?"

"Not my actual words."

"The point is, you actually *are* guilty. That's the great thing about you. Somewhere along the line, you actually *have* been radicalised."

"Thanks for the vote of confidence."

"Come on, John. It's not the bloody army. We're *supposed* to be individuals. Grey doesn't get that. My guess is they're still living in the days of Sir Vernon George Waldegrave Kell, KCMG, and the 'War Department Constabulary'. This case against you doesn't stand a chance. It's not even premised securely. Enjoy it while it lasts. See it as a chance to reminisce and reflect."

"Let's talk about you, shall we?"

They reached the Red Lion. They went straight to the bar and waited to be served. The usual postprandial crowd sat about on stools and chairs, chatting and drinking, or just looking blankly at the floor.

"What are you having?" Mordred asked.

"It's my turn to buy," she said. "You bought in the Duck and Waffle last month."

"You paid for the pizza in Mrs Hennigan's."

"You pay, then. Let's not argue. I'll have a fresh orange juice with ice, please. Get one for Edna too."

"Two iced fresh oranges and an American Cream Soda, please," Mordred said when the barman came over.

"I'm - " the barman said, looking flummoxed, "I'm not sure … We may be out of American Cream Soda right now. Let me go and look. I won't be a minute. Just one second."

"Don't worry, that's fine," Mordred said. "I'll have a shandy instead. Please."

The emergency ended, the drinks were supplied. Mordred took them to the window-seat where Annabel was.

"No American Cream Soda again?" she said.

"They may have it, they may not. I decided not to wait."

"Wise decision."

It wasn't secure for them to talk here about anything professional, so Annabel lapsed into a complete, comfortable silence. She had the capacity to do that at any time, and when she did, you were just left alone, as if you didn't exist. Mostly, it was when work-related topics had been exhausted, or she judged there might be risks to unguarded talk: store cameras, CCTV, or stationary unidentified strangers. That was the difference between her and Phyllis, though. With Phyllis, under the same circumstances, the conversation would simply switch to the TV or the weather, or plans for the weekend. Annabel didn't seem to think those things worth airing. Which they weren't, not really. The problem was, he was itching to find out why she'd called him as a matter of urgency earlier that day.

"Could we drink outside?" he asked.

She looked at him as if he'd woken her up. "Have you any idea how difficult it is to get a proper seat in here? And what about Edna's orange?"

"We can take it with us."

She smiled. "Oh, I see, yes. Sorry, I said I had a plan, and I neglected to tell you what it was. And now you're busting with excitement. Let's go, then. I think there's a pavement table, if it's not taken."

They went outside. The sun had come out, but it went in again as soon as it saw Mordred, and stayed there. He finished his shandy and held the empty glass. The picnic table was taken, so they stood by the front door like a couple of smokers. Annabel did a scan of the area to satisfy herself they weren't being watched.

"In three days' time," she said, "Daldalian-Hasque is holding a party on the twenty-eighth floor of One Canada Square. Edna's got an invite, and I'm going with her, as her PA. Since I won't know anyone there, no one will notice when I disappear halfway through the evening."

"What's Daldalian-Hasque?"

"Architects and surveyors."

"How did Edna get an invitation?"

"Do you really need to ask, John? All you've got to do with Edna is put her in place and make her amenable. She unlocks any door. I'll tell you the details if you want – a bit of research by me into upcoming events in 1CS, an 'accidental' bumping into Mr Daldalian himself – literally – then an *oh, I'm so sorry* on Edna's part, a *gosh, aren't you the gold medallist* on his, etcetera, etcetera, one thing leading to another, and all culminating with an *I'm one half of Daldalian-Hasque and we're having a party*

- but I warn you, I'm quite boring when I start talking minutiae."

"I think I've got the picture. Thanks."

"Shall we go back inside now?" she asked. "Where do you think Edna actually is? I'm going to end up having to drink her orange at this rate."

"What if someone tries to chat you up?"

"What are you talking about? In the Red Lion?"

"At the Daldalian-Hasque bash," he replied. "Then they'll be interested in you and they'll notice if you disappear halfway through the evening."

She frowned. "Are you just trying to make conversation? Because I am a professional, you know. I don't need coaching."

"Sorry. I was only saying. Men do tend to notice when a very attractive woman leaves the room, even a mere PA. That's not a piece of sweet talk. I'm just warning you."

"Thank you for the advice. So I'll make myself vastly less attractive. Happy?"

"Do you want another drink?"

"I've got Edna's."

Suddenly, Edna appeared from the crowd two hundred yards away, walking briskly towards them. Hopefully, she'd provide some sort of pretext for him to get away. He could tell he was starting to get on Annabel's nerves. Once you'd fussed her, she took against you. You couldn't un-fuss her in an attempt to put things back the way they'd been. The genie - albeit a stupid one - was out of the bottle.

"All that signing, I've got cramp in my wrist now," was the first thing Edna said. "Nice to see you again, sir. I mean, John."

"How was Belgium?" Mordred asked.

"Grim," she replied. "Very grim."

"Here's an orange juice," Annabel said. "John bought it. Drink up and we'll move on."

"Where do you want to go?" Mordred asked.

Annabel shook her head, as if the answer was obvious. "Back to base. I want to find out what Ian and Phyllis know about Planchart and Durand, and what our next move is. My feeling is that if you don't get in at the beginning on these things, you tend to get a bum job. Actually, I think you should stay here, John. Come along later."

Was she joking? Probably not. "I'll probably have another drink then," he said. "Join you presently."

Edna looked as if she'd rather stay here, but she was still a junior agent and had to look enthusiastic, so she didn't have a choice. She downed her orange juice while Annabel looked at her watch. Then they left together, without looking back.

"Another shandy, please," Mordred told the barman.

"Coming up, sir!" the barman replied, as if anything was preferable to the hell of an American Cream Soda.

His phone rang. *Annabel.* "I was only joking, John," she said. "I thought you were behind Edna. We're on our way to the tube. Come on."

"I'm going to ring Alec," he said, although the thought had only just occurred to him. "I'll catch up with you in ten minutes."

She hung up. He went to contacts and selected Alec, more out of a sense of duty now than because he wanted to. If Belgium had got Edna down, there was no telling how it would have affected Alec. Right now, he was probably full of bitter, black frustration. *Call.*

"John," Alec said, cheerily. "I hear you've been flagged up as vulnerable to radicalisation. Classic. I laughed so hard I thought my socks would never dry. Where are you now?"

"The Red Lion in Westminster."

"Weeping into a glass of milk?"

"Something like that. I've bought you one if you're in the vicinity."

"Funnily enough, I was about to ring you, suggest the same thing. Phyllis is busy debriefing Young Ian now. Apparently, there's been some sort of development in the Holland case. She suggested I come and see you as a way of me getting up to speed. We can kill two birds with one stone. Milk plus info."

"Infomilk. Suits me."

Alec hung up. Mordred's phone beeped. A text message. *Unknown caller.* 'I'm in trouble. Sorry I doubted you. Help me now, please. Sarah.'

Finally. How to play it, though? He'd mentally rehearsed getting this sort of message a dozen times, but he still didn't know. He went to her number and pressed call, but it was switched off.

That needn't be a problem, though. Now he had her contact details, he could get Tariq to put a trace on her phone. A matter of priority.

He called Alec. "Change of plan," he said. "Something's come up. Meet me back at Thames House as soon as you can get there."

Chapter 14: Good Ol' Tim Again

That was the great thing about Alec. You could turn an already bizarre phrase – 'Milk plus info' – into an invented word – 'Infomilk' – and he wouldn't bat an eyelid. He might even store it up to use again with you on a similar occasion. For reasons Mordred couldn't quite put his finger on, it was that sort of thing that made life worth living.

He walked down Parliament Street, turned left at the junction, descended into Westminster tube station and boarded the first open carriage on the eastbound District Line. He guessed he was probably one or two trains behind Annabel and Edna, which was good. It meant he'd been telling the truth when he said he'd catch them up in ten minutes. Which he hadn't been at the time, but he now was.

Halfway there, he realised there was a faster way to locate Sarah Riceland. He didn't need to be physically at Thames House to see it through. If he rang ahead, maybe he could arrange for the results to be ready for his arrival. He called IT.

"John," Tariq said when he answered. "How lovely to hear from you."

Mordred was never sure whether this kind of greeting was ironic or not. For a long time, Tariq had imagined they were rivals for Annabel's affections, and he'd never quite got over it. Or maybe he had, and he really did think it was lovely to hear from him. Who knew? Best to take it at face value.

"Thanks," Mordred said. "I love you too. I need a trace on a phone. I'm on my way back to base."

Tariq sighed. "Send me the number and I'll see what I can do."

"Bye." He hung up and texted him the number, adding a smiley-face emoticon, just in case.

Trouble was, there were just too many smiley-face emoticons nowadays. Difficult to get the nuance right. Impossible, sometimes.

Oh, for the good old days.

He stepped off the train at Victoria to change for Pimlico and began walking to the correct platform. He became aware of someone behind him. A stupid sensation, surely: there were hundreds of people behind him, of course there were. But this was a single individual, intent on harming him, and his instincts weren't usually wrong.

Always a first time, though, and maybe it was Alec. Best not turn and look, otherwise you alert whoever it is to your suspicions. Just carry on as normal. Someone was following him. He took out his phone, went to apps and selected the anti-glare mirror. From the rear, it ought to look as if he was just checking his screen.

Good God. It was the man from the City, the one he'd punched unconscious. Hard eyes, fastened unrelentingly on Mordred; heavy frame, neat brown hair, good suit, every bit the amoral financial boy. Obviously here to resume work. No sign of his partner anywhere, but then it probably took a little longer to recover from a dislocated kneecap. Timothy Manners, that's right: supposedly ex-Grey, now working for Horvath.

The fixity of his gaze almost certainly meant something was going to happen right *now*. The only thing someone in his profession could usefully do down here was push someone else into the path of an oncoming train. Which meant – bloody hell – whoever was behind him, or even if he was working alone … Someone must be desperate.

Maybe he was paranoid. If it was Grey – they wouldn't dare murder someone within their own overarching organisation, would they? And Horvath wouldn't dare take on the might of MI7, surely? It *couldn't* be that – could it?

He was ready. That gave him the advantage. He just had to sidestep, but he didn't want to throw his opponent onto the rail, which could happen. He liked winning a fight, but not that way. Not murdering a murderer, even though sometimes there was no option.

Only one thing for it. Turn round, and go up the escalator. Hope for a less lethal confrontation outside. He stopped to put some money in a busker's cap, then double-backed, sweeping towards Manners before he had chance to adjust. As he made towards the escalator and the exit, he saw Manners's momentary indecision then watched him retreat. Mordred was the pursuer now.

A hand landed hard on his shoulder. He wheeled round ready to defend himself – and found himself face to face with a tall, square shouldered man, about forty, with receding black hair. *Alec.*

Except that Alec hadn't come to say hello. He pulled Mordred out of the way and went after Manners. The Horvath man realised he'd been identified and began to run. He bounded up the escalator with Alec just behind. Mordred went after them, clearing two steps at a time.

One by one, they vaulted the turnstiles and ran up the steps to the exit. Mordred was closing the distance between himself and Alec, and Alec, his camel coat flying, was closing on Timothy Manners. They ran through the station, slaloming, thrusting past bodies, almost losing their footing on the smooth surface, and out onto Terminus Place.

There was a screech of tyres as a large 4x4 rammed its brakes on and jerked to a halt, and Mordred saw Manners get pitched sideways along the street. Alec went from sprint to stationary in less than a second and stopped hard up against the car's passenger door. Mordred changed purpose and direction. Whoever the man had been, he was in trouble now. Inside the car, a white bag inflated. The horn blared.

Mordred knelt down next to the victim. Still conscious, he was breathing, although he didn't look to be in a good way. Mordred took out his phone and went straight to the emergency call function. He heard himself give the location and a terse instruction: *ambulance*.

To one side, the 4x4 driver got out, hysterically blurting apologies, and Alec began keeping onlookers away. A second later, the sound of sirens.

Manners was trying to speak. His words emerged in an inaudible hiss of bubbling blood and saliva. Mordred put his ear close to his mouth.

"You're dead, John Mordred," he whispered. "John Mordred, you're dead."

Amazing how the first green shoots of compassion immediately withered and died when someone said something like that to you.

Mordred smiled. "I don't suppose you'll be the one to actually kill me," he told him quietly, "given how utterly useless you've been on both occasions we've met. But thanks for letting me know. I'll keep an eye out." He patted Manners vigorously on the shoulder. "Incidentally, Timothy, just remember: I know where you live. Right now, a lesser man than me might think, 'Maybe I should go round to Mr Manners's house while he's in hospital, since he says he's going to kill me. Give him something worth killing me for'. What I'm trying to say, Timothy, is it's *over*. You're completely exposed. The only reason I haven't come after you so far is because I thought you'd have realised that. Sadly, I'm beginning to think I've been too nice."

As he spoke, he saw Manners's eyes widen, first with surprise then fear. Interesting how those two expressions remained the same, even in a face struggling to manage pain and stupor.

He stood up. The police arrived, then the ambulance. Mordred called Thames House and got them to make the necessary obfuscations. The paramedics loaded the victim onto a stretcher and drove him away. A policeman asked Mordred and Alec questions – but tactfully: the message from base had obviously got through fast. Then another text. *Unknown caller*.

Bloody hell, Sarah Riceland's number again. 'Please, please call me'.

He turned away from the policeman and went to return call. This time it rang. Just once, then he heard her voice. "Damn it, John, where have you been? I've been trying and trying and *trying* to get you. I'm in serious trouble. Really *serious deep shit*. Are you alone? Come and get me, please, but come alone."

"I'm afraid I can't do that," he said.

"Do what?"

"Come alone. Look, what you may not realise - "

The phone went dead.

He swore under his breath. He called Tariq.

"Nice to hear from you again, John," Tariq said. "Riceland's in Canvey Island. Ruby Parker's sending a helicopter over to pick you and Alec up. You're to proceed to the top of the T-Western building on Royale Street. They're expecting you at reception. If the Riceland moves, I'll let you know. Otherwise, call me when you arrive."

"Will do."

"Oh, and John?"

"Yes?"

"Thanks ever so much for the emoticon. Very nice."

He hesitated. Irony – or not? He didn't know.

"Glad you liked it," he said.

He put the phone down.

It rang again in his hand.

Tariq. What the - ? He picked up. "Is that - ?"

"Sorry, John," Tariq said, sounding hurt, "I hadn't quite said goodbye. One last thing. We've just had a message from the paramedics who took Timothy Manners away. The police alerted them to the national security angle, so they're probably a little over-keen to pass stuff on. It seems Manners is desperate to get a message to you. They want to relax him without the use of an anaesthetic, so I said I'd help out. Just in case you two meet again - "

"I think I already know what's coming," Mordred said. "Is it by any chance, 'John Mordred, you're dead, you're dead, John Mordred'?"

"No, it's, 'Tell him I'm sorry. Tell him please not to hurt my family. Tell him it's over'."

Mordred didn't know what to say. "Well, er, that's nice."

"You can hang up now if you like."

"Bye, then."

"Bye."

Chapter 15: Fun in Canvey

Mordred grabbed Alec. They ran to T-Western on Royale Street and entered the building just as their flight arrived on the helipad one hundred and eighty metres above ground-level. Ninety floors in a soundless lift, then they climbed onto the two seats next to the pilot and ascended high into the air. Below them, Royale Street, Tower Bridge, Buckingham Palace, Trafalgar Square like toys. Then fast forward and gone.

It took twenty minutes to reach Canvey Island and *en route,* none of the three occupants exchanged a word beyond their initial greeting. They landed in a field and Mordred and Alec jumped out while the blades roared. The helicopter ascended as soon as they were clear then accelerated in the direction of London like it couldn't wait to go home.

"Ever been to Canvey Island before?" Alec asked.

But Mordred was already on the phone to Tariq. "We're here," he said. "Where are we supposed to be heading?"

"Forty-three Fairbrother Crescent," Tariq replied.

Mordred hung up and used his phone to get a map. "That direction," he told Alec. "About two streets away."

"You still haven't briefed me, but I guess that'll have to wait."

"Thanks for your help back there."

"I saw you about two minutes before. Then the guy following you. At that point I realised you'd seen him too. I take it you knew him?"

"Timothy Manners. Ex-Grey, allegedly, now works for Horvath. But that's just what we 'know'. I'm inclined to take it with a pinch of salt. I don't really know what's going on."

"Should make for an interesting briefing."

"Oh, it'll be *that* all right."

"So forgive me for asking, but why are we actually in Canvey Island? First time I spoke to you, it was come to the Red Lion, then go to Thames House, now here. Reminiscent of classic disorientation techniques. We'll make a spy of you yet."

"Thanks."

"At my expense, I'm afraid."

"Frances Holland, MP and Brexit advocate, has disappeared. Phyllis is in charge of investigating that. Out of the blue, she and I saw Pierre Durand in central London. We gave chase, I caught him, a team of prestigious lawyers sprung him from custody. The other day, I was attacked out of nowhere by the man we just chased into the path of a 4x4, plus one other guy called Shafiq Effanga. I hypothesised that Durand's presence in London might be linked to the Holland case. I went to interview Charles Planchart, MP and friend of Holland, when I was approached by an *Independent* journalist called Sarah Riceland, who claimed to know something. When we finally caught up with her, she had photos of Holland and Durand together. Then she disappeared, but not before I gave her my phone number. About two hours ago, Ian saw Planchart meeting Durand. Now Riceland's called me and asked for my help. I don't know what sort of 'help' she wants, or what sort of danger she's in, but Ruby Parker thinks there's a significant possibility she's working against us. That's why you're here. Tariq traced her phone to Canvey Island. Oh, and we think Grey's declared war on Red."

"Takeover bid, eh?"

"We don't know."

"Grey's always had ambitions to absorb the whole organisation. Remember, I worked there a lot longer than you. It was always coming up, usually in a jokey kind of way. Farquarson was the first head who wasn't up for it – even the waggish suggestion - and look at the good it did him."

They climbed over a stile and entered a fully parked suburban road of 1950s semis, each with its own gated or hedged front garden. Overhead, the sky looked like a sheet of white paper, perfectly uniform. There were no people about and no sounds: no traffic, no birdsong, nothing at all to indicate life.

"This is Montacute Road," Mordred said. "Fairbrother Crescent's right ahead, turn left."

Alec stopped dead, and put a hand out to stop Mordred. "We need a plan. How are we going to play this when we get there? You go front door, I go back?"

"Let's just both knock at the front. If she runs away, we'll soon catch her again."

"Unless she ditches her phone, which she could do."

"I don't want to spring anything on her. I said I couldn't come alone. I don't want her to think I've changed my mind then later reveal there's two of us."

"Can't you just say, 'It's me. My friend's round the back'?"

"It makes it look like I think she's going to do a runner. Like she's unreliable."

"And isn't she?"

"Maybe. But."

"You're being a wuss." They began walking again. "Okay, we'll do it your way. But don't say I didn't tell you. I take it you think she's got more information? Things beyond the Durand-Holland meeting?"

"Possibly. The other thing - " He tugged Alec's sleeve to make him cross the road at the junction rather than turning left.

"What?" Alec said without breaking stride. He looked. "Oh, right. That."

Fairbrother Crescent was considerably less parked up than Montacute Road, hence they were able to see a Volvo saloon parked opposite one of the houses with two men inside.

"Even numbers that side," Mordred said. "Meaning they're parked opposite the odds. Stop when we're out of view and we'll do a little recce. This could be more complicated than we thought."

"You can be pretty damn sure if someone's got the front covered, they won't have left her an escape-route at the rear."

"True, but I can only see two men at the front. If we split up to allow one of us to check the back, we concede parity of numbers."

"Just because you can only see two, doesn't mean there aren't four, six or eight."

Mordred took out his phone and called her. A single ring, then she picked up. "John?"

"Sarah."

"What's going on? Where are you?"

"The junction of Montacute Road and Fairbrother Crescent."

"Don't mess me about. This isn't funny."

"Look out of your front window. Of whoever's house you're in. Whose house are you in?"

"My friend's. Cara's. Look, John, they'll be listening in to this conversation. I don't know who they are, but they tracked me here. They tried to kick the door down, but we barricaded it and Cara called the police. We only just stopped them getting in, but they're outside and I'm pretty sure they're just waiting for nightfall. Now *where are you?*"

"What have you got that they want?"

"I don't *know!*"

"If they're listening in, the best - " The line went dead. He looked at the screen. *No signal.*

Mordred heard a car door slam. Alec heard it too. Run – or stay? They looked at each other. Alec shrugged.

"Just follow my lead," Mordred said. "And be ready to thrash them when I put my hand on my hair."

"What?" Alec looked baffled for a moment, but then as if he was willing to try anything once.

Two men rounded the corner, looking aggressive. They were both young and tall, but that, and a bullish demeanour, was all they had going for them. They were mainly padding.

"What do you want?" one of them said.

"What do you mean, mate?" Mordred said in a cockney accent, grinning ingratiatingly.

"I'm not your *mate!*" the first said.

"I only wanted to know what you're spying on my little sister for," Mordred went on. "You can't do that, pal."

He saw the two men inwardly relax and escalate their act to compensate. They'd obviously expected something more difficult to handle than this: one guy who kept trying to befriend them and another who seemed determined to stay out of it.

"He said get lost, Loser!" the second yelled, as if he could blow them away if he wanted to.

Mordred grinned inanely again, showed his palms like he was surrendering, and made as if to back away. Then he touched his hair. He lurched at the first man, locked his head between his arms and fell to his knees so as to bring the man's forehead down hard onto a garden wall. He met no resistance; all he detected was a sense of horrible surprise. He didn't see what Alec did, but when he got up, both their opponents were unconscious, and Alec held a set of car keys.

"Do you want to drive or shall I?" he asked.

"You," Mordred said.

They ran back to the car, beckoning to the women to leave the house. They didn't need extra encouragement. Cara was a small, fat woman in pyjamas and flip-flops. She had a tattoo of a rose on her arm. Within a few seconds, they were all in the car, the women on the back seat, and Alec was running through the gears as they left Canvey Island at speed.

"Careful," Alec said. "This car could be bugged. If they've got any sense, they'll have taken precautions to cover even the unlikeliest of scenarios. We'll ditch it in a minute and burn it, along with all our mobiles. Until then, keep schtum."

"Our *mobiles?*" Cara exclaimed. "But mine's got all my *apps* on!"

"It's a question of whether you want to die with apps, or live without them for a while," Alec said.

"Die with them!" she bellowed.

Alec pulled the car to a halt. "Better get out then."

"But," she said, "but I - "

"Get out of the car!" he yelled. He waited a second and held his hand up. "Or you can give me that phone. Put it this way, I'm going to be parking this vehicle permanently in a minute, and if you refuse to do either, you're on your own. Given that we're fleeing any number of professional thugs, you may not make it very far."

She struggled inwardly for another half-second then handed her phone over.

"I suppose that means mine too," Riceland said. She surrendered it without a fight.

"I bloody *hate* you now, Sarah," Cara said. "I wish I'd never said I'd help out. I might have bloody *known* you'd be trouble."

"Smash them," Alec said, tossing them to Mordred. "And yours as well. They've probably all been compromised." He put the car back in gear and pulled out into the traffic again.

Mordred set about pretending to break the phones, beginning with his own. He hoped Alec was concentrating on the road and that he trusted him.

This was typical bloody Cunningham, of course. First sign of an emergency and a bit of responsibility, straight into simple and brutal mode: obtuse solutions, barked orders and a little Taekwondo for good measure.

Cara sobbed and made semi-coherent attempts to explain that all her photos of her dad, and little Liam, and the cats were on there. Sarah put her arm round her. Meanwhile, Mordred surreptitiously pocketed her phone – with its little 'I love Canvey' Union Jack on the back - while Alec was looking for the signposted speed camera.

And Sarah's phone, that had to be saved too. It might have a transmitter inside, but it probably also had information. He hadn't come this far to throw it away. Alec be damned; he'd been in sodding Belgium. What right did he have coming back here ordering everyone about? Anyway, they'd reach base soon. They could deal with it there.

"We need petrol," Alec said. "I'm going to pull in here, John, and I want you to go inside, buy a canister and fill it. Fast as you can."

Mordred bit his tongue so as not to say 'Yes, sir'. He bought the petrol and they drove to a wide flat patch of wasteland down by the Thames.

"The railway station's over there," Alec said, pointing. "Walk as fast as you can, and I'll be along in a minute. Has anyone brought any money?"

The two women shook their heads. He'd ordered both their phones broken; they weren't going to let him add insult to injury by admitting to money he could use as well.

"I've got my cashpoint card and forty pounds," Mordred said.

"Get going," Alec told them.

A few seconds later, they heard a faint whoosh behind them. They turned to see Alec striding away from a torched car, head down. Behind him, the sun was setting against a thin strip of clear sky. Above, dark clouds hovered, threatening to burst. It looked like a scene from the end of the world.

Mordred fell back ten paces from the women to allow Alec to catch up. He got the impression they were glad to see him go – providing it wasn't too far. When Alec drew level, he didn't look happy.

"Okay, John," he said, "where are the phones? And don't tell me you haven't got them. They weren't in the car, you didn't toss them out of the window – you're too much of a goody-goody to go 'dropping litter' – and you certainly didn't ditch them at the petrol station. Where are they?"

"In my pocket."

"Smashed or intact?"

"The latter."

Alec nodded sagely. He didn't look as angry as Mordred expected. Quite the opposite. "Before I congratulate you, just reassure me: this isn't some misguided feeling of compassion for ladies' apps, is it?"

Mordred smiled. "Not at all. Well, ninety per cent not. Okay, eighty. Whatever. The important thing is, it can be justified on professional grounds. And that's how it'll appear in my report."

Alec slapped him solemnly on the shoulder. "I wasn't thinking. Luckily, that's the difference between you and Young Ian. He'd have just done what I told him. And when we got back to Thames House, Ruby Parker would have had me for breakfast. Thank God you're a milksop."

"I've been radicalised, that's all."

Alec sighed. "We shouldn't joke about that, John."

"Take my word for it, I wasn't trying to be funny. How was Belgium?"

"I'll tell you something. I *was* going to vote to come out of the EU on the grounds that it's too pink. It's not going to be pink any more. Brussels is starting to see where decades of tolerating no-toleration movements gets you. I'm not saying the Belgian capital *is* the EU, obviously, but its ethos definitely influences the way the Commission thinks. In future, an EU based there might just be worth belonging to. Which way are you going to vote?"

"I don't know."

"But you are *going* to vote, aren't you? Because, as I recall, you've a history of abstaining."

"Right now, I think it's more important to discuss our next move. If whoever's following us can locate these phones, we could still be in danger."

"Maybe we should have kept the car."

"On the other hand," Mordred said, "it could have been packed to the hilt with location transmitters. We probably did the right thing. Do you think we should split up?"

"You take the women, you mean, and I go it alone with the phones?"

"The other alternative is to call base and get them to send the helicopter over. Would there be enough room?"

Alec smiled. "It's a seven-seater EC135. That's not the problem. The problem's the length of time it would take to get here. And whether it, or the pilot, is available. We could be looking at forty-five minutes minimum, during which time we'd need to keep moving. A lot can happen in that time. Plus, if we're mobile, it may not necessarily be able to find us. Or land."

"I that case, we split up," Mordred said. "But not your way. I'm not prepared to leave you alone with two phones – three, if you count mine - "

"You mean you didn't even destroy *yours?*"

"All of which could make you a sitting duck."

"So what's *your* interpretation of 'we split up', genius?"

"We check the women into a hotel somewhere. Without the phones, they're probably untraceable, and we can come back for them later. Before you point out that they could do a runner: I know: that's a risk we'll just have to take, but we'll have taken it because we prioritised their safety. Afterwards, we've got two pairs of eyes, and if push comes to shove, two pairs of fists."

Alec tut-tutted. "Fighting talk. Not what I expect of John Mordred."

"So what *do* you expect?"

"A suggestion to the effect that we love our enemies, maybe share a quiche with them."

"I haven't got a quiche."

"What about a gun? Have you got one of those?"

"No."

"Sur-bloody-prise." He sighed. "Me neither, as it happens."

The women had stopped in their tracks, and it quickly became obvious why. The patch of swampy grassland across which they were walking was bounded on three sides by embankment, and on the fourth by the river. On the three elevated sides, men appeared by stationary cars and vans; men small enough to be silhouetted, but all looking in their direction. Mordred turned around to see if the water offered some hope of escape. But there were also men facing them on the opposite bank of the Thames. Altogether, he counted twenty. But that could just be the tip of the iceberg.

The women walked back and stood next to Mordred and Alec as if four was a number in which there might be safety.

"Don't anyone panic," Alec said.

Mordred glared at him. The truth was, this looked like a good place for murder. Kill someone here, and you could probably be assured of complete privacy. After which, you could bury the body where it had fallen. It might be months or even years before anyone discovered it. Or it might never be discovered.

They were aware of a roaring sound, growing in intensity. For a surreal moment, it sounded like a tidal wave headed in their direction. But it was coming from overhead.

The helicopter suddenly swooped down like it had seen all this coming long ago, and had only waited so long because it wanted to inflate their gratitude.

"I was given instructions to wait in the area for when you wanted to come back," the pilot said, as they climbed aboard. "Base monitored your movements and guessed you were in trouble. Don't forget to fasten your seatbelts, please."

The men on the embankments had started in on them, but they were years too late now. The helicopter rose into the air like someone had catapulted it vertically, and their would-be killers and their cars and vans became so many knickknacks.

In another second, they were gone. Mordred's phone rang. *Ruby Parker*.

"Thanks for the rescue," he told her. "It was a hell of a close shave. I'm pretty sure Sarah Riceland's ready to talk now. This could be the breakthrough we've been hoping for."

"I take it you haven't had the time or the opportunity to catch up with the national news," Ruby Parker replied. "Frances Holland is dead."

Chapter 16: Sarah Riceland Spills the Beans

In the event of the premature death of a high-flying politician, key civil servants considered it sadly inevitable that the public should devise conspiracy theories. The prevailing wisdom was that, left unchecked, these would hamper a police investigation and damage the government's reputation. Small, rarely-convened working-parties in Whitehall were therefore on permanent standby, charged with devising and disseminating an official version of the victim's last days and hours, and managing its ramifications. Probably none of those involved in this would have described it as 'spin' – it would have seemed tactless – yet that is what it was.

The known facts surrounding Frances Holland's death were these. She had disappeared in the middle of April, and was last seen at King's Cross Station looking 'unhappy'. Fourteen days later, her body was discovered in an advanced state of decomposition in the single bedroom of a self-catering cottage on the Isle of Skye. There were no indications of a struggle. A forensic examination of the contents of her stomach revealed she had taken an overdose of sleeping tablets. Estimated time of death was eight to ten days before the discovery of her corpse.

That still left between four and six days unaccounted for, during which no one on the island could recall having seen her. Moreover, the cottage had not been booked in her name, but that of a 'Mr T. Robinson', who had paid over the phone in February with a company credit card. One thousand and ninety-eight pounds was charged to a financial services firm called Dobson-Fresenius whose head office was a plaque screwed to a disused office door in Zurich. The company had 'branches' in Jersey, Luxembourg and the British Virgin Islands.

The aim of the official version was to release the first set of facts *post-haste* and temporarily conceal the second from public view. That way, the investigators would have more time in which to work unencumbered by hysteria. The crucial point was that no one was suppressing anything. Quite the opposite. Without the efforts of the investigators, the truth would remain hidden at the bottom of a deep hole. In time, when the fuss died down, everyone expected *all* the facts – minor and major, irrelevant and central - to emerge. Just not now.

Because Frances Holland had died in the Inner Hebrides, the investigation was conducted under the auspices of the Scottish Procurator Fiscal rather than a Coroner. There was a Fatal Accident Inquiry rather than an Inquest, and unlike the English system, the process was to be conducted in private. In Westminster, this was generally considered providential. No one sought to override it, partly – so the official version went – because of the sensitivity of the 'nationalist question'.

MI7 knew all the facts from the outset. Since Mordred had been left with Sarah Riceland, he had only the vaguest idea what action it was taking. He put the whole thing out of his mind.

One thing at a time.

His interviews with Sarah Riceland were scheduled to take place in an *en suite* room at the Majestic Hotel in Covent Garden. Only he, Ruby Parker and Phyllis knew she was here. It was considered unnecessary to post a watch to prevent her leaving. Her meals were brought by staff and left outside her door with a knock. The empty plates and cutlery were picked up in the same anonymous way. Her friend, Cara Fowler, had gone to stay with relatives. Cara's house had been broken into by whoever had been staking it out, though nothing had been taken. It was expected that whoever was after Sarah Riceland would now leave Cara alone. As a parting gift, Mordred returned her phone along with some money for a new front door lock.

He visited Sarah Riceland at 10am the day after their narrow escape on the banks of the Thames Estuary. Her room had a deep pile beige carpet, a single bed, a TV on a wall bracket, a dressing table – containing her medication, courtesy of Red department - a wardrobe – containing four different outfits in her size, courtesy of ditto – a small dining table, and two chairs all in oak. The central light was a candle bulb in a frosted glass shade. When Mordred went in, she was dressed, the TV was on – *Homes Under the Hammer* – and she sat at the table with a cup of tea in front of her, eating cereal. She wore a black pullover and jeans.

"Bit different to my real home," she said forlornly. "Mind you, I'm behind with the rent now. It's probably not mine any more. Plus those bastards have likely trashed it."

"We've taken care of the rent," he told her. "There would no point in them wrecking anything. They'll have searched it thoroughly long ago."

"I'm prepared to tell you anything and everything now," she said. "Just ask."

Mordred sat down opposite her. "So who were 'those bastards'?"

"I don't know. I thought you might." She looked at him and grinned slightly. "What are you looking at me like *that* for? I'm telling the truth!"

"I wasn't looking at you like anything."

"Yes you were. You were looking at me like this." She opened her eyes wide and stuck her chin forward.

He laughed. "If that's how I looked at you, I didn't mean to. Anyone can look like that by accident."

"Sure. Your second question, please." She stopped eating and her smile dropped. "Look, I'm sorry if I'm acting like all the cards are in my hand. They aren't. I haven't got any cards any more, okay? Or I have, but I'm going to give them all to you and your pals at Spy Centre One. As for who the men were, I honestly don't know. *Oh yes, but you must have a theory* you'll say. Well, yes, I have. I think Planchart hired a private army to come after me. But I only think that because I want some sort of handle on everything. Soon as I start thinking about it, it's a stupid idea."

"Why would Planchart want to come after you?"

"Look, I've just said I've got a deck of cards and I'm going to give it to you. So instead of sitting there asking about what shade of red the hearts are, and whether the knave of clubs has a snub or a Roman nose, or whether it's a standard fifty-two deck or a Tarot Nouveau, *why don't you just ask me to hand them over?* Surely, then you can check for yourself?"

"When you said 'pack of cards', I assumed you meant information. What else have you got?"

"What about those photos you saw when we were having dinner in the Gherkin? Don't you want to see those again?"

"We've got all morning. Just because they're not at the top of my agenda … There is such a thing as easing an interviewee in gently. You're a journalist. You must know that."

"I'm of the 'go straight for the jugular' school."

He sat up and folded his hands on the table. "Okay, you're in charge. What have you got?"

"Get me a laptop, and I'll show you."

Seventy photos in all, the sort of project you'd initiate if you didn't like working as a team, or thought you had a potential scoop on your hands and wanted to guard exclusivity, or both. All were photos of the seven members of The Get Out Clause in various locations, taken with what looked like a telescopic lens. The kind of pictures a spy might take, which made him immediately suspicious – until he began to look at them. She went to manual slide show, and gave a running commentary.

"Now look," she said, "the first thing you'll want to do with these is download them, so you choose the 'save as' location when we've finished. I expect you'll want to pass them on to your techno department to make sure they haven't been mocked up. Not that there's any need. You can simply put any one of these in front of Planchart. I don't think he'll deny it. Doesn't have to. He's not doing anything illegal."

After the first twenty photos, it became obvious they had a running theme. As Ashbaugh had claimed, Planchart and his fellow TGOC members had been meeting with the leaders and emissaries of continental right-wing Eurosceptic parties. The *Dansk Folkeparti*, the *Partij voor de Vrijheid, Alternative für Deutschland*, the *Kongres Nowej Prawicy* were all represented, and Riceland knew the representatives by name. "It took me quite a long time researching them at first," she said, "but once I established a pattern - anti-EU conservatives - it became easier. Sometimes, I had to try and get physically close to them, see if I could detect the language. Others, it was just a question of following the interpreter, asking him or her a few questions at the right moment. There was a lot of Googling, or Binging, as I call it. The only guy I wasn't able to place was your Pierre Durand, and for some reason that made him the most interesting of all. Then one day, I saw you chasing him through town. I thought, 'Oh boy, this is finally it'. I thought I'd found the key, the touchstone, you know?"

"Sadly, he's as mysterious today as he was then."

She went to the next picture. It showed Planchart staring straight at the lens. "This is one of the most recent. That's when he spotted me. I guess it was inevitable sooner or later. Anyway, immediately afterwards is when my troubles began. Which is why I said a moment ago: those men yesterday: maybe his doing? Of course, it could be any one of them."

"Any one of who?"

"The Get Out Clause. I don't think they really care whether we're in or out of Europe. They just see the whole referendum thing as a chance to grab power."

"What makes you say that?"

"Because they're *all* doing it, all politicians. Whether or not you're on the winning side on June the twenty-third is going to determine your political future. Not because of what it means in itself, but because it's an ideological expression of where you stand in relation to the established faction in your party, and to your leader. That's what it's really about for most MPs. Not what's best for Britain, but what's in their own short-term job interests. It's a game of roulette. And, like it or not, they all have to play."

"From what I've heard, Frances Holland was a conviction politician. There must be some of those. They can't all be time-servers and careerists."

"I can't believe she committed suicide. It doesn't ring true. Why now?"

Mordred had to be careful here. She only knew the official version. Any mention of T. Robinson or shell companies could complicate matters to the point where they became unmanageable.

"They were *her* tablets," he said, "and she doesn't seem to have been involved in a fight. Maybe she needed to think things through, that's why she booked the cottage. Then she decided not to come home. I love the Scottish Highlands, don't get me wrong, but it's rainy and dark and cold up there a lot of the time. For someone who's already suffering from depression, that may not be a helpful cocktail."

"I suffer from mental illness, and her committing suicide strikes me as odd."

He smiled. "There's more than one type of mental illness."

She shrugged.

He looked around for some way of changing the subject, then found one.

149

"Who's that guy in the background?" he asked, pointing to her thirty-fourth photo. She was flipping through them without much comment now. He got the impression she'd told him everything important. "I've seen him before."

"Seen him where?" she asked.

"I don't know. Go back. I think, in some of your other photos."

"Damn, I thought you meant in real life. For a moment, I thought we might be on to something." She went back to 25/70, then to 18/70. He was also in 15, 12, 9, 8, 7 and 1. "He's probably in a lot of them," she said.

"I take it you know who he is. I mean, given the quality of research you've done on just about everyone else in here."

"I got close enough to listen in to a lot of their conversations. I say listen; I mean, 'catch snatches'. He wasn't a major player, by any means. He just hung about in the background most of the time. In fact, nearly all the time. And he's English. I came to the conclusion that he's irrelevant. Probably some sort of special adviser, or a junior civil servant, or possibly a constituency apparatchik. He always seemed quite friendly, not like the rest of them. Because of that, I concluded he was probably a complete nonentity. Such is the world."

"Go forward to nine."

She obliged. A picture of Frances Holland, Charles Planchart, a middle-aged woman from *Alternative für Deutschland*, and in the background, the mysterious man.

"You don't know his name?" Mordred asked.

"Like I said," she replied. "I assumed he was of no account. Are you now telling me I'm wrong?"

He wasn't obliged to share his insights with her, but he still needed to download her photos, and he'd been incautious enough to pique her interest. He couldn't go into reverse now. Too late.

"Go to the first photo."

" ... Right."

"Now the fifth ... Go to nine again ... Now forward to twenty-five."

She put her face closer to the screen. "What am I supposed to notice?"

"The way he's looking at Frances Holland."

She repeated the sequence. "Yes, I see now," she replied. "Affection."

"I'd say it's more than that."

"I'm pretty sure she was having a fling with Planchart. At least that's the rumour. So you're thinking maybe unrequited love? Where does that get us?"

He sighed. Time to put her out of her misery. "Look, Sarah, I'm not a detective. There can't be an 'us' in the sense you want – an investigative duo. For your own safety, there are going to be lots of things I can't share with you. You were almost killed yesterday, and if you keep pushing the envelope as regards Planchart, that may not be finished. We can't be a team. That's why you've got to give me everything you've got. Only once they're sure you've done that will they leave you alone. They don't do revenge attacks."

"But they'll know – or think they do – that I've got the capacity and determination to put a story in print. Killing a journalist, even after they've given away everything they know, is rarely about revenge. Unless said journalist has already put the incriminating evidence into the public domain, there's still every reason to stop her. And in giving it to you, I'm not doing that, am I?"

"No, but you haven't got a story either."

"Which may change. I've got I.I.C., as they call it. Ideology, intent and capability."

He almost betrayed himself with an overt double-take. For a moment, he thought he'd misheard her. Ruby Parker that first day back after Durand. *You've been flagged up as vulnerable to radicalisation. The accusation is that you've got I.I.C. Ideology, intent and capability.* Was Sarah Riceland making fun of him?

Trying to send him a message? Who was she? What did she know? Suddenly, he was all at sea.

Test her micro-expressions, that had always worked in the past. Often, the sardonic semi-revelation preceded a physical assault, but she didn't look inclined to that. Maybe she had someone outside. He went to the window and looked out. No one he could see. Not that that meant anything.

In any case, they needn't be out on the street.

"What's the matter?" she asked innocently. "Did I say something wrong?"

It could just be coincidence. Paranoia.

"Tell me your name," he said.

She stood up slowly. "What do you mean? Why? What's going on?"

"Your name. What is it?"

"You know who I am. I'm Sarah. Sarah Riceland!"

A lie. The leaning away, the subtle shake of the head, the movement of the eyebrows, a million other things.

"Are you from Grey department?" he persisted.

"No! No! I mean, I don't know what you're *talking about!*"

Another falsehood. He'd walked into a trap. Fast as an express train, he reviewed his association with her. Until recently Grey or Horvath, or whoever, had simply wanted to rough him up. That skirmish outside the Lord Mayor's – if they'd wanted to murder him, they could have. But yesterday, something had changed. Timothy Manners: *You're dead, John Mordred.* They'd decided to kill him. He had to get out of here.

He suddenly became aware of a movement down in the street. Someone coming towards the hotel at speed.

His phone rang. *Ruby Parker.* Bloody hell. He picked up. "John, listen carefully," she said. "I need you to get out of the Majestic right away. Just get out and - " He hung up.

Shafiq Effanga. Good God, that dislocated knee had healed quickly. Six weeks it normally took. He'd already entered the hotel now. Probably seconds till he got here.

Leave Sarah Riceland – yes or no?

Yes.

No. Play along with the idea that it was her they were after. Then find out who she was. If she knew now she'd been exposed, he'd never see her again. Or her photos – which, come to think of it, were probably all worthless too. Probably? Certainly.

"We need to hide you," he said. "There's someone here to get you. An old enemy of mine. A hit man. If I don't make it, his name's Shafiq Effanga."

"Shafiq Effanga," she repeated. She looked genuinely scared now, not like she was putting it on. Maybe she and Shafiq didn't get on. Or maybe she was squeamish, didn't like seeing someone like Mordred get murdered in broad daylight in a nice hotel in Covent Garden.

That had to be it. She'd had all morning to murder him, and she hadn't. She wanted it done; she just didn't want to be the one to do it. Or see it.

Well, if it got to that point, she'd have to. She was right behind him, so he grabbed her wrist. He needed to watch out now, on all fronts. She might be unhappy about killing him, but she clearly had no qualms about delivering him for that purpose. A sudden push down a flight of steps, or a deft trip while they were running – they'd serve her purpose. She could be off and away when the death-blow was dealt. With two people after him, both bent on his elimination, one of which he had to keep close, he rated his chances of survival at around twenty-five per cent. It was an odd realisation. 25: maybe the last number he'd ever think of.

She made no show of resisting. Obviously, she was as determined to play along with him as he was with her. They slipped out into the corridor and he closed the door behind them. She took out a key, locked it and put it into her bag. He hadn't noticed a bag before. Could be ominous, but he'd lost the capacity to consider ominous any more.

He ran along the corridor looking for an escape-route. The stairway he'd come up was at the other end. But there had to be something at this end too, surely. You needed a variety of fire-exits nowadays. Health and safety, good ol' -

"Here!" she yelled. She pushed a door he thought was the entrance to a room, and revealed a staircase.

"Stay behind me," he said. "Or go in front."

She looked at him as if she thought he was having a breakdown, then went in front. These weren't steps for guests' use: they were concrete and functional. At the bottom, double doors with panic bar latches. She pushed down and went outside. He followed, but he could hear someone hot on their tail.

Suddenly, he was outside in an alleyway. Four wheelie bins had been pushed up against each other at each end, blocking the exits. He'd stumbled into an ambush. Sarah Riceland was nowhere to be seen. The only other presence was a dark-haired, ex-army looking man of about Mordred's age wearing a brown suit and carrying an umbrella. Probably Effanga's accomplice, though he looked curiously reluctant to advance. A trainee Grey, perhaps, here solely to watch and learn. Probably he who'd arranged the wheelie bins.

Too late to worry about that now. He turned to meet Effanga as he emerged, and slammed the door hard on him when he was halfway through. He went down. Mordred fired a kick at his head, but, after his slip-up in the City and what had happened to Manners, Effanga clearly wasn't in the business of underestimating opponents any more. He caught Mordred's foot and turned it through ninety degrees. Mordred lurched on to his side in an attempt to stop his ankle breaking.

Effanga bounced to his feet like a gymnast and suddenly the positions were reversed, Mordred on the floor. He attempted a roll into the hit-man's legs, but Effanga casually reversed and pulled a gun fitted with a silencer from his inside pocket. He raised his arm to shoot, and suddenly the fire-door flew back and Sarah Riceland was there. She smacked the gun out of his grasp as if it was made of putty. Before he had chance to register what had happened, an umbrella handle came out of nowhere and almost took Effanga's head from his shoulders. He slumped unconscious – or possibly dead.

Mordred lay on the floor, gasping. Sarah Riceland put her hands on her knees and panted. Only the man with the umbrella looked unruffled. He extended a hand to help Mordred to his feet.

"Thanks," Mordred said, accepting the favour. "You … er, saved our lives." He brushed himself down. Odd that his chief emotion was pleasure. The revelation that Sarah Riceland wasn't a bad guy, after all.

But she certainly wasn't who she'd claimed to be. Of that much, he remained certain.

"Are you two … ?" He didn't know how to finish the sentence. Together? Journalists? Secret agents? What?

The former Sarah Riceland and the man in the brown suit exchanged looks. She nodded solemnly, bowed her head again and went back to panting.

"I'm Nicholas Fleming," the man said, offering a handshake. "And this is my wife, Marciella."

Chapter 17: It's Not a Fiefdom

"It's all getting very complicated," Alec said, as he and Mordred breakfasted in the canteen two days later. "Tell me again: who is she, and what's she doing in the middle of our investigation?"

"Her real name's Marciella Fleming," Mordred said. "She used to work in this building. For Blue. Then she retired. I don't know the circumstances or what she did while she was here. Ruby Parker met her a few times, but her brother also used to work here. A 'Jonathan Hartley-Brown'."

"Bloody hell. She's Jonathan Hartley-Brown's *sister*?"

"The name did ring a bell. I recall you mentioning him before once."

"He was the old you. Heart first, then head. Died an avoidable death in the line of duty. Hero in some ways, complete berk in another."

"That does sound a lot like me. Thanks."

"So she once worked for Blue? Who's she working for now?"

"White. And herself. This is where it does get complicated. Her father's Sir Anthony Hartley-Brown, the former cabinet minister, now distinguished backbencher. He and a few of his colleagues don't trust Charles Planchart, and they wanted him watching. Since his daughter's a former spy, it seemed like a good idea to hire her. After all, you can always trust family, and in the espionage business, trust is a valuable commodity. They got together with White department, and agreed an in-the-interests-of-national-security deal where White would take care of the false documentation and set the parameters and the Party would provide the finance and Marciella. Of course, White wouldn't have looked twice at her had it not been for her MI7 record."

"Must be pretty impressive."

"Her friend, Cara, from Canvey Island, was also a White agent."

Alec gave his tea a single stir and put the spoon back on the saucer. "Figures."

"Her husband used to work here too. Marciella's, not Cara's."

"Which department?"

"Ours," Mordred said. "Red."

"So they both left together. Presumably, to get married. Nothing suspect then."

"Probably not. Ruby Parker seems to think highly of them."

"What's happening now?" Alec asked. "Are they off the case?"

"I doubt it. Two highly trained former intelligence officers who've already got further than us? We need all the help we can get."

Alec chortled. "I bet Phyllis is over the moon."

"It's not a fiefdom. It's an investigation. The sooner it gets solved, the better she looks. Like *The Apprentice*. It's not *how* you do it, it's *whether*."

"Does 'Marciella' know you've been flagged up as a possible radical?"

"I don't know and I don't care."

"How's that going, incidentally? Heard anything yet? Like 'you're fired'?"

"Very funny," Mordred said.

"Just trying to continue the Alan Sugar theme. Sorry, insensitive."

"Apology accepted. No, I've heard zilch."

"I can't speak from personal experience, but there probably comes a point at which you just want it to be over with. Even if it does mean being fired."

"True, and I'm only young. The world's my oyster."

"You could go and live in an Ashram, like a true hippy."

"I was thinking more about getting a dog."

"You could get married," Alec said. "You could call Naomi Klein and propose."

"Naomi Klein?"

"The writer. You told me last year she was your ideal woman."

"Right. What I find interesting is that you'd remember that."

"We're supposed to be friends. Of course I would. Why wouldn't I?"

"When's my birthday?"

Alec shrugged. "September? May? Sometime in June?"

"You see, that's why it's so interesting. Anyway, she's married. And abroad. And it'd probably be difficult to engineer an introduction."

"There are other women in the world. So I've heard."

"On another subject entirely, do you know how Annabel and Edna got on last night at One Canada Square?"

"Complete success, apparently."

"Meaning what, in this context?"

"They both got out safely; Annabel downloaded all their files. We now know Simpson, Musgrave and De Groot are linked to Charles Planchart and The Get Out Clause."

"And what about the Lord Mayor, William Chester?"

"The full analysis won't be complete until midday, but nothing yet. Surely, you should know that? You shouldn't be asking me."

"I'm effectively off the investigation. At least, as a foot soldier."

Alec nearly swallowed his bacon the wrong way. "What are you talking about?"

"I had a very brief conversation with Ruby Parker yesterday afternoon. Brief because she's still interviewing the Flemings. In her view, I'm better off in Thames House. Since this investigation began, there have been two attempts on my life

– three if you count the City incident. She thinks we can't allow another. Either Grey are implicated or they aren't. Whichever way, I'm safer here. They wouldn't dare strike in this building. They'd be hanging themselves up naked by the feet."

"What about at night? Are you allowed to go home?"

"I've orders to sleep in the pods in the basement."

"What about the odd cocktail? What about Netflix? What about having a friend round to watch *Godzilla*?"

"We must do that sometime."

"Bloody hell, John. What about your human rights?"

"Her idea is that I'm mainly a linguist and a detective. Those skills can be as easily practised here as outside."

"So how long does she intend keeping you under house arrest?"

"She didn't say. Until the investigation's over. Or more likely, the war with Grey's reached a satisfactory conclusion."

"Could be forever then."

"Don't worry, I've got a plan."

Alec laughed. "You're going to tie your sheets together and get out through the window."

"Even more cunning than that. I'm going to see her this morning and persuade her she's wrong."

"To be fair to her, she does tend to listen to reason. She's not the 'I'm the boss and you'll do as I say and like it' type. How are you going to persuade her?"

"I'm going to tell her I've got a plan."

"A *further* plan? Plan *to the power of* plan? I thought your plan was to go and see her? Anyway, you'd better make sure it's not anything someone else can carry out. One problem I've always found with telling someone in authority my 'plan', is that, once I've finished talking, they're likely to go, 'That's an excellent proposal, Alec; however, I'm not sure you're the best person to execute it. How about insert-name-of-office-boot-licker-here?' And, for fear of looking bitter and envious, I'm

obliged to go, 'Oh joy, that's just what I was thinking!' Be careful. You might find 'Marciella' gets more of this investigation
than anyone's bargained for. Then we'll all be sorry."

"I keep telling you, it's not a fiefdom."

"It *is*, John. That's exactly what it is. It's what every investigation is. A fiefdom. And this one's Phyllis's. Remember
that."

He finished his cereal and read the papers. Two days on and
still 'Death of the Brexit Queen', 'Tragic demise of key Brexit
player', '"Police not considering foul play": report', 'Frances
Holland: her life in pictures', 'Holland's cause of death determined but undisclosed'. Alongside other news: the US
Primaries, the continuing fightback against IS, another Taliban
attack on Christians. Did the papers always make it sound as
if the world was coming apart at the seams, or were the times
just very 'interesting'? He couldn't remember. Once you'd
read a paper, it tended to get forgotten as new ones piled on
top of it. Probably all the same, all the time.

Wait a minute, though. 'Justin Bieber becomes first artist to
hit 10 billion views on Vevo'. A crumb of good news, surely?
If you liked him. But what the hell was Vevo? He ought to
know: he was a spy.

He buttered a slice of toast and ate it while reading about
The Get Out Clause. Then he got up and went to see Ruby
Parker. He'd made an appointment at ten mainly because he
knew Phyllis would be questioning the Flemings then. He
looked at his watch. 9.56. Ample time, assuming Grey hadn't
poisoned his Coco Pops.

He went to Basement One, knocked and went in on her
command. She sat at her desk looking unrelenting. She obviously knew what he was here for, and considered it best to begin as she meant to go on. She put her pen down, sat up, folded her hands on the table in front of her, and permitted her-

self a faint you've-no-hope smile. Implacable, but polite as well.

"Sit down if you like," she said, indicating the chair.

He accepted. No point exacerbating matters. She was only doing what she thought was best for him.

"State your case," she said. "And make it as fast as you can. I've a lot of work to do. You want to be allowed out again. I assume that's what you're here for."

"I'd like to begin by asking a few questions."

"If they're about the case, you're probably best advised to see Phyllis."

"I understand she's meeting the Flemings now. Otherwise, I would have done."

"Go on then."

"What about Pierre Durand? Has Planchart seen the photos?"

"All of them. He claims he's met European politicians from a variety of ideological backgrounds over the last few months. Given his position as leader of TGOC, it's inevitable that at least the majority would belong to Eurosceptic parties. He says that any attempt to read a significance into the photos beyond that is mischievous. He says it's the sort of thing *The Sun*, the *Daily Star* or the *Mirror* might do. He doesn't expect it of MI7. I happen to agree with him. As for Durand, he claims to have thought he belonged to the French *Front National*. He can't remember what they talked about, except in very general terms: how to roll back the influence of Brussels. He challenged Phyllis to prove that he *doesn't* belong to the FN. Which of course she can't."

"What about Annabel's burglary? Alec tells me Planchart's linked to Simpson, Musgrave and De Groot."

"So is TGOC. So, unfortunately, are lots of people. Simpson's kept on a retainer, with bills coming in to TGOC quarterly. We've just reached the end of the last quarter, which means there's still two months and twenty days till a new one. If this particular service – springing Durand - has been itemised yet, it's not on the system. Right now, since we've no evidence against Durand – we only want to question him – there's no way we can make them tell us the name of the specific client at whose behest he was released. Planchart will probably say it was the FN, but will hedge that round with caveats to the effect that he's only speculating and it's really none of his business."

"Presumably, we can find out whether Durand belongs to the FN?"

"I've asked Interpol to investigate, but of course, we can only find out whether he's a member, not necessarily whether the FN's employing him. Any such employment might be in-direct."

"Links between the FN and Simpson?"

"None. At least nothing direct. In any case, John, nowadays the FN is a respectable political party, and one of the largest in France. So what if we *do* establish a link? It's not the bad old days of Jean-Marie. His daughter's completely revamped it. It's mainstream now."

"Point taken."

"The real problem is, we've probably lost the Frances Holland connection, which was one very important pretext for this investigation. If it's true that she committed suicide – not-withstanding T. Robinson and the mysterious shell company - there may be nothing left for us to investigate. Or very little. We need a new lead, and we need it fast."

"The nub of this investigation, as I see it, is Pierre Durand. If there was nothing to hide, they wouldn't have got him out of police custody and off the face of the earth so quickly. Somehow, he's at the centre."

"And that gets us precisely … where?"

He smiled. "You have to admit we're in desperate straits."

"I just have admitted it," she said frostily. "Repeat: what's your point?"

"Let's say I had a plan to make progress, and the success of that plan would be increased, even ever so slightly, by my personal involvement, you'd have to consider it, yes?"

"I take it this 'plan' involves you leaving the building."

"Sure does."

She sighed. "I might as well hear it then. But don't build your hopes up."

"Did Marciella Fleming tell you about Mysterious Background Man?"

"Well done for spotting him so quickly. And?"

"Did you – Phyllis – ask Planchart about him?"

"Yes, and he didn't bat an eyelid. He's Ian Talbot, a sixty-one year-old politics lecturer at Sussex university. He's writing a book about the EU referendum."

"Have we spoken to him?"

"On what pretext? He's not in any of the pictures in which Durand appears."

"I see your point, but did Marciella - "

"'Marcie'. She'll be upset if you keep calling her Marciella."

"I take it we're meeting again then, she and I?"

"She may be joining the investigation. Sorry, what were you about to say before I so rudely interrupted you?"

"Simply that in all the pictures in which he appears, Ian Talbot seems to be looking at Frances Holland with undisguised … tenderness."

"On that basis, what questions could you possibly ask him that would have any bearing on our investigation? Most likely, he'd deny it. Even assuming you're right, John – and you may not be - it's just a *look*; it's not an incriminating document or a smoking gun. And in any case, as I've just said, this probably isn't an investigation into Frances Holland any more. As you so rightly pointed out a moment ago, our sole point of interest now is the intersection – if any – of Simpson, Musgrave and De Groot, TGOC and Pierre Durand."

"In order to discover a point of intersection, it's sometimes necessary to look at the behaviour of the surrounding bodies."

"I'm not sure what you mean."

"Like in the 1840s when Pluto was inferred from disturbances in the orbit of Uranus."

She smiled thinly. "I meant, in the context of this case."

"The way in which Durand's role may be inferable from anomalies in the orbit of Frances Holland and her associates."

"Specifically, Talbot, you mean? It's a very, very long shot."

"Seven point five billion kilometres. But still worth sending a spacecraft up for. Why is Marcie Fleming still interested in TGOC?"

"Why wouldn't she be?"

"From what Alec told me, she was spying for the Conservative party. Her photos proved Planchart was hob-nobbing with dubious foreign powers. Mission accomplished, surely? What more does she want?"

"You're to blame for that, I'm afraid. It *was* very much a case of done and dusted - until she saw you chasing Durand through Central London. Then she realised there was more to what she'd discovered than met the eye. Look, John, I've got a lot of time for you, but I'm also very busy. Tell me specifically what you want, and I'll think about it."

"I want to go to Frances Holland's funeral and see if Ian Talbot's there. If he is, and if he's as devastated as I think he is, I'd like your permission to ask him a few questions."

She sat back and looked at the ceiling. "I'll think about it," she said eventually. "Go to your desk and start familiarising yourself with the results of Annabel's latest break in. I'll let you know when I've considered all the pros and cons in peace. Give me half an hour."

Thirty minutes later, she called him at his workstation. "I suppose it'll get it out of your system," she said. "And it can't do any harm. Be careful leaving the building, and come straight back afterwards. If you suspect Grey – or anyone else

- is following you, I want you to turn around and come back to Thames House, is that understood? If necessary, phone for a car. Don't do anything stupid."

He smiled. "Thank you."

Chapter 18: Talbot on the Run

The day of Frances Holland's funeral, Mordred dyed his hair black by way of disguising himself and left Thames House via the emergency underground exit at Pimlico. It was the height of the morning rush hour and Kevin was waiting for him in a black London taxi at the end of Lupus Street. They drove for two hours in silence to West Wittering on the Sussex coast. Just after ten o'clock, they arrived at a church called St Michael's, where Frances Holland had been confirmed and married. The funeral was scheduled for eleven, although lots of people were here already, most, by the looks of it, to satisfy their curiosity rather than express their condolences. After a short service, the coffin was to be laid to rest in the churchyard.

It took Mordred a long time to find Talbot, and the crowds were large enough to make maintaining an unbroken sight-line almost impossible. The lecturer was alone, a red haired balding man with large wire-framed glasses and a pale complexion, and although all six remaining members of The Get Out Clause were among the chief mourners, he made no attempt to effect a reunion; in fact, he seemed eager to keep out of their way. The sky was full of large individual clouds, but a high wind kept them moving and ensured the sun got a frequent look in.

"You'd think he'd be keen to get a seat in the church," said a woman's voice from behind Mordred. "Planchart and company could probably guarantee it. Why's he hanging back?"

He turned round.

Marcie Fleming. She was as disguised as he was – or maybe this was how she normally looked. Nothing like Sarah Riceland. Mind you, she was in mourning gear, including a veil. But her make-up was completely different, and even the way she stood and spoke. They could have been two completely different women.

"My father was a friend of Frances Holland at one time," she said. "I say 'friend': I'm pretty sure they slept together. Years ago now. Still, huge age-gap. Obscene, some might say. Anyway, I'm here with him. I'll probably get a seat indoors."

"What do you want?" he asked. "From me?"

"I wouldn't have agreed to accompany my father here if it wasn't for you. I came to tell you I'm taking a back seat. I'll do what I can to help – Daddy's already killed your absurd 'radicalisation' inquiry: Red department will find out officially tomorrow, and you'll be informed sometime after that – and I can be very useful to you tackling Grey. All I'm looking for in return is whatever truth you finally come up with about TGOC, and Ruby Parker's already pledged me that via White. My offer's unconditional, in other words, so best of luck, and thank you for saving my life more than once. I may occasionally have got in deeper than I should have." She shook his hand and kissed his cheek. "Goodbye, John."

She turned and left before he could reply. A few moments later, he saw her enter the church on her father's arm.

Meanwhile, Talbot had become quite emotional. He'd come only half-dressed for a funeral – black coat and tie, but violet shirt, beige trousers and brown brogues - and it was clear he wasn't expecting a welcome. He wiped his eyes on his sleeve and walked out of the churchyard with the determination of one who has made a sudden decision to get as far away from the action as quickly as possible.

At the end of the road, he climbed into a red Peugeot and pulled out at speed, almost knocking a clutch of pedestrians over.

This was it. He was in a state of high sentiment. If he had anything to tell, it was now.

Mordred got into the back of the black taxi. "Follow that car," he told Kevin.

They pulled out much less dramatically, but it didn't matter. Whatever Kevin's faults – and it was difficult to pinpoint them since he never spoke, at least to Mordred – he wasn't one for getting thrown off the scent. They left West Wittering and made for the M27. When they joined the motorway, Talbot accelerated until he was doing 120 mph and stayed there, overtaking everything in his path.

Was he determined to get caught by the police? You didn't do that sort of speed without knowing you'd draw attention to yourself.

More likely, he'd realised he was being followed. Kevin tried to keep pace with him, but a London taxi doing that sort of speed was unheard of. He slowed to 60 and switched on his satnav. The screen showed their car, but it also showed another – Talbot's, presumably – way in front. A few moments later, it turned onto the A36 for Salisbury. Mordred put it at about five miles ahead now, and it slowed, as it would have to on that sort of road. Still, the way it was moving in spurts, it was obviously still doing a lot of overtaking. How long till the police got wind of it?

Kevin started speaking. At first, Mordred thought he might be trying to start a conversation, but then he noticed he had Bluetooth. Presumably, he was talking to base, but since he was a completely unknown quantity he could just as easily be ringing ITV1 to book an audition for *Emmerdale*. Best leave him be.

When he'd finished speaking, Mordred's phone rang. *Ruby Parker*.

"Kevin's just called me to say Talbot's driving dangerously," she said. "He suspects he may have been drinking. In any case, he's contacted the police. They'll probably take him into custody – I'll see what I can do – and you'll get a golden opportunity to act as his guardian angel. Let me know as soon as you're finished with him. Kevin has orders to bring you straight back to London afterwards."

"Understood."

"Listen, Talbot has a wife and two teenage daughters. From what I understand, it's a happy marriage. Don't say anything to him that he could interpret as blackmail. You're DI Jonas Eagleton again. The police will be expecting you. Kevin's got your papers in his glove compartment."

Chapter 19: Possibly Young Conservatives

Mordred and his driver went to a service station while, seven miles further up the road, Talbot was flagged down by traffic officers, arrested and taken back to Salisbury to be charged. Mordred ate a vegetable slice in *Mike's Kitchen Garden* while Kevin sat in the taxi with a flask of coffee and a beef tongue sandwich. Like all motorway cafés, the outside was cold, noisy and windswept with the passing of cars, and the inside was anonymous and somehow dominated by the toilets. Afterwards, they went to find the police station.

When Mordred walked in, the officer at reception – a young WPC with a bob - was expecting him. "Mr Talbot's in a cell right now, sir," she said. "Would you like to wait till he sobers up, or do you want to deal with him right away?"

"As soon as possible, please," Mordred said, putting his card back in his pocket. "I'll speak to him alone at this stage, keep it as informal as possible. Do you have an interview room available?"

"It's all arranged, sir. Would you like a cup of tea or coffee?"

"That's very kind, but no thank you."

She introduced him briefly to some of the other officers – a matter of etiquette - then took him straight to the room where Talbot was waiting, seated at a table. She closed the door as she left and Mordred sat down. Talbot looked at the floor. His eyes bulged manically.

"You're a university lecturer, I understand," Mordred began. "This probably isn't going to look good for you. 120 miles per hour, eh? What were you trying to prove?"

Talbot shrugged. He wiped his nose on his sleeve, avoided eye contact and said nothing.

"However, I'm not here to talk about that," Mordred went on. "I'm here to talk about Frances Holland. The woman whose funeral you just attended," he added, to prevent a quibble. "I know you two were having a relationship."

Talbot seemed to wake up from a dream in which he'd decided to be uncooperative. "Er, what?"

"Are you denying it?"

"Wha – how? Who are you?"

"A friend of hers."

"Here, in the police station?

"DI Jonas Eagleton. When I say I'm her friend, I don't mean I knew her personally. I mean, I'm on her side. And I'm not sure you are."

"How dare you? She and I were always friends. *Always.* I've known her since she was at university."

"Is that when you started sleeping with her?"

Talbot deep breathed for a few moments, then relaxed as if a weight had been taken from him. He spent a few seconds swallowing his indignation, then sat up. "For what it's worth, it wasn't a crime in those days," he said meekly.

"Granted. It isn't now."

Another long pause, then: "It wasn't even considered unethical. We were in love. Correction: I loved her. She didn't love me." He grinned acrimoniously. "Obviously, I was younger and better looking in those days. What was your name again?"

"Eagleton."

"Do you – suspect anything?"

"About what?" Mordred asked.

"You tell me."

This didn't come out as a declaration of defiance. It came out as 'You go first'. Tell me what you know, and maybe we can help each other. How to respond?

"I'm not convinced she committed suicide," Mordred hazarded.

"Me neither. In fact, I'd stake my life on it."

"Except I don't have a theory. I'd be glad of any assistance in that department, which is why I'm here."

"I'm being blackmailed."

No point in trying to conceal his surprise. "Blackmailed? By who?"

"I don't know. They say if I … Yes, I do have a theory. I guess it must be close to the truth. But I'm not allowed to say anything."

"Did you sleep with Frances Holland recently?"

"Depends what you mean by 'recently'. Once. A mistake. Old times sake. She was unhappy, and we'd been drinking - "

"And someone filmed it."

"So they say. I haven't seen it, but I can't afford the risk. Emily would leave me. My wife."

"In my experience, if someone hasn't shown you the goods, that's because they haven't got them. In this case, they never filmed it to begin with. They just heard about it somehow. Think about it. Copies are easy enough to make. You'd want to make at least one, for insurance's sake. Where exactly did you have sex?"

"In the toilets at East Chisley Conservative Club. Look, I know that sounds implausible. Mad, even. But Frances *was* mad. When she was on a low, she was in complete stasis, but when she was on a high, she threw caution completely to the wind. Like she was two different people."

"Presumably, you chose the toilet cubicle at random. It wasn't pre-planned?"

"No. No, of course not. She didn't plan – *anything* when she was in that mood. And any plans *you* had, she deliberately trampled them."

"Okay, think about it then. Think about the logistics of setting up a camera to record something like that."

"It could have been an opportunist. Everyone films *everything* on their mobiles nowadays."

"So – what are you saying? This is the Conservative Club, let's remember that. Someone comes into the toilet, presumably because they need to, and they hear a couple having sex in a cubicle. They don't think, 'This is disgraceful. I must tell the club chairman' or 'I really need to urinate. I hope they don't hear me and think I'm a peeping tom'. No, they get out their phones and film it. Like it's a secondary school."

"I see your point, but there were lots of Young Conservatives in that night. Everyone knows they're not quite right in the head."

"I'm sure they'd have put it on Youtube by now. They wouldn't have handed it over to some anonymous gang of blackmailers. No, what happened is that someone probably *did* hear you that night, and word *did* get out, and that's how the blackmailers heard. You're in the clear, if you ask me. When the chips are down, it's your word against theirs. And they won't dare throw into question the reputation of a fine, upstanding politician like Frances Holland, as they'd have to, like it or not. Even less so, now she's dead. It would backfire on them pretty much big time. They're bluffing."

"Maybe."

"Okay, I've done enough talking now. Now I need to know your theory. You said you'd stake your life on the notion that Frances Holland didn't commit suicide."

"That's right, she didn't."

"So ...?"

"Planchart killed her. Charles Planchart, the MP. Her Parliamentary colleague."

He nodded in an attempt to conceal his disappointment. "I have to say, on the face of it, that's highly implausible. He was in London the entire time she was in Scotland."

"Look, yes, I know it sounds barking. I'm just going to tell you what I *think* I know now, okay? I don't actually *know* it in the technical sense. I can't provide hard evidence. But I 'know' it like you know ... I don't know ... that I was telling the truth

173

about me and Frances at the Chisley Conservative Club just then."

"Just tell me what you strongly suspect then."

He took a deep breath. "Okay. Okay. Well, for a kick off, Frances wasn't at all what most people thought she was. In most people's view, including that of her constituents, and the cabinet, and the party, she was Little Ms Dependable, supremely rational, a bit of a cold fish, bluestocking, young fogey, spinster, what have you. All those things.

"But in reality she wasn't like that at all; the mental illness saw to that. She wore a mask. She kept it in place with great difficulty, and most of the time, she was petrified it would slip. But not all the time. Sometimes, when she was in one of her euphoric periods, she would behave recklessly: sex with strangers, inappropriate practical jokes, theft, even – on one occasion - arson … So I've heard. It rings true.

"I knew her at college. I was one of the lecturers on her course. We had a fling, I suppose you'd call it. I didn't realise she was seeing Bill Ashbaugh at the same time, who also went on to become an MP. Labour. You may have heard of him."

"I've already spoken to him."

"In hindsight, her thing with Bill was probably much more serious than her thing with me. Must have been. She was all set to marry him, apparently, political differences notwithstanding – although they weren't *that* different in those days – but he … Well, I can't say. It's just what I heard. Let's just say that when I heard he'd been fiddling his expenses the other year, I wasn't surprised."

"Financial misconduct. That's what split them. At university."

"Combined with a strong dose of two-timing. Poignant: she was cheating on me, and he was doing exactly the same to her. The odd thing is, had it not been for their love affair and the car-crash way it ended, I really think they'd have ended up in the same ideological place. Pink or pastel blue, one or the other. What happened instead was that their mutual repulsion had an impact on their outlook. She became dark blue, he became deep red.

"Except he didn't. Just like her, he put a mask on. The difference is, his mask was there to conceal his moral bankruptcy. Whereas, ironically perhaps, she retained her idealism. You may have heard her called a 'conviction politician'. That's true. For all her impetuousness, in public she only championed causes she believed in.

"And in the end, that's what did for her. Have you ever come across a satirical magazine called *Private Eye*?"

"I've heard of it."

"Basically, it's a mixture of satire, cartoons and serious behind-the-scenes journalism, most of the latter in a font so small you can barely read it. It focuses on corruption in the British establishment. I mean the whole caboodle: the newspapers, the local councils, the City, the health service, agriculture, and, of course, the mother of all cesspits: Parliament. *HP Sauce*, it's called, and there's usually an entire page of it, sometimes two.

"Now just about everything that appears in *Private Eye* is way ahead of Reuters and the like. It's mostly what you'd call 'breaking news', although it rarely creates a scandal: thanks to the fact that there's a disgraceful level of apathy amongst the public. The point is, though, to work something like that, you need sources. Spies, more than journalists. People who care about the public good enough to risk their necks disseminating information the establishment would rather you never knew about.

"Step forward Frances Holland. She began with the intention of exposing Bill Ashbaugh, but once she'd done that, she got a taste for what I'd call *the spying life*. Everyone can see the attraction. Look at the following *Spooks* had. Look at *The Night Manager*. Divest yourself of your identity; become this secret person filching hidden files and popping them into the hands of your controllers, shedding light on darkness. The irresistible glamour of becoming no one.

"Pretty soon, she wasn't just spying on her political opponents; she was spying on everyone. And because of who she was, how occasionally self-destructive and unrestrained she could become, she was spying on The Get Out Clause too. I counted four separate articles on Planchart and his cronies this year. Of course, they've dried up now."

"Can I ask how you knew she was doing all this?"

"Back a bit. When I heard that she was part of TGOC, I hastily claimed funding for a book that would allow me to shadow her for 'research' purposes. Part of me was still enamoured of her, you see. Anyway, she got me in, and used me to bounce ideas off. Pretty soon that extended to sex in a toilet cubicle and desperate revelations concerning things I didn't necessarily want to know about. She was fully aware I didn't like the fact that she'd turned out all Mrs Thatcher – us full-time academics tend to be a fairly left-leaning lot – so she thought she'd mitigate it by letting me see her human side. As in, telling me what she was doing for *Private Eye*, among other things."

"I assume you're going to say Planchart found out."

"She overextended herself. I didn't discover what it was she eventually found out and tried to give to *Private Eye* – she said it would blow my mind if I knew. But I also know she was becoming paranoid about my book by this time. In a stupid, completely unrealistic way. Like it was going to be some definitive kiss-and-tell, disclosing everything I'd undergone with TGOC in every last detail, and thus wrecking her career. Bit by bit, she stopped trusting me. I last saw her precisely two weeks before she disappeared. She asked me to stop shadowing TGOC and stop writing my book. I said I could do the former. I couldn't do the latter. She became utterly uncontrollable. I had a black eye for nearly a week."

"I assume you didn't go to the police."

"Absolutely not."

"This 'mind-blowing revelation' she had. How did she tell you about it?"

"Phone. It was the last conversation we ever had." He smiled sourly. "Not counting the two-word text."

"This conversation. Before or after the black eye?"

"Just after. And she told me Planchart had found out."

"How did he do that? Do you know?"

"She took the information, whatever it was, to *Private Eye*, but apparently it was such a grandiose claim, and there was so little evidence to substantiate it, that they couldn't put it into print. They have a good team of lawyers over at Carlisle Street, but they're not omnipotent. However, it was a serious enough for them to want to pass on to the police, just to cover themselves. And someone in the Met went straight to Planchart. He had an informer, in other words."

"Surely, the police would have wanted to interview him anyway?"

"You're a policeman yourself, DI Eagleton. You're investigating Frances Holland's death. And yet you've no idea what I'm talking about. Have you?"

It was a good point. True, he wasn't who Talbot thought he was, but if the police knew about it, then as a member of MI7, he'd have been told. "No," he said.

"So there we are. It must have been taken to the police – if *Private Eye* say that's what they did, then that's what they did – but someone in the police saw it, sat on it and had a quiet word in Planchart's ear. 'Someone': I'm guessing, another freemason."

"Planchart's a freemason?"

"They all are. Tossers."

It was beginning to sound like a conspiracy theory. Still, not wholly implausible. "How did Planchart kill her then?"

"This is speculation now," Talbot continued, "but it fits with what I know about him. Once he found out from the police that Information X – we might as well call it that – had reached the police, he knew there was only a limited number of people who could have passed it on. It was someone in his immediate circle. He then trawled through six months' worth of *Private Eye*s, and realised that revelations were being made about people and organisations connected to various people, but all with only one common denominator. Frances Holland. He confronted her, then he threatened to expose her."

"How would such 'exposure' work?" Mordred asked. "Given what you said a moment ago: that no one in the country cares about what *Private Eye* thinks and says?"

"The public, by and large, don't. The politicians and the press, they do: very much so. No one likes having their peccadilloes held up to ridicule in print."

"So Planchart would have 'exposed' her in a more limited sense than the usual – to her colleagues."

"That's all he needed to do. She'd have been finished. And I don't mean just her Westminster career. Powerful people would make sure there was no cosy job in industry waiting for her at the end. No boardroom consultancy, no advisory post, no well-paid column in a national newspaper. They're a vengeful lot, on the whole."

"I still don't understand how he's supposed to have killed her."

"Back to my story. He's blackmailing her now. He pretends to be her friend. *Listen, I have a cottage in Scotland. Two weeks. Best leave now, lie low for a while. I'll try and smooth things over while you're away, but I can't promise anything.* So off she goes, defeated and alone and facing a dark future. Once she gets there, there's no car, probably limited wireless, no one she knows, and to cap it all no anti-depressants. Planchart made sure they went missing somewhere between King's Cross and Skye."

"How do you know that?"

"I don't for certain. But, like I said earlier, I received a two-word text message from her, the day after she disappeared. That was the last I heard of her."

"What did it say?"

"*No Citalopram*. Plus an emoticon. A sad face. It's still on my phone, if you don't believe me. Which was confiscated when I arrived here."

"And how did you respond?"

"Best check my phone for the details. I haven't deleted anything. A combination of 'Where are you?' and 'Let me help', and variations on those themes."

Mordred tried to take stock. So maybe Planchart had sent her to Skye. That would at least mean he'd been lying throughout the period of her disappearance. And maybe she'd had something big and incriminating but unverifiable on him. And maybe he'd arranged for her antidepressants to vanish as soon as she'd left London. Perhaps he'd even foreseen where that would lead. Any one of those things currently looked hard to establish. Together, they were an Everest.

At least in so far as pinning Frances Holland's death on him was concerned. But the bigger issue was probably what did she uncover, and why was it momentous enough to merit her extermination?

"I'm surprised no one's looked into who booked that Skye cottage," Talbot said. "Dig deep enough, I'm pretty sure you'd discover it was Planchart."

"And the reason you didn't go to the police with any of this," Mordred said, "was because you were being blackmailed. I assume you've met the blackmailers at some point?"

"They phoned me at work."

"Pretty amateurish."

"If I'd gone to the police, I'd have had to confess to having had sex with Frances. And given how leaky the police were first time round ..."

"Just one more question." Mordred reached into his inside pocket and put a picture of Pierre Durand talking to Frances Holland on the table. "Do you know this man?"

"I saw him a few times, but I don't know him by name. I don't think I ever spoke to him. Who is he?"

"That's what we're trying to find out. You don't know anyone you could ask?"

"My association with Frances means all my bridges with TGOC are now well and truly burned, I'm afraid."

Mordred stood up. "Understood. Don't worry, nothing will get out this time round. I'll need your phone, I'm afraid, and a guarantee that you'll cooperate if we need to ask further questions. You're not in a position to ask for anything in return. You were driving dangerously under the influence of alcohol and innocent people could easily have been killed. However, given the circumstances, and your invaluable assistance with a major inquiry, I'll do everything in my power to see you're released with a caution. We'll take you home. You can pick up your car from here tomorrow morning. Never again, though."

Talbot got to his feet and accepted the handshake. "Agreed. Th – Thank you."

Chapter 20: The *Private Eye* Connection

Mordred sat in Briefing Room One with Ruby Parker, Alec, Phyllis, Annabel, Edna and Ian, around a square table designed for twice their number. He outlined his conversation with Talbot and awaited questions.

"Before we start get down to Planchart and what to do about him," Alec said, "I'd just like to congratulate John. Personally, I think it's a shocking decision: they obviously don't know the first thing about him – but I'm pleased he's going to be with us a little bit longer. At least until someone makes another radicalisation complaint."

"I'm desperately sorry," Ian said. "I'd only just joined - "

"Forget it," Mordred said for the thousandth time.

"It was *your* fault, John," Annabel said. "You can't assume that everyone shares your sense of humour. Especially when you haven't yet been properly introduced."

"Well done, John," Ruby Parker said. "Now let's return to business. It's pretty clear Planchart's up to his neck in this, whatever it is. Without hard evidence, I don't think we're going to get any more out of him, and I think returning to him will set alarm bells ringing. *Private Eye*'s our obvious next port of call, but before we tackle that, has anyone any other ideas?"

"How about we despatch someone to Skye to check out the GPs' surgeries?" Mordred said, after a silence. "Let's say Frances Holland knew that without her medication she was in danger. Isn't it possible she'd have tried to get help? Even knowing it was unlikely?"

"The press have been crawling all over that area," Alec said. "I don't think they'll have left a stone like that unturned."

"I disagree," Phyllis said. "I mean, I agree with John. Let's say I'm Frances Holland. I go to a doctor's surgery to try and get a specific drug, one they can't do over the counter. I might get into a bit of an altercation. Probably not with the doctor, because doctors tend to hide behind their receptionists. The problem is, once the press arrive, no receptionist's going to say, 'I remember Frances Holland: she was the lady I turned away when she came in here begging for antidepressants'. If that's what you did, you're probably going to keep your head down."

"What I find suspicious," Annabel said, "is the absence of a suicide note. That might implicate whoever discovered the body. If Frances Holland thought her reputation was on the line, she'd probably want to write one, wouldn't she?"

"Not necessarily, if she was depressed enough," Edna said.

"We need a full list of everything in that cottage at the time of death," Alec said. "And also of what she left behind in London. We need to know when she was last prescribed antidepressants, what they were, and when and where she picked up the prescription, if at all. And as far as possible, we need to reconstruct her journey from King's Cross to Skye."

"We're going to end up relying pretty heavily on the police," Ruby Parker said, "but that needn't be a problem. They don't always like us giving them orders, that's all."

"Tough luck," Phyllis said. "If Talbot's right, they've got a case to answer."

"Which just leaves *Private Eye*," Ruby Parker said. "Anyone any ideas? Because they've already been to the police and nothing happened. They're going to wonder why it's taken all this time. DI Eagleton appearing alone at the front desk in Carlisle Street isn't going to reassure them, with or without ID. They'll just think 'journalist'."

"The mention of DI Eagleton tells me you think this is another job for John," Alec said. "With respect, can I ask why no one else round this table has been considered?"

"Don't address that question to me," Ruby Parker said. "It was Phyllis's call."

"I assumed no one else would want it," Phyllis said curtly. "John's a subscriber. I assumed the rest of us would either be ignorant of *Private Eye* or hostile to it."

"Who on earth would be hostile to it?" Mordred said.

"Me," Phyllis said. "I would."

They looked at each other for a second. In the background, Frank Sinatra sang, *'Twas goodbye on the Isle of Capri.*

"Why?" he asked. "I'm not looking for a fight. I'm genuinely interested."

"Don't upset her," Alec said. "You might not get the job."

Ruby Parked turned a withering look on him. "That was an idiotic remark."

"Apologies," Alec said. "I didn't mean it to come out like that." He shrugged. "Communists in toilets. Everyone's allowed one."

Edna tried to suppress a grin by looking at the table.

"I'm interested too," Ruby Parker said. "What's wrong with *Private Eye*, in your opinion? It's an academic question, so you're not obliged to answer."

Phyllis leaned back. "Let's say I'm a broadsheet journalist, and I want to write an article on some backbench MP. Let's say he's a villain according to *Private Eye* – it's published several articles about him and his doings. Because there's no searchable database of past issues, even for subscribers, me finding out about it's an uphill struggle. Of course, once I publish my article, it'll run a piece ridiculing me: *she didn't even know … As the Eye reported as long ago as last June*, etcetera. My guess is it's protected by some very knowledgeable lawyers, and, for those who fall foul of it, it's a waste of time and effort suing: everyone knows the offending issue will effectively disappear the week after next. A kind of implicit contract between the magazine and the establishment, in other words. We'll fling mud at you, but don't worry, it won't be very sticky."

Annabel let out a laugh. "You know you and John are actually quite suited," she said. "You both over-think things."

Mordred and Phyllis looked at each other. Annabel laughing out loud in a meeting? A once in a lifetime experience.

"Does 'you're quite suited' mean …?" Alec said, pointing to Mordred then Phyllis and back again.

"I think it's time to re-focus on the investigation," Phyllis said. "And, with all due respect: none of your business. Who votes that John – *subscriber* John - should make our first approach to *Private Eye*?"

Everyone raised a hand except Alec and Ruby Parker.

"Those against?" she said.

Alec raised his hand.

"Abstain?"

Ruby Parker raised her hand. "I think Alec and I are thinking the same thing," she said. "John may have passed his radicalisation inquiry – my sources tell me that was more a case of intervention from on high than anything he said in his interview – but that doesn't mean the war's over."

"I'm sorry," Annabel said: "those two hit men? I can't believe anyone within this organisation's trying to kill him. It's outrageous."

"Grey denies the hit men," Ruby Parker said. "Remember, I didn't originally say they were Grey. I said they were Ex-Grey. What made me think I might be wrong was that they appeared as part of a pattern. First, the formal accusation against John. Second, the fact that Grey appear to be spying on us."

"What does Timothy Manners say?" Alec said. "What does Shafiq Effanga say?"

"They've disappeared. Manners discharged himself from hospital a few hours after his arrival, and before we could interview him. In our defence, we were told he wasn't in any fit state to be released. Whoever came to pick him up was obviously pretty determined. And Effanga's still at large. Again, someone came to pick him up."

"Someone keeps collecting people we want to talk to," Mordred said. "First, Durand, then Manners, now Effanga."

"We're acting on the assumption that someone wants John dead," Phyllis said. "Which may not be correct. We've no real evidence that Manners wanted you dead," she told him. "Just repeating 'you're dead' over and over may not mean anything. Men say it to each other in pubs every night. And Effanga may have been after the artist formerly known as Sarah Riceland."

"It may have been about her all along," Annabel said.

"What could anyone have to gain by killing John?" Phyllis asked.

"You kill him before he finds out who you are and exactly what you're up to," Alec said. "He may not be Jack Bauer, but he's our most talented detective. Probably. Another attempt on his life would clarify matters. We'd know for certain he was the target. But can we afford to risk it?"

"I can't keep hiding out here," Mordred said.

"Why don't we try to draw them out?" Phyllis asked.

Ruby Parker said nothing. She had her hands folded in front of her and she looked hard at the table. She clearly wasn't ready to speak.

"Remember when this investigation began," Phyllis went on. "The reason John joined my team was because it was unlikely there were two things of such magnitude going on in London at the same time. Our working assumption had to be that they were linked. Well, that also applies now."

"Assuming someone *is* trying to assassinate him," Ruby Parker replied. "Annabel may be right. Maybe it was Marcie they were after all along."

"Except for the attempt to strong arm him away after his visit to the Lord Mayor," Alec said. "That's when it started. And don't forget, two people round this table made that visit to Mansion House. Only one was assaulted."

"I was forgetting that," Ruby Parker said. "Thank you, Alec. You're right."

"John's right about one thing," Phyllis persisted. "He'll have to leave the building undisguised sometime."

"So what's your plan?" Ruby Parker asked.

"The suspicion is that Grey's spying on us," Phyllis said. "We broadcast it internally as loud as we can that he's leaving on foot for Carlisle Street. It's a half hour journey. Abingdon Street, Whitehall, Leicester Square, Dean Street. And we get all available hands to keep a watch on him. It may yield nothing, but it's worth a try."

"And what about the next time he leaves the building undisguised?" Ruby Parker said. "And the time after that?"

"I don't know," she replied.

Ruby Parker sighed. "Very well, let's give it a try. If he is subsequently killed and we haven't undertaken this particular exercise, we'll be doubly sorry. Only not Carlisle Street. I don't want anyone knowing about the *Private Eye* connection, or anything about any of our leads. We'll send him to the Shard to meet an unnamed journalist. We won't say what it's about, and we'll do everything we can to create the impression that he's acting on a personal hunch, one he hasn't yet shared with us. That should pique their interest. If anyone is after him, and if they're listening in, we should be able to trap them."

"I don't get it," Annabel said. "If Grey are denying any involvement, why don't they just team up with us in an effort to get to the bottom of it? That would demonstrate their innocence better than anything could."

"It's not within their remit," Ruby Parker replied. "And they certainly won't feel any need to prove anything to us. We may share a building, but Red's small fry as far as they're concerned. Our problems are our problems, and ultimately insignificant."

"So if I've got the whole department behind me on the draw-'em-out decoy-thing," Mordred said, "Who's going to call on *Private Eye*? Time may be of the essence."

"Leave *Private Eye* to me," Ruby Parker said. "I think I know a way in."

"It's a great plan," Mordred said, "but I'm going to make one small adjustment. I'm not going to the Shard. I'm going to Mansion House, unannounced, for another meeting with the Lord Mayor. This time I'm going to ask him outright why he looked so scared that day. He may or may not answer, but at least I'll have tried. And if we're looking to pique their interest, hey, that's got pedigree."

Chapter 21: Up on the Roof

The good thing about all the precautions against terrorism nowadays was that most buildings had very strict entry requirements. Theoretically, between Thames House and the Lord Mayor's residence, there were ten or twelve places a sniper could set up, but in practice, only one or two at such short notice. Moreover, the few flat roofs along the route could be covered by a combination of satellite surveillance and high-altitude drone-copters.

In reality, though, it seemed unlikely anyone would attempt something that melodramatic. This was London, England. Hit-men here spiked your drink, or set a pit-bull on you, or knifed you, or menaced you and hoped you had a coronary. They didn't go climbing ten flights of stairs with a high velocity rifle and start focussing telescopic sights on the back of your head. It just wasn't done, even by gangsters.

That left street-level. There were lots of ways a determined assassin might come at you there. Abduction and subsequent murder elsewhere was the most obvious. After that, a knifing; then a swift lethal injection. Lower down the list came the classic car-mounts-pavement technique. Or the brutal push from behind into the path of an oncoming vehicle. At bargain basement level, you could even be dispatched by a drive-by shooting - although your murderer would either have to be desperate, or a big fan of rap music. Again, it wasn't terribly English, and too much like hard work.

Mordred set off for Mansion house at precisely 10am. He checked out at the desk and lingered long enough for a short conversation with Colin Bale, the head receptionist. Then he descended the steps onto the street.

Phyllis and Edna were already in place on the rooftop of a restaurant in Lombard street overlooking Mansion House and with a good view of three other rooves and five out of six possible approaches. They were disguised as painters. Alec and Ian tailed Mordred at a distance of ten and fifteen metres respectively. Annabel kept a watch from the balcony of Thames House. Inside, technicians kept tabs on his movements via the capital's CCTV network. Red department agents were placed at intervals along his route and everyone was in mutual contact by Bluetooth.

The calculation was that if Grey were after him, they'd launch any assault either immediately after he left Thames House, or just before he reached his destination. There were too many routes for them to cover all possibilities, and they'd want as many personnel on the job as they could spare. Once he'd left the broad environs of Thames House, Annabel would pack her things and head for the Lord Mayor's part of town. He was expected to reach Mansion House at 10.20.

"I'm nervous," Phyllis said as she backed into the shadows for the fourth time to use her binoculars. "I don't know how my investigation became this, but it has."

"I thought Ms Parker was responsible for the Grey-Red thing," Edna said.

"I *feel* responsible. Probably because it's John. I don't mean especially him. It'd be the same if it was you or Annabel. I never knew Frances Holland. But this is personal. A slip here has more than merely professional significance."

"I totally get it, yes. And I also think it's this part of London."

"What do you mean?"

"Look down in the streets. They're nearly deserted. Look at Mansion House. It doesn't look like it's been cleaned since it was built. Those net curtains at the windows – talk about grimy. Weird for a supposedly prestigious part of one of the most prestigious cities on earth, don't you think?"

"Maybe."

"Hang on," Edna said, pointing to the street. "Look."

A large white van had stopped at the junction of Poultry and Princes Street. The driver, a well-built young man in jeans and a windcheater, put his hazard lights on and jumped out. He looked both ways cautiously, then opened the rear doors and shouted something. A stream of about ten men emerged with a purpose and poured into the adjacent building. The man got back in the van and it pulled away.

Phyllis went to *override all channels*. "I think we've a problem," she said. "Ten men inside Wilson's Exchange Building."

"We caught them on CCTV too," Ruby Parker said. "Stay in position until my order."

"Were they armed?" Edna asked. "I didn't see."

Phyllis shrugged. "They'd only need one gun. They'd assemble it up there, so we probably wouldn't see it. I can't believe they've decided to play it this way. *Sniper*, bloody hell. The Iraq War coming home again, probably. Maybe I'm wrong: maybe they're nothing to do with John."

"The way they got out of that van ... We're not wrong."

"I damn well hope someone's given him the order to abort."

"They must have guessed we're monitoring them," Edna said. "Or at least something of what we're doing."

"Why do you say that?"

"Because, as you pointed out, they only need one shooter. Why bring ten men?"

Phyllis swallowed. "... Unless they're expecting to meet resistance? Shit, you're right."

"I don't think they can be *expecting* it exactly. Otherwise, they wouldn't have come at all. They're just covering their arses. Someone fires and misses. You've got another man in the wings with a blade, and five or six more to cover all John's possible escape routes."

190

"You're quite good at this spying business, Edna. You're thinking like a real pro."

"Thank you, ma'am."

"Please don't call me 'ma'am'. I know it's *per* the book, and this isn't the time to be having this conversation, but it makes me feel ancient." She looked through the binoculars again and returned to *override*. "It's a definite. There's a man assembling a rifle. Assuming we haven't done so already, we need to instruct John to stand down."

"If we do that," Ruby Parker said, "they'll know we're onto them. Annabel's nearly there. Ian's just round the corner with Alec. Pick up your firearms and get downstairs. Annabel's in charge."

"Why Annabel?" Edna said, when they were on their way down to the street. "Just out of interest? I thought you'd been in the army."

"Ask me afterwards. Although I doubt you'll have to. Let's just say she's fully ambidextrous, I'm not."

When the reached ground level they halted, removed their Bluetooth and sauntered out onto the street as casually as if they were going for a tea-break. Alec leant against one of the columns of the stock exchange, wearing a trilby and reading a newspaper so he couldn't be identified from above. Ian, just outside the Bank of England, pretended to speak on his phone and chuckle.

Suddenly, Annabel arrived in a taxi, carrying a holdall. She got out right in front of Wilson's Exchange Building. She went up to the front door and knocked. No answer. She stamped her foot and pretended to be a little girl, frustrated. She knocked again, harder.

A man opened the door and was halfway through telling her to get lost, when she kicked the door onto him, drew a pistol, shot him, and went inside. She hauled the holdall after her and beckoned her colleagues to follow.

Her victim lay on the ground, bleeding and unconscious, but breathing. "It's only his shoulder," she said. She unzipped the holdall and closed the front door. "Guns are in there. Try not to kill anyone. Aim for shoulders, arms or legs. Remember, we're supposed to be on the same side. Me-Phyllis-Alec-Me, that's how we'll advance. Any questions?"

Annabel took two guns, one in each hand, and went first. They took turns clearing six floors without incident, and gathered together on the narrow topmost, before the double door of what was obviously the entrance to the rooftop. They looked at each other for a nod. Annabel knocked. No need to burst in: they'd be expecting their friend's return.

The man who opened the door didn't have time to look surprised. She shot his leg and kicked his head, and suddenly she was on the rooftop, firing in both directions. Alec and Phyllis came in at a lower level to avoid friendly fire, but ready to give her backup.

They didn't have to. Including the man she'd just shot, three men were down, two with pistols lying in front of them. Another eight had their hands in the air. The only one who didn't look ready to surrender was the guy with the rifle. He'd obviously spent some time assembling it, and was wondering whether he could raise it and pull the trigger before Annabel did the same.

But then he realised there were four other pistols already trained on him. He dropped his gun with a sardonic grin.

"What the hell do you think you're doing?" a well-built man of about forty yelled, advancing fast on them. *"What the HELL do you think you're up to?"*

Their commander in chief, obviously. He'd obviously worked out that they weren't going to shoot him in cold blood, and he thought weapons were all they had. As he strode forward with his jaw out and his muscles flexed, Annabel calmly came to meet him. She punched him so hard with her revolver grip that, despite his forward momentum, he momentarily reversed before he fell on his back. She trained one of her guns on him.

"Be polite," she said. "Next time you decide to murder one of my friends in cold blood, I may not be so forgiving."

He shook his head like he was punch drunk and sat up.

"As I hope I've demonstrated, I'm a very, very good shot," she said. "So before I pistol-whip you, you'd better start explaining. There may be eleven of you up here, but we're a long way up. Even if you all scream together, no one will hear you."

The man on the ground chuckled like he couldn't believe what had just happened. He spat a little blood onto his wrist and looked at it like it was some kind of black magic. His attitude changed.

"Okay," he said. "Maybe we need to talk."

"*You* do," Phyllis said.

"I take it we're both talking about the same guy," the same man said. "A certain 'John Mordred'. I'm Geoff Prebble. I'm in charge of these men. We're Grey, and if you're who I think you are, we seriously outrank you." He registered Annabel's derisive little smile and put his hands up. "Of course, right now, that gun outranks everything."

"Just like five highly skilled operatives outrank ten musclebound amateurs," Phyllis said unnecessarily.

One of the men made a lunge for his pistol. Annabel shot his arm and he fell back bleeding and gasping. "I still haven't heard anything approaching an explanation," she said levelly. "Alec, go round and collect their guns, please. Ian, you go downstairs and bring the holdall. Prisoners, get in a well-spaced line facing me. Drag yourselves if need be. Edna, frisk them. You," she said, addressing Prebble: "stay there and start talking. And I don't mean more phoney indignation, or bull-shit about rank. This is your last chance."

Alec obliged while the Greys walked or hobbled or helped each other into the semblance of a line. They looked at the ground like the last little flicker of fight had gone out of them.

"Okay," Prebble said. "It's like this. We weren't going to kill your man. The intention was to maim him with an ankle shot. We've tried a few times before to incapacitate him, but just lately, it's got a little more serious. The investigation we launched into his activities was spiked from on high. The spike came from outside MI7, and we've reason to believe it was tied to an agenda."

"What 'agenda'?" Annabel asked.

Prebble looked her straight in the eye. "Your agent's spying for the Chinese. Has been for about two years now, ever since he went on a mission to Siberia. It was there he met a woman by the name of 'Dao-ming Chou', real name Wan Chunmei. She'd been sent by the Chinese Ministry of State Security to entrap him with sexual inducements. From what we've been able to piece together he fell in love with her. After his return to Britain, the Chinese managed to create the illusion that she was a member of Black department, thus conveniently disappearing her at the heart of our own organisation. Brilliant idea: no questions need ever be asked. Except that we now know it was a lie."

"So you're saying John – *John Mordred's* been passing secrets to *the Chinese?*" Alec said incredulously.

"Obviously, it's why we started to investigate him," Prebble said. "We also think he's best ... incapacitated while we go through the tiresome formality of getting the whole thing up and running again. If he's guilty, and we think he is, we will get him. Until then, it's best if he's not part of any investigation whatsoever."

"I don't believe it," Phyllis said.

Prebble shrugged. "The novelist EM Forster once said, 'If I had to choose between betraying my country and betraying my friend, I hope I should have the guts to betray my country'.

Does that sound to you like the sort of thing your John Mordred would say?"

"Maybe he wasn't joking to Ian in the toilets that day," Alec said. "No, no, sorry. I can't believe it. *John Mordred?*"

"You're a spy," Prebble said contemptuously. "You should *know* the depths to which people will sink when they think they're 'in love'. And remember: he's being aided and abetted by people in high places, that's why his radicalisation inquiry was quashed. Chinese steel, Chinese nuclear power, Chinese meetings with the royal family. It's all China, China, China nowadays."

He paused for a moment to allow all this information to sink in. He looked round at their faces. When he resumed, it was with the confidence of someone who believes they're getting through.

"Put it another way," he went on: "everyone knows the nuclear plants the Chinese are supposed to be building at Bradwell and Sizewell may come with an inbuilt spying capacity. No one in Whitehall gives a stuff. If they don't care about that, they're not going to care about a few paltry tidbits going Wan Chunmei's way. All part of the grand kowtow. But *we* in MI7 don't have to think like that. They're what used to be called 'traitors' before the word became redundant. All of them."

Alec had made all the guns safe and put them in the holdall. He zipped it shut and picked it up at one end. Ian grabbed the other. They were ready to go.

"Look," Prebble said. "I think we understand each other now, yes? Let's make a deal. Pretty soon, Grey's going to assume full control of the Holland case. We tried to limit Mordred's involvement, but you wouldn't let us, and this is where it's got you. Now all you can do is twiddle your thumbs and wait till something else comes along. Just keep Mordred out of the loop of whatever you're assigned to next, okay? And preferably don't let him out of your sight. Definitely don't trust him. If you can agree to that, then *we* can agree not to put him in hospital. It doesn't exactly please me, but I'm willing to be reasonable for the sake of peace between the departments. Done?"

Annabel nodded. She wasn't the type to admit the other side might have a point, and especially not the sort to go making deals with losers. But this was different. She signalled a withdrawal. Within a few moments, they were all in a taxi, heading back to Thames House. None of them spoke. Phyllis rang Ruby Parker and made a full report. She fielded a few questions, but didn't go into detail in her answers. She just wanted to sit quiet and hug her knees.

When she hung up, her face was ashen. "It's just been confirmed," she told the others. "Red's been ordered to stand down from Holland and everything connected with it. A clean and complete break. As from this minute, Grey's assuming full and exclusive control."

Chapter 22: The John Mordred Show

It was an eerie feeling walking through the city alone, knowing all kinds of eyes were fixed on you, some with your welfare in mind, others – possibly – out to wipe you from the earth's surface. And having to pretend it wasn't happening, like you were just taking a stroll. Mordred picked up a copy of *The Epoch Times* from a metal dispenser and folded it up and put it in his pocket. Falun Gong, you couldn't but like them. He'd read it later.

He had faith in his colleagues, but knew enough about this sort of escapade to realise the ultimate responsibility for his safety lay squarely with him. If his enemies were any sort of professionals, which they were, they'd have budgeted for guardian angels nearby, and devised a strategy to bypass them. Meanwhile, he needed to focus all his attention on reading as many micro-expressions as possible – anxiety, stress, fear, heightened emotion - and those whose incongruously lowered heads might suggest they were trying to hide something. Passers-by all took on amplified significance, and after about half a mile, he felt like he'd taken some sort of mind-altering drug. It should have felt unpleasant, but instead he floated in a euphoric haze. Like watching himself in his own show.

They'd all agreed back at Thames House that the main danger-points were (1) just as he left the building and (2) just before he arrived at his destination. But of course, he couldn't take anything for granted. He wore a bullet-proof vest, and carried a telescopic truncheon at Annabel's insistence, although whatever happened, he probably wouldn't use it. You probably needed to be accustomed to a weapon before it became your first, instinctive recourse in moments of crisis. Otherwise … well, you might not get two chances. Things tended to move quickly when someone was trying to murder you.

He could take his time, of course he could. That was allowed. Look natural. He'd been instructed to cross the river and go via the Imperial War Museum. The best alternative - along the Victoria Embankment – left any would-be shooters too much leeway on the other side of the river. Not that they expected shooters. You wouldn't get *American Sniper:* you'd get the Kray twins.

They'd allowed twenty minutes, but everyone except him was in mutual touch. Phyllis and Edna, at the finish line, would know if he was going to be late. They wouldn't worry. He stopped for a good look round him, stretched, pretended to be enjoying the sunshine. Couldn't see Alec or Ian. But then, they were pros. Or Alec was. And Ian was supposedly behind him.

The ostensible mission – the one beneath which this weird little game of cat and mouse might or might not be going on – was ridiculous really. *Going to see the Lord Mayor at Mansion House*, like that was where he actually lived. Of course he didn't. He probably lived in a semi-detached in Bermondsey with Mrs Chester and a King Charles Spaniel. Or more likely still, a private apartment in Belgravia. Or even a country house somewhere fancy like Buckinghamshire. Or a castle in Westeros, complete with five towers and a moat.

As the twenty minutes wound down and he closed in on his destination, paradoxically he began to feel relaxed. Here was where the battle would commence, if there was to be one. And it probably wouldn't involve him because he didn't have Bluetooth. All he had to do was knock on the front door of Mansion House – or more likely put his head in at the enquiries desk downstairs if the big blue gates were bolted – then clear off. Stroll a few streets and get a taxi back to where he'd started. End of what was starting to look like a wasted twenty minutes.

He approached his destination alongside the Bank of England on Threadneedle Street and kept sweeping his eyes to either side. All at once, it occurred to him that the gunshot – if that's what it was – might actually come from within Mansion House.

Unthinkable … and yet that's what made it so possible. Phyllis and Edna wouldn't necessarily see where it had originated. And there were lots of available exits. There might even be – probably were – underground doors to one or both of the two nearby tube stations. The perfect spot.

Suddenly, all his attention was on the Lord Mayor's official residence. He'd completely lost interest in the rooftops now.

Then he saw something move within the building. His heart jumped and he almost broke stride. The net curtain at the window next to the front door moved. Then drew right back.

Good God, it was Chester. The Mayor himself, looking right at him, like he expected him. His expression showed he wasn't looking forward to the visit.

It was all over in a split second. The grimy curtain fell, and for all the world Mansion House looked the way it always did: like an abandoned soon-to-be ruin.

Where had he gone? Mordred stepped up his pace. Somehow he knew – second sight, or intuition - the Mayor was on his way outside. Which must mean he was due somewhere. Or maybe he was a lure, to draw a murder victim.

Or maybe neither: maybe the heightened sense of awareness that came with this particular journey had filled Mordred's brain with endorphins to such an extent that he was imagining things that couldn't conceivably be. *The Lord Mayor as bait to some kind of contract killing?* What the - ? Maybe he hadn't even seen Chester, there at the window. Maybe it hadn't been him at all. Maybe it hadn't been *anyone*.

He stepped up his pace and did a circuit of the building, aware that, if there were assassins lurking, he was behaving exactly as they'd like him to, but also that he couldn't stop. He was caught in a kind of play, acting the part of the – well, what? Down Walbrook, round the back along St Stephen's Row, up Mansion House Place and back to the intersection of the Bank of England, Mansion House and the Stock Exchange. No one. Weird, weird part of town. Eight and a half million people in this city. Even looking around now – you could have counted the passers-by in all directions on your fingers.

What did Alec think of his behaviour? Surely, the mission was over. Time for him to show himself if he thought Mordred was behaving oddly, or departing from the script somehow. Which he was. Or Phyllis and Edna? Where were they?

They'd gone.

Suddenly, he was sure of it. He was absolutely alone. Good God.

He didn't have time to ponder his predicament, because suddenly he saw the Lord Mayor – or the brain-phantom that was impersonating him – walking briskly down Princes Street, right opposite him. He felt himself caught up in a literal nightmare – the sort of surreal, defiance-of-physics-and-logic scenario you'd have when you'd eaten an entire baked camembert and your pillow was too soft.

He set off to follow him. He had to: the nightmare dictated it, but even if it hadn't, there was a mystery here and it was his professional duty to investigate it. The Lord Mayor *had* looked at him. Now he was outside, apparently fleeing.

Where to? Bank tube station was just across the road from Mansion House. If Chester was going any distance, that should have been his first port of call. He could have nipped out of the front door while Mordred was at the building's rear and been underground and away, and Mordred would have been none the wiser. True, Alec would have seen him, or Phyllis and Edna –

But he was forgetting: they'd vanished. That's what made everything so intensely otherworldly and sinister.

Did Chester know that? That they'd been here, and now they weren't? It was beginning to make sense. Alec and Phyllis and all the rest of them had been nobbled somehow. The reason Chester hadn't taken the underground was precisely because he *was* a lure. He was luring the last agent standing to his death. Mordred looked up at the surrounding buildings. He was a sitting duck here. Too late to call the chase off. They – whoever they were - would know as soon as he turned round that he'd twigged them.

They probably could have killed him by now. They knew he knew. They were stringing it out, playing with him. That upwards look had been a big mistake.

The other best option was to run. Run forward, zigzag a bit, and catch up with the Mayor. Maybe haul him into a taxi or a bus or something. In the last resort, flag a passing car down. Even if he couldn't do that, the two of them together – they'd make a more difficult target ... probably. And more incriminating for Chester.

Not that that mattered. There'd be a cover-up. If it was Grey, there definitely would.

Suddenly, the nightmare became hyperreal. A car – black, expensive-looking - mounted the pavement. It slapped Chester off his feet and against the wall of the Bank of England, then accelerated towards Mordred.

But it wasn't aiming for him. The driver's eyes were fixed hard on the road now. It passed Mordred at speed and went straight through the red light at the junction and off down Lombard Street. CJ15 AXK, Black Mercedes, one occupant. Its tyres didn't even screech as it took the corner.

Meanwhile, people had emerged from nowhere, running towards the victim. Chester lay prostrate and motionless. Mordred ran and knelt over him as two more men approached at speed.

The Lord Mayor lay awkwardly and a huge contusion was already emerging on his head, but he was alive. Mordred loosened his clothes. A woman had her mobile pressed to her face, begging for an ambulance. People gathered helplessly, murmuring about *that poor old guy*, with the emphasis on 'old'. No one knew who he was.

But that was the point, it always had been; and now it had returned to haunt him. He was the Lord Mayor of London. Not a personality, not even any sort of regular in the *Evening Standard*, but a semi-invisible facilitator for people like Barclays and Goldman Sachs and Pricewaterhousecooper. Useless at a time like this. Just some poor old guy.

Ruby Parker's office had been built to accommodate five people plus a desk. On the whole, she didn't welcome visitors. So much so that she'd had a fish tank installed to reduce the available space. She wasn't a public figure, and wasn't expected to entertain stakeholders or carry out PR. People came to see her only if they were in her department, and then only if they were directly connected to the business of the day. There were six people in her room right now, and she couldn't tell whether it felt like five too many or one too few. Because the subject of the meeting was missing. She sat in her chair. Annabel, Edna, Phyllis, Ian and Alec all stood.

"They told you he was spying for the *Chinese?*" Ruby Parker said.

"Has been for about two years," Alec said. "Since our Russian excursion. He's been passing secrets to 'Dao-ming Chou', real name Wan Chunmei. Quote: 'She'd been sent by the Chinese Ministry of State Security to entrap him with sexual inducements'. Then he fell in love with her. That last bit rings true."

"He never denied it," Annabel said.

"They then somehow created the impression that she worked for Black," Phyllis said. "Funnily enough, when they said 'and she wasn't', that's what made me think."

Ruby Parker leaned forward. "Explain."

202

"Consider how young she was," Phyllis went on.

"Probably a year or two younger than John," Alec added.

"To be fair," Ruby Parker replied. "Neither of you had extended contact with her, and given what she managed to pull off – the prevention of a third world war – there's every reason to believe she was highly skilled. I know next to nothing about Black, but I'm willing to wager it's not a gerontocracy. They'll take the best personnel as and where they find them."

"The question," Annabel said, "is, what are we going to do?"

"And it's complicated," Ruby Parker said, "by the fact that we don't actually know where he is."

Alec's eyebrows jumped. "Er, what? I thought he had orders to touch Mansion House then make his way back here!"

Ruby Parker shook her head slightly. "Well, he hasn't. And I don't know where he is. And there's no reason to think there's anything suspicious in that."

"Maybe he knows his little secret's out," Alec said. "I'm just trying to look at all sides of the question."

"How could he?" Phyllis said. "And why would it make him disappear? This isn't the Cold War. He wouldn't make for the airport and a reserved seat on an *Air China* flight." She frowned at what she'd said and added: "Not that that was ever a thing."

"What do we actually know about this 'Dao-ming Chou'?" Annabel asked. "She did work in Red very briefly, didn't she?"

"Everything I thought I knew about her turned out to be false," Ruby Parker replied. "Two things strike me about Grey's claim. Firstly, MI7's not the kind of organisation from which you can 'steal secrets'. The reason we switched from the old MI5, MI6 setup in the first place was that – quote - 'intelligence must be intelligent'. Parallel distributed rather than serial processing; emergent rather than programmed capabilities. The other thing is that Grey can't be a hundred per cent certain he's involved with the MSS, otherwise he wouldn't still be working at Thames House. They certainly wouldn't be looking to resuscitate their investigation into him. There must be room for doubt. The question then becomes: what makes them suspect such a thing?"

"And is it true?" Phyllis said. "Excuse me, ma'am, do you mind if I ask a rather brutal question of the group?"

Ruby Parker shook her head once, firmly. "It would be normal for someone in my position to say, 'that depends what it is'. But we're all involved in this. Go ahead."

"Raise your hand if you think John's guilty," she said.

No one responded.

"Now if you think he's not," she went on.

Alec, Edna and Ian raised their hands.

"Abstentions?"

Ruby Parker and Annabel raised her hands.

"I've learned enough in life not to trust my feelings," Annabel said.

"I'm afraid I can't afford not to keep an open mind," Ruby Parker said. "And before you object, I know you're only asking for a provisional leap of faith, not a firm declaration of allegiance. In any case, a vote's not terribly helpful if you can't give reasons. Phyllis, you initiated it. Let's hear your thinking."

"Dao-ming Chou was briefly in Red," she replied. "From what I understand, we didn't expose her. She just disappeared one day. If she'd wanted to spy on us, she could have done it herself. From inside MI7, she could have turned agents in other organisations – the CIA, say, or the French DGSI - or even mined their secrets herself."

"Maybe she knew her fabricated background had a short shelf-life," Alec said.

"So what's your theory?" Annabel asked.

"He's got too much stake in his life here," Alec said. "Good job, one or two friends, big family. I just don't think he'd give all that up for an infatuation. That's what it would have to be if she was making him deceive his colleagues."

Annabel scoffed. "Any spy worth her salt knows from the outset that infatuation won't get her very far. If she's in to that sort of thing at all, she'll quickly supplement it with the security of blackmail. After which, there's no way back."

"Edna?" Ruby Parker asked.

"I think Mr Cunningham's right," Edna replied. "Even if it ended up in extortion, it would have to have *started* with infatuation, and Mr Mordred's very much into human rights, charity, kindness to animals and so on. Fifty years ago, you could get idealists onto the Communist bandwagon by talking about the class struggle and the deferred possibility of a just world, etcetera. But no one believes China's in the vanguard of anything like that, not nowadays. It strikes me as just too improbable that someone like Mr Mordred would start passing secrets to a regime that still reveres Chairman Mao – whatever the incentive. Added to which, he's a bit religious. I think."

Annabel nodded. She didn't reply.

"Ian?" Ruby Parker said.

"I'm not sure China's our enemy," Ian said. "Not in the old sense Russia was. It may want to know things about MI7, but cyber-spying's the thing nowadays. If Beijing wanted a mole, it would probably have chosen someone with better IT skills. I don't mean any disrespect to Mr Mordred, but I'd say his knowledge of computers is probably about average."

Ruby Parker put her fingertips together and looked at the table. "This is what we're going to do," she said eventually. "We're going to have to act quickly. Tonight, if possible. One of you needs to waylay John, take him out somewhere. I want the rest of you to search his flat. Leave no stone unturned – take up the carpet if possible. Annabel, you're in charge of the search. It won't be a burglary, because it's an MI7-approved property, and I have a key. I'm sure I don't need to tell you:

make sure you leave everything *exactly* as you found it. He's a trained spy, so keep that in mind at all times."

"Hairs across the door closures, as in *Dr No*," Ian said.

"I wouldn't put such a thing past him if he thinks Grey are after him," Annabel said. "Which he does. And given that, isn't it likely he'll have hidden or destroyed anything incriminating – assuming it exists?"

"We can only try," Ruby Parker said. "On the other hand, you might actually find something exonerating."

"Like what?" Alec said.

"He's John Mordred," Ruby Parker replied. "If I've learned anything about him, it's that he has an uncanny knack of surprising you. Now who's going to do the waylaying?"

Everyone in the room turned to look at Phyllis.

"I think that would be your job," Alec said.

"Remember Capri," Annabel said.

Phyllis rolled her eyes. "It's nothing to do with Capri," she said. "But yes, I'll do it. When he gets back from wherever he is, I'll look all cut up about us being taken off the Holland case. I won't have to act too hard, that's for sure. Somebody then needs to suggest to him that it might be kind to take me out somewhere expensive, help me get over it. *Because that's what boyfriends do, John.* He might not cotton on otherwise."

Annabel smirked. "So he's your boyfriend now?"

"You made this particular bed," Phyllis replied. "Now I've got to lie in it."

"I can think of worse beds," Annabel said.

Ruby Parker brought her hand down on the table just loud enough to make a noise. "That's enough. Sort the details out between yourselves. Keep me updated as regards developments. We'll talk again tomorrow morning."

Chapter 23: Alien-Possessed Phyllis

Mordred couldn't tell what it was, but there was something about the way they all looked at him when he came back from helping the police over the Chester hit-and-run that meant something wasn't quite right. They'd disappeared when he'd been most vulnerable, and now here they were again, but not quite who they'd been before. It felt like *Invasion of the Bodysnatchers.* Alec, Annabel, Phyllis, even Edna and Ian – *even* Ruby Parker for God's sake: they'd somehow exited the planet while he'd been out, and now alien creatures animated their bodies.

He noticed it first when he got to his desk. Phyllis was waiting for him. She was *furious*, apparently, that they'd been taken off the Frances Holland case. And for a few moments, he shared her anger. Until he saw it was bogus. Not entirely, but hidden so deep beneath something more important as to be worth discounting as the cause of her present frame of mind.

Then Alec: *she's upset, don't you think you'd better do something to cheer her up, maybe dinner ...* Like it was normal for Alec to start caring about people's feelings or offering dating advice. Where was *we're off the Holland case, so coming up to the canteen?* for example, or *now we don't have to worry about Frankie Holland any more, fancy celebrating?* said ironically with the overriding implication of alcohol?

And Edna and Ian, so quiet.

Only Annabel was normal, but that was because she was Annabel. She didn't do easy-to-read. Or even in-any-way-readable.

He might have put it down to nerves. He'd been in a pretty weird mood walking over to Mansion House. The twenty-minute long sensation of thinking a bullet might go through his brain at any moment had seen to that.

But then he'd been in to see Ruby Parker. He explained where he'd been, how the police had plied him with tea and questions, and how he hadn't been able to ring base. To give her credit, whatever alien was inhabiting her body, it must be a pretty top-notch one, because it alone seemed conscious he might suspect something was up. 'She' told him they were off the Holland case, and tried to put a mixture of indignation and resignation into her tone, but it fell flat.

By this time, he had a plan. He found Phyllis – two strides away from his desk, talking to Annabel and so suspiciously findable – and told her he'd like to take her out to dinner to cheer her up. Annabel moved off like the trap was sprung.

"Oh, that's really thoughtful of you!" alien-possessed Phyllis replied.

"I didn't think you'd say yes!" he replied.

"We did agree we'd go out before Capri. Just to prove I'm not trying to pull a fast one. I really do like you, John."

"Thank you, and I like you too. Are you sure you want to go out?"

"Absolutely."

"I thought you'd say, 'No, sod off, I just want to sit around in my pyjamas and mope'. I mean, that's what I'd do if my investigation had been stymied. And I'd try to think of ways I could re-open it."

She shrugged. "Maybe we could do that together. You're supposed to be the Saint Jude of failed investigations. Why don't you bring your pyjamas round to my place?"

Nice reply, but hang on, this was moving too fast for Phyllis. For a moment, he was wrong-footed.

"I'm offering *you* dinner," he said, to test the waters. "You should come to *my* place."

"I don't think that's a good idea," she replied. For some reason, the temperature had just dropped a notch. Suddenly, an idea occurred to him.

"How about *Burger King* at Waterloo station?" he asked as innocently as he could. "I really want to sample their vegetarian menu."

She smiled. Relief. "Okay!"

"I was only joking," he said. It felt cruel. Even an alien didn't deserve Waterloo *Burger King* as a first date. "I want it to be a surprise."

She put a hand on her extra-terrestrial-infested chest. "Phew!"

Right. Something was up. Phyllis + Burger King + Alec Being Nice + My Place But Not Yours + Annabel Exits Stage Left = ?

Phyllis was a decoy. For some reason, Annabel was about to burgle his flat.

They ended up at The Counting House, just because he couldn't think of anywhere else. Because he was still supposed to be living at Thames House, Amber gave him a suit, and he went straight from his desk at 8pm. It was packed as usual, but he'd rung ahead, and it was a weekday, so it felt fairly routine. He had potato gnocchi and she smoked haddock, and they drank wine and tried to make conversation.

But it was never easy, relaxing with someone who can't relax but pretends it's not an issue. Or relaxing when you know your flat's being burgled and the person sitting opposite you is in on it. For a while, he'd toyed with sneaking home and setting traps for the intruders – a *Dr No* hair or two – but decided against it. What was the point? He had nothing to hide. If they wanted to search his stuff, good luck to them. Maybe they could tidy up a bit while they were on.

Although, no: he did have things to hide. He hadn't been home for some time, and last time he had, he'd left in a hurry. He should probably have vacuumed, and the bathroom was in a bit of a state. And the kitchen: that teabag in the sink, and the stuff he should have put in the pedal-bin before setting out for work that morning.

Bloody hell. He had a lot to hide.

The thing is, normally she would have known he was distracted and called him out on it, but being a decoy means making yourself amenable, so she was being doubly alien. Even he was being alien now.

"How's the gnocchi?" she asked.

"Great. How's the haddock?"

"Lovely."

"That's good. How's the wine?"

"Very nice. How's yours?"

"Tasty."

End of conversation. On any other date, this would have set a big neon sign flashing, and it would have read INCOMPAT-IBLE. But there weren't any rules here. They could still be perfectly matched for all anyone knew.

"Do you know what I like about you, John?" she said suddenly.

"The way I'm house-proud."

"That, yes. But I mean, what else?"

"My curly blond hair."

"And the fact that your clothes always look freshly ironed."

That was another thing. He'd forgotten to put the ironing board away. Bloody hell, he couldn't even remember whether he'd unplugged the iron now. Fine meal this was turning out to be. Mind you, with a bit of luck, his flat might have burned down.

And that clump of hair in the bath.

"Thanks," he said.

Annabel unlocked the front door and entered quickly, looking at the door closure. She gestured Alec, Edna and Ian in and switched the lights on. They removed their shoes and coats and pulled on latex gloves.

"We've got two hours," Annabel said. "Phyllis is taking him back to her place afterwards, hopefully - although we can't count on it. She's convinced he suspects something, and I agree with her."

"What are we looking for?" Edna asked.

"You know the hypothesis," Annabel replied. "'This flat's occupant is working for the Chinese'. Anything of relevance, however tenuous. Now, John doesn't do online banking, so the first thing we need to do is find his bank statements. Absence of them would count as suspicious. Next, to access his home computer. We've got Tariq on duty back at base. He's going to discover John's password and check bank account details from John's statements. Direct debits, that kind of thing. Everything you find, report it to me. Be gentle. You've all got phones. Photos, if necessary, are good. Otherwise, use your initiative. Any questions?"

They all shook their heads.

"Let's go," she said.

"How's the gnocchi sauce?" Phyllis asked.

He'd had enough of this. "Fine. It's a kind of tomato creamy thing with spinach and mozzarella."

"I didn't ask *what* it was," she said tetchily. "I said, 'how'."

"And I said 'fine'."

"Look, what's wrong with you this evening, John? I thought we got on, but you're behaving very strangely."

"Well, so would you be."

She took an affected sip of her wine. "I'm afraid I don't follow."

"If Annabel was burgling your flat."

"Er ..."

"I built a webcam into the wall," he lied. "It transmits to my watch."

She looked at him. A mixture of embarrassment and fury. She didn't know which to give precedence to, because she didn't know whether he was bluffing. But then nature decided for her and she blushed.

"You're making that up," she said with only 95% conviction, and as if there was still hope for the charade.

"You do realise I'm an expert in reading people's faces? And good at detection. I've been sitting here all evening thinking, 'Maybe I should tell her I know'. But another part of me says, 'No, whatever it is they're after, it's probably for your own good, and - as Billy Joel says - you're an innocent man. Just do what she's doing: talk about your gnocchi and her haddock. Humour her.' But I don't want to humour you any more. Every time I do that, I'm patronising you. It doesn't feel right."

She sipped her wine again. "So you're confronting me because you respect me."

"Correct."

"I can live with that. It's rather flattering, actually. Now, before I ring Annabel and tell her the cat's out of the bag, a few questions."

"Fire away."

"Although since you're so clever, perhaps you can ask *yourself* those questions, *and* answer them, and I'll just sit here and listen and maybe take a few notes."

"I'm not that clever."

"So you don't know why we're burgling your flat?"

"No, but then I *would* say that. I'd have gone home before Annabel arrived, removed everything incriminating, and now I'd be sitting here, pretending I didn't know what it was about."

"*Do* you know what it's about?"

"No."

She sighed.

"But then, I would say that," he added. "Don't make that face. You brought this upon yourself."

"Sel*ves*. I'm not working alone."

"Who else? Although no, hang on, I *do* know that. Alec, Edna, Ian and Ruby Parker. And that's not a guess, before you ask."

"You can see them through your watch-thingy."

"That was just a lie. I made it up."

She sighed again and put her knife and fork together on the plate. "Okay, you win. Let's get down to business." She caught the waiter's eye. "Two more glasses of the house wine, please. Large."

"Ask me anything you like."

"Are you working for the Chinese?"

He laughed. "No."

They sat in silence looking at each other. Then it hit him. That wasn't a starter-question, a canard designed to disorient him so that when the real question came it would be like a punch out of the blue. No, it was *the* question.

"Bloody hell," he said incredulously.

"What?"

"You're serious."

"Deadly."

"Who says I'm working for the Chinese? Grey. It must be Grey. It can only be Grey, right?"

"It's Grey. I'm not even sure I should have told you that."

"So let me see ... They must have told you this sometime between me setting off for Mansion House, and me getting back to Thames House. But they can't be sure, otherwise they'd simply have presented Ruby Parker with the evidence. I'd be out on my ear, and possibly in the clink. So they don't *know*. Which of course they can't."

"All spot-on so far. With the possible exception of the final sentence."

"Now they wouldn't have told you unless they had to, because that's not Grey's style. So you must have somehow compelled them. In some way, their suspicions leaked out against their will, and they decided the only way they could limit the damage was by admitting you to their confidence but swearing you to secrecy. And we've all been removed from the Holland case as a way of reducing my sphere of influence."

"Keep going. I'll tell you when you're getting cold."

"Now Grey wouldn't have asked you to investigate me. They wouldn't have hauled us off the Holland case if they thought we could work together. So the only reason Annabel's round at my flat is because you want to find out for yourselves."

Their wine arrived. They cheers-ed each other.

"Has it occurred to you," he asked, "that if there was any burgling to be done, Grey would probably have done it long ago? If there was anything to find, they'd have found it?"

"A flat's a dynamic entity," she replied. "New things arrive every day. Besides, you might know they'd been round. You might even have been expecting them in advance. Now they've gone, you might not be anticipating another visit."

"Expecting burglars is part of being in MI7. Every time I leave home, I hang up my stocking and put out a carrot for Rudolph."

"Don't joke, John."

"Now my questions. One: what makes them think I'm working for the Chinese? I assume you compelling them means you at least got to the bottom of that."

"We don't know precisely. We know their theory. We don't know how much evidence they've got to substantiate it."

"They can't have much. What's their theory then?"

"Dao-ming Chou, who we met in Siberia, is a Chinese agent. She lured you into a honey-trap, and you're still in there."

"It was Ruby Parker who told me she works for Black."

"According to Grey, her real name is Wan Chunmei. And Ruby Parker admits that everything she once thought she knew about her turned out to be fabricated."

"What sort of secrets would I be giving her? As far as I know, the Chinese want technological secrets, especially military ones. The US C-17, the Black Hawk, the Humvee. Their espionage tends to be of the good old industrial variety. Seriously, what could I give them?"

"I don't know."

"Think about it. Think of the great British moles."

"Donald Maclean," she said.

"Kept the Russians informed about US energy policy. Helped them rate the relative strength of their nuclear arsenals. I couldn't do anything remotely resembling that."

"Guy Burgess."

"The Marshall Plan negotiations. Kim Philby: details of Anglo-American cooperation. And Anthony Blunt passed secrets the British had decrypted from the Germans during World War 2. And now, John Mordred, the sixth man. What does he pass?"

Phyllis sat for a while. The waiter took their plates away. She slowly sipped her wine. Eventually, she met his eyes.

"You're right," she said. "It makes no sense whatsoever." She took her phone out.

"What are you doing?" he asked.

"What do you think? Ringing Annabel. I'm going to put it on speakerphone."

It rang for a few seconds.

"Hi, I - "

"Phyllis," Annabel interrupted. "I was just about to ring you. John's in the clear. Bloody hell, all these different direct debits he's got. Greenpeace, Amnesty International, Reporters Without Borders, Shelter, PETA, Oxfam, MSF, the RSPCA ... Anyway, it turns out he made two fairly big donations to Falun Gong last year. You know, the Chinese meditation and exercise cult? Weird, but he is a bit weird. Anyway, everyone agrees that Beijing regards Falun Gong as enemies of the state. The consensus over here is that he couldn't be both passing secrets to the MSS and cash to its enemies unless he was clinically insane."

Mordred took the phone. "I did it because I felt sorry for them."

Silence. Annabel was obviously re-adjusting. She must be pretty rattled, because the process wasn't usually lengthy enough to register as an audible pause.

"John," she said calmly, as if it was the nicest surprise in the world. "Apologies for referring to you as 'a bit weird'."

Chapter 24: Spies Within Spydom

Edna, Ian and Alec sat on Mordred's sofa watching *Avengers Assemble*, each with what looked like a burger on a plate. They looked up briefly to greet him. Alec wolf-whistled at Phyllis, said, "Look at you!", then Edna said, "Oh, I love this bit", and they went back to eating and watching the film.

"Where's Annabel?" Phyllis asked.

"Kitchen," Alec said. "And before you start, I didn't lock her in there. She likes to cook on burglaries, everyone knows that." He turned to Mordred. "And before you start accusing us of pinching your stuff, Ian went to the shops."

"It's a burglary," Mordred replied drily. "Why would I think you were stealing?"

Alec rolled his eyes. "It was in a good cause, and we did agree we'd wait till you got back to start drinking. Pass me a beer, Ian, there's a good man."

"Speckled Hen?" Ian asked. "Or Hobgoblin?"

"What's the difference?" Alec said.

Annabel came out of the kitchen with a veggie burger on a plate. She gave it to Mordred as if he'd ordered it when the shop was just about to close, then talked to Phyllis. The two women drifted to the far side of the room for what was clearly a top-secret conference to which he wasn't invited. On the near side, the only other occupants watched Marvel superheroes. Mordred stood alone and ate his burger. He was already full of gnocchi, but it seemed only polite. Times like this, he wished he had a dog.

"I might go to bed," he announced when he'd finished eating.

Everyone stopped what they were doing and turned to face him. Alec put the TV on mute. "Excuse me?" he said, as if it was Mordred's fault they were all here, and given how much he'd inconvenienced everyone, the least he could do was stand in complete solitude without complaining.

"I mean, now everyone's satisfied I'm innocent," Mordred added.

"We need to decide what to do next," Annabel said. "Nobody's going to bed yet."

"Presumably, any decision is Ruby Parker's department," he replied.

Annabel shrugged. "I've been in contact with her. As long as she's satisfied you're innocent – which she now is – she's happy for matters to take their course. She has no personal investment in the Frances Holland case. The way MI7 works, Grey has precedence over Red, orders are orders, and Red's been ordered by Grey to stand down. It's virtually a syllogism with one conclusion: all our hard work over the past few weeks has been wasted."

"Hey, that's intelligence," Alec said. "And police work. In fact any kind of investigation that isn't a *this time it's personal* cliché. John's innocent, that's all that matters."

"What do you think, John?" Phyllis asked.

He smiled. "I think you and I should pretend to toe the line, but maybe take a bit of 'leave' with immediate effect to go and see Annabel's place in Capri."

"It would be a very good time to put in for time off," Annabel replied. "Old investigation killed, no new one on the immediate horizon, you might get a few days. And of course, the weekend's coming up."

"And under cover of taking leave," Mordred went on, "I think we should continue the Holland investigation."

Alec sighed. "*John Mordred: this time it's personal.*"

"Has it occurred to you that Grey is trying to frame me?" Mordred replied. "Before you answer, consider the following. They can't *know* I'm communicating secrets to Dao-ming Chou, obviously, but I don't see what grounds they can even have for suspicion. When Ruby Parker first informed me I was going for a radicalisation interview, she said it was – quote – a 'thinly disguised attack on her department', and actually nothing to do with me. Then you, Alec, said Grey is always looking to take over the whole of MI7. Now you've burgled my flat and reassured yourselves I'm a nice guy, you're all happy. You've lost the wood in the trees, if you ask me. If I'm framed, you might be next."

"Hang on, John," Annabel said. "I was the one who just stopped you going to bed. Going to bed's essentially giving in."

"Apologies," Mordred said.

"So you and Phyllis are going to continue the Holland investigation?" Alec asked. "How does Phyllis feel about that?"

"She's right behind it," Phyllis said.

"And what are the rest of us going to be doing?" Alec went on.

"Covering for us two," Mordred told him. "Stop news of our real activities reaching Ruby Parker. As far as a lot of people connected with the Holland case are probably still concerned, Red's their first port of call for new information. Grey will gradually work to change that, but the transition may not be complete for a few days. Meanwhile, anything that comes in, you pass it straight to Phyllis or me, and if possible delay it getting to Ruby Parker or Grey."

"That would probably be Tariq's department," Annabel said.

"Interpol should be about to report back regarding Durand," Mordred went on. "It's crucial that we're in on that, and that we get to pick over whatever they've discovered before Grey gets a look in."

"If you go to see Interpol," Edna said, "how are you going to stop Grey finding out? They're going to know, then they're going to tell Ruby Parker."

"After which, you'll be in deep shit," Alec added. "I'm not saying I won't help. I'm just saying let's go into this with our eyes open. An unauthorised meeting with Interpol's going to be pretty tough to explain anyway, especially so when you're meant to be in Capri. And it would also mean Tariq ends up in trouble."

"Alec's right," Annabel said.

"So we've got to find some way of making it look like the there's been a breach of security and I'm the sole culprit," Mordred said.

Phyllis sighed. "Maybe we should cross that bridge when we come to it."

"The likelihood is I'll be found out anyway," Mordred went on. "True, I'm not prepared to stand round waiting for Grey to drop the axe, but frankly, I'd rather not take you down with me. I should do this on my own. Forget Capri. I'll put in for leave to go and see my parents."

"The Holland case is mine," Phyllis said. "No *way* are you doing this on your own."

"I'll talk to Tariq," Annabel said. "He could say you ordered him to send you any information from Interpol direct. That would put a bit of a firewall round him. He'd be gullible rather than dishonest."

"I think you're forgetting something," Ian said. "If Grey wants rid of Mr Mordred and they find out he's gone to Interpol, then bang goes their little *we'll leave him alone if you keep him out of it* agreement. They won't complain to Ruby Parker, they'll just come after him with a gun."

"In many ways, I'd prefer that," Mordred said.

They looked at each other. Suddenly, it seemed that everything worth saying had been said.

"John's made a decision," Alec said. "I propose we support him, but keep in touch, keep the whole thing under review. I also propose we call this meeting to an end. We've made a decision of sorts. We need to sleep on it."

Mordred saw everyone out like it was a dinner party that had gone on too long. Phyllis waited till everyone had gone and kissed him hard on the lips. "Go and see Ruby Parker first thing when you get in tomorrow," she said, "and ask for leave for both of us. Tell her you need a rest. Tell her you feel conscience-bound to absent yourself for a spell, to give Grey free rein for their investigation. Tell her about Capri. Tell her you're hoping to surprise me by proposing a preliminary visit. Tell her you've cleared it with Annabel. Tell her you'll be back in good time for any second interview. Make her feel very, *very* guilty for doubting you. Find me as soon as you're done."

After they'd left, Mordred went to bed, but couldn't sleep. He wasn't entirely surprised. When your mind raced, you became exhausted, but its racing had an independent impetus. It wouldn't apply the brakes while it was busy pressing the accelerator, no matter how much you might need it to.

The last time he'd been in this position, it was because some insight had lain just out of sight of his consciousness. He had the feeling it was the same now.

Why *had* they run the Lord Mayor down today? Who were 'they', anyway? Grey?

There'd been plenty of time to ponder all this at the police station, and he'd used it pretty fully, but hadn't emerged any the wiser. Since then, things had moved on so fast, he'd lost interest. Probably impossible to answer right now. Something would happen, soon maybe, and he'd know. But it hadn't happened yet. That wasn't what was troubling him.

He got up, just like last time, and made himself a coffee. He wandered through the flat looking for things that might jog his memory, set a train of thought going. He switched the TV on and watched the news on mute. That sometimes did it. He yawned repeatedly. 4am. His mind kept galloping.

Then it hit him. He went into his bedroom and opened his wardrobe door. He got down on his knees, pushed the bottoms of the shirts and jackets out of the way, and groped beneath the linen pile of old sweatshirts.

And there it was. His precious collection of *Private Eye* back-issues.

Chapter 25: HP Sauce

Mordred dressed in an oxford shirt and new sweater with brown cords and brogues and brought his passport and driving licence into work, plus a few other essentials. He left his phone with Annabel and bought a pay-as-you go in Vauxhall Bridge Road. After a quick, matter-of-fact interview with Ruby Parker, he left the building to buy flowers, then went straight to Phyllis's desk to give her his new number and break the good news.

"She gave us seven days," he said.

"A *week*? Oh, wow."

"Seems very reasonable to me. You can't just jet into Capri then jet out again. Consider the jet lag."

"Either way, it's wonderful."

"When would you like to fly?"

"Asap. Tomorrow. Tonight, even, if there's a flight. Not budget, mind: I'm one of those people who does meaningful luggage."

"*Compos mentis*, I think they're called. I'll call you as soon as I've reserved two seats. You see Annabel, get the address and the key."

"Will do. And, John?"

"Yes?"

"Thank you - for the flowers as well."

She actually did look very grateful. So much so that, as he walked away, he wondered whether something had failed to get through. Crossed wires? Maybe she genuinely believed they were going to Capri, not just trailing round town after Planchart's buddies and waiting for Interpol to call.

No, that wouldn't make sense. She was good, that's all.

He left Thames House by the main entrance and noticed he was being followed by man of about thirty in a business suit and sunglasses. He turned left onto Horseferry Road, then right onto Marsham Street. There were two of them now, taking it in turns. On Great Saint Peter Street, he got into a taxi. He saw both men do the same behind him, climbing into a single cab one after the other.

"Charing Cross Station, please," he told the driver.

Since the invention of smartphones, it had become much easier to evade a tail. You Googled whatever train was just leaving and hopped out of your taxi with no time to spare. If your pursuers were anything more than ten seconds behind, they wouldn't stand a chance. And you'd alight at the first stop and come straight back by another means. Taxi was preferable, but expensive. Bus was next best.

He asked the tax-driver the fare while they were slowing and added a tip. He jumped out as soon as they pulled up, then ran through the station and got on the train to Hastings.

When his two pursuers arrived at a brisk walk, he was already on his way. He watched them through the rain-smeared window as they disappeared into the distance.

Or rather, as he did.

Two hours later he was back in London. He got off the bus in Oxford Street, drew a thousand pounds out of his bank account and walked one and a half miles to the House of Commons central lobby. It was just gone lunchtime now, and he hoped to catch his quarry in the same manner he'd caught Ashbaugh. As always on these sorts of occasions, he had a picture in his pocket to aid the identification.

And here he came. Sauntering from the Westminster Hall side in conversation with a woman of about his age. Obviously colleagues they looked to be in their late fifties. Arguing, but in a civilised way. Suddenly, their attitude changed. They smiled at each other, hugged, and parted. Mordred's cue.

"Mr Hignett? Mike Hignett?"

As before, with Ashbaugh, the little twitch of the right hand: an instinctive need to shake hands restrained by the split-second-later onset of suspicion. Hignett was a tall thin man with grey hair, black plastic-framed glasses and a bulbous nose. He wore a light grey suit.

"I'm not a constituent," Mordred said as quietly as he could. "I'm a police officer. Jonas Eagleton, DI. I met with Bill Ashbaugh about a week ago. I'm here to talk to you about what could be a sensitive matter."

He took a square of paper from his pocket and handed it over. Hignett unfolded it and turned pale. The front cover of that fortnight's *Private Eye*.

"I'm not here to embarrass you," Mordred said, "much less to expose you to your colleagues. Should we find somewhere private to talk?"

"My office," Hignett said, the way a headmaster might.

Much better than Mordred had expected. Much better, for example, than Hignett asking to see his ID: because that was at Thames House. An appeal to Ashbaugh had been the contingency plan in that eventuality. But he'd calculated a simple mention of *Private Eye* would suffice to break down all barriers. And it had. Never underestimate the power of a nasty shock to open doors.

Hignett's office was upstairs and just along the corridor from Ashbaugh's. Small but tidy. The usual desk, PC, phone, bookcase, magazine rack, desk lamp and filing cabinet.

"Sit down," Hignett said, gesturing to a chair. He went to sit behind his desk and folded his hands. "What do you want? Be quick, if possible. I was on my way somewhere."

"I'm investigating the death of Frances Holland."

"And?"

"Apparently, she used to be a source for *Private Eye*."

"I won't pretend I didn't know. But we didn't collaborate, if that's what you think. I never even met her to talk to. How did you find out? No, wait a minute, that's the wrong question. What I really want to know is how did you find out about *me*?"

"I'm a subscriber. I went through my past copies and referenced events reported, on the one hand, to MPs on the other. A simple process of elimination. In the end, you were the only possibility."

"Why should I believe you?"

"I'm not sure what choice - "

"What's *Private Eye*'s press section called?"

"Street of Shame."

"Politics?"

"HP Sauce."

"Television?"

"TV Eye."

"The pseudonym of its literary reviewer."

"Bookworm."

Hignett nodded. "Okay, I believe you. Provisionally. What do you want to know?"

"One of our sources made a claim you may be able to cast light on. He said Frances Holland regularly passed information to *Private Eye* about the shenanigans of The Get Out Clause. Most of it made it into print, with the exception of one item. Whatever it was, it was considered outrageous enough for the editors to pass to the police."

"The police, yes. Which raises the question, why don't *you* know what it was?"

"I'm investigating the possibility that there was a cover-up."

"Within the ranks of the Met? That would be a very, very serious matter. It would also mean there was some truth in Frances Holland's 'information'."

"Not necessarily. Someone might have been trying to protect her reputation, or that of The Get Out Clause."

"True, so whichever policeperson it was had a sly chuckle and binned it. That's not a cover-up. Let's get to the point, shall we? I take it you want to know *what* this information is – or was. I'll tell you. It was a 'plan' by The Get Out Clause to blow up the Channel Tunnel after the EU referendum. A completely ludicrous attempt to pull the wool over the eyes of the good folk at *Private Eye*. Apart from anything else, the Channel tunnel's been built to withstand an earthquake. A terrorist bomb might well kill a lot of people but it wouldn't compromise the structural integrity of the passageway. *Private Eye* knows that. The editors thought – probably justifiably, I have to say - she was trying to take them for a ride. A few tasty tidbits of information, and ultimately for what? In order to sneak the Big Fabrication in, that's what. The Big Fabrication goes into print, someone sues, someone wins, Lord Gnome gets egg all over his face. Mission accomplished. The only problem is, it was painfully transparent."

"But not *too* painfully transparent?"

"Don't assume your average Tory has any sense of what counts as plausible in the real world, DI Eagleton."

Mordred wrote his phone number down on a slip of paper and stood up. "As far as I can tell, you've answered all my questions. Thank you very much for seeing me, Mr Hignett. If you think of anything else, give me a call. I'll show myself out."

Two hours later, he ascended a set of concrete steps to the second floor of a multi-storey car park in Hackney. Outside, high rises, tenement blocks, busy roads and patches of grassland. The sky was grey. Phyllis sat where she said she'd be, in the driver's seat of a blue 4-door Ford, checking her phone. He went over and tapped on the window.

"Rear door's unlocked," she said in a bored tone without looking up.

She didn't look anything like Phyllis. She wore no make-up, she had her hair tied on top of her head and she was dressed in the sort of clothes she'd never normally be seen dead in: trainers, black cotton leggings, a T-shirt with 'Obey' written on, and a pale blue hoodie top.

He got in the back, as instructed. "Absolutely sure you weren't followed?" she asked.

"Absolutely," he replied. "But don't forget, Grey's probably got access to the nation's CCTV network."

"Better keep your head down then. There's a blanket and something of a disguise in the back."

He lay down on the back seat and pulled the blanket over his head and upper half. She started the car and left the car park at a leisurely speed. She put the radio on. *The Archers*. The upholstery smelt of dogs.

They drove for about half an hour, during which he changed awkwardly into the disguise. Baseball cap, glasses, trainers, jeans and a leather jacket. She made no attempt to converse. Eventually, he felt the car decelerate and stop.

"You can sit up now," she said. "Get out quickly, come round the back and help me out with the shopping like we've lived here all our lives."

They were in a long street with six-floor blocks of flats on either side. Young, evenly spaced trees stood in a wide band of uniform grass that went all the way round the buildings. The window frames were white plastic, the brick a kind of off-pink and the front doors bulky and functional. Wide pavements ran either side of the road, and a small parade of shops stood at the northern end.

Five carrier bags. They removed them from the boot and went in through the entrance nearest their car. Up three flights of steps, along a corridor and in through a solid-looking brown front door. Phyllis led the way into a dimly-lit kitchen and dumped her bags on the table. He followed suit.

"Welcome to Capri," she said. "I'll put the kettle on. You put the stuff away in the cupboards."

Cans of beans, a loaf of bread, soap, shampoo, disinfectant, washing-up liquid, instant coffee, teabags, soup, a packet of disposable razors, bathroom odour-eliminator.

"I was going to buy bedding," she said, "but it may not be necessary. Interpol's been on the phone."

He stopped what he was doing. "And …?"

"We're going to meet them. Tariq sent the message straight to your phone, and Annabel passed it to me."

His mobile rang. *Unknown number*: could be anyone. He pressed answer. "Hello?"

"DI Eagleton, I presume."

Bloody hell, Hignett. What did he want? Surely his cover wasn't *already* blown?

"Speaking," Mordred said.

"I've been on the blower to my overlords at *Private Eye*. It seems I may have given you a merely partial account of the truth. Probably doesn't change anything, but it turns out Holland believed there was a plot to *demolish* the channel tunnel after the referendum. 'Demolish' may not have meant an explosion, not in the first instance. Possibly it meant dismantle, by any means possible, initially by attacking Eurotunnel shares on the stock exchange."

"I see."

"Still highly implausible, though. Doesn't change anything, in my view."

"Thank you for getting back in touch."

"I like to think of myself as a conscientious citizen, Detective Inspector. Good day." He hung up.

"Who was that?" Phyllis asked.

"Mike Hignett, MP. It's a long story. Last night I trawled through my *Private Eyes* - "

"Bloody hell. You're one of those nerds who collects back issues?"

"I don't collect them. I hang on to them. It's different. I've got a notebook. Occasionally, I jot - "

"Yes, get the picture. Carry on."

"I worked out that Hignett's one of *Eye*'s spies. I went to ask him what this piece of evidence was that Holland passed to them that they gave to the police."

"And?"

"It was a report – presumably fairly vague, otherwise they'd have sat up – that The Get Out Clause was planning to demolish the Channel tunnel after the referendum."

She shrugged. "Sounds pretty plausible to me."

"How so?"

"Everyone knows Planchart's using TGOC as a lever to filch the PM's job. If that works, as it may, he'd have the power to do whatever he wants."

"Probably too speculative for *Private Eye*, though. And us."

"Unless 'after the referendum' means 'in any event', 'whatever happens'. A modern-day Gunpowder Plot."

"Except that everyone agrees the Channel Tunnel's unblow-up-able."

"Who agrees that?"

"Everyone. I haven't time to name them. Wikipedia."

"Wow," she said drily.

"Look it up on your phone. Google 'Can the Channel Tunnel be blown up?' That's what I did. I didn't just take Hignett's word for it. Look, forget about whether it's plausible for a moment. Even if it is, what are we going to do? We can't just go to Planchart and present him with a 'you've been rumbled' card."

"At least we'll know where to look."

"White department are continually on the hunt for people making bombs. That's pretty much all they do. If they haven't found anything, we've no chance."

"Maybe they're looking in the wrong place. At Islamic extremists rather than Tory politicians."

"I don't think that's how they work. Besides, Planchart wouldn't make a bomb himself. He'd get someone to do it for him. And that's where they *would* be looking."

She sighed. "Now you've just said that, I've realised how very implausible it is."

"Where does Interpol want to meet?"

"France."

"France?"

"Our suggestion. Yours, officially: Annabel and Tariq using your phone to impersonate you. We didn't want them coming over here. All the palaver of an official visit: introductions, tea and cakes, hotel rooms, etcetera? Too risky."

"Which part of France?"

"Calais. We can be there in no time, long before our appointment. Look, stop fretting. I was an MI7 officer long before you were. I know the ropes. And before you ask why we came back here, I signed the tenancy contract before Interpol rang. And after I picked you up, I had to drive round a bit to make sure we weren't being followed. And now I'm going to look outside to see what I can see in the way of suspicious characters." She looked. "No one. Happy?"

"Do you want to drive, or shall I?"

"I'm hungry, and I'm guessing you probably are. It's dangerous to drive on an empty stomach, so make me something to eat and use that kettle to make me some tea, and if I'm happy, I might let you drive the first fifty miles while I take a nap. You've got fifteen minutes."

Chapter 26: Yves Robillard the Slightly Annoying

They arrived in Calais at 6.30 that evening for an interview at eight, parking the car on a city centre street overlooked by the square tower of the Église Notre-Dame. Phyllis was keen to eat at a restaurant, but they spent forty minutes looking in shops in the Place d'Armes, and eventually settled for two cartons of chips from a street-corner *friterie*. Then they sat in the square, people-watching. Mordred put his arm round her. They were supposed to be going to Capri together, after all: hardly a liberty to get some basic intimacy going. She put her head on his shoulder. "I feel like an utter tramp," she said.

At 7.55, they walked to the Commissariat de Police on the Place de Lorraine and announced themselves at reception. Phyllis had brought ID, and a *femme officier* took then to an interview room on the second floor where she introduced them to their Interpol liaison. Yves Robillard was a small, thin man of about forty in a maroon jacket, grey trousers and bow tie. They exchanged names and job titles. He appraised their appearance, made a distasteful face and shook hands with them, releasing a waft of expensive perfume. "I take it you're working undercover," he said in French with a strong Lyon accent.

"No, we always dress like this," Phyllis replied.

Mordred looked at her. Then at him. Mutual contempt at first sight if he'd ever seen it. He'd have to be at his diplomatic best here.

They sat down.

"I understand you've found Pierre Durand," Mordred said.

"Not *found* him, Monsieur, no," Robillard replied. "I thought I was clear about that in my communiqué."

"My mistake," Mordred replied, trying to smooth the waters. "I apologise. We came out here in a hurry. We're anxious to get to the bottom of it, as I'm sure you understand."

"It seems an odd detail to overlook," the Frenchman went on. "If you imagine we have him in custody, presumably you're expecting to take him away. I'm afraid - "

"Monsieur Mordred is here as my assistant," Phyllis said brusquely. "I'm afraid I haven't familiarised him with all the details. He tends to start speaking first because he's a man and you're a man, and he thinks you'll be on the same wavelength."

Robillard looked at her as if he thought it was an insane explanation, which maybe it was.

"He's also rather tired," Phyllis said. "I won't go into the details. Please tell us what you know about Pierre Durand, Monsieur Robillard. We'd like to get back to London."

"Not that we don't love France," Mordred added. "And apologies for our clothes. We meant no disrespect. You're right, we've been working undercover."

"Sorry I was sarcastic," Phyllis said. "We got off on the wrong footing earlier. Let's begin again – please."

Danger. Robillard didn't know whether they were making fun of him. The thing to do now was maintain eye-contact without smiling. Luckily, Phyllis had recognised the hazard at the same time as him. Both their pairs of eyes bored into Robillard's. Suddenly, he looked slightly afraid.

"Until three weeks ago," he said, obviously anxious now to get it over with, "Monsieur Durand was working for a freight company called *Godolphine*, a subsidiary of Eurotunnel. We have no reason to think his business there was in any way connected to any of the previous activities for which the British secret service flagged him up. Officially, he worked in the clerical department, but, given his background, and our discoveries, we think he was probably engaged in industrial espionage."

"So working against Eurotunnel?" Phyllis asked.

"Against *Godolphine*, Mademoiselle," Robillard said as if it ought to be too obvious to state. "Likely he was employed by a rival freight company. Whichever it was, it wouldn't have been looking to undermine Eurotunnel. Rather, for ways to undermine *Godolphine*'s relationship with it and replace them as contactors."

"The only reason I ask," Phyllis persisted, "is because in Britain, we were given evidence to suggest a plot to 'demolish' – and we're not entirely sure what that word means in this context - the Channel tunnel."

Robillard looked thunderstruck. He removed his hands from the table, put them on his thighs and leaned back. "That is the first I have heard of it!"

"We've only just found out," Mordred said. "We thought you might as well get it from the horse's mouth."

"And you two are the horses, yes?"

"We discounted it," Phyllis said, "for a million reasons I can't go into here. Apparently it's impossible to demolish the Channel tunnel anyway. We had reasons to think it was false information intentionally designed to mislead us."

"Mislead you about what?" Robillard asked.

"Islamic extremists," Mordred said, before Phyllis could speak.

Robillard chuckled. He put his hand back on the table. "ISIS? With respect, Monsieur, Pierre Durand may have done some bad things, but he's hardly a genocidal monster."

"I only mention it to explain why my colleague raised the possibility of Durand working against Eurotunnel," Mordred said. "She was merely thinking aloud."

Robillard sighed. "He *could* have been spying on Eurotunnel. I do not want to go on record as having ruled it out as impossible. The police obtained a warrant to search the relevant premises and also interviewed senior *Godolphine* executives, but they came across no evidence of Islamic extremism. I will pass your concerns on, though."

"You talked earlier of your 'discoveries' regarding Monsieur Durand?" Phyllis asked.

"Ah, the *piece de resistance*," Robillard said, as if this was what he'd been waiting for all along, and if only they'd asked him about it to start with, instead of talking about horses and ISIS, he'd have been much more amenable. "We do know he was in regular contact with some very important people across the continent, and in Britain."

"In what capacity?" Phyllis asked.

"Taking delivery of consignments of 'equipment'," Robillard said. "Some, but not all of it, bound for Britain."

"You mean – guns?" Mordred asked.

"Not that we've so far been able to discover," Robillard said. "Transporting large quantities of firearms across France and through the tunnel would be exceptionally difficult. No, we were only able to intercept one consignment of said 'equipment', and that only because it was somewhat late and bound specifically for Calais with no instructions to transfer it to the United Kingdom."

"And?" Phyllis said.

"Second-hand clothes."

Phyllis and Mordred exchanged quizzical looks.

Did you just say, 'second-hand clothes'? Mordred asked Robillard.

Robillard looked icily at them without speaking. Written on his face were the words: "I won't repeat myself for a couple of imbeciles."

"And these … clothes were actually meant for Calais?" Mordred asked. "With no instructions to transport them elsewhere?"

Robillard nodded. But just once, and obviously as a concession to politeness. "We will, of course, inform you if there are any other developments," he said. "I apologise if you feel you've had a wasted journey, but I did, after all, offer to come to England."

There was a knock at the door. Without waiting to be invited in, the same *femme officier* who had conducted them here entered hurriedly carrying a piece of paper which she handed to Robillard. She didn't wait for his reaction but exited in the same rushed manner.

Mordred saw the Interpol officer's features change, and knew at once what it was. A dispatch from Grey. Somehow, they'd found out what was going on.

The likely course of events during the last five minutes flashed before his eyes at the speed of light. An urgent fax from Thames House had arrived downstairs. It identified Mordred and Phyllis as impostors and carried instructions to the *Gendarmerie* to desist from all further communication with them. The *femme officier* had taken it to her superior. He or she had sent the same *femme officier* to inform Robillard while he or she – the superior - buttonholed a couple of officers to make the arrest. Depending on how many officers were on duty at this time of night, and how quiet the city was, he and Phyllis had between ten and thirty seconds to get away. Added to which a personal visit from Grey might already be imminent: presumably they had access to that seven-seat helicopter, among other things.

He grabbed Phyllis's arm and stood up, raising her with him, to her surprise. "Er – *John?*" she exclaimed.

"We've got to get out of here. Grey."

"Just wait a minute, Monsieur!" Robillard said angrily.

They left the room, turned left and walked briskly along an empty corridor. From in front, they heard footsteps ascending a staircase. They turned around and went the other way. Hopeless. The only one thing to do in a situation like this was make straight for the exit and try to plough your way out by brute force.

But that wouldn't work. One person might make it, by a miracle. Two, never.

There were stairs at this end of the corridor. They pushed through a set of double doors, but personnel were coming at them from downstairs here as well. They were surrounded. Might as well surrender. Although …

Tariq would know what had happened. He was monitoring unusual signals sent from Grey. If that was what this was …

"Upstairs!" Phyllis said. She grabbed his hand, and tried to pull him. He stood his ground and she almost lost her footing as her attempt to drag him failed.

"What's the point?" he said.

"Where there's life there's hope! We can get onto the roof!"

"And *then* what?"

"Bloody hell, John, *both our jobs are on the line!*"

"Walk downstairs, like we're leaving."

"*What?*"

He grabbed both her arms and looked into her eyes. "Keep calm," he said, "and trust in Tariq."

She seemed to grasp his meaning. She closed her eyes and frowned and swallowed. They walked downstairs and into what looked like a veritable rugby team of *Gendarmes*, none of whom looked like they were susceptible to being ploughed through. At their head, stood a uniformed woman with short hair and a supercilious expression. The 'superior' in his fleeting vision of unfolding events.

"Maybe you can explain why you're in such a hurry," she said.

"We're on our way home," Mordred said calmly. "What seems to be the problem?"

She smiled. "You're not going anywhere. Not yet, anyway. Maybe never."

Silence. Everyone waited to see what *bon mot* the British couple would come up with. Mordred put on his best perplexed expression.

Suddenly, the *femme officier* appeared with a new piece of paper. She pushed through the French rugby scrum looking unhappy, and passed it to her superior. The superior read it with obvious fascination then made a perplexed expression every bit as impressive as Mordred's, the difference being that hers was presumably genuine.

"I don't understand," she said quietly, as if to herself.

"If it's what I think it is," Mordred announced, with confident authority, "it's happened before, and I can only apologise on behalf of the British secret service. I suspected the old problem might have recurred when I saw Monsieur Robillard's expression change in our interview, and I signalled to my colleague that it might be best for us to leave. Last time it happened, a few months ago in Amsterdam, we weren't released from the police station for a full six hours. It's a countermand, of course, and it comes as a consequence of the layer on layer of security we have to have nowadays. My colleague and I will give you our passports and you can confirm our identities with the *Direction générale de la sécurité intérieure* in Paris. They have our details on file. Again, my apologies. I realise it makes us British look thoroughly amateurish, so I'm embarrassed as much as frustrated. I only hope you can improve on the six hours of the Dutch, though obviously I realise we have no right to expect anything whatsoever. For the remaining duration of our stay here, we're completely in your hands, and we'll try not to get in the way."

The superior looked at him and her attitude softened. "If it's a simple matter of a phone call to Paris, Monsieur, I think we can improve on six hours. Meanwhile, perhaps you'd like tea."

He smiled. "That would be wonderful. Thank you so much."

Two hours later, they were released. Not a moment too soon. As they walked away, an English car pulled up in front of the police station and four men got out, one of whom Mordred recognised as Shafiq Effanga. He and Phyllis stepped up their pace, got into their car and drove south, since they reasoned that was the opposite direction to which their pursuers – they almost certainly had pursuers now – would expect them to go. Phyllis drove. When they were passing through Inghem, Alec called Mordred's phone.

"Just checking you're okay," he said.

"Dandy, thank you."

"I take it Tariq's message got through. We've just had new information. Remember you said we should send someone to Skye to interview doctors' receptionists. Turns out to have been a good idea. It was just as you said. Frances Holland walked into Dunvegan health centre in the north of the island, looking 'extremely distressed' and seeking anti-depressive medication. She left before she could be properly dealt with."

Mordred nodded. "So we've got the 'how' of the murder. Just like Talbot claimed, she's put in a position where the likelihood of her taking her own life increases to a significant level, and she's given enough time for the statistical probability to work itself out."

"Looks that way. Now we just need the why."

"Tell Tariq I'd send him another emoticon, but this phone doesn't do them."

"When are you coming home?"

"We're being chased south by Grey at the moment, and probably the French police."

"Had sex with Phyllis yet?"

"What the hell's that got to do with anything? Aren't you worried about us?"

"Yes or no?"

"No. It's not high on my list of priorities. Or hers. We're being chased by men with guns. Doesn't that mean anything to you?"

"It's what you signed up for, so count yourself lucky. Or would you rather be reading junior agents' reports? Look, we're doing what we can, John. We're all sticking our necks out for you here. Let's not get too po-faced. Keep calm and be professional."

He nodded and sighed. It was Alec who'd trained him after all. "Understood."

"Good man. Stay safe."

"News?" Phyllis said, when he'd hung up.

"Frances Holland tried to get anti-depressants in Skye. She was turned away."

They drove along in silence for five minutes into the deep countryside. The road grew narrower and the lights fewer until all they could see anywhere were their own headlights and the vague outlines of trees in the middle distance. Mordred couldn't tell what was going on, but something about Phyllis had changed. She was ruminating urgently on something. He couldn't tell what, but an unreadable emotion kept flashing across her face.

After a few minutes fruitlessly trying to divine her, he gave up and considered Pierre Durand.

"What are you thinking about, John?" she asked.

"Those clothes in Calais. Why would anyone like Durand need piles of clothes?"

She slowed down and pulled off the road onto what looked like a dirt track. No signposts, and still nothing to indicate life anywhere beyond their own headlights. She pulled into the side and switched them off. She turned to him. Whatever emotion she felt, it had intensified to breaking point. "We need to get some practice," she said hoarsely.

"For what?"

"Capri."

Suddenly, he realised what she meant. She was already taking her clothes off as she got out of the car. He joined her and they kissed and fell and clawed and made it to the long grass. She'd been in the army, so what followed had something military and heat of battle about it; he could feel her physical power beneath and around him. As always, it was nothing like what happens in films, couples becoming unthinking copulation machines: the comic always threatened to burst through and even sabotage it. A fleeting vision of Alec announcing 'mission accomplished', a quick pastiche of EL James and *Fifty Shades – Over and over again, he tried to reverse his mile-long Winnebago into her tiny little car park* - a parade of misplaced limbs, asynchronisms, lying on things that shouldn't have been there and definitely wouldn't have been in a movie. But it was joy as well as biology and discomfort. At least, for him. He half expected that when it was over – which it was, after about ten minutes – she'd get dressed as if it hadn't occurred and tell him never to mention it again. That happened a lot in films too.

But she didn't. She lay across him panting, then laughed. Then she sat up in the almost complete darkness, clasped her hands and whooped. She said hoarsely, "I can't wait for Capri", and fell back onto the ground, still laughing.

At that moment, he realised he was probably in love with her.

Chapter 27: The Decisive Arm-Wrestle

It took them twenty minutes to find all their clothes again, and, as Phyllis pointed out, that was probably because they didn't want to find them. Not because they desired another round of sex – they were too exhausted for that – but because they couldn't face getting back into the same downmarket kit without at least washing it or themselves. "Still," she said as she retrieved one of her trainers from the grass, "*C'est la* spying *vie*."

"What now?" he said. "We can't just keep on driving. We're going to need fuel soon too. They'll know that. They'll have passed our details to all petrol stations within a fifty-mile radius. It's not like they won't take it personally. We escaped from under their noses. They're probably furious, and they'll want revenge."

She laughed. "*John Mordred: this time it's personal*."

"Not quite what Alec had in mind."

"I trained for this sort of situation at Sandhurst. First of all, we're going to get some sleep, then at four in the morning, we're going to find somewhere to hide the car. A screen somewhere: probably behind trees or a disused barn; or last resort, cover it with brushwood. Then we're going to don whatever disguises we can cobble together. Probably not much: swapping one or two items of clothing, pulling our hats down. Then we're going to split up and make our way cross country back to Calais. We'll be much harder to identify separately, and they'll already have CCTV of us leaving the city. They probably think we're heading for Boulogne, or possibly Dieppe or Le Havre. I've got Euros in the car. We'll buy new clothes in Calais, improve our disguises a bit, get a room and plot our next move. Our services are probably no longer required at Thames House."

"Remember, these sorts of organisations tend to think, *They'll suppose we expect them to go south, so they'll come north to wrong-foot us.*"

"Maybe, but what if they're even cleverer? What if they think, *They'll imagine* we *think* they *can pull off the double-bluff by coming back to Calais, so they'll probably go south to wrong-foot us!* Or a quadruple bluff, where we end up going north again? Don't forget they probably haven't much imagination. They're angry. They'll be using the reptilian part of their brains. Let's keep things simple."

They got back in the car and drove further down the track they'd been following. It was a cloudy moonless night and the dark was complete enough to feel tangible. They could be any-where except civilisation. Phyllis had 4G, but it wasn't work-ing. Ideally, they'd have dumped the car now and headed off for Calais before sunrise, only there was no way of telling which way was north. They'd end up going round in circles.

"I think it would be a good idea for one of us to keep watch while the other sleeps," Mordred said. "The moment the sun comes up and we can get our bearings, we can hide the car."

"Maybe we should drive some of the way back to Calais," Phyllis said. "It could be a hell of a distance."

"This is the first place we've come to where there are no lights at all. It must be pretty out of the way. The trouble is, the further we go back, the more civilisation there's going to be, and the harder we'll find it to conceal the vehicle."

She shrugged. "So?"

"As soon as they find it, they'll know we can't be far. They'll get the sniffer dogs out, and even if we make it to the city, they'll have redoubled their efforts."

She pulled into the side of the track and turned the engine off. "What if we drive to a railway station? They'll think we've taken the train."

"CCTV will tell them we haven't."

She nodded and sighed. "Sorry, John, I'm not thinking. I'm very tired."

"I'll take the first watch."

"It's cold, and you probably need rest as much as I do. If we take it in turns, that probably means about two hours each. Less, because you can't nod off when you're icing over. No, we'll sleep together. Our body clocks will tell us when four o'clock comes."

They both awoke together at 3.50, but there was no sign of the sun. The sky had cleared and the stars were out, and their night vision allowed them to make a limited assessment of their surroundings. They were surrounded by fields. There were a few trees, but so far apart as to make screening a car impossible. They climbed off the back seats and got in the front. Phyllis started the engine.

"Wherever this road goes, it has to lead somewhere," she said.

"We're looking for a glint."

"Going to be difficult with no moon."

He meant a lake, preferably a large one. Putting a car underwater wasn't very eco-friendly, but it was the most effective means of concealment. After about a mile, when the sun still showed no signs of showing its head, Phyllis pulled into the side, and they climbed into the back for more sleep. They weren't overly tired now, but trundling along a bumpy road with no end in sight and hardly anything to see seemed a waste of petrol. The gauge said almost empty.

They next awoke at seven. The sun was on its way up now, and it looked like the beginnings of a beautiful day. No clouds anywhere. Also, an ideal time for sun glinting on water.

"There!" Mordred said.

She started the engine. It was more or less straight ahead, and after a mile, the road met the lakeside and began to follow its outline. The car spluttered and died. Phyllis put her foot on the clutch, and they freewheeled for ten yards and stopped.

"I think it's made its choice," she said. "I just hope it's deep enough here."

Getting a car to submerge in a lake wasn't as easy as the movies sometimes made it look. The water needed to be deep enough, for a start. Then you needed a really good run-up. Anything less than 100% wouldn't do. Once you got stuck in the shallows, you were probably stuck for good. Your initial momentum had to be great enough to overcome that. But, well, Phyllis had been in the army.

They got out and wheeled the car through a three-point turn so the bonnet was facing the water. Phyllis took a wad of Euro notes from the glove compartment and put it in her pocket. Then they cleared a runway to the lake, about five metres away. The ramp down to the water was quite steep, but maybe too much so. What if the car somehow caught on something and somersaulted?

"What do you think?" he asked.

She grinned. "I think God's on our side. We wouldn't be here otherwise."

It was the sort of thing she obviously thought would win him over. Or maybe she was actually coming to think like him. Either way, touching.

"Okay, push as hard as you can, as far as you can," she said. "I'll steer."

"No, I'll steer," he said.

"Why?"

"Because if it goes wrong, you could get run over."

She smiled. "What you actually mean is, you think you're stronger than me."

"I think we should at least put it to the test."

She gave a 'we don't have time for this' sigh.

"Look, I'm sorry," he said, "I don't want you getting run over. Lie down. We'll decide it with an arm-wrestle."

"You can't be serious."

"I'm being rational. Afraid you'll lose?"

She rolled her eyes and got down reluctantly on her stomach. He lay down opposite her and they locked grips.

"Ready?" he said.

"One, two, three."

The epic battle of grips and muscles began. Their elbows bit into the road, their veins bulged, the sky darkened, thunder and lightning blasted the earth, the ancient gods of war put their hands over their eyes, the foundations of Valhalla trembled, civilisations rose and fell. Phyllis railed as the back of her right hand hit the dust.

"You win," she said simply.

That was the great thing about her. She didn't hold grudges.

Although, if she was anything like his sisters, he'd probably hear about it later.

"Let's have a re-match," she said. "Left hand."

"You can't be serious."

"Okay, you grab the steering wheel. I'll wind the windows down to let the air out, then I'll push from behind. But *be careful*. It's not just about muscles."

They counted to three again and charged the car down the slight hill and in through the water. It didn't seem happy about what was happening to it, but went under better than either of them expected, before apparently stopping at roof level. But that was just the air bubbling out. Ten seconds later, it gave up the ghost and disappeared from sight.

"As someone who habitually recycles," Phyllis said, "I can't begin to tell you how ambiguous I feel right now."

Mordred dusted his palms together. "Me too."

"I guess this is where we go our separate ways."

"What time is it?"

She looked at her phone. "Five past eight."

"Aren't you worried someone might trace that thing? I mean if Tariq could find Marcie - "

"It's not mine, dummy. It's a posh pay-and-go. I simply transferred my address book. Where shall we rendezvous?"

"How about the *Musee de la Guerre* in the Parc Saint Pierre?"

She looked impressed. "I take it you know Calais quite well."

"We once went on a family excursion, years ago."

"I'll find it. It would help if we knew where we were now. I still haven't any 4G and my battery's almost dead. How about yours?"

"It conked out straight after my conversation with Alec."

"There's a moral somewhere in that statement."

"The *Musee de la Guerre* at eleven o'clock tonight. Wait twenty minutes, and if I don't turn up, return to the same spot at nine tomorrow morning."

She divided her wad of Euros and gave him half. "Going by the sun, north is that way. I reckon we were travelling for just over forty minutes last night. The speed we were going probably makes Calais between forty and sixty miles away. Beyond reasonable hiking distance. We're going to have to get public transport. The bus rather than the train."

He looked at what she'd given him. "Bloody hell, how much did you bring?"

"Two thousand. You?"

"A thousand pounds. But I didn't get time to convert it."

She sighed. "It's finally beginning to sink in."

"What is?"

"My little MI7 job, spying for the Queen and Britannia. I loved coming into Thames House every day, the adventures, and I loved all my friends: I mean you and Annabel and Alec and Edna and ... Sorry, I'm going to start crying soon."

"And after that, you're going to realise it's all actually my fault. I'm sorry. I know that isn't - "

"If we could go back in time, I'd make the same choice. It's about being able to live with yourself. We'll fall on our feet, don't worry. True, we're redundant, but I doubt they'll be able to charge us with anything, even under the Official Secrets Act. Annabel's villa's probably out of the question now, though. Unless she's in as much trouble as we are, which seems unlikely."

"We don't need Capri," he said.

"Which is what I told you in The Counting House, remember? That was never what this was about. I mean, you and me."

"I'm an optimist."

She looked at him and half-laughed, half-cried. "... And?"

"Something will turn up."

She seemed to forgive him for talking bullshit, and they kissed.

"Good luck," she whispered, "and be careful." She disengaged herself gently, smiled and walked away without looking back.

When she was out of sight, he began to walk back the way they'd come. He'd wheel north in about twenty minutes, minimise the chances of bumping into her.

He felt horribly guilty. But not despairing. He'd think of something.

He avoided the roads north without losing sight of them. He crossed meadows and skirted the sides of fields and followed streams to where a bridge let him cross. The sun rose and became overpowering and he was forced to rest beneath a tree for thirty minutes. He thought about Phyllis, how old she'd once looked, and how young now. The first time he'd really talked to her was on that mission to Siberia, two years back. She'd sat on the flat roof of a Russian hotel in a bearskin hat and a fur coat talking airily about global politics; and she'd seemed somehow the archetypal Tory ice-queen, full of pontifical aphorisms, faintly intolerant of difference, insufferably English County. As he'd got to know her, she'd somehow grown younger and more vulnerable, until today, as they'd parted, she could have been eighteen and desperate for help. He shouldn't have let her go alone. They should have stayed together.

But that wasn't right. How he saw her didn't mean much. Somehow, she was all those things, and God help him if he forgot it.

He'd landed her in deep trouble, and now he had to get her out of it. Why would anyone like Durand need piles of clothes? That was where the solution lay. In finding the answer to that question. Perhaps.

Why would *anyone* need piles of clothes? You wanted to dress people up, presumably. You were going to disguise them.

As what? Well, there couldn't have been any common theme to what was in the warehouse, or Robillard would have mentioned it. So – just dress people up in second-hand clothes? What possible purpose could that serve?

Maybe they weren't being used *as* clothes. Maybe they were padding for something. Or insulation.

Or maybe they meant nothing at all. Maybe Durand had realised Mordred would sooner or later come looking for something, and he'd left a pile of clothes. Something to throw the authorities off the scent.

Just after noon, a village came into view, dominated by the tall *flèche* of a country church. With clothes so much on Mordred's mind, he realised it would be better to get a change here – while he was still relatively far from Calais – than anywhere further along the route. A new outfit would open new possibilities. Once he no longer looked like a tramp, he could spend his cash freely without arousing suspicion. It was that first significant purchase that might raise eyebrows.

Accent and manners would help him through. The village turned out to be well stocked with shops, nearly all surrounding a cobbled square with a statue of Chateaubriand at the centre. He walked into a tailor's, and adopted a Parisian accent.

"Excuse me," he told the assistant, a little man with grey eyes and a receding chin, "I'd like to buy a ready-made suit. I'm here from Paris and I've just been invited to a friend's daughter's first communion. I didn't bring anything appropriate with me, but I've a budget of five hundred Euros and I can pay in cash."

Within a few moments, the assistant was his happy collaborator, charmed by his perfect diction and courtesy. A suit was provided and paid for, and a matching hat was acquired to go with it. Mordred left the shop with his old clothes in a bag. He wandered out of the square and flagged down a taxi.

"Ardres," he said, remembering one of the signposts they'd passed last night.

The driver didn't bat an eyelid. "Very good, Monsieur," he replied.

Fifteen minutes later, he stepped out of the car a stone's throw away from the town's Chapelle des Carmes, and went to find the shops. He dumped his old clothes in a bin, bought a bottle of dark brown hair-dye, a pair of sunglasses, a newspaper and a new mobile phone. He checked into an anonymous-looking inn on the town outskirts for one night, and went upstairs to his room, a small, square space with a washbasin, bed, mini flat-screen TV on the wall, and a dressing table. The toilets and showers were communal and at the end of the corridor.

On the bedside table, which doubled as a kind of brochures cupboard, there were maps of the area and public transport timetables. Calais was sixteen kilometres away: about twenty-five minutes by taxi; an hour by bus. He showered, then dyed his hair, tying a plastic bag round his head and sitting on the bed watching TV while it set. He could get a bus in an hour's time and arrive in Calais in good time to book a five-star hotel room and meet Phyllis at eleven. It was her money, but he'd pay her back. No point in trying to scrimp and save. All the spy manuals agreed parsimony was bad tactics. Invisibility lay in the highest echelons of society. That was always where state surveillance was least intense.

He hoped she was okay. He'd kept his old phone and the charger, and there was a plug adapter in the drawer. He plugged it in, looked up her number and called. It went straight to voicemail.

He sat with the phone in his hand for a moment and his head suddenly emptied of all thoughts, like someone had pulled out a bathplug at the bottom of his brain. Then there was an equally abrupt rushing in of fresh thoughts from above, and he had what felt like the beginnings of an epiphany. Alec! *Alec, when he'd phoned last night!*

My God, maybe he could get through to him now. On one reading, it was risky, but on another, not at all. He went to 're-call last number'. It rang three times.

"Hello?" Alec said suspiciously.

"Mordred here. Just thought I'd ring to tell you I'm okay."

"John. Good God, you scared me. You probably shouldn't - "

"I just wanted to know how you were."

"Me?"

"And Annabel, and Tariq, of course."

"We're fine, idiot. Look, we can't afford to make courtesy calls. Only call me when you've something important to say."

He hung up.

That was it then. Suddenly, the whole thing made sense. Of course. The bits of the jigsaw puzzle arranged themselves in his mind.

But that five star hotel was out of the question now. He'd have to grab Phyllis as soon as she showed up and bring her back to Ardres. They were probably in even more serious danger than they'd imagined.

Chapter 28: Friends Reunited

That glamorous woman standing outside the *Musee* – well, at this time of night, it could only be … Yes, it was. Thank God. She'd had the same idea as him. Maybe she'd even booked them into an exclusive hotel. He wouldn't put it past her.

The museum was long closed. Phyllis stood at the end of a short path flanked by stone planters. With the main building and a shrubbery just behind her and a lime tree above her, she was hardly visible from a distance. He could probably have chosen a better place, although in some ways it was perfect. It was lonely here now, and abandoned-looking, and if it rained, she had a fair way to walk to shelter, but she'd see anyone hostile a mile off.

He approached her briskly, hands in pockets looking at the ground. She came to meet him from the semi-shadow, and slipped her arm through his as naturally as if they'd only been apart for five minutes.

She wore a long camel coat, a headscarf and heels. To anyone looking, they might have been any couple walking home after a night at the opera.

"I hope you haven't booked us a hotel," she told him.

"I haven't. I've only just got here."

"Good, because we're going to spend the night at *La Réserve Calais-Nord*. It's five star and it's got all the trimmings. I thought we might as well go out with a bang."

"When did you arrive?" he asked.

"About three. I got a change of clothes in Ardres."

He stopped and turned to face her. "Bloody hell, not the tailor's on the square?"

"The *boutique*, not the tailor's. But yes, on the square. Shit, I take it that's where you got yours. How long – maybe - before they start talking to each other? Two customers, hours apart, both the same age, both – fitting the descriptions."

"And then the police. But it's not a foregone conclusion."

"They'll never think of looking in a swanky hotel," she said. "Although, yes. Yes, they will when they hear what kind of kit we bought. We'd better get out of here. Oh, what a disappointment!"

"Don't worry."

She chuckled darkly. "Is that another of your 'I'm optimistic' remarks? Because they don't seem to be coming true."

"I've hired us a boat. We're going back to England and we're going to get our jobs back."

She smiled indulgently. "I take it you've got a 'plan'." The significance of her words seemed to hit her and she stopped and turned to face him. "Wait a minute, I'm forgetting. You're John Mordred. On the one hand, you're completely insane; on the other, most of your plans seem to bear fruit. I take it you're not joking."

"Although, quite honestly, I doubt we ever lost our jobs to begin with. I'm pretty sure that, as far as Ruby Parker's concerned, we're sunning ourselves in Capri. Or we would be, if it wasn't midnight in Italy right now."

"Go on. I'm interested."

"In five minutes we're going to get in the taxi I've got waiting for us, and we're going to *Le Gris Nez*, where there's a motor boat moored just offshore to take us to Folkestone."

"Who owns this motor boat?"

"A Maths teacher from Margate. Doesn't speak any French. Not interested in current affairs. Likes a life on the ocean wave, and comes here at weekends and holidays to stock up on booze. Anyway, I showed him my passport, we got talking, and I said I'd like to surprise my girlfriend with a midnight trip back to Kent. I'm a city broker so it cost me a thousand pounds. And before you ask, no, I haven't handed it all over yet. I gave him a deposit."

"I'm not really interested in that part, although well done. What really interests me is the bit where you said you were going to get our jobs back. Although you also said …"

"We never lost them to begin with. That's right."

"Okay, well, that's the bit I'm interested in."

"I didn't think about it till today," he said, "but last night Alec rang - "

"And told you something you didn't tell me."

"Er, maybe let me tell the story? No, he didn't."

"Tell it a bit more quickly then!"

"It's what he *didn't* say that struck me," he continued, speeding up. "I saw Shafiq Effanga and his men arrive at the police station just as we were leaving, which means news of Tariq's countermand must have reached Grey shortly afterwards."

"And?"

"If that actually happened, Grey would have been straight on the phone to Ruby Parker, who would have been straight on the phone to Alec, Annabel and anyone else she suspected of being involved. And all that would have occurred at more or less lightning speed."

She hmm-ed and nodded. "I think I see what you're saying."

"Alec rang us at least thirty minutes after we left Calais, and he hadn't experienced anything. I rang him today and he still hadn't. Everything was fine, he said."

"So what's your theory?"

"There's a mole in Grey. Someone high up and in control of communications, especially inter-departmental. He's also managing a coterie of thugs who are passing themselves off as Grey agents in order to perfect the illusion. From our point of view, it looks like Grey's taken against us. But I'm willing to wager the head of Grey doesn't know a thing about it."

"Wow, that's some conjecture."

"It would explain why people like Shafiq Effanga know so much about me – Dao-ming Chou, for example, and exactly where we are at any given time, and also why Tariq was able to pick up on Grey 'spying' on us, and just about everything else. But it would also explain why Grey didn't intervene earlier, why it's taken such an oblique approach to stopping us."

"And what's this high-up person's motive?"

"He's somehow connected to Planchart and Frances Holland and Pierre Durand."

She nodded. "It fits. There is another possibility, however."

"Go on."

"Brace yourself. Grey's discovered you're interfering again and decided it's time to stop pussyfooting around."

"You mean, kill me."

"*Us*, probably, now. And make it look like an accident. While we're on the Continent and supposed to be in Capri. How embarrassing it'll be when it turns out … Well, when it turns out you were passing secrets to the Chinese all along. A few classified documents on your corpse, evidence of a trip to the Chinese embassy, and to make matters worse, you turned another MI7 officer. Me."

"Think about what you're saying. You used to work for Grey. I know our two departments don't always see eye to eye, but do you *really* think they'd stoop that low?"

"Well, we've - "

"Got into the habit of thinking they would, I know. But only since I was admitted to the Holland case."

"You're forgetting something else. It would take a mighty big hand to pull the wool over Ruby Parker's eyes. She made it clear in no uncertain terms that, on Grey's direct orders, we were off the Holland case. She wouldn't have done that if there'd been the slightest shadow of a doubt."

"So you'd think. But her decision followed a specific conjunction of events which made an error forgivable. Even for her."

"You'll have to remind me."

"We'd spent a long time setting up a scenario in which I walked from one side of the Thames to the other under the benign supervision of virtually her whole department. Our assumptions concerning what was happening were completely overturned on that rooftop, and you and Annabel and Alec were given information that only someone within Thames House could know. Then Ruby Parker was given a direct order from the lower floor to cease and desist. Excruciating embarrassment followed by unconditional command. Two reversals in Red's fortunes apparently emanating from the same place. I can appreciate why she might have preferred *not* to ring downstairs and check the details. What would be the point? She'd be rubbing her nose in her own humiliation. And that was exactly what they were counting on. Simple psychology."

"What about the clothes in the warehouse?"

"That, I'm not sure about yet. I've got the beginnings of an idea, but I'd have to talk to Robillard again. And he'd have to be a bit more receptive this time."

She closed her eyes while she walked as if it might help her concentrate better. "Okay, let's assume you're right so far. What are we going to do about it? We can't just go downstairs into Grey and demand to know the truth. It's a thousand per cent off-limits. And it's not like we can look the department head up on one of his or her days off. No one knows who he – or she - is. We don't, anyway."

"Someone might."

"Ruby Parker."

"Absolutely not. No, at this point she'll be more concerned that we've apparently gone rogue. Ringing her up with a speculative hypothesis when we're meant to be in Capri isn't going to do her or us the slightest bit of good."

"So who?"

"Our old friend Farquarson."

"You know where to find him, I take it."

"I happen to know he's a regular at one or two London clubs. The Bulletin's his favourite. He'll be there tomorrow night."

"And you know that – how?"

"I used my phone to call Marcie Brown. She asked me to, if I was ever in trouble. Her father's intimately familiar with the WGP scene. She tapped him for me."

"WGP?"

"Whitehall Gentleman Pensioner. Apparently."

"So we're going back to London for a pow-wow with Farquie."

"Don't forget, he owes us after that shambles with Durand. *I completely forgot I used to be a head of section and before that, in charge of recruitment and training,* were, I think, his unconditionally sarcastic words. *So thanks awfully for your wise advice.* Or something along those lines."

"Added to which, he loves us."

"You're right. That's got to count for something."

It was time to get in the taxi. He held the door for her and went round the other side once she was inside. Best to be as traditional as possible when you were dressed like this.

The motor-boat owner was a thin, fifty-something man with a grey beard, a puffa jacket and trainers, called Lionel Hamilton. He was waiting on the beach for them with a couple of inflatable dinghies tied together bow-to-stern with a short rope. He shook hands with Mordred, who introduced him to Phyllis, then took receipt of the remaining portion of his thousand pounds before installing them both in the larger of the two dinghies. He pushed them out to sea, got into the smaller vessel and started rowing, towing them to where *Lucky Sam*, his motor-boat was anchored. They all climbed aboard. It was small – not really big enough for three people to stand up in without unbalancing it, but not too small. It didn't look overly weighed down.

"You two just lie down in the back," he said cheerily. "You're going to need that coat tonight, love. Weather's going to be very calm, but cold. It's going to be very cold. If you want to come back to Calais – if it gets too much for you – just say. I can happily turn around. Now just one thing before we cast off. You *have* both got your passports on you? I don't want to sound like a stickler for the details, but I'll need to see them now. If we get stopped by the coastguard and you haven't got them, I'll be in deep shit. Not just my boat, but my lovely teaching job too."

It was clear he was anxious for Phyllis to say more than a few words. An English tourist falling in love with a foreign migrant in Calais, then trying to smuggle her into England under cover of darkness with a forged passport – it might happen quite a lot for all Mordred knew. She seemed to twig as well.

"This is really kind of you," she said. "I'm totally looking forward to it. We'll get the train straight to London once we get there. We can pick up our things next week."

"You'll be hard-pressed to find a train at three in the morning," Lionel said. "Where are you staying in Calais?" he asked, changing the subject.

"*La Réserve Calais-Nord*," she replied. "We've got a fortnight. They probably won't notice we're missing at the hotel, but I'll let them know once we arrive, just in case. Which part of England do you teach in, Lionel?"

He scrutinised their passports, looked happy and passed them back. "Margate," he said.

"Oh, I love Margate," she replied. "The Turner Contemporary - wonderful. And there's a jazz festival in June, isn't there?"

He visibly relaxed. "You know it!"

"I had an auntie used to live there. She moved to Romford about two years ago."

"I used to teach in Hornchurch."

She smiled. "That's just to the south, isn't it?"

"About five minutes."

Mordred put his arm round her while she talked to Lionel. He could tell they were both enjoying themselves, so he didn't interrupt. The sky stayed clear and they were wafted towards England by the gentlest of breezes. Had it not been for the cold and Lionel's obsessive talk about boats and where he'd been in them, and his subtle attempts to prise Phyllis away from Mordred to join him for an all-expenses-paid trip to Portugal in the summer holidays, it would have been perfect. They reached a beach near Folkestone at three. Phyllis had already called a taxi. There was no public transport to London at this time in the morning, and they were running low on funds. They found a cash machine, checked into a Travelodge and went straight to sleep. They were in London with the rush hour crowds at eight the next morning.

Now all they had to do was lie low for twelve hours.

Chapter 29: Farquarson's Big Chance

Both of their places were probably under surveillance, so either was out of the question. Which meant another Travelodge, this one in King's Cross. On their way, they bought a *New Statesman*, a *Spectator*, a selection of broadsheets, and some snacks. They showered, spent the morning in bed, sent out for a Chinese at lunchtime, then drank tea and read their newspapers during the afternoon. At seven they bathed again and dressed to go out. Mordred put the TV on while Phyllis stared into her mirror and applied her make-up.

"I don't know how you can watch *Goldfinger*," she said absently. "I got bored with it after the fifth time."

"There's nothing else on. And it's a classic."

"What about *Line of Duty*? That's good."

"True, but it doesn't start till nine."

Her mobile rang. *Annabel*. She put it on speakerphone.

"We're in London," Phyllis said. "We'd have rung to let you know, but Alec said it'd be best to wait for you to contact us."

"Alec," Annabel replied as if it was a sigh. "Still, he's probably right: walls have ears. How was Interpol?"

"Not terribly useful. We got away by a hair's breadth. How are things at your end?"

"Oddly normal. I thought we'd have been bollocked and possibly sacked by now, but not a whisper."

"How does Ruby Parker seem?"

"It would be nice if John was here to read her micro-expressions, because as far as I can tell, she's behaving completely normally. Which means they must be biding their time before informing her. We're all just awaiting the inevitable. Alec, me, Tariq, even Edna and Ian – walking on eggshells."

"Unless it's *not* inevitable. John's got a theory."

"Pray tell," Annabel said drily.

261

"It's not Grey."

"What isn't?"

"Who we're dealing with," Phyllis replied.

"How the hell does he figure that out? Is he there? Put him on."

"Hi, Annabel," Mordred said.

"I assume you've got it on speakerphone. You heard my question?"

"Yep."

"Are you mad? Think about what they know about you and about all of us. Think about the fact that Tariq caught them spying on us. Think about the fact that they've known our every step since day one, and finally, think about the fact that they got in direct touch with Ruby Parker just after our little rooftop fiasco. Then explain to me why you think it can't be Grey."

"Well, to - "

"On second thoughts, don't. Walls have ears, I've just said that. You'd better be right, though. How confident are you?"

"There are still a few loose ends I need to account for."

"On a scale of one to ten?"

"Seven."

She sighed. "When might you know for sure?"

"Sometime tomorrow, I hope."

"It must be some completely out-of-this-world theory to account for everything I've just mentioned."

"Thank you."

"It wasn't necessarily a compliment. You'll get one of those if and when you're proved right. What are you doing now?"

"Getting ready to go out. Strictly business. We're not going clubbing."

"How very encouraging to hear. Let me know as soon as you refute or confirm. I don't normally suffer from anxiety, but I'm suffering now. The exact minute you find out."

"So we're allowed to ring you? And what if we need help?"

"Obviously. But only at this number."

She hung up. Phyllis sat down on the bed, plumping her hair. She wore the full skirted blue dress and fake fur overcoat she'd had on last night, and she looked ready for another fake night at the opera.

"I think we ought to be careful going to see Farquarson," she said. "Since we're on the run, so to speak, it's likely they'll have tried to cover a number of bases. Farquarson would be one of them. They may even have got him on board."

"He's nothing to gain from helping a mole, and he's too well connected for a mole to fool him for long. He probably knows the current head of Grey. Chances are he'd mention the whole thing to him over dinner."

"I think you're discounting the possibility that he may have been paid. And before you say he's not that sort of guy, no one is. Until they are. Remember, pensioners can be very hard-up. Especially when they have club memberships to maintain."

"Possible, but we have to take some risks."

"I'm not saying don't. I'm saying, let's keep the danger to a minimum."

"How?"

"Instead of going to meet him at his club, we maybe need to follow him on his way out. Make sure no one else is tailing him."

"If you're right," he said, "somebody *will* be. Then what do we do?"

"Hit them, obviously. We've got the element of surprise, and we can call Alec and Annabel in. Possibly Edna and Ian too, although I'm not persuaded it's wholly ethical to get the juniors involved."

"I've a better idea. I'm going to ring him."

"At his club?"

"Why not?"

She thought about it and shrugged. "Can't hurt, I suppose. Anything's probably preferable to getting shot. He won't believe it's you, though. He'll probably want to speak to you face-to-face. Anyone can imitate someone else, and as an ex-head of Grey, he's a man worth getting to."

"I'll put you on the line."

"The same applies."

"Yes, but it'll reduce the uncertainty. You wouldn't get two fabulous imitators on the phone in one call."

"Depends what the stakes are. Besides, sometimes people on the phone don't sound like they do in real life. Or they do, but the person on the other end just doesn't hear them right."

"That may be - "

She rolled her eyes. "Oh, let's just *do* it, all right? We've got to do *something*, and this looks like the safest option. If he does want to see us, well, we were going to go and see him anyway. And at least when we go over there, we won't be cold calling."

He picked his phone up. Fully charged. Phyllis put the TV on mute and found the number on her phone. "Put it on speakerphone," she said.

"Good evening. Bulletin Club. How may I help?" said a young male voice on the other end of the line.

"Good evening, my name is John Mordred," he said affecting an upper-class English accent. "I'd like to get an urgent message to one of your members, Sir Ranulph Farquarson. I'd be very grateful if you could ask him to call me back on this number at his earliest convenience. Mordred, John. M-O-R-D-R-E-D. We were supposed to be meeting for drinks this evening at about eleven, but something's just come up in the House, and I'm obliged to be there."

"He's not available at the moment, sir. He doesn't usually arrive until after eight. However, I'll make sure he gets your message as soon as he gets here."

"That would be very kind. Thank you." He hung up and turned to Phyllis. "Just a question of waiting now."

They didn't have sex because Phyllis had spent so long getting ready and they might be called out at any moment.

They lay on the bed and watched *Caravanner of the Year* followed by *Line of Duty* then *Normal For Norfolk*. Halfway through the ten o'clock news, Phyllis turned to him. "I don't think he's going to ring."

"He'll ring."

"Quote: 'He doesn't usually arrive until after eight. However, I'll make sure he gets your message as soon as he gets here'. Unquote."

"'After eight' could also mean 'after ten'."

"It could mean the day after tomorrow, for that matter. Or next year."

"Put it this way. If he gets our message and he's not been nobbled by Grey, he'll ring back. It's only polite, and he's not known for his discourtesy. If he has been nobbled by Grey, he'll phone because they'll want to know where we are. Either way, he'll phone."

"Unless he's trying to protect us. Maybe you should ring them back."

"And say what?"

"How about 'drinks are back on'?"

He laughed. "Let's have a look at your phone and find out when the Bulletin closes. That should give us a good idea of when to start worrying."

She flicked through her phone. "We're *already* worrying. Or I am. Eleven-thirty."

"So he's still got an hour and a quarter."

His phone rang. They both jumped and he almost threw it in the air in his haste to pick up. "John Mordred."

Farquarson's voice, midway between indignation and puzzlement. "What 'drinks' are you *talking* about, John? Surely you know we're not supposed to meet!"

If Mordred had been asked to come up with an ideal opening gambit, a few words optimally calculated to dispel his suspicion, he couldn't have come up with anything better than this.

"I need to talk to you as a matter of urgency," he said.

"About?"

"Grey department."

"It may have escaped your notice, but I'm not in charge of anything any more. What precisely were you going to say, just out of curiosity?"

"Last I heard, they wanted to shoot me through the ankle from a London rooftop. But the time before that, I'm pretty sure they wanted to push me under a train. And now I think that's what they've reverted to."

Farquarson paused. "Trying to kill you," he said incredulously. "Right. Where are you, John?"

"I can't say."

"Well, I know Grey and Red have different *rationales*, but it'll be a sorry day when we start trying to murder each other. How much have you had?"

"I'm not drinking. I've got Phyllis here with me."

"With respect, that doesn't necessarily prove anything. I was there at The Counting House, remember? You two were at the sauce like the world was about to end."

"We had an appointment with the Lord Mayor."

"Oh, of course," Farquarson chortled. "That would explain it."

"All I want you to do is ask whatever contacts you have left in Grey – I'm sure you can't have broken all connections – and ask them whether there's any truth in what I'm saying. Whether there really has been a plan laid to assassinate me."

"But it's ridiculous. Why don't you simply ask Ruby Parker to find out? I don't like loose cannons, John, and that's what you are sometimes: a bit of an *agent provocateur*. I like to do things through official channels, especially when they're as odd as this."

"She agrees with me."

"I don't believe you."

"I can prove it."

"How?"

"I'll bring her to meet you at the Bulletin club in an hour if you promise to use your connections to investigate the question so you've got something to say to her."

Farquarson laughed. "You're telling me you think you'll be able to drag Ruby Parker out here - "

"Don't forget Pierre Durand. You owe me one."

"Oh, I wondered when you'd throw that particular chip onto the table. Listen, let's make it interesting. You say you can get her out in an hour. I'll give you till quarter to midnight. The place shuts at eleven-thirty, as a rule, but it stays open till twelve for members. I bet fifty pounds you can't get Ruby Parker over here."

"If I get her over there, you need to provide hard information. If you do, you owe me nothing. Otherwise, you have to pay me."

"Sounds fair."

"In that case, let's make it two hundred."

"Three."

"A thousand," Mordred said.

Farquarson guffawed. "Really? Have you actually *got* a thousand?"

"I'm an officer now. I was promoted last year."

"Egad, John Mordred, an officer. What's the world coming to?"

"In addition, I've never lied to you. You know that. I'm a man of my word. And finally, Phyllis is here to back me up."

"Put her on. Phyllis, have you been listening?"

"Intently, sir," she replied.

"Are you willing to act as a guarantor for Officer Mordred?"

"Absolutely. But I'm pretty sure I won't have to."

"You actually think he'll be able to get Ruby Parker to come *here*? At *this* time of night?"

She chuckled. "I don't think he's got a cat in hell's chance, but I do happen to know he's got a spare thousand pounds, and who am I to complain if he wants to throw it away?"

"Quite. What do you think about this assassination business?"

"I know he believes it, and so does she. And it's probably worth a thousand pounds to put their minds at rest."

"Very well, you're on. You've got precisely one hour and a quarter. I'll tell the concierge to expect you, just in case you *do* pull off a miracle. Otherwise, you can hand over the money in the waiting area of Lloyds Bank, Regent Street, tomorrow morning at eleven. *Don't be late.*"

He hung up. Mordred stood up and put his phone in his pocket.

"Do you really think I haven't a cat in hell's chance?" he asked Phyllis.

"I wouldn't put it that strongly," she said. "But we were hustling him. Weren't we?"

He pulled his coat on. "I don't know. I really don't know."

Chapter 30: A Trip Across London

Whoever was after them couldn't know they were in London, otherwise they'd have attacked already. A budget hotel in the middle of a big city was ideal for a murder.

If those people didn't know they were in London, they couldn't know they were decamping.

So it wasn't reaching Thames House that would be the problem. It was what would happen afterwards. Like Phyllis had said, they'd have predicted a set of next-moves and covered each with a handful of personnel. One such was the personal approach to Farquarson. Another was the midnight slink back into Thames House.

Pull up quickly enough outside, though, run up to the entrance, and you'd probably take them so much by surprise they wouldn't have time to do anything significant. But they'd be waiting for you on the way out. Then there'd be more of them than when you went in. All of them, in fact. To make things worse, if there really was a mole in Grey, they'd know all about the secret exits.

It was raining when they emerged from the Travelodge. Their taxi was waiting for them in the road. They climbed in and closed the screen between them and the driver. Mordred sat in quiet reflection. Phyllis squeezed his hand. "What are you thinking about?" she asked.

"*Goldfinger,*" he replied.

She drew a deep breath, then laughed humourlessly. "Well, at least we'll arrive prepared for the inevitable showdown."

"Could you get me the telephone number of a hotel in Calais?" he asked her. "It's just a hunch I've got. It may be nothing."

She shrugged and switched her phone on. "333 2196 6941," she said after a few seconds. "Do you want to borrow mine to ring?" she asked testily.

"This'll do."

He put the call through.

"*Hotel Calais Horizon,*" came a male voice at the other end. "*Comment puis-je être utile?*"

He sat back. "*Je voudrais réserver une chambre pour la vingt-troisième de Juin, s'il vous plaît. N'importe quel salle.*"

The male voice went silent for a minute, then returned sounding disappointed. "*Non, je crains que ce soit impossible, monsieur. Nous sommes complet à cette date.*"

"*La vingt-quatrième?*"

Another pause. "*Non, je crains que non. Pardon. La vingt-cinquième semble correct.*"

"*Non, ça va. Merci quand même.*" He hung up.

Phyllis held her hands up. "I know you're renowned for not voting, John, but a hotel in Calais on referendum day seems like a lot of trouble to go to."

"Give me another number."

"In Calais? 333 2196 4444," she said in response to his nod.

He tapped the number in and again tried to book a room for the twenty-third then the twenty-fourth, and again failed. He rang Annabel.

"Where are you?" he asked her.

"Thames House," she replied. "Sorting reports. I thought of going home, but I don't think I'd be able to sleep. Why are you calling?"

"Is Ruby Parker there?"

"Upstairs. Don't ask me why. It's not as if anything interesting's happening here."

"She must suspect something's wrong."

"Repeat: *why are you calling?* I assumed you must have news."

"We're on our way back to Thames House. I need you to leave the building on the pretext of going home, get on the Tube and come back in disguise. Ideally, get Alec, Ian, Edna and whoever else you can round up to do the same. If they're at home, bring them in. In about thirty minutes, Phyllis and I are going to leave the building with Ruby Parker and we're almost certainly going to come under attack. I need you to secure us safe passage."

A pause while she digested this. "I suppose it beats filing," she said.

The taxi pulled up sharply outside the entrance to Thames House. Mordred had paid a minute earlier, and he and Phyllis leapt out, ran up the steps and went inside through the code-locked side door with their cards showing. After the security guards had okay-ed them, they checked in with a thirtysomething woman with spectacles, feathered blonde hair and a blazer, and waited while she logged their entry on the computer.

"Ms Parker wants to see you," she said.

Phyllis turned to Mordred. "How did she know we were coming?"

The receptionist spoke before he could answer. "It simply says here, 'As soon as they return'."

"I take it she's in her office," Mordred said.

In response, she picked up the phone and made a call. "Mr Mordred and Ms Robinson here to see you, Ma'am," she said. "Of course. Right away."

Mordred looked at his watch. An hour to go. Every second counted now. The receptionist put the receiver down as if there was no hurry whatsoever. "She's in her office, yes."

They took the lift down to Basement One, and walked briskly along the short corridor to her door. Phyllis knocked.

"Enter!" came an irritable voice from within.

They went in. Ruby Parker sat behind her desk apparently sorting a pile of papers. It took her a whole second to look up at them. When she did, it was with a kind of controlled anger. "How was Capri?" she asked sardonically.

"We didn't go," Mordred said, before Phyllis could speak. "We never had any intention of going. The people who are chasing me aren't Grey. When you were ordered off the Frances Holland case, that wasn't Grey. The men on that rooftop weren't Grey. We've been duped throughout. There's going to be a *coup d'état*. In this country. It's going to happen so subtly that no one's going to recognise it as such, but that's what it's going to be. I haven't time to explain, I've a bet to win. You're coming across London with Phyllis and I to meet Sir Ranulph Farquarson at the Bulletin Club. He's waiting for all three of us as we speak, and there's a thousand pounds riding on it."

Ruby Parker's mouth popped open slightly as she continued to glare at him.

"Er, I meant, *please*," he said to cut the silence.

"Are you – *drunk*, John?" she asked. It was a genuine question. All her irritability had dissipated and she looked concerned; pitying, even. "They've re-opened your radicalisation inquiry," she said grimly, as if this might throw cold water on him.

"Awesome," he said.

"I can confirm he hasn't been drinking," Phyllis said. "Mad: well, I'm not so sure about that. What do you mean, '*coup d'état*', John?" she asked. "I don't remember us discussing that at all."

"I've been ringing hotels in Calais," he said, as if this explained everything. "Trying to book a room for the twenty-third of June. No joy. I might ring a few more on my way over. Sorry, I know I'm not making the slightest bit of sense. I'm excited."

"Sir Ranulph really is waiting for us," Phyllis said. She tried to say another sentence, but failed, and admitted exasperatedly, "I'm afraid I've no idea what John's talking about with his 'Calais hotels', either. We watched *Goldfinger* tonight, or he did ..." She tailed off and her face filled with the dismay of someone who realises she's not making any more sense than the person she's trying to defend. "Oh, my God," she said. "I've become you, John."

"I love you," he told her. "I should have said that in France, but better late than never. I hope we get married and have ten children."

She laughed and frowned at the same time. "I promise you he hasn't been drinking, Ma'am," she said again. "At least, not that I've seen."

Ruby Parker was putting her coat on. She sighed. "Let's just get this over with, shall we? For good or ill, I do need some air right now. Then we need to sit down and have a serious talk."

They got no farther than twenty metres outside Thames House – through the secret entrance within Pimlico tube station – before she seemed to realise they might actually be in real danger. A man in a suit carrying a briefcase and a barely-concealed knife came casually but determinedly at them, while two others approached at the same speed from angles designed to foreclose escape. A small well-dressed woman with blonde hair materialised from the crowd, grabbed the knife, kicked the assailant's jaw hard enough to dislocate it, then took the legs of the other two from beneath them. She sashayed off in the direction of Rampayne Street leaving the tube personnel still wondering how to intervene and the attackers prostrate. Two Chinese students, not having seen what had led up to it, knelt to help. Mordred and Phyllis covered Ruby Parker in front and behind on the descending escalator.

Phyllis looked at her phone. "Alec's at Victoria," she said. "He's already made six hostiles. Even with Edna and Ian, that's more than we can handle."

"Six against six," Mordred said. "And they won't be expecting us to expect them. We'll have the element of surprise. Just."

Phyllis shook her head. She put her phone to her ear. "Annabel intervened. That means they know we know." She spoke into her mobile: "Alec, you need to get everyone out of there. You're in acute danger." She put it back in her coat pocket.

"I'm taking command from here," Ruby Parker said. "We'll going south to Brixton, the stop after next. That should wrongfoot them."

It seemed the best plan out of a handful of tawdry alternatives, but at least she was finally on side. The only other possibilities were turning round and leaving Pimlico now, either to get back into Thames House, or to take an alternative mode of transport to Whitehall, or to stay on the train at Victoria and alight at Oxford Circus, or even somewhere way up the line like Seven Sisters. All of those, they'd have foreseen. They'd probably factored in the Brixton possibility, but it just might be too late for them to get personnel over there. Even if they did, they might be too thinly spread. They'd obviously put most of their eggs in the Victoria basket.

"What are we going to do when we get to Brixton?" Phyllis asked.

"I've got relations there," she said. "They'll put us up for the night."

They cleared the escalator and went through onto the southbound platform. "Impossible," Mordred told her. "We've got to meet Sir Ranulph at eleven forty-five."

"I don't particularly approve of gambling," Ruby Parker replied. "I was going to say, 'Especially when it concerns speculation about me', but thank God I've never been in that posi-

THE NEW EUROPEANS ~

tion before. What's going to happen now is that you're going to give me a full explanation, then I'm going to ring Sir Ranulph and speak to him in person; put an end to this apparently lethal charade."

"John doesn't think it's Grey that's after him," Phyllis said.

"I got that bit," Ruby Parker said sardonically, without looking at her. "Cut to the chase."

"What happened when we were supposed to be going to Capri was that we actually went to talk to Interpol at the Commissariat de Police on the Place de Lorraine in Calais. It turns out that Durand did some clerical work for *Godolphine*, a subsidiary of Eurotunnel, although Interpol thinks he was more likely involved in industrial espionage. That doesn't matter for the moment. What happened halfway through was that 'Grey' discovered what we were up to and sent a message telling the French to stop blabbing and detain us. Luckily, we got away. We - "

"How?" Ruby Parker interrupted. "*How* did you get away?"

"Smoke and mirrors," he replied. "It's irrelevant right now - "

"Tariq," she said incredulously. "You've obviously got Annabel on board, and Alec and Edna. It would be odd if he wasn't. And he's the only possibility. He sent a message from within Thames House countermanding the original order. Is that right?"

They turned to each other. They nodded, conscious that they probably looked like naughty children.

"Good God," Ruby Parker said.

Mordred sat up. "The point is," he began, mustering as much dignity as he could, "is that - "

She held her hand up. "Stop talking. I need a moment."

There was a loud bing-bong. "*This is a passenger announcement,*" a loudspeaker said. "*Due to unforeseen circumstances, this train will now stop at* Vauxhall. *Passengers for* Stockwell *should board the northbound train for Victoria Station and proceed by way of the District or Circle lines to Embankment, then board the southbound Northern line train. Passengers for* Brixton *should leave the station and wait to be directed to the coach. We apologise for the inconvenience. Please note: these are unusual conditions* beyond our control. *Repeat: this is a passenger announcement. Due to unforeseen ..."*

They exchanged looks. Hardly worth speaking, since the truth was written in all their faces. They'd fallen into a trap.

"We'll take the train north," Ruby Parker said. "Has either of you got a gun?"

Phyllis shook her head.

"I tend not to carry them," Mordred replied.

"For what it's worth," Ruby Parker said, as the train began to slow. "I can see you may not be wrong about who's after you. Grey would know they'd been bamboozled. They'd be on the phone to me faster than a bolt of lightning. But they weren't. Why?"

"Because it would have to be a personal call from the very top of the chain of command," Mordred said. "No one other than the Head of Grey would be remotely qualified to give the Head of Red a ticking off. By contrast, an order such as 'You're off the Holland case' can be relayed impersonally, in writing. Which incidentally, means the mole, whoever he or she is, must occupy a fairly senior position in their communications hierarchy."

"A one-to-one conversation's always fairly risky if you're pretending to be someone else," Phyllis added. "Your interlocutor might ask something unexpected, or she might refer to some point of knowledge you're both supposed to share, but with which you're completely unfamiliar."

"I need to ring Sir Ranulph," she said. "Why did you tell me it was impossible a moment ago?"

Mordred sighed. "The bet's for a thousand pounds. I don't expect any money to change hands, but I had to induce him somehow, and I happen to know he likes a flutter. The idea is that if I deliver you to the Bulletin Club before eleven forty-five, he owes me. But if he can use his connections in Grey to prove – what he's convinced of – that it's not Grey that's after me, I owe him. Result: he and I are quits; and secondly, you have irrefutable proof that my hypothesis is correct and there's a mole on the floor beneath ours. Win-win. Right now, he'll be ringing round everyone that can possibly throw any light whatsoever on the question, just so he's got security. A call from you will defocus him. We can't afford that, especially as it's beginning to look very much as if we aren't going to make it."

They stood by the sliding doors now, looking out at the platform.

No one. Complete emptiness from one end to the other.

But obviously, that's what you'd expect. This was where the train terminated. Any assailants would be at the various exit-points.

Too late to ring for reinforcements. Even the police wouldn't get here in time now. The only question was, how many of them would they attempt to kill?

Probably not Ruby Parker. That would open the gates of hell on them.

And the course of events over the last few weeks showed Phyllis didn't mean as much to them as she probably should.

Just him.

But they probably wouldn't even kill him. Even that stunt with the knife at Pimlico had probably been a scatter-tactic rather than an assassination attempt. They were plotting a *coup d'état*. They'd want to know how much he'd learned and by implication how much he could have passed on. Only then could they know whether to proceed or abort. Killing him would be their least preferred outcome.

Which meant – if he played his cards right - he could conceivably persuade them to abort.

The doors hissed open and the handful of people aboard stepped off and went their separate ways, half making to the surface via the escalators, the other half pushing onwards to the opposite platform. The northbound train was waiting with its doors open, presumably the last of the evening. Once this left, they'd have to close the entire line, because that was how it worked.

He, Phyllis and Ruby Parker went in and sat down next to each other. There were only five other passengers in the carriage right now. Two women in hoodies, deep in conversation; a bearded man of about forty with a collie, and two teenagers, sitting apart. All five had earphones in. The teenagers and the women were looking at their mobiles.

"Where are we aiming to get off?" Mordred asked.

"We're going to stay on for as long as we can," Ruby Parker said. "Unless either of you has a better plan. That's a genuine offer, by the way."

Two stocky middle-aged men in smart overcoats appeared on the platform. They swept the carriages with their eyes and alighted on Mordred and his companions with a glint of satisfaction. They got on the train and sat down together facing them.

"Are you going to make this difficult?" one of them asked Ruby Parker. He took his phone out and pressed dial.

"That depends what you're talking about," she said.

He raised his phone to his ear. "We're sitting opposite them on the northbound train. I'm going to need assistance, though." He put it away and smiled. "Mr Mordred's going to accompany me and my friend. You're going to stay here."

Ruby Parker removed the gun from her pocket. "I don't think so."

They sat facing each other without speaking. The man continued to smile, as one by one he and his comrade were joined by ten clones.

"I don't think you've enough bullets in that thing for all of us," he said. "And don't forget: we've got guns of our own, pointed right at you."

Mordred stood up. Time to go.

Two men flanked him. As he stepped off the train, he felt a little jab in his thigh. The conventional sleeping drug, of course.

Behind him, he heard Phyllis protesting. The doors swished shut. He heard the train pull out. Then darkness.

Chapter 31: Gilded Prison

Sleeping drugs were the preferred tool of amateurs, so it was with an ambiguous sense of reassurance – a sense of reassurance, none the less - that Mordred felt a needle in his thigh. He might be wrong, it might be poison, but he dismissed that even before succumbing: the number of men involved, and their determination to separate him from his friends made murder unlikely – at least at this point in their game. They obviously had a bigger plan.

What made an anaesthetic so amateurish was that firstly, and most obviously, you'd need to haul your victim to wherever you were taking him. Which would self-evidently arouse suspicion. Secondly, you'd have to wait for him or her to wake up. Especially if you were seeking information, any artificial means of arousal - a splash of cold water, or a few slaps in the face - wouldn't cut it. So long as the victim was still under the influence, anything he or she might say could be the drugs talking.

Thirdly, and most importantly, because the interrogator had await the course of nature, the victim could sometimes pretend to be asleep for a short while after he'd awoken. If they were within earshot – which they could well be, given that they were amateurs – then that victim might glean insights into what was going to happen next and how to manage it.

When you did wake up, you'd nearly always be in a single predicament in one of two locations. Predicament: tied to a chair. Location: either an empty warehouse or an over-furnished Mayfair flat. Villains didn't usually have much imagination. They got their ideas from literature and TV.

The first thing Mordred heard, before he'd opened his eyes, was:

"J'aime vraiment le son de ce John Mordred. Je voudrais que vous me disiez de lui avant plutôt gaffeur avec des fusils et des menaces. Nous aurions pu trouver une façon beaucoup plus civilisée de le gérer." I really like the sound of this John Mordred. I wish you'd told me about him before instead of blundering in with guns and threats. We could have found a vastly more civilised way to manage him.

"Il est encore temps." There's still time.

Not quite what he was expecting, but that was the problem with sleeping drugs. Sometimes, you really did wake up in a semi-delirium. The drugs talked, but they talked to you and told you, no, you weren't sitting in a chair, you were lying down. And no, you hadn't been restrained with cords, or kicked while you were unconscious just for the sake of it; and no, that voice over there wasn't menacing: it was quite nice. It sounded just like the hotel manager you'd rung in Calais, on the way to Thames House, the first one.

He opened his eyes just enough to see through his eyelashes. An East Asian woman of about his age leant over him.

Good God. Dao-ming Chou.

"I think he's coming round," she said in French.

"Put him back to sleep," came the man's voice. Again, no hint of menace. "We need to finish deciding what to do with him."

Mordred reached over to her. She evaded his touch and he felt another needle. His arm this time – probably. Just as well. He was with Phyllis now. He loved Phyllis.

"I love Phyllis," he told her, as he sank. "Phyllis Robinson."

When he next awoke, it was with the same sense of unreality. Dao-ming Chou was still by his side; he was still lying down. The voices had gone. He opened his eyes.

He was in a large bed in a room that actually looked like a bedroom. Furnished in the antique-style. Probably a Mayfair flat. Certainly not a warehouse.

A chandelier hung from the ceiling. A single window with drawn velvet curtains looked out onto - sky: so he was probably above ground floor level. There was a dresser and a wardrobe, and a variety of superfluous tables all of different heights, some with plants on, others supporting vases or figurines. There was a smell of the past.

There were two occupants in the room. Dao-ming Chou and a tall, absurdly handsome man of about fifty with grey hair parted at the side, and a matching suit. He had his hands in his pockets and looked at Mordred with mingled amusement and curiosity.

"Let Monsieur Mordred wake up," he said.

"How are you, John?" she asked.

She wasn't Dao-ming Chou: just someone cleverly done up to look like her. It was two years since they'd last met, but, just like everyone else, Dao-ming Chou's personality tended to express itself in the physical act of speaking. This wasn't her.

"Who are you?" he asked.

She smiled. "You must remember me."

He shook his head.

"Dao-ming?" she persisted.

The man on the other side of the room laughed and came over. "Leave him," he said. "He's already seen through you. From what I understand, he's an expert in facial tics. Unless you've met the real Dao-ming Chou, there's no reason to expect you to be able to replicate them. Good try, though. Off you go, and thank you."

The Chinese woman, whoever she was, instantly lost interest in Mordred. She stood up, shrugged amicably and let herself out of the room.

"We just wanted to make you feel at home," the man said. "My name's Jean-Paul Crevier and I'm going to be your host for at least the next twelve months. We're on the second floor of a very elegant château in the south of France. You don't need to know precisely where, but I own it, and I live here with my family: my wife and four lovely daughters, all of whom you'll meet presently."

Mordred sat up. Not as groggy as he expected. "Twelve months?"

"At least. You'll be well looked after. To all intents and purposes, this is your room from now until next May. You're my guest. It's only fair to warn you, though, that you'll be watched at every moment of every day - bathroom activities excluded, of course: even the most rigorous surveillance has to have moral limits. Trying to escape is utterly futile, although I expect you to attempt it frequently, especially in the early stages."

"Why do you want to keep me here? What are you hoping to obtain that'll take a year to get?"

Crevier smiled. "You. Your allegiance. We'll talk properly after dinner." He looked at his watch. "Which will be served in precisely one hour, Monsieur Mordred. Take a shower, get dressed and I'll see you in the lounge at six-fifty. Garnier will 'show you the ropes', as the English say."

He walked casually out of the room and closed the door behind him.

Garnier was a small man with a thin horseshoe of black hair surrounding an otherwise bald head. Mordred followed him to the shower where another servant gave him a towel, a bathrobe and a sponge bag. Twenty minutes later, he returned to 'his' room. A suit had been laid out on the bed. He felt desperately hungry now and his mouth was dry. A clock on the dressing table said six-thirty. He changed into the suit on and sat down on the bed and thought about how he'd got here. That late-night rush to rendezvous with Farquarson; the final, hopeless denouement; Phyllis's protests as he fell unconscious.

How much time had passed since then and now? He looked round for anything that might give him a clue, but this place was ageless. Crevier had talked about a twelve month period, apparently ending 'next May'. That would have to mean he hadn't been here long. It would also mean a month, probably, before the EU referendum. Still time to prevent the takeover. If he could get out.

The trouble was, when obviously intelligent people like Crevier said *attempting to escape is futile*, he was inclined to believe them. This wasn't the 1930s. Then, you only had jailers, sniffer-dogs and biplanes. Nowadays, you had CCTV, location-trackers, drones, infra-red binoculars, heat-seeking this, that and the other, satellite photography. And it wasn't like sniffer-dogs had gracefully retired. Nowadays, they probably had genetically modified noses. No one escaped from house arrest any more.

But that probably wasn't the right attitude.

He went to the window. A long ornamental lawn with a lake. In the distance, oddly random screens of trees, hedgerows, fields of green and brown and yellow, a wisp of smoke. No sign of any rival human habitation. The land extended without apparently rising an inch until it met the sky an infinite distance away in a little hazy band of grey. The sun was sinking now, somewhere behind the château, and cast long shadows.

A knock at the door. He opened it to find Garnier waiting to show him the lounge.

Madame Crevier was in her late forties, a slim woman with gentle features and her hair in a bun. She greeted Mordred like an old friend, said she hoped he'd slept well, she understood he'd be staying for a long time, he was very welcome, he must do the tour of the house tomorrow. From her remarks, it became subtly obvious she knew he was a prisoner of some sort. There were no suggestions of trips to the local village, queries about where he'd come from, polite enquiries about life plans. He was a man on his own: he existed here and nowhere else. The daughters, Brigitte, Caroline, Virginie and Sylvie – eighteen, seventeen, sixteen and fifteen – were similarly minded. He guessed they got a lot of 'guests' here, and had at least some sense that their father was a kidnapper. They didn't seem bothered by it. Meeting the family was probably some sort of test. Because they all seemed so pleasant, he wanted to pass.

Within the limitations of the shared but unspoken acknowledgement that Mordred was a hostage, dinner was entertaining. At first, he wondered whether the mother and daughters might be paid performers, brought in to create a sense of normality and make him more talkative, but they enjoyed each other's company too much for that. They ate Chicken Gruyere - in the normal course of things, Mordred was a vegetarian, but he wasn't above eating meat for politeness's sake - and spoke animatedly about how they'd each spent the day. They had innocent in-jokes, shared mannerisms and the kind of easy synchronicity that only comes from a long time together.

He met their restricted conversational gambits with courtesy and good humour. It wasn't their fault he was stuck here, even if they were complicit on some level. After dessert and three bottles of wine between them, the women went their separate ways, leaving Mordred alone with his host. Time to get down to business.

"Come with me, please," Crevier said.

Mordred followed him along a corridor and up a spiral staircase. They emerged into the outdoors. A flat tower-top with a view of the entire world. Two deckchairs had been laid out, facing each other. It was cold now, but Garnier was waiting with two heavy overcoats, which he helped each man into. A pair of patio heaters burned, one on either side of the chairs.

Crevier gestured for Mordred to sit down. On a table in between them, a flagon of brandy and two glasses. Garnier poured each man a large measure and disappeared from existence.

"I'd like the thank you for being so civilised at dinner," Crevier began. "I expected to find you a little sulky. My wife and daughters obviously enjoyed your company. They don't always warm to my guests."

"I'm a vegetarian," Mordred said. "I wouldn't normally insist on it when I'm being accommodated for free, but this is different."

"A mistake on my part. It won't happen again. Now, shall we talk frankly about more serious matters?"

"What did you do to my two – companions on the tube after I left them?"

"You mean, Ruby Parker and Phyllis Robinson. Nothing at all. We'd already decided to cut our losses. We realised we could limit the damage so that it stopped at Cheswick. So we sacrificed him."

"Who's Cheswick?"

"Martin Cheswick was the head of information technology in MI7's Grey department. He it was who initiated your radicalisation enquiry, he who worked together with Horvath and one or two other private security agencies to create the illusion that Grey itself was after you and crush the Holland investigation. Once we realised you were back in Britain, we calculated you'd concentrate all your efforts on exposing him. The mass pursuit was merely our way of keeping you focussed, so you wouldn't divulge what I'm pretty sure you'd already worked out. Once we'd removed you from the frame, we could relax, or at least hold our collective breath and wait to see what happened. And the good news is, nothing happened."

"Oh, that is good news."

"On the night in question, we allowed your two colleagues to pass unmolested to the Bulletin club. There, they found Ranulph Farquarson with David Morris, the head of Grey department. Of course, Morris knew nothing of an attempt to commandeer the Holland investigation, certainly nothing of a direct order to Ruby Parker to stand down, much less of a co-terie of armed men on a London rooftop. Pretty soon, they all worked out that there was only one man it could be. By this time, Martin was already in Paris. Alas, poor Yorick, he had to die. The important point is, everyone you care about is fine."

"When you say, 'nothing happened' …"

"I meant, as regards Planchart. The project to frame John Mordred was a trifling side-show. If I'd known the slightest thing about it in advance, I'd never have allowed it."

"Really."

"I swear. Why do you think you're alive now? Only because I took charge. I could have sent you the same way as Cheswick with all the ease of scratching my little finger."

"Why didn't you?"

"Believe it or not, Monsieur Mordred, I haven't missed Mass once in over ten years. I find killing evil men easy. But I won't murder a good one, no matter how much of a threat he may pose."

"'Call no one good except God alone', Mark ten-something."

Crevier laughed. "Are *you* a Christian?"

"I'm a little bit of everything. Christian, Hindu, Muslim, Jain, Buddhist, Atheist. The full English breakfast."

Crevier kept laughing. He slapped his thigh.

"Whereas I see you as more of a croissant," Mordred said.

Suddenly, Crevier was giggling and he couldn't stop. He leaned forward in his deck-chair in an effort to regain control. After thirty seconds, he was red in the face. He giggled twice more in quick succession and swallowed. "I think we're going to get on," he said hoarsely.

They sat without saying anything for a few moments. It was always difficult when the bad guy creased up and couldn't uncrease. Especially when what you'd said to provoke it wasn't particularly funny. It never happened to Jason

Bourne. Meanwhile, he noticed a few flying insects getting ready to bite.

"Tell me seriously," Crevier said at last. "How much do you actually know?"

"Well, I hope this doesn't sound big-headed, but probably everything."

"Astound me."

"I was watching *Goldfinger* on TV the night you kidnapped me. That bit where Bond defuses the bomb stuck in my mind and just wouldn't go away. I put it together with Frances Holland's apparently bizarre claim that The Get Out Clause was going to blow up the Channel Tunnel, Durand's stint in *Godolphine*, the used clothes in Calais, and Planchart's Prime Ministerial ambitions."

Crevier nodded noncommittally and smiled. He folded his hands and lay back.

"Given the amount of surveillance nowadays," Mordred went on, "it's probably impossible to plant a bomb capable of destroying the Channel Tunnel. But not to plant *any* bomb. If I were say, a *Godolphine* employee with access to otherwise restricted parts of the tunnel, I might just get away with planting a small one. Detonated in conjunction with a bunch of armed immigrants apparently crossing *La Manche*, it might just inspire media hysteria."

"Very good," Crevier said. "I'm impressed."

"Of course, just as the explosion wouldn't be quite what it seemed, neither would be the immigrants. They'd be hired hands, some on this side of the channel, some in Dover, some on the outskirts of London, the latter primed to stage an 'invasion' of Westminster. Which would be feeble, of course, but it'd afford Planchart a great photo opportunity. Cobbling a citizen militia out of nothing, reclaiming the streets of Great Britain for the British, imperious demeanour on every front page, a true Horatius at the Bridge. And then, thanks somehow to his heroism, the 'immigrants' would go 'home'. They'd evaporate. Only, not before they'd made everyone in the country hyper-paranoid about something they've so far only been conventionally paranoid about: the prospect of being swamped by Johnny Foreigner."

"The sole problem with your analysis so far is that you're talking in the conditional tense. Change 'would' to 'will'."

"And of course, some of his citizen militia would be British policemen. Someone in the Met helped suppress what Frances Holland found."

"Policemen everywhere can always be bought. It's no job for an idealist. But go on."

Mordred shrugged. "In the run-up to the Conservative Party conference in October, Planchart's cronies will propose him for leader. With everyone else tainted by pro-Europeanism, he'll be the only game in town. He'll ride to victory on the power of nightmares. And of course, he'll be Prime Minister for a very long time. Everyone's scared of Europe at this point, so that makes the Labour party unelectable."

"Scared of one version of Europe, that's all."

"Somehow, I prefer it to any version likely to be put forward by Charles Planchart."

"That's because you haven't seen Charles's version."

"I can guess. A big emphasis on law and order. Re-introduction of capital punishment and possibly flogging. Abolition of the dreaded human rights act. Britain for the British, war is peace, freedom is slavery, ignorance is strength."

"He had something of an epiphany a year ago after reading Chapman Hill's *The Social Magus*. He's one of those rare beasts: a convert from a prior conversion. Started red, went blue, now he's red again, only hardly anyone knows it."

"Probably best. For him."

"He wants to begin by renationalising the railways. Then he's going to push a massive housing programme. No more excuses. If what you're building isn't affordable, you're not building it. Confiscation and redistribution of foreign-owned property-for-investment in the capital. The City brought to heel. Resuscitation of public transport, the revival of scientific research and manufacturing, more money for the National Health Service, more power to farmers."

Mordred laughed. "And yet he's still officially Conservative."

"His party colleagues will come round, once they realise it's a long-term ticket to power. Besides, all this right and left wing nonsense. So twentieth century, don't you think?"

"I'll believe it when I see it."

"Which is why you're staying here for one year, John. Precisely so you can see it with your own eyes. I said I wanted your allegiance. I've learned a lot about you in the last few weeks. I've been told that, given a choice, you'd prefer the morally right but treasonable outcome to the iniquitous but patriotic one."

"Possibly. But I don't think life's ever that clear-cut."

"But this *is*. Planchart's an honourable man, and his programme is for the immeasurable good of your country – including, incidentally, the royal family, to whom you owe your nominal allegiance. Don't you see? You could, in theory, outwit me and sabotage Planchart's chances, but you'd be doing wrong. You'd be depriving a lot of vulnerable people, the very weakest people in your own society, of a meaningful future."

"I don't get it. You're French. What do you get out of it?"

"Planchart's just the first of the few. We're new Europeans. Confederates rather than Centralists. This is about the revival of a great civilisation, John. Probably the only great civilisation there's ever been. China was interesting and fairly inventive, but it wasn't going anywhere; America's blossomed, but it was always an outgrowth of us. And the rest of the world was only ever – at best - a sequence of brilliant moments. No, the future lies, as it always has, with Britain, France, Germany and Austria, Italy, the Low Countries, the Scandinavians and the Polish at a pinch, and of course, Russia."

"Sounds like a recipe for another war to me."

"That, I doubt."

"The Russians don't like sharing power, never have. The British are the same, and the French and the Germans. In fact, it's probably only the Americans that have kept us from cutting each other's throats."

"Well, we'll see. I didn't expect quite this level of pessimism, I must admit. From what Planchart told me about you, I assumed you'd be more sanguine."

Something suddenly hit Mordred. "You said he wants to bring the City to heel. Is that why the Lord Mayor was knocked down by a hit and run?"

"William Chester's a friend of mine. Or was. As the owner of *Godolphine*, with interests in the City, I even helped back him for Mayor. Last year he came to stay with me here as my guest, along with a few other people. Let's just say he overheard more than I intended him to, or he probably wanted. When I heard he was entertaining MI7 agents, I overlooked it for a while. I gave him a warning. But when you set off for Mansion House a second time, and in such a hurry, I realised he had to go."

"So you got someone to run him down."

"Tush, he'll recover, but not till after Planchart's in power. By that time, of course, there'll be a new Lord Mayor: I understand it's merely a one-year tenancy."

"You see, this is what I don't like. The means. When the means isn't good, it's difficult to see how the end can be any better."

"If there's anything good in human history, scratch the surface and you'll find it's only come about by dubious methods. Ancient Greece via the Delian League; Rome by the destruction of Carthage; Jesus Christ as a long term consequence of Joshua's slaughter of the Canaanites; The United States through destruction of the natives and slavery; Great Britain by permanent warfare and global profiteering. I hardly need go on. Planchart's only duping a few people. He's not a mass murderer. In the historical scale of bad means to noble ends, it hardly even merits a ticking off. Let's not be squeamish. Or overly precious."

"You killed Cheswick. And Planchart killed Frances Holland."

"Cheswick knew the risks when he signed up. That's not an injustice. As for Frances Holland, she killed herself. We simply gave her the tools and conditions to do it honourably. She was a traitor."

"Can I ask what makes you think Planchart will 'play ball', as the Americans put it? I mean, why should he help you create your 'new' Europe? Especially once he's got what he wants."

"Ironically, I have a significant amount of influence with the present French government, and so do my co-conspirators. When we put our minds to it, we tend to get our way. Once Planchart leaves the EU, I can persuade Hollande to revoke the Treaty of Le Touquet if I feel let down. That means we'd end British border controls in Calais and allow migrants to pass unchecked across the Channel. Planchart wouldn't survive that. Just as we built him up, so we can bring him down."

"It doesn't sound like you trust each other."

"Trust doesn't mean throwing caution to the wind. I trust my car to get me to work, but I insure it all the same."

"You don't blackmail the driver, though."

Crevier chuckled and changed the subject. "I'll wager you can't show my one great writer or thinker in your country alive today. I certainly can't think of a French or German one. We're not building a perfect Europe, John, just a better one. What we have now is insipid and mediocre. It breeds bland, inoffensive, and yet somehow unforgivably *vain* men and women."

There didn't seem too much left to say. Let Crevier have the last word; they were never going to agree.

"Too much for you to take in in a single sitting," the Frenchman said eventually. "But at least now you know what's at stake. I have one year to bring you round."

"And if you don't?"

"You're free to go. But the world you choose to re-join will be very different to the one you left. It'll have moved on, and you may not find it as congenial. However, the choice is yours. In any case, I have a busy day tomorrow. You'll forgive me if I turn in for the evening. Thank you for being such a charming conversationalist. I did not expect us to see eye-to-eye, but nor did I expect you to respond to my explanations with such good grace."

He stood up, bowed slightly from the neck and left. Garnier arrived and escorted Mordred back to his room. When he arrived, he found a freshly-ironed set of old-fashioned pyjamas - jacket and trousers – laid out on the bed.

Then, outside the door, he heard the key turn in the lock.

Chapter 32: Drawing and Plotting

Over the next few days, Mordred had confirmation that his world was defined by the château boundaries and populated only by the people inside. Its outposts were guarded by men with dogs; he was never left unattended; his movements were monitored by cameras; people with walkie-talkies watched him from afar.

Within this world, there were only eight people (the guards didn't count). Jean-Paul Crevier was the most congenial – in the evening they drank brandy and discussed European polit-ics - but frequently absent from home altogether; Amandine Crevier, his wife, only ever talked about her family, the bur-dens of managing household domestics, and food; Garnier was unknowable. The four teenagers, Brigitte, Caroline, Vir-ginie and Sylvie, were shy and preferred each other's com-pany, although, after the third day, they started to open up.

His duty to Queen and Country was to escape. Which looked impossible on the surface, but probably wasn't. They might be pretty stringent about guarding him now, but it would be difficult to keep that up for a year.

In an espionage novel, he wouldn't even question his patri-otic responsibility. He'd immediately start digging a tunnel or trying to turn the guards, and he'd practice Kung Fu in the pri-vacy of the bathroom, where there were supposedly no cam-eras. And whenever he despaired, or began perversely to en-joy the life of a prisoner, he'd stab himself in the palm to focus his mind. He'd demand regular meetings with Number One and make himself as obstreperous as possible.

Somehow, none of that seemed worth it. Yes, he felt affec-tion for the Queen and he liked being British, but so probably did Planchart. And this wasn't supposed to end in the destruc-tion of the UK: rather – well, what? Planchart sounded like an old fashioned socialist, primed to pull off the Trojan Horse of the century. Renationalisation of the railways sounded damn good thinking, for a start.

On the other hand, your duty was only your duty because you'd made it such. You couldn't back out just because things didn't look apocalyptically grim.

Luckily, none of this mattered, because he had a more urgent motive for escape.

Phyllis.

She probably thought he was dead in a shallow grave somewhere. Pretty soon, she'd forget him. Someone else would come along. Toby, probably. She'd fall back in love with Toby and they'd marry. *The world you choose to re-join will be very different to the one you left. It'll have moved on.* Selfish though it might be, he couldn't allow that. He had to escape. Queen and Country were merely a bonus.

There were eight people in his world, five of whom were members of the opposite sex. According to the spy manuals, your correct strategy in such a scenario was seduction then blackmail. Get at least one of the women to fall in love with you, promise her the earth, then take advantage of her.

That wasn't for him. The Crevier women hadn't done anything wrong, and he was above using them as a means to an end. Besides, he'd been warned against it in all his psych-tests, as all his colleagues were so fond of reminding him. Play to your strengths. Romantic duplicity wasn't one of his.

The next best method was to play along with your captors and lull them into a false sense of security. Sometimes, you made a few dummy attempts to escape then a show of giving up, the idea being to fool them into thinking they'd broken you. Here, that didn't seem appropriate – everyone was so civilised - and there probably wasn't time. In a year, if Crevier was a good as his word, he'd be getting out anyway. A meaningful escape would be one that included the possibility of stopping Planchart, however ambiguous that might make him feel. It needed to happen soon.

And he did feel ambiguous. Because they chimed roughly with his own convictions, he could feel Crevier's powers of persuasion working on him. There were no contrary arguments. God help him, he was becoming radicalised. In the daytime, he was more or less alone. Amandine and her daughters kept their distance as if somehow he might be a corrupting influence. He gradually found out why. They knew more about their father's views and ambitions than Mordred had assumed, and each saw herself as integral to his success.

On the third day, the youngest daughter came up and sat next to him on the bench in the shade of an old beech. The sun shone and cloudlets peppered the sky. The only sound was of an overhead plane. Had it not been for his confinement, it would have been a perfect afternoon. He watched a group of ants in a dust-clearing in the grass. Suddenly, he became aware of a presence in front of him. He looked up to find fifteen-year old Sylvie. Jeans, plain T-shirt and sandals. Long, narrow eyes, a tiny chin, prominent cheekbones, long dark hair in two plaits.

"Is it okay to sit down?" she asked.

"I'd be glad of the company," he replied.

"My sisters and I have a question."

"Fire away."

"Are you *really* English? Papa says you are, but you don't *sound* it."

"I'm just good at languages."

"Say something in English."

"Like what?"

She laughed. "Anything!"

"The quick brown fox jumped over the lazy dog," he replied in English.

"You could have learned that by heart," she said, also in English. "What about 'the zebras are body-popping in the shopping centre whilst eating chocolate'?"

"I don't think they'd do that," he replied, reverting to French. "Most zebras are allergic to chocolate. The body-popping bit rings true, though."

She gave a semi-shriek and laughed. "*Oh, my God! Caroline! Virginie!*"

Her sisters, a year and two years older than her, emerged from behind a tree. Caroline was slightly plump with a round, pleasant face, a smock-dress and bare feet. Virginie, at sixteen, looked a little like Sylvie, but with darker, wider eyes. She wore a Chapman Hill and Morgan Smith T-shirt with *There Will Always Be a Real Alternative* written on. They bounded over and stopped in front of their sister without looking at Mordred.

"I said to John," Sylvie said breathlessly, "'say something in English', and he said, 'The quick brown fox jumped over the lazy dog', and I said, 'You could have learned that by heart; say something in English like "the zebras are body-popping in the mall whilst eating chocolate bars"'. And do you know what he said? He said: 'that can't be true because *zebras are allergic to chocolate*'!"

Caroline and Virginie made a demonstration of laughing heartily. They were probably pleased rather than amused. The Englishman had at least the makings of a sense of humour. They may choose not to hang out with him – they probably thought he was a bit puerile - but at least he wasn't going to be unpleasant to them.

"So you *are* English?" Caroline said.

"British," he corrected her.

"Is it true that the British are obsessed with *owning houses?*" she asked. "And they mainly watch programmes about property and cooking?"

"Is it true that lots of British people drink a bottle of wine *each* every night?" Virginie asked. "And not even with *food?*"

"Is it true that people in England judge each other by their *cars?*" Sylvie asked.

"Is it true that some of your politicians have never held real jobs?" Caroline said.

Sylvie held her hand up. Enough questions. Let him speak. He laughed. "All true."

Virginie turned on her sisters. "France is no better! It's easy to laugh! We're just as bad – and not always in different ways!"

They began to argue, not with the basic premise, but about the precise areas in which it applied. Then they moved on to the Germans, the Italians, the Belgians and finally, the Turkish government. They stood in a circle and hurled sweeping national generalisations at each other focussed on the Mayor of Molenbeek, Recep Tayyip Erdoğan and Angela Merkel. They seemed to have completely forgotten Mordred's existence.

Yet on another level, it was clearly a show put on for his benefit. He could tell from their body-language that this was a discussion they hardly needed have. What they were doing was setting the ground for their future association with him. From now on, it wouldn't involve any more chocolate-eating zebras.

The château was built on a slight slope, with a huge garden leading down to a lake which formed its boundary on one side. Beyond that, there were fields and distant farmhouses. The other borders were similar: declivities but with different features at the bottom: a fenced-off vineyard, what looked like an orchard, a complex of stables where the car was kept.

It was on the slope down to the lake that Mordred met the oldest daughter, Brigitte, the next day. She sat with a pad of cartridge paper drawing something in the distance. She either didn't notice his approach or preferred not to acknowledge it. She was tall and thin with delicate features and suntanned skin. Her long black hair was tied behind her head with an elastic band. She wore a long paisley dress and tennis shoes. At her side there was a tin of lead pencils of various types and three charcoal sticks. She didn't look happy with what she was doing.

They'd been introduced over dinner on his first proper day, so he didn't feel the need to shy away. Besides, he suddenly realised she had something he might need. Paper.

"Is it okay to sit down?" he asked.

"I'd be glad of the company," she replied as if the opposite was true. "Don't comment on my drawing."

"It's good." She'd drawn the view down to the lake, but beyond that she'd put a huge Tolkeinesque castle. The perspective was excellent, but it was clearly more of a rough sketch than a finished article.

She smiled. "I said, don't comment."

"When someone tells you that, and you don't, it can come across as a criticism."

"Not with me."

"If you want to know what a bad drawing looks like, let me try."

"You haven't anything hard to lean on," she said.

"I can get something from the house."

"I can't promise to be here when you get back."

He got up. "You *can* promise to leave me a piece of paper," he said as he left her.

When he returned with a large book to lean on, she'd gone, but she'd left him a sheet of paper beneath a stone. He sat down, took it up and began to sketch.

Half an hour later, she returned. She sat down next to him without saying anything and looked at what he'd done.

"Don't comment on my drawing," he told her.

They sat in silence for a few seconds. "It's terrible!" she said at last, and laughed.

"It's awful," he agreed.

She spent the rest of the afternoon giving him a drawing lesson. They talked, in the restricted way he was getting used to here, of each other's lives and interests. He managed to interpose the fact that he had a 'long-term' girlfriend, and although that was more hope than reality, at least it might prevent her developing any romantic attachment to him. He was a drawing companion and a temporary friend, that was all.

Behind him, watching both of them from one of the upstairs windows of the château, Mme Crevier stood wringing her hands.

Mordred quickly worked out that there was no wireless access in the house or anywhere within the grounds. There was a landline phone in the front hallway. There was one internet-connected computer in the living room. It was left unplugged when anyone wasn't using it. Its plug was of the British type and inserted into the wall with an adapter which was locked away - he never discovered where - when not in use.

Whoever was responsible for guarding him had made two elementary mistakes. Firstly, all the trousers and jackets they'd provided for him had pockets, which made hiding things easier. Second, contrary to what he'd been told, he quickly discovered there weren't cameras watching his every move. They were absent in most of the rooms where the family spent a lot of time. The reasons were obvious: as Crevier himself had said, even the most rigorous surveillance must have limits.

Although Mordred had no intention of seducing any of the Crevier girls – and no idea how successful he'd be if he tried – clearly the possibility had occurred starkly to their mother. As of course was only natural. A young man thrown together with four females in the first stages of womanhood, with no other eligible males in sight; the dangers were clear and present. After two days of relative indifference, suddenly Mme Crevier became solicitous and eager to spend time with him. He was glad to accommodate her, and quickly became her principal companion.

It took him three days to discern a pattern to her daily routine, but then he realised he could use it. She awoke at eight and breakfasted with him and her daughters (and Jean-Paul if he was at home): toast and jam, a pastry, or cereal, all served with coffee. At ten, she opened the post and pored over every item at least twice, even apparent junk mail. At eleven, she walked briskly around the château grounds for an hour, usually in company with one or more of her daughters. She read a novel at midday. At one, lunch was served: again, the whole family. At two, she sat on a chair in the entrance hall and spoke on the landline to friends in Paris, Nice and Lyons.

Between three and six was her favourite part of the day. She went into the living room, plugged the computer in and trawled the internet for bespoke food outlets, planning the meals their invisible cook would prepare in the coming days and weeks. She made lists of orders, but because there wasn't a printer – Mordred's chief gaoler having apparently decided that if, by some miracle, he ever did get a few unattended moments on the internet, a printout of such click-bait staples as '10 ways to get out of prison', 'You won't believe these ways of outwitting surveillance cameras' or 'These four ways of digging a tunnel will make your jaw drop', might be invaluable to him – she copied everything she needed longhand onto a scrap of paper torn from a little notepad: name of supplier, supplier's phone number, specific ingredient to be supplied, recipe web address. Presumably, since she never cooked herself, and only ever spoke on the phone to her friends, these were passed on to someone whose job it was to take care of them. She always used a pencil, probably borrowed from Brigitte. Stationery was hard to come by here as well (presumably because also useful to spies). At five-thirty, she folded her piece of paper over and switched the computer off. She pulled the plug out, and conscientiously, but with daily increasing discomfiture, took the adapter out of the room and back to its hiding place somewhere in the house. Five minutes later, she returned and took her scrap of paper away, leaving him alone. At half past six the family ate dinner.

During all the time Mme Crevier was on the internet, Mordred sat in the chair by the window, drawing. Brigitte had bought him a pad and a tin of pencils, and gave him lessons. She arrived every day at four in the afternoon and left precisely an hour later. She seemed to regard it as an interesting responsibility with no personal ramifications.

His plan was a simple one. Every day before Brigitte arrived and after she left, he spent part of his time trying to catch a glimpse of what Mme Crevier was writing down, and trying to reproduce her script on one of the middle pages of his sketch-pad. One day, when she left the room to take the adapter away, he picked her paper up. He put it face-down on his pad and rubbed his thumbnail up and down across its reverse. That night, he kept the back of his pad to the camera in his room, and obsessively traced and re-traced the imprint while pretending to do more drawing. Good attempts, but none perfect. He knocked to be allowed out to the toilet where he tore them into bits and flushed them away. He knew someone was examining his waste-basket. The next day, he took two pieces of paper from the back of Mme Crevier's pad.

Most of the perimeter guards checked off at about sunset. The château was in the middle of nowhere, and there probably wasn't too much to worry about in the way of break-ins. Every evening, around about eight, he'd excuse himself to go to the bathroom. He opened the window and used the lid of his pencil-tin and the central light to flash Morse code across the fields. It was the sort of thing the manuals recommended, but it felt silly. He wasn't remotely sure he was doing it properly. Or whether that was even possible.

All his drawing didn't go unnoticed by the Creviers. It became obvious they thought he was infatuated with Brigitte.

Which was ideal, because she was clearly a million miles from feeling anything for him. The perfect cover, and he could play it up.

Two weeks later, he was ready. That night he took one of the scraps of paper he'd stolen from the pad, and, under the pretence of drawing, compiled a list of suppliers plus phone numbers. At the bottom, he added a recipe website, all in Mme Crevier's hand.

The numbers were MI7 emergency contacts. The next day, when Mme Crevier left to secrete the adapter, he switched papers. She picked the substitute up without noticing and he flushed the real version away an hour later.

The next day, she came into the room with the paper. He could guess from her expression what sort of a conversation she'd just come from. The cook had probably told her he'd tried to contact the various purveyors, but none had answered. He'd have given Mme Crevier the slip back so she could try for herself. Mordred was now about to discover what had gone through her head as she looked at it.

There were lots of ways the internet could go wrong. Among other things, your computer might have a bug, a website might be down, the search engine might misdirect you, the online store might change its details. If you didn't know much about that sort of thing, you might assume the fault was yours. But you'd probably check.

Mordred sat drawing a line of trees on the far side of the lake. Mme Crevier greeted him as usual and got on her knees to plug the computer in. She stood up, brushed herself down, then looked at her slip of paper. She frowned slightly, sat down and logged on. She knew enough about the internet to go straight to her history folder.

Mordred sat waiting for the time-bomb to go off. She was shaking her head and tut-tutting. After about half an hour, Brigitte arrived with her pad and pencils. She looked at what Mordred was drawing and nodded approvingly.

"You're getting better," she said. "Still not there though. You need different patterns of hatching and crosshatching to map out the different planes, like I showed you."

"I must be going senile," Mme Crevier said.

"What's the matter?" Brigitte asked her.

"I made one of my lists yesterday and gave it to Karl. You know my shopping lists? One of those. Anyway, he brought it back today and said he couldn't contact any of the suppliers. And I've just checked it and *none of the places on the list is one I wrote down!*"

Brigitte shrugged. "You're not going senile."

"What's your explanation then?" her mother asked.

"Isn't it obvious?" Brigitte replied. "Karl either lost your original list and fished out one of your older ones to cover his tracks, or he mislaid it and got it mixed up with one of the old ones. He probably doesn't throw them away. You might query something."

"I'll have to tell him to be careful."

"Be tactful. Good chefs are hard to come by."

"It's never happened before," Mme Crevier said. "Maybe I should let it go."

"Wait and see if it happens again."

"But he said none of the suppliers could be contacted!"

Brigitte chuckled. "But he *would! Obviously* he would!"

They looked at each other for a second and laughed. Mrs Crevier rolled her eyes, shook her head, and went back to surfing. Brigitte began teaching her daily lesson. Mordred resumed breathing.

That night, after he'd gone through the motions of sending his usual SOS from the bathroom, he noticed something out in the gloom.

… Flashes?

It was. My God. About half a mile away? H-O-L-D … T-I-G-H-T.

Its significance sank in. His stomach turned over and the blood rushed to his head. He hadn't expected it to be this quick. My God, my God.

He had to act. Now.

Chapter 33: Back at Thames House

After Mordred was frogmarched off the tube, and the train pulled away, Ruby Parker and Phyllis Robinson phoned the police. Then they went straight to the Bulletin club. Ranulph Farquarson stood at the entrance with David Morris, the head of Grey. Fact swiftly disowned fiction, and Martin Cheswick, Chief Coordinator of Grey's IT strategy, was identified as the mole. By now, he was in Calais *en route* south. As it later transpired, he had destroyed all leads to any possible co-conspirators.

Four days later, in an apartment on Paris's 19th Arrondissement, he was shot dead. None of the neighbours saw or heard the killer. Because there was nothing obvious to link the corpse to MI7's Most Wanted, the police took three days to identify it. Among Cheswick's few personal effects was a plane ticket for Rio de Janeiro, and a false passport in the name of Cyrille Desmarais.

Thus the most promising trail to Mordred ended.

At the end of the first night, Phyllis went home to her flat and cried bitterly. She was as much angry as distraught. That she'd had to sit and watch while he was just marched to his – well, honestly: probably his death – was unthinkable.

It might not have happened yet.

Three o'clock in the morning. The Bulletin Club had gone on and on and *on*. Valuable things had come out of it, but Cheswick was likely to stay one step ahead.

What had John been trying to do, ringing Calais?

Attempting to make sense wasn't an option right now. Ruby Parker would want to see her in the morning, first thing, pick her brain. She needed to be fresh. She probably knew things she didn't even realise. She warmed herself a cup of milk in the microwave, threw her clothes off in a temper and got into bed.

She was convinced she wouldn't be able to sleep, but she did.

Her body-clock awoke her at 7am. She didn't feel tired at all now. The key was to let routine take over. She'd lost colleagues before. This was different, both in quality and degree, but she had to forget that, or try to. Her coping strategy simply had to be more intense. Turn herself into a robot: fully-functioning on the outside, lights off inside. Likely outcome: either success or a breakdown. She wasn't in the mood to care yet. Anything to crush the mingled guilt and grief, let her think rationally, clear her memory.

She showered, called a taxi – she couldn't face the tube again - and arrived at Thames House at eight-thirty, ready to sit out the half-hour before clocking on.

But Ruby Parker was already here. She'd left a request for an urgent meeting. Phyllis went straight to her office, almost running along the corridor.

As she expected, there were no polite preliminaries. She sat down in the seat reserved for her and the interview began.

"I've written down the essentials of what John told me when he arrived here last night," Ruby Parker said. "I need you to confirm and correct as necessary."

"Go ahead."

"He began by talking about a *coup d'état*. In this country. As I recall, he said it would happen 'so subtly that no one's going to recognise it as such'. You then said it was something you hadn't discussed. You didn't seem to know what he was talking about."

"The first time I heard about any *coup d'état* was when he mentioned it to you."

"Have you had any insights since?"

"No, but if he's right, it would probably involve Charles Planchart."

"I agree. I think Planchart's in this deep. We're officially following his movements now, but there's nothing concrete to tie him to any wrongdoing whatsoever. We can't connect him to Frances Holland yet, and until we discover some wrongdoing by Durand, he's completely untouchable. To make things worse, if he is involved, Cheswick's almost certainly warned him to don the whiter than white for a while. We probably won't catch him out now."

"Not until he stages his *coup*."

"Assuming John meant him. And that he was right. Even then, we may not know. Remember John's 'so subtly'. Let's move on. Those Calais hotels."

"He got me to ring two in the taxi over here. He asked them for a room on the twenty-third of June. Both were booked. For the twenty-fourth as well."

"Did he use your phone or his own?"

"His."

"And what were the names of the hotels?"

"I can't recall offhand, but they'll be in my browsing history. But I don't think it matters. He made me select them at random."

"What did you make of that?"

"I made a quip about him wanting to get out of Britain on referendum day. I was trying to get him to explain. But we were in a hurry."

"Do you have any ideas now?"

"He seemed to set huge store by it. My guess is that he connected it to the other big mystery we uncovered. Why Pierre Durand stockpiled a ton of second-hand clothes in a warehouse in Calais."

Ruby Parker put her pen down. "Here's what we're going to do. My guess is that John thought *all* the hotels in Calais would be booked on the twenty-third. That's the only explanation consistent with two random requests, as far as I can see. We'll check, and if so, we'll find out who's behind the bookings: if a small group of people, what they've got in common. Perhaps they intend to stage a riot. Together with Frances Holland's claim that someone's planning to set a bomb off in the Channel Tunnel, it may be time to start worrying. Either way, this may be our best chance of finding John."

Cheswick's death three days later foreclosed one avenue of investigation, but it quickly became apparent that the other was likely to prove productive. All the hotels and inns in Calais and its surrounds were mysteriously reserved on the twenty-third and twenty-fourth of June. By contrast, on the twenty-second and twenty-fifth, and all dates before and after, demand was exactly normal for the time of year. Someone was planning something.

Nearly all the rooms had been block-booked, in conglomerates straddling particular venues, by relatively small groups of European and Russian oligarchs. The French secret service was informed and a joint French-British investigation was launched. So far, those on MI7's list had done nothing wrong, so bringing them in for questioning would probably do more harm than good. The plan was to put the key players under observation and see where that went in the run-up to June 23, then – if there was still no breakthrough - to saturate the streets of Calais with police officers. The only member of the group who could not be found was a Frenchman called Jean-Paul Crevier.

Crevier was of particular interest because he was linked to Durand through his ownership of *Godolphine*. He owned a large number of properties across France and abroad, but not all of them in his own name. Given that he could not be found at any of his usual addresses, he might be anywhere. Finding him became a top priority.

Meanwhile, there was neither sight nor sign of John Mordred. The discovery of the block-booking and the oligarchs seemed like solid progress. But then things stagnated. Those under observation behaved impeccably. Crevier showed no inclination to re-appear.

To make matters worse, Toby Mansfield found out that his former girlfriend's new beau had walked out of her life three days after the tube catastrophe. He assumed it was a normal break-up, and Phyllis was in no position to correct him. He bombarded her with flowers and phone calls and texts, and came round to her flat every third evening to talk. She turned him away, but after nearly a month, as she sat alone in her flat at nine in the evening, she began to wonder what she was doing.

In some ways, she'd only really known John since The Counting House that day. They'd known *of* each other for ages before that. They'd even held conversations. But that was their first real meeting. That was where it had begun. All because of Annabel and her lovely, stupid villa in Capri.

That was the weird thing. She'd even admitted it that first day. She didn't want the villa in Capri. She wanted the holiday with John. She hadn't felt anything much then, except that it'd probably be fun. She certainly hadn't felt attracted to him.

And yet, in a strange way, she had. None of us had any free will really. The brain made its own decisions. They were nearly always for the best, and 'you' usually only found out about them later. She'd seen *Horizon* programmes about it. Your mind thought it was in charge, but the real shots were actually called by your little grey cells. Bits of matter as solid as this table or that chair.

She sat on the armchair, holding a glass of gin and facing the TV, and told herself aloud what she should probably have accepted at least a fortnight ago. John was dead. No point pretending otherwise. All they'd wanted from him was information. They'd have got it, and then killed him. He wasn't in any position to refuse. It wasn't like he was betraying anyone. Quite the reverse: he might be forestalling a revolution. Forewarned, they might just hold off.

Except that they hadn't. The bookings hadn't been rescinded.

But that was probably a loss they could afford to incur. They were bloody oligarchs. They probably oozed cash. Likely, come the twenty-third, no one would show up in Calais.

They knew MI7 was onto them. And John Mordred was dead.

It happened a lot in this job. She'd known that when she signed up. They all had, John too, obviously.

She was a mess. It was time to let herself cry. Cry bitterly, get it out of her system and move on.

And Toby wasn't such a bad guy. A bit of a macho poseur but so were most men. She could do worse. She tossed her gin back and poured another one. Make yourself weep, girl. Think of how wonderful JM was and feel devastated for your poor pathetic self, no one to really love you any more, and you just a child really, and –

Her phone rang. She picked it up lethargically, expecting Toby, and looked at the screen. *Thames H.*

"Yes?" she said.

"Drop whatever you're doing and make your way over here as fast as you can," Ruby Parker said. "John's alive."

She took the tube for the first time since she'd last been with him, and on the way, she laughed and cried alternately. Everyone in the carriage looked furtively at her. This immaculately dressed woman who probably still looked like the almost-supermodel she'd once been, drunk as a skunk and not afraid to show it. Thank you, God. Oh, let it be true. Thank you, please. She raced off the tube at Pimlico and ran up the escalator on the left hand side as if she had a plane to catch and seconds to spare.

When she arrived at Thames House, everyone was in. She wasn't the only one who was laughing-crying. Everyone was at it: even Alec and Annabel. She felt so much at home she almost went into overdrive. But it was okay. God, it was all going to be okay. Thank you, thank you, thank you. Stupid as being back in infants' school again, but thank you, Lord and Father! She sat on her chair at her desk and took a few moments to hyperventilate. Everyone ignored her. In a nice way.

Twenty minutes later, everyone went to Lecture Room One. The euphoria had worn off now, and mild embarrassment was the order of the moment. People talked about the weather and how tired they were or avoided speaking altogether. Brian had created a fabulous new Powerpoint and Ruby Parker was scheduled to talk everyone through it. No big deal.

The lecture room was packed. Not just people from Red, but from other departments too. That was the way MI7 worked. Normally, a kind of competition, but when someone was down, distinctions went out of the window.

At ten-thirty, she mounted the steps to the podium. The doors were closed and the lights went down. Phyllis smiled. The last time this had happened, she'd been sitting next to John. He'd opened a bag of popcorn and offered her some. Alec had been on her other side, eating Doritos. She didn't want those either.

On the screen, a large château in sunshine in immaculately kept grounds.

"This is the Château de Les Sablonnières in Auvergne," she said, "where the Lyonnaise billionaire, Jean-Paul Crevier, and his family have been staying for the last four weeks. That is, since officer John Mordred's abduction at Vauxhall tube station. Yesterday, we received five separate emergency signals, all phone calls, from its rough environs. All of the calls were to numbers which Mordred learned as part of his training and are unique to him. Once we determined the area from which they had been sent, we began to cast about for significant local properties. It turns out that the Château de Les Sablonnières is owned by none other than Dobson-Fresenius, a financial services firm whose head office is a plaque screwed to a disused office door in Zurich. If that rings any bells, it should do. It's the same firm that stumped up for Frances Holland's fatal 'holiday' in Skye.

"John Mordred has been seen walking around the château grounds, and is alive and - as far as we can tell - well. For those of you who may be wondering why he didn't contact us earlier, the residence boasts over two hundred CCTV cameras, twenty-five full time guards, all armed, and a large pack of well-trained dogs. The château itself is in a wireless blackspot, and connected to the outside world by a single landline phone, and one hardwired computer terminal.

"In a joint operation with French special forces, we aim to secure the house tomorrow night. The intervening time is partly to allow reconnaissance and partly to allow Monsieur Crevier to return home. His current whereabouts is unknown, but he is expected at the château late tomorrow afternoon in time for dinner. His wife and three teenage daughters are permanently on the premises.

"In addition to having transmitted signals, it may interest the more traditionally minded among you that John Mordred has been attempting to send Morse code. His success in that department has left much to be desired.

"The rescue operation is essentially a French police affair, but in the spirit of the *Entente Cordiale*, we have been invited to participate. I have selected a small team of John's closest colleagues for that purpose. Officers Robinson, Cunningham, Gould-al-Banna and agents Watson and Leonard are instructed to repair to Briefing Room One at the end of this presentation. The reasons are rational and practical. It is my firm conviction that the successful resolution of all the conundrums surrounding what used to be called The Holland Affair stand their best chance of resolution if John Mordred is returned to us safe and well. His most loyal friends are best placed to secure that outcome. Thank you."

Everyone applauded before getting up to leave. Rare for this kind of thing, but not unheard-of. If nothing else, it showed the euphoria had not quite dissipated.

Chapter 34: Up, Up and Away

Hold tight. As he stood in the first floor bathroom of the Château de Les Sablonnières, Phyllis was Mordred's first thought. Nearly a month had passed, but it felt much longer - like a year or even two. Almost impossible to remember what *a month* felt like in the real world. Not that this wasn't the real world, only there was some sense of an authenticity-contrast between here and where he'd come from. Which was the more real? God, he didn't even know where he wanted to be. With Phyllis, yes. In France, though? Or back in London?

He'd been radicalised. Really. The possibility had occurred to him earlier, but now it was more than that.

He didn't feel upset about it. But that was one of the symptoms. You'd changed, but imperceptibly, even to yourself. Now you were possessed by what you took to be some sort of moral imperative. Nothing could override it. Friends, family, personal safety, nothing. You were all alone in a cold tunnel with a clear view of eternity.

He went downstairs into the Study. Crevier sat with a glass of brandy, reading a day old copy of *Le Monde*. He folded it in two when Mordred walked in, smiled genially and gestured for him to sit down. He indicated an expensive-looking green bottle and an empty balloon glass on the coffee table.

"I thought we'd continue your Gallic education with a glass of Danflou 1865," he said.

"You've got to get out of here," Mordred said. "The police are about to break your doors down."

Crevier looked at him. A little embarrassed: if this was an escape attempt, it wasn't very kind. Not when your host was offering you a priceless brandy.

"I'm serious," Mordred said.

Crevier sat up, looking a little paler than a split second ago. He rose, opened the door and invited two burly men in leather jackets in. For the first time in over a week, it struck Mordred as unusual that such men were always at hand.

"Stay here," Crevier said. He closed the door behind him.

Mordred remained standing. He didn't know precisely what was going to happen now.

He did know it wasn't in Crevier's interests to put up a fight. Certainly not with his family to hand. He'd either make a run for it or surrender. *Abduction:* good for a few months in prison, possibly even a suspended sentence if you had Masonic connections and no priors. He'd probably surrender. Not from cowardice. From prudence.

He returned after five minutes, looking wan and older. "It's true," he said. "Out, out," he told Mordred's guards, almost in a gasp. "Get Amandine and the girls. Tell them to drop everything and come straight to the Study."

"What are you going to do?" Mordred asked.

"How did you find out?" Crevier asked. "I mean, that we were surrounded?"

"I can't say. I'm a spy. You should have expected it."

"Why are you warning me? You must know I can make a run for it. I know this countryside far better than any Parisian gendarme."

"You won't want to look as if you 'turned chicken', as the Americans would say."

"No, no," he said frantically. "That's right. A bad example. The girls have got to get used to dealing with the police. If they want to be the women I've brought them up to be."

He looked like someone who didn't know what he thought, but wanted to appear in control. One minute he was all for escaping; now he was determined to stay for the girls' sake. Mordred had the weird feeling he, Mordred, could suggest anything at all right now, and backed with half-sufficient reasons, Crevier would accept it.

Crevier didn't matter. That's why he wanted to save him.

"Can I suggest something bizarre?" Mordred said.

"My God, this is *surreal!*" Crevier replied feverishly.

"Your plot to install Planchart could still work if you kill me. I'm probably the only one that knows the whole plan. Why don't you?"

Crevier laughed hysterically. "From surreal to *hyper-sur-real!*" he exclaimed. He swallowed. "For your information, Planchart has ways and means of knowing what's happening here. He'll be fine."

At that moment, his family burst in. They all looked even more panicked than him. He put them at a slight distance from himself and made a short announcement about what was about to happen. Nothing heroic. Straight to the point. The police were about to burst in. They were here to retrieve John. No one should be frightened. Just do what you're told.

Mordred expected despising looks, possibly a slap or two and a blob of spit in the face, but no one even made eye-contact with him. Virginie cried. Despite Crevier's instructions, everyone looked frightened.

Then it happened. A battering ram somewhere outside the room but only just, lots of yelling, stomping boots, men on radios shouting 'secured'. One final whirlwind, then they stood in the room, ten menacing gendarmes in flak-jackets and protective headgear with short rifles. Crevier, his family, Mordred and the two guards all had their hands up.

It was over. One of the policemen came forward, took off his helmet and shook Mordred's hand. "Pleased to finally meet you, Monsieur," he said with genuine enthusiasm.

"Thank you for your help," Mordred said. "I wonder if it would be possible to order me a helicopter? I have to get back to England as soon as possible."

Suddenly, Phyllis stepped from between the personnel. She bowed low, swept his hand up and kissed it. "Your carriage awaits," she said.

He smiled. "Is it a helicopter?"

"It can be anything you want it to be," she replied.

A two-seater was all they could muster at such short notice, which meant leaving all his colleagues behind. He was tempted to wait for a larger one, but that would be another hour minimum. He'd be safer with Phyllis, Annabel and Alec – they'd all been trained in ways he hadn't – but time was of the essence. On the way, Ruby Parker debriefed him by radio, and – on Mordred's advice, after three hours - alerted the police in London. A warrant was issued for Charles Planchart's arrest. The British police prepared to launch a raid on his house, and the several other properties he owned in London and Berkshire. Mordred asked for a list, and after ten minutes of wrangling over protocol with Scotland Yard, Ruby Parker supplied it.

Mordred smiled. As he suspected, it was a list of places Planchart wouldn't be. Whoever in the police had seen fit to bury Frances Holland's *Private Eye* material was still at large. They'd warned Planchart.

There was only one place he could be now. Somewhere he had to go.

"I need you to take me to Portcullis House," he told his pilot. Several hours had now passed, but Planchart wouldn't be in any hurry.

Thirty minutes later, the helicopter swooped on Parliament Square just long enough for Mordred to alight, and then ascended while the police were still calling for back up. Mordred reached the sightseeing/ theatregoing/ late night drinking crowds before anyone could stop him. He used all his training to fade into the background, and crossed the road to Portcullis House.

Locked. There was no business in the House tonight then.

But then it opened electronically. Someone was expecting him. It couldn't be Planchart, because he'd be upstairs in his office.

He went in. He heard the door lock behind him, and walked straight out into the internal courtyard. There were two security lights on, but most of the illumination came from the moon, directly above the glass ceiling.

Only the police would have the power to disable the alarms. Assuming he survived, it ought to be possible to discover who was responsible for doing so, although they were probably on their way abroad now, with at least five other Met officers. Ruby Parker would know who they were. In getting the police to apprehend Planchart, she'd almost certainly set a snare of some kind.

"Good evening, John!"

The conventional bad-guy welcome. Shafiq Effanga. He was coming leisurely down the stairs from Planchart's office. In his hand, a large knife.

Mordred understood immediately. It had to be a knife rather than a gun, because even with the best will in the world, the latter might kill too quickly. After the repeated humiliations, Effanga wanted to make sure of a happy ending. In his world, that involved torturing the discomfiter to death.

This was going to be messy. No point in attempting *repartee*, or even trying to hold his position. Heroics was for strongmen. Effanga outmatched him in weight, combative centre of gravity, and weaponry.

Mordred backed off towards the commercial section. A restaurant, a coffee shop with tables and chairs outside, a post office. All closed, obviously.

The key would be to stop that knife, but more to prevent Effanga getting a grip on him anywhere.

In a film, Effanga would have come at him slowly, like a zombie, trying to maximise the horror. And smiling. But

Mordred was running. And Effanga bolted down the stairs and came after him.

As soon as Mordred reached the dining area, he started hurling tables and chairs. Effanga ducked and ducked again, but Mordred had the element of surprise, and in the end, through sheer persistence, a chair hit his target on the side of the head.

It seemed to shake Effanga's confidence in the blade. He put it into his belt for later, and picked up one of the tables Mordred had thrown. As if to show that anything Mordred could do, he could match four times over, he sent it screaming back like a bullet. Mordred ducked. It flew over his head and through the window of the restaurant. There was an inward explosion of glass.

Effanga laughed and slapped his hands together theatrically. He picked up a chair and repeated his performance. What still remained of the window shattered violently.

Mordred leapt into the restaurant. He probably looked cornered in here, which would give his opponent added heart. Make it look like the endgame.

Lots of condiments beneath the counter. Oil, olive oil.

He found it with a gasp of relief. He began picking up anything he could find – salt and pepper pots, bottles of ketchup, HP Sauce, Branston Pickle, gravy pourers, everything – and throwing it at Effanga. Effanga grabbed a table and held it in front of him like a shield, laughing. Everything ricocheted off and burst into smithereens on the floor between them. Finally, Mordred threw the oil with grunts of affected desperation.

Then nothing. Mordred made a play of running out of missiles and of suddenly realising his predicament was hopeless. Given that he was cornered, the one thing Effanga couldn't permit was that he leave the restaurant. He charged forward as if to exit. Effanga emitted a yell of victory and charged to head him off.

Effanga rushed straight onto the oil and slipped onto his back. Mordred grabbed a chair and leapt out of the shop in the full knowledge that keeping his balance wasn't a done deal. No room for error now. Using the chair to maintain his poise, he landed perfectly and slid the four metres between him and Effanga at lightning speed. He thrust the aluminium leg into the soft tissue underneath Effanga's chin. He drove his adversary backwards across the oil and smashed his head into the concrete planter, bringing them both to a violent halt. The chair leg burst through the bottom of Effanga's skull and entered to a depth of what looked of about four inches.

Whether Effanga knew he'd lost, Mordred never found out. As far as he could tell he'd died instantly.

Planchart. Mordred forgot Effanga, bounded up the stairs then walked as calmly as he could to the MP's office. He was still suffering from the shock of the killing.

He opened the door to find exactly who he was seeking. Only pointing a gun at him.

"I take it you've eliminated Shafiq," Planchart said. "I thought you might." He paused to allow Mordred a witticism and when it didn't come, he went on: "Well, if he can't kill you in fair combat, I'm not going to kill you in cold blood. I don't want to be remembered as a coward."

Mordred made as if to advance, but Planchart stopped him with a gesture. "I don't have to kill you to stop you crossing the room," he said.

The office was in darkness, and Planchart was dressed in an overcoat with a briefcase by his feet. Outside, police sirens. Presumably, the bad guys at the Met had been flushed out and the helicopter pilot had passed the message on: *your guy asked me to drop him in Parliament Square.*

"It sounds like it's over," Mordred said. He was still shaking slightly.

Planchart smiled. "I've no intention of escaping. It's why I came here, back to Portcullis House."

He calmly put the gun in his mouth and pulled the trigger.

Chapter 35: Final Bits and Pieces

The next day, Mordred arrived at Thames House at 8.55am as usual. He mounted the steps to reception, checked in and went straight to Basement One for his debriefing. He didn't expect it to last long. Most of it had already been done in the helicopter *en route* from France. He wanted to get the loose ends out of the way, meet Phyllis in the canteen for breakfast – or even take her round the corner to the café, if she felt like it: get a bit of privacy – before revisiting the hell of filing junior agents' reports.

He knocked on Ruby Parker's door. She bade him enter, and he went in. For once, she was standing behind her desk, instead of seated. "Well done, John," she said. "Everyone's pleased to see you back. You did an excellent job." They shook hands.

He wasn't used to her praising him. A simple "thank you" was the appropriate response. He said it and sat down.

She read aloud the details of the statement he'd given her last night, and he confirmed it and added details where necessary. Standard procedure, and a little dull. But her fulsomeness at the start had made him uneasy.

They interrupted their discussion for the 10 o'clock news on Radio 4. Another senior Met officer had been arrested, bringing the total to ten. As part of the conspiracy, Planchart had offered them significant benefits in what they'd all mistakenly imagined was the future. At least two other arrests were expected in the next twenty-four hours.

"We found the 'bomb' you deduced," Ruby Parker told him. "Once we knew where *Godolphine* had been, it didn't take long. You were right: a flash, smoke and a loud bang – that would have been all. But enough to spark speculation and panic."

"Any word of Durand?"

"None."

"What about Crevier's collaborators?"

"All disappeared into the woodwork. And Crevier won't go to prison for long. He might not end up there at all. Good lawyers, influential friends at the highest levels of government, a kidnap-victim who can't take the stand for security reasons; he holds a lot of cards."

The de-brief took ninety minutes, much longer than he'd anticipated. At the end, Ruby Parker printed him a copy of his statement, then asked him to read and sign it. He knew not to treat it as a formality. He took ten minutes before passing it back.

"As I told you at the beginning," she said, "you did a brilliant job."

"Thank you," he repeated. Here it came.

She sighed. "There is something else."

He already knew what it was. Let her tell him, though; in this sort of scenario, it didn't pay to go leaping in with educated guesses. He should look suitably surprised when she revealed it.

"Jean-Paul Crevier claims you warned him we were coming," she said.

He nodded. Bang on.

"Why?" she asked.

A series of excuses flashed through his mind. *Because I didn't want anyone to get hurt; because I knew I could overpower him if he grabbed a gun; because I felt sorry for the other members of the family; because —*

All false. "I don't know," he said. The only true thing.

"I appreciate you not making something up," she said. "It'd have been easy to do. I talked this whole thing over at an early morning meeting with David Morris, the Head of Grey. We agree you should attend a ... counselling session."

"You mean a radicalisation interview," he said. "Only, a real one this time."

She smiled. "I should emphasise that there's not the slightest possibility of you losing your job. It's a formality, a chance for you to come to terms with your experience at the Château de Les Sablonnières. You were there for a long time, John, in congenial company with intelligent people whose views must have struck you as not a million miles from your own, but which were, by any yardstick, radical."

He nodded. This was only the morning after the whole forced vacation thing. And the truth was, he'd enjoyed himself there, albeit in a tense way. God help him, he actually missed the Creviers now. In some ways, theirs had been an ideal world: chaste, cultured, all material comforts, good conversation, every day sunny and verdant. Who could tell how much more he'd miss it tomorrow, in a week's time, next year?

Maybe not at all, but it had to be looked at.

"You do realise why Planchart came back to his office last night?" he asked her.

She didn't look pleased by his apparent diversion. "I assumed it was to erase his hard drive," she replied patiently. "That's the usual motive in these sorts of cases. And of course, to put his suicide as close to the physical centre of British government as possible. The final grand political gesture for his cause."

"You sound uncertain. About the hard drive."

"Unfortunately, it doesn't seem to fit. As far as computer forensics can tell, he didn't so much as delete a file."

"His purpose was to add files. His actual manifesto, as opposed to his pretend one. He wanted posterity to know who he really was. Or could have been."

It seemed to take her a moment to digest this. "That would also explain the annotated copy of *The Social Magus* we found in his desk drawer," she said, awkwardly, like a person only

325

half-aware that she was stating the obvious. "I notice you subtly changed the subject."

"I'm making the point that I can see that *now*, when no one else yet can. I can think myself into Planchart's shoes, in other words. That may be dangerous, or it may not." He smiled and added, "I admit, it merits an interview."

A week later he sat in a Harley Street consulting room whose Victorian décor, including a desk and a chaise longue, made it a caricature of Viennese psychoanalysis at its most photo-genic. A woman of about forty in a pastel blue jacket and grey trousers sat opposite him asking the usual questions about cases he'd been involved in, people he'd met, feelings he'd ex-perienced and still possessed, possible perspectives on world affairs, vegetarianism, the various charities he supported. She made no attempt to catch him out and actually seemed quite chummy in places. Which didn't stop him keeping his guard up. As he spoke, he realised he actually did sound quite rad-ical. Not necessarily a bad thing.

After their interview was apparently over, she sat at her desk, writing, for about twenty minutes.

"What we're going to do now is something a little like what's called 'the talking cure'," she said at last. She chuckled. "Not that I'm implying you need to be *cured* of anything. 'Free association' might be a better term. I simply want you to speak for about sixty seconds on the question of what the word 'rad-ical' means and how and whether it applies to you."

If he'd been the touchy sort, he might have walked out. *Talk about why someone sent you here and I'll listen?* On the face of it, how patronising.

But he was close to getting out of the door. In a week or so's time, he'd be in Capri with his fabulous girlfriend, and this would be a memory.

"I suppose most people go through life not thinking," he began. "They don't *see* themselves as doing what they're told, but that's probably what they *are* doing. 'Radical' means you're different to that, not just a little, but very. It needn't imply you're inclined to violence. Only that you've thought about where you're heading - not just in this life but through all eternity, even if there isn't a literal one. If you have principles and you stick to them then, sooner or later, you'll be perceived by some as a threat. But it may not last. Just as others will move away from you occasionally, so, later, they'll come back. And then they'll move away again. Or not, depending on the wind-direction. Sometimes you'll find yourself labelled as a radical, sometimes a middle-of-the-road traditionalist, sometimes nothing. It's not about *you* and what *you* are. It's about society. And we happen to be living in a very conformist age. In some ways, right now, it's arguably a person's duty to be a radical."

She smiled and wrote something down. "Very good," she said. "I think that will be all, Mr Mordred."

She stood up and offered a handshake. Over her shoulder, on her desk, he saw her report. On the bottom, she'd written, *No cause for concern.*

He would celebrate by ringing Phyllis. They could meet for a cup of tea and a slice of Victoria Sponge. Nowhere too fancy, nothing too exotic. He'd had enough radicalism for one day.

Books by James Ward

General Fiction
The House of Charles Swinter
The Weird Problem of Good
The Bright Fish
Hannah and Soraya's Fully Magic Generation-Y *Snowflake* Road Trip across America

The Original Tales of MI7
Our Woman in Jamaica
The Kramski Case
The Girl from Kandahar
The Vengeance of San Gennaro

The John Mordred Tales of MI7 books
The Eastern Ukraine Question
The Social Magus
Encounter with ISIS
World War O
The New Europeans
Libya Story
Little War in London
The Square Mile Murder
The Ultimate Londoner
Death in a Half Foreign Country
The BBC Hunters
The Seductive Scent of Empire
Humankind 2.0
Ruby Parker's Last Orders

Poetry
The Latest Noel
Metals of the Future

Short Stories
An Evening at the Beach

Philosophy
21st Century Philosophy
A New Theory of Justice and Other Essays

CPSIA information can be obtained
at www.ICGtesting.com
Printed in the USA
LVHW111633260721
693715LV00009B/173/J